MINDSCREW

Book Three of the DEVOLUTION Series

Part 1

Future and past

Are the stories we fashion

A mad distraction

From the one thing happening now.

-Chairman Zeitgeist, *"Charismatic Megafauna"*

Chapter 1

The end of the modern world began in New Jersey. This proved a number of people right, who asserted that New Jersey sucked, a capacity which, it might well have been argued, grew very suddenly to encompass the entire globe.

At least, the portion of the globe whose lives were impacted directly by the whims and fancies of the US dollar, a population which included almost every human on the planet, minus a token tribe or two of hunter-gatherers.

The trouble was that almost nobody knew the world was ending. Not even the guy who had helped begin its ending.

Especially not him.

He just thought he was getting rich. Right guy, right place, right time. Right on.

The whole thing wasn't even his idea. He was kidnapped, coerced, and cajoled into using what was by any standard a rare skill set. His task: to reapportion ownership of certain virtual financial assets.

In short, he was made to steal things. Crypto-currency, to be precise, something he hadn't heard of until the time came to begin stealing it.

Domingo Mondragon was his name, but he was known far more widely by his *nom de guerre*, Sabot. He was a hacker. He had Anonymous, Antisec, Lulzsec, and various other credits to his name.

Arcane monikers notwithstanding, those were meaningful credits. He was damn good.

Equally meaningful was the fact that Sabot's real name – Domingo Mondragon – appeared on another list, one that contained the names of the Federal Bureau of Investigation's stool pigeons. He was a rat, and there were just shy of two dozen people who were Big House guests on his account.

He was also on a list of convicted felons.

And a list of FBI employees.

And, now, Sabot occupied the top slot in Special Agent Sam Jameson's Biggest Bastards list.

She knew the world was ending. Or, if "ending" was too dramatic a term for the kind of economic subjugation that was occurring second by second as a single server in a single cluster in a single data center — in New Jersey — steadily and inexorably redistributed a controlling percentage of the world's wealth, Sam at least recognized the magnitude of the problem.

Freaking huge.

It was the kind of wealth that would make the Queen blush. Maybe Louis the Fourteenth, too.

A little blinking light on a little box full of semiconductors, situated in a server farm in a dark cave that used to be the main dig in the Naughtright Mine, protected by millions of tons of rock, cooled by spring water piped in from the nearby stream, was a terrifically poor indication of the mayhem being unleashed in the digital domain within.

The machine didn't know Sabot, didn't know Sam, and didn't

know anyone called Archive. It certainly didn't know the Facilitator. And it also didn't know that its simple script, which it repeated several hundred times per second, performed a task that tilted the entire socioeconomic world on its axis.

It just knew that its system diagnostics reported a clean bill of health. So it continued to work. Find new account, unlock new account, remove money, repeat.

The light blinked on, placid, content, oblivious to the destruction it wrought.

Chapter 2

Terencio Manuel Zelaya absently swatted a mosquito. The annoying buzz of parasitic wings had a lower pitch in the jungle, owing to a larger wingspan than city mosquitos, evidence of a larger supply of blood to suck. Zelaya had swatted thousands of mosquitoes, during thousands of hot, sweaty Central American evenings, on his way to thousands of jungle interrogations.

He was good at interrogations, and in spite of his deeply religious upbringing, or maybe because of it, he rather enjoyed them. A 1983 graduate of the United States Central Intelligence Agency's "Human Resources Exploitation Course," and an ex-member of the Honduran death squad known as Battalion 3-16 – the biblical reference wasn't lost on him – Zelaya had so much to hide that hiding was impossible, and intimidation was the only remaining defense mechanism in a society that increasingly frowned on the kinds of political murders that had been Zelaya's bread and butter for nearly four decades.

He was well beyond nightmares. The atrocities he had committed over his long but insufficiently lucrative career had woven themselves into the fabric of his persona, and were as much a part of his identity as his scowl, his scars, and his ghost-white head of cropped hair, unusual for a man of Honduran descent, but not unusual for an American product.

Zelaya was both. He'd only been to the States a few times,

always to attend CIA training courses, during which he had applied his unusual memorization skills to chapter and verse of the KUBARK, a politically toxic tome that distilled the state of the art of coercive interrogation techniques. It existed to train generations of crusaders and ideologues in the arcane arts of pain and extortion. Zelaya was a star pupil.

Many of his compatriots enjoyed the sadism, and many more merely endured it for its utility, but Zelaya had the perfect combination of zeal and twisted proclivity to enjoy a long career as a pipe-swinging, throat-slitting, mind-screwing utility man.

The politics were complicated and ever-changing, of course, but there never seemed to be a shortage of *them* for *us* to fight. Near as Zelaya could tell, the Americans were interested in the region for what seemed like a silly reason: Honduras grew the shit out of some bananas. Bananas, as in the bright yellow phallic fruit, though the country had its share of the other kind of bananas, the kind of mental insularity and infirmity that produced civil and international strife lasting decades.

There was an even sillier reason that the gringos had come south, with their large words and their even larger impositions. This related to the uniquely gringo delusion that the entire world would be better off under a new religio-political system, called (drum roll, please) Democracy. Like Truth and Beauty, it was self-evidently, axiomatically, undeniably *good.* Better than everything else, even.

At least to the gringos.

Zelaya hadn't bothered to point out that if Democracy needed the same kinds of goons, assassins, spies, shills, and puppets that supported socialism, communism, dictatorships, and other lesser forms of government all over the globe, perhaps the idea wasn't really all it was cracked up to be.

Making such an observation would have been counterproductive, however. While the gringos were clearly naïve and misguided, they were also dizzyingly well-resourced. And their interests appeared to align more or less with his own, a happy coincidence which, together with the open-faced American gullibility for anyone who murmured the right ideological pet phrases at the right time, formed the backbone of a long and symbiotic relationship.

But here he was, in his sixties, still traipsing through the Central American jungles on the way to a prisoner camp to inflict grievous emotional, psychological, and physical harm on yet another human being, one who was unfortunate enough to find himself positioned by fate on the wrong side of a social or conceptual divide.

Surreal.

Old.

But it was remarkably commonplace in Zelaya's world, where borders were short but bitterly contested, and seemingly drawn to ensure that political divisions bisected as many familial and historical alliances as possible. There were more beefs per square foot than even Europe at its most truculent.

Job security.

And even in the relatively peaceful times, such as the era after the cocaine wars, the Americans' need for politically palatable places to conduct "enhanced interrogations" kept Zelaya plenty busy. Most of his reluctant guests over the last few years had been religiously misaligned gentlemen of Middle Eastern descent. They usually had little knowledge or concern regarding any nascent terrorist networks upon their delivery to Zelaya's care, but that didn't stop him from performing the proper due diligence.

Zelaya had expected the sudden gringo money problem – the dollar seemed intent on implosion, and appeared to be on the verge of tumbling into an inflationary oblivion of Dinar, Drachma, and Weimar Deutschmark proportions – to have unfavorable cash flow implications for him, but that hadn't turned out to be the case. A dear old Agency compatriot had called just days after the global meltdown had begun, in need of short-notice service for three Americans, two of whom happened to be female.

It was work, and it was of the lucrative variety, due to the political sensitivities involved, and Zelaya rarely turned down an opportunity. He had his eye on a small villa befitting a man of his loyalty and service, but not quite fitting within his means at the moment, so Bill Fredericks' call had been most welcome.

Zelaya reached his destination, swatted another mosquito, and rapped three times on a tree trunk to announce his arrival. A hollow echo resounded with each rap, affirming that he had chosen the right tree trunk. It had been hollowed out and resealed with a plaster-coated door designed to replicate the gnarled bark it had replaced, providing a suitably clandestine entrance to a well-used but well-hidden underground facility.

The subterranean entranceway was even muggier and more uncomfortable than the stifling jungle air, lacking the benefit of an occasional breeze to wick sweat away and replace the sickly sweet smell of decomposing organic matter.

With the door safely closed and locked behind him, Zelaya descended an earthen stairway leading to a narrow passage. He swiped his hand in front of his face to find a dangling string, a yank upon which caused a feeble overhead bulb to glow, helping him avoid the gnarled roots protruding through the cavern floor. Tripping hazard. He would mention it to the lieutenant, who would undoubtedly take the hint.

He felt the familiar downslope begin to level off, meaning he had descended the full twenty feet below grade, and was now on the top floor of a two-story underground interrogation and detention facility built by American contractors in the Reagan era. Talk about bananas. An underground prison with a Tolkien-like entrance in a hollowed-out tree? Couldn't they have just put a wall around a cabin in the jungle? Zelaya shook his head for the hundredth time at the boundless gringo zeal.

But it was tough to argue with success – in the facility's lengthy existence, Zelaya was aware of no security breaches. Perhaps there was a method to their madness.

"Our guests arrived safely, I presume?" Zelaya asked, striding with nonchalant authority into the facility's control center, of which he was undisputed master.

"Si, Señor." Lieutenant Alvarez was bright, competent, and dedicated. But not mean enough, in Zelaya's judgment. "Mother, girl, and target. They thought they were on their way to Costa Rica," he said with a derisive laugh. "All in separate cells, currently undergoing preparations."

Zelaya nodded. Preparations, as they were euphemistically called, entailed various measures that were designed "to induce psychological regression in the subject by bringing a superior outside force to bear on his will to resist." It was as if a business school graduate had written the Agency's exploitation manual, except that the sentences in the KUBARK sometimes actually made sense.

A superior outside force. Zelaya had always liked that phrase. It was a fitting personal and organizational description, he fancied, as well as a goal worthy of continuous aspiration. Part of his DNA now. The CIA-recommended techniques were varied and voluminous, including prolonged constraint, prolonged exertion, extremes of heat, cold, and moisture, deprivation of food or sleep, solitary confinement, threats of pain, deprivation of sensory stimuli, hypnosis, and drugs.

In all, nature had provided a rich palette of available techniques to place the human psyche in an agreeably compliant condition.

He looked at his watch. Almost dawn. In a few hours, it would be time for an introductory visit with each of his new subjects.

Chapter 3

Turbulence awoke Special Agent Sam Jameson. She had the kind of nasty taste in her mouth that she always got when she was awakened too early from too little slumber. She looked at her watch, which confirmed that entirely too few minutes had passed while she was unconscious. Just shy of an hour, to be exact.

Her watch was still set to Mountain time. It was a couple of steps behind. Along with her compatriots, who together comprised the entire passenger manifest of a US government VIP jet transport plane, she had left the Pitt Meadows Regional Airport in British Columbia, Canada, and was hurtling down the American Left Coast through the darkness toward Costa Rica.

It was a long story.

It involved what she had come to regard as a colossally bad idea, which had spawned a shockingly successful conspiracy. One of the perpetrators happened to occupy a seat on the airplane. He went by the unlikely name of Trojan, and was busily pecking away at a laptop computer, trying to unscrew what he had so well and truly screwed.

Trojan was part of a group of extremely competent, and in some cases, extremely prominent, illuminati who had become of a mind, collectively, to disable the US banking system. They were pissed off, near as Sam could tell, about the US socioeconomic system's steady descent into oligarchy, to be remedied only by the destruction of the oligarchy's lifeblood: the US dollar.

By all indications, they had pulled it off.

Their success had added the Mighty Greenback to a long list of failed or failing fiat currencies, a result that produced just the sort of economic and political upheaval that re-drew maps and invited newly-self-appointed Masters of the Universe to try their hand at wrestling society's reins from whoever used to hold them.

And *that*, in turn, was why Sam, a busty, beautiful, brash, and somewhat bombastic redheaded Homeland Security agent, found herself jetting toward a Central American country in the middle of the night.

Messy.

But what else would she have been doing, if she weren't saving the world from the bastards? Writing memos? Informing stakeholders? Adding value to a value-added team in some value chain somewhere? No, thanks.

She'd rather catch spies, despite the sleep deprivation it sometimes produced. And the near-death experiences. But those things kept life interesting, and she figured that they just came with the territory. After all, was the threat of a violent physical death really all that much worse than the certainty of a protracted and painful death caused by cubicle-induced boredom? Sam had given the matter plenty of thought, and she thought not.

She looked over at Brock James, the man whose bed she'd shared for what was entirely too short an episode in her life. He was, for lack of a better word, perfect. Not in the usual bullshit, starry-eyed sense, but in the sense that all of his jagged edges fit all of her jagged edges as though they were complementary pieces carved from the same sarcastic, intelligent, athletic, and doggedly determined block. Their relationship worked in the way that gravity worked. There was almost nothing they could do to *stop* it from working.

In addition to the economic meltdown of global proportions, the past week had seen a kidnapping, too. Brock's. Those were three of the worst days of her life. But Sam's bull-in-a-china-shop tenacity and her Kimber .45 had saved the day, and while his bedroom athleticism was temporarily diminished by a gunshot wound to the thigh, Brock had survived the ordeal.

Thank god for that. She loved that man and his bedroom athleticism.

She could go for a little of that right now, she thought, watching his beautiful face as he slept. *Alas.* She resolved to take advantage of him sometime when they weren't confined in the presence of subordinates, criminals, and other unsavory people.

Unfortunately, a cozy bed wasn't anywhere on the agenda. They weren't exactly headed to Costa Rica on vacation. It had taken convincing, cajoling, and even a little coercion, but Sam had eventually wrestled the destination of Domingo Mondragon's chartered jet from the Obsidian Air charter service's desk clerk. An American government badge didn't go far in Canada, but Sam had found an exploitable pressure point. Thanks to her above-average persuasion skills, they subsequently found themselves winging their way toward Juan Santamaria International Airport in the little banana republic's capital, San Jose.

She chuckled to herself at the absurdity of the situation. She was on a plane with her deputy, her lover, and an international criminal responsible for helping to castrate the world's banking and monetary system, flying to the Central American jungle to chase down a felon and FBI informant, turned FBI employee, turned rogue Bitcoin thief.

You can't make this shit up.

The sound of clicking computer keys interrupted her reverie, and she looked over to see Dan Gable's face illuminated in the blue-white glow of a laptop screen. Her deputy was built like a bodybuilder, though one who had perhaps enjoyed a few too many ho-ho's. His physique made his uncommon computer skills seem a bit incongruous. He was putting his geekery to good use, searching for digital clues left on a laptop in the warehouse they'd searched just a couple of hours earlier. By all indications, this was the very laptop that Mondragon had used to steal tens of thousands of Bitcoins.

Those were worth about seventy gazillion dollars, now that the dollar had inflated beyond recognition. This week's dollar, Sam reflected, was worth quite a bit less than last week's penny.

More clackety-clack, caused by Dan's meaty fingers typing excessively hard on the keyboard. He was, in her estimation, the sole trustworthy individual in the Department of Homeland Security. She loved him like a brother. Sometimes he was an annoying brother. But he was nothing if not effective.

Their relationship was extremely close, but always professional. He'd touched her naked body once, and had even put his hands on her bare chest, but that was in an attempt to restart her heart, which had stopped beating on account of her very recent death. Thankfully, death didn't take, and she returned to the realm of the living with a few scars and an outrageous story.

Dan noticed her looking over at him. "Found something, boss," he said, turning the laptop so she could read the screen.

Sam saw instant-message artifacts from several conversations that occurred between someone named Sabot – Mondragon, she assumed, since Sabot was his pre-incarceration hacker moniker – and a person who called himself Balzzack011. "So it looks like this wasn't really Sabot's idea," she summarized after reading the message traffic between them.

Dan nodded. "The reluctant genius, kept chained up in a warehouse, stealing a fortune in Bitcoins. But who's pulling the strings?"

Sam shook her head and scowled. "The fact that there's a master of any sort is a bit disconcerting. If Mondragon was just a random hacker with a bright idea about how to get over on the world, that would be much easier to deal with. But this sounds a bit like coerced theft, which means that someone understood the importance of Bitcoins after the dollar pancaked, but lacked the technical skills to actually steal any."

Dan assented silently.

Sam pondered. There was no shortage of megalomaniacal bastards in the world, it turned out. It was simple probability math. One in twenty-five denizens of Planet Earth had sociopathic tendencies. A fraction of those were also narcissistic. And a slice of that cohort had the intellect and social skill to manipulate their way to real power. The sudden rise of the Bitcoin market in the wake of the dollar's implosion was a juicy motivator, and Sam didn't doubt that it had brought the nut jobs out in force.

So she had no clue about who might have been running Sabot, the hacker-thief. "Any clues about why Mondragon ran?"

"Maybe," Dan said. "I found something in the ftp history."

"The history of what?"

"Are you completely computer illiterate?"

"No," Sam said. "I can program my vibrator."

Dan frowned and shook his head. "You can use the internet to transfer files directly between computers, without sending them in an email. It's called file transfer protocol, or ftp. It leaves less of a trail than email, which is the digital equivalent of petrified wood."

Sam nodded. She'd typed angry before, and had clicked send, which was how she had learned that email was forever.

"Our guy deleted the ftp history, which is a great indication that he's got something to hide. Porn, usually, but in this case, it turns out that Sabot transferred the scripts that were behind all the Bitcoin thefts to a server farm in New Jersey."

"How did you figure that out if he deleted the history?"

Dan smiled. "A few tricks of the trade."

"Constitutionally dubious, no doubt."

"No comment."

Sam smiled, shaking her head. "So he made a copy of his own program for his own use," she summarized. "I suppose that might be grounds for a falling out, given that this 'Ball Sack' guy seems to think that Mondragon works for him."

Dan nodded. "He must have been pretty scared. He took his girlfriend and her mother along with him."

"There's a ton of money in play. I can see why he was concerned. How about the list of Bitcoin accounts and passwords?"

"It's hidden behind 256 encryption," Dan said.

"Which will be child's play for the decryption bug that destroyed the Fed," Sam said, gesturing toward Trojan.

Dan nodded. "Exactly right. So I don't expect trouble hacking in."

"So we just un-steal the coins. Done. No more threat of world domination. Right?"

Dan nodded. "And we should be able to work the same magic on the mirror operation hidden on the New Jersey server." He smiled. "Makes me wonder why we're flying all the way to Costa Rica."

"Great point. Who ordered this expedition? She should be fired. But humor me, maybe, and un-steal a few zillion Bitcoins ASAPly, just to prove we can."

Dan opened the decryption program, briefly consulted with Trojan, the international computer criminal whose virus had brought down the banking industry and whose help they now enjoyed, and clicked a few more keys.

"Oh, shit."

Sam: "What's up?"

"I just opened the Bitcoin transaction ledger to get an idea of which private keys to go after."

"English, please."

Dan explained that a Bitcoin wasn't really a physical or digital object. Instead, it was an entry in a public record of private transactions. Each transaction involved a public key, which was otherwise known as the account name, and a private key, which was akin to its password. "I was looking for the right accounts to hack into."

"Should be easy, right? Aren't they using thousands of new accounts to receive the stolen Bitcoins?"

Dan nodded. "They are. But it looks like there's a parallel operation going on to disperse the cash through a bunch of different, new accounts, too." More clicking, and a low whistle. "Tens of thousands of accounts."

"Sounds inconvenient. But you can crack them all, right?"

"Fairly easily, if we use Trojan's network of slave computers. Disregarding the legal problem with using a network of virus-infected private computers to do federal government work, of course."

"I don't think Uncle Sugar has the luxury of splitting hairs at the moment," Sam said. "Besides, these guys are making a play for the kind of wealth that will buy any government they want. I think I can ask forgiveness."

"Let the record reflect that I am breaking the law on the suggestion of my immediate supervisor."

Dan squinted his eyes and examined a few new windows, a frown deepening on his brow. "Shit. This isn't going to work."

"What's not going to work?"

"It looks like they have their funds in continuous movement. In the time it will take us to decrypt an account's password, they will have easily established a new account and transferred all the Bitcoins out of the old one."

More clicking. "It's actually kind of brilliant," Dan continued. "They've found an elegant way to stay ahead of the tracing problem. Every Bitcoin transaction is public and traceable, so they're making every transaction utterly meaningless by keeping the money constantly in flux, establishing new accounts every second or two."

Sam frowned. "How wily of them. Any way we can maybe anticipate the account names, to get inside the time cycle?"

Dan shook his head. "Each account name has thirty-four random digits, each of which can contain letters or numbers."

"So looks like it's down to good old fashioned spy catching."

"Looks that way."

"I guess flying down to Costa Rica wasn't such a bad idea after all."

Dan smiled. "I hear it's pretty down there. And the cartel beheadings have slowed down a bit, too."

"See? It'll be fun."

Chapter 4

Domingo "Sabot" Mondragon slumped on the dank concrete floor, his wrist chained to the wall above his head, the shower above him still dripping ice-cold water. His clothes were soaked. Despite the stifling jungle air, he was shivering uncontrollably, and he was completely exhausted. Every time he came close to feeling remotely less miserable, he received a blast of frigid water.

They hadn't asked him any questions. In fact, he hadn't seen another human since the charter jet's passenger door had opened on the tarmac hours earlier.

The particular humans he saw then weren't friendly. They had loud voices, automatic weapons, black hoods, duct tape, and a rickety van that bounced and jostled for an eternity before coming to a noisy halt in someplace that smelled and sounded like a jungle.

Not that Sabot knew what a jungle smelled or sounded like. He was from Queens, and had lived most recently in Seattle. But it was tough to mistake the loud buzz of insects and the shrill calls of nocturnal creatures as anything even remotely urban. And the sweet stench of both life and decay was another solid clue that they weren't in the city.

Chained up in a wet, dark cell, it was all he could do to keep his wits about him. His penitentiary time had fostered a stronger-than-normal aversion to captivity, and the sound of Angie's soft, fearful sobs echoing in his memory were working his emotions into a frenzy.

Because it was probably all his fault.

It probably wasn't just a random third-world kidnapping. This one probably had his name all over it, all because of a single decision he'd made.

He'd decided to skim a few hundred thousand Bitcoins for himself, in addition to the hundreds of thousands he was stealing for his employers, whoever the hell they were.

But that wasn't the problem. The problem was, they *knew* he'd done it. He'd covered his tracks exceedingly well, but they'd somehow gotten inside of his decision loop. They'd somehow managed to sneak a spyware program onto that damned black market laptop he now deeply regretted buying, the one he'd used to make a copy of the automatic script he'd written for his employers to swipe Bitcoins from tens of thousands of individual accounts. They'd had a ringside seat for his treachery.

So here he was, incalculably rich and growing richer by the second, yet chained to the wall in a third-world jungle, freezing, afraid, exhausted, and unable to stop imagining all of the horrific things they were probably doing to Angie and her mom, whom he hadn't seen since the kidnappers threw a hood over his head and kneed him in the balls.

His throat hurt, too. Not because of the cold. It hurt because he'd swallowed a USB drive, wrapped in a cute little heart-shaped waterproof container. It was like swallowing a rock, and the pointy edge had scraped his esophagus in a few spots on the way down. It was probably going to get stuck somewhere in his innards, a condition which would undoubtedly suck a tremendous amount. But not nearly as much as it would suck if they – and he still had no idea who the hell *they* were – ever got their hands on the device.

It had been an exceedingly risky move on his part. Because his face was covered by the hood, he had no idea if any of the kidnappers had been watching him while he fished around between his sock and his leg, where he'd stashed the drive for safekeeping, and then brought his duct-taped hands together to his mouth.

He'd swallowed the damn thing as quickly as he could, fearing they'd figure out what he'd just done and fish it out of his mouth before he could get it safely into his stomach, and it was this haste that undoubtedly contributed to the discomfort he now felt in his throat. It had felt like he was swallowing broken glass, and it took forever for peristalsis to carry the jagged little thing down to his gut.

An excruciating bout of acid reflux told him that it had breached his esophageal sphincter, but took its sweet time making it all the way through to his stomach.

No matter, he told himself. It was as important a thumb drive as ever existed, at least as far as he knew. He could put up with a little pain. More than a little, in fact, given the size of the bounty awaiting him in the accounts it contained.

He heard the pipes rumble, and braced himself for the drenching that followed, sputtering and cursing as the frigid water splashed down on top of him.

Chapter 5

"You don't slice someone's head off because you believe in a cause." It was the kind of proclamation for which terrorism expert Harv Edwards was famous, one that presaged a pithy punch line, a penchant for which he was equally well known. He paused, dumpy and rumpled in his aircraft seat, looking expectantly at Sam with a trademark twinkle in his eye.

She dutifully arched her eyebrow to elicit the inevitable follow-up.

"You join a cause so you can slice off heads," Edwards said.

Sam smiled. Harv was disagreeable in almost every important way, down to the annoying fact that, in Sam's experience, Harv was almost never wrong. His unrelenting unlikeability and his prescience were the two things Sam loved most about him. He'd been a last-second addition to the unlikely entourage of federal agents and international criminals. Harv had been summoned by Sam's superiors from a vacation in the Oregon wilderness to join the team charged with stopping the unfolding fiscal calamity.

"So we become what we always were," Sam said.

"But more so."

"And you're implying that the same principle applies to our friend Sabot Mondragon in some way, I presume?"

Edwards smirked. "No, I just wanted to impress you with my terrorism Zen."

"Fail," Sam said, her eyes suddenly weary. "Focus, please. On a scale from zero to damned tired, I'm way up there, and I want to get some sleep before we land."

"Our friend isn't unaccustomed to big, risky plays. He once shut down a Middle Eastern country's computer network from his kitchen in Queens, if memory serves."

Sam nodded, and Edwards continued. "But he's not a joiner. The causes he's supported seem random. Near as I can tell, the only unifying theme between his crimes is a slightly anarchic penchant — picking on big business, oppressive but largely harmless governments in remote parts of the world, that kind of thing — but there's otherwise no guiding principle at work."

"Other than opportunity," Sam said.

Edwards nodded. "Seems like all of Mondragon's victims are slightly disagreeable from an ideological standpoint, but I think he only attacked them because he found a weakness that he could exploit. There wasn't anything really ideologically significant about any of his hacks."

"So your conclusion is?" Sam prodded, weariness showing.

"He's an egotistical opportunist. He's willing to pull the trigger on a big play that lands in his lap, then sort out the consequences later."

A skeptical look crossed Sam's face. "His time in the penitentiary didn't scare him straight?"

Edwards laughed. "Does it ever?"

"Good point."

"And don't forget my guiding principle," Edwards said in an

annoyingly didactic tone.

"Once a condescending asshole, always a condescending asshole?" Sam asked pointedly, arching one of her pinup-model eyebrows in Edwards' direction.

"Touché. But in our case, it means that our man Sabot probably isn't a card-carrying member of a cohesive group of hackers, thieves, or ideologues. He probably just saw an opportunity and took advantage of it."

"So instead of installing himself as Commander of the Universe, the richest thief in the world will probably just buy fancy sports cars if he gets away with it?"

"Seems likely," Edwards said. "Mondragon seems shady, egotistical, and totally Screw-The-Man, but I don't think he's a megalomaniac."

Dan Gable, listening at the periphery of the conversation, caught Sam's attention. "I don't think it's just a rogue hacker we're worried about. Sabot may not have had revolution on his mind when he stole all that Bitcoin, but nothing says that his employers weren't eyeing more than just fancy cars when they contracted him to steal that money."

Trojan hefted his laptop and turned the screen toward Dan and Sam. "Dan's right," he said.

"What am I looking at?" Sam asked, too tired to squint at the page full of text on Trojan's computer screen.

"Server logs, from the data centers that saw account activity from Sabot's Bitcoin op," Trojan said. "I've noticed a particular IP address snooping around the servers."

"How'd you notice that?" Sam asked.

Trojan looked questioningly at Dan, who nodded assent. "Hacked in for a peek," Trojan admitted.

"Figured we could argue exigency, if it came down to it," Dan said by way of explanation for authorizing Trojan's illegal computer maneuver.

Sam shook her head. "I'm hoping it doesn't. Tell me why the IP address thing is important."

"I wanted to see whether there were any usage patterns in the affected stacks," Trojan said.

"English," Sam prodded. "And pretend you're speaking to a retarded child, or an MBA."

Trojan smiled. "I mean that if anyone else were onto Sabot's play, following his Bitcoin moves around the country through random accounts on various computer servers, that evidence would show up in the logs."

"The server logs keep track of which other computers have asked for information," Dan added helpfully.

Sam cocked her head. "And you've noticed a pattern."

Trojan nodded. "One computer, in Banff."

"Canada?"

"How many other Banffs are there?"

Sam scowled. "Could it be coincidence? Maybe some Bitcoin geek following transactions who happened to discover Sabot's merry-go-round scheme?"

Dan shook his head. "Those are extremely thin odds. Mondragon's operation looks tiny to each individual victim, even small enough to go unnoticed, and it's only in aggregate that the scale becomes evident. And he's done a brilliant job of using slave computers to do the dirty work for him, which left a confusing mess of several thousand IP addresses to sift through. It would take months to investigate them all."

"Insider, then," Sam concluded.

"Someone familiar with the op," Dan agreed.

"I'll get on the horn to Washington," Sam said, lifting the in-flight phone from the seat in front of her. "We need to get someone back up to Canada to poke around."

She began to dial, but was interrupted by an announcement from the flight deck, something about seat belts, tray tables, an imminent landing in a small Central American country, and the end of the in-flight Wi-Fi and phone service.

She closed her eyes and sighed, feeling exhaustion wrapping itself around her consciousness, wondering when her next opportunity for sleep might come, and wondering whether the cell phone system in Costa Rica was compatible with her US government-issue phone.

Chapter 6

The old man called Archive awoke from a fitful slumber, neck sore, slumped over in a posh leather chair in the media room at the Lost Man Lake Ranch in the mountains of Colorado.

At first glance, the lodge and surrounding acreage looked like any other mountain vacation property owned by someone with ridiculous wealth. It was elegant, well-apportioned, isolated, and expansive.

But it was also off the grid, almost completely self-sufficient, and designed from the ground up to weather the sort of political, economic, and social storm that Archive himself had set about creating.

The wizened tycoon rubbed his eyes, trying to wash out a weariness that had settled upon him some years ago, which had only worsened as he and his coterie of fellow luminaries and oligarchs brought to fruition their highly improbable plan to rid the world of what they believed to be its greatest ill.

They had succeeded in grand fashion. Unfortunately, there had been some unsavory side effects.

The news feeds droned on, video loops showing riots and violence in familiar American cities. The newsies seemed particularly fond of footage of a riot at the entrance of the Federal Reserve Bank on Constitution Avenue in Washington, DC, showing what looked like angry middle-class white people lobbing empty water bottles at the addled Fed Board of Governors as they assembled for yet another emergency meeting.

If not dead already, the US dollar was surely dying. The Greenback had been, Archive and his cohorts concluded, the largest scam in human history, but the bubble had burst. *He* had burst the bubble. Game over.

But the chaotic aftermath, which they had anticipated would be painful, was testing his nerves in a way that Archive hadn't accounted for. He groaned, feeling disdain for the pompous Fed clowns as he watched them exit their limousines in front of the Federal Reserve edifice, but also feeling the weight of responsibility for the unrest.

His guilt wasn't without cause. One might reasonably argue that regardless of their intentions, he and his cronies had blood on their hands. Hundreds had died over the past several days in the rioting, lawlessness, looting, and unrest that had erupted across the country as the populace realized that their life savings — if they could access the money at all, which most couldn't — would probably not pay for two weeks of groceries. The rug had been pulled from beneath them, and they were more than a little pissed off.

That hadn't really been the idea. Archive and his group of shining lights had surmised that the degradation of infrastructure during most of history's revolutions had caused the lion's share of violence and upheaval, so their plan left intact all of the physical infrastructure underpinning modern society. They had just struck at the fiat currency that had lubricated the machinery of commerce and government, a currency that had been manipulated beyond all recognition and turned against the people it ostensibly served.

Archive had sought to end the silent oppression, the tacit reapportionment of wealth further in favor of the wealthy. He wanted to end the theft. There was no other name for it, he had reasoned during many of the late-night thinking sessions and conversations he'd held in the posh study in his DC mansion, pondering first whether, and then how, to take matters into his own hands to restore some semblance of equality.

Slogans and election-time charades notwithstanding, Archive believed that the people had been subjugated, unaware, to serfdom. The modern version was far subtler than the medieval incarnation, but it was a form of slavery nonetheless. Pricing the means of modern survival — shelter, transportation, even food — beyond the common man's grasp, then inducing him to borrow against his future to pay for those goods today, represented an indenture no less thorough than in the feudal system of old.

So Archive had used his mammoth wealth and even more impressive influence to slowly assemble the right people to perform a surgical strike at the heart of the beast. And they had won.

Whether society could survive the victory was another matter entirely.

Protégé entered, coffee in hand, wearing a flannel shirt and cargo pants. Archive was most accustomed to seeing the young executive in a hand-sewn suit and power tie, but the casual attire served to underscore the fact that the world had changed. Profoundly, in fact.

"Do you have any figures for me?" Archive queried, surprised by how tired he sounded even to himself.

Protégé nodded, exuding the kind of calm, confident competence that had propelled him to the helm of the General Electronics Corporation's Government Services Division at the tender young age of forty. At least, that's the position he used to hold, before he stole the GE technology that hobbled the backbone of the global monetary system.

"I'm not sure how reliable these numbers will be," Protégé said, "given that only half the police officers in any given city have reported for duty. The National Guard has the same problem. Most people ignored their orders and stayed home to defend their families from looters and thugs."

The old man winced at the mention of hooliganism. Atavistic behavior was unavoidable in a time of chaos, but the reality of it was hard for him to watch. He'd set them loose, and he was impatient for the chaos to run its course, eager for people to realize that the only change brought about by the dollar's implosion was a change in the agreement between them. Crops still grew, machines still functioned, bridges still spanned rivers, technology still worked, people's homes still sheltered them from the elements, and, most importantly, the talent and genius of humanity remained as powerful a force as ever.

A smile crossed Protégé's face. "But honestly, I'm encouraged by the figures," he said. "Maybe three thousand serious injuries. Far fewer deaths."

Archive didn't share Protégé's optimism. "The first death was one too many."

"But you knew it was highly probable, and maybe even inevitable. And you — we — all of us… We chose to move ahead. 'The mantle of responsibility,' and all of that."

The old man nodded. "Far less egregious in theory, but I'm finding it hard to stomach the losses."

Protégé nodded. "There have been some horrible scenes. But we need to put those episodes in perspective. It's a numbers game. There are three hundred million US citizens, and probably another thirty million illegals. At least a third of a billion of us. If one half of one percent of the population are complete bastards, and the chaos removed the social restraints keeping them in check, it means that just over a million and a half assholes broke loose to channel their inner caveman."

Archive's visage darkened further. "That's supposed to be consolation?"

"It certainly should be, when you consider that the remaining three hundred-some-odd million of us will eventually subdue them," Protégé said. "And it's already happening. The crime rate appears to be dropping. Ad-hoc citizens' groups are springing up all over the place, and they're restoring order. It looks like the neighborhoods are starting to recover from the initial shock of the dollar crash, and people are starting to work together again. We're not out of the woods yet, but things appear to have taken a turn for the better."

"I certainly got a different impression from the news channels," the old man said.

Protégé sneered. "Those bastions of objectivity and truth? I'm shocked."

Archive allowed himself a tired smile. "I suppose I should place less stock in what remains of our journalistic enterprise."

"Come downstairs with me," Protégé said. "You need to see something."

* * *

The journey to the underground portion of the Lost Man Lake Lodge took less than a minute, but it was like crossing into a different dimension. Protégé typed his PIN into a wall-mounted keypad in the rustically-apportioned basement lounge, and an entire section of wall retreated into the foundation to reveal the entrance to a spacious bunker dug into the side of the mountain.

Another keypad-activated door led to the computer center, where an athletic man named Vaneesh, whose pseudo-quantum decryption program had made child's play out of the Federal Reserve's state-of-the-art firewall, leaving the entire banking system utterly exposed and vulnerable to the subsequent cyber attack, sat perched in front of a wall of monitors.

"Our fearless leader has been watching too much propaganda," Protégé announced. "So I've brought him down for a dose of the unvarnished truth."

"I think you'll like the news, honestly," Vaneesh said. "I've gained access to all of the street corner video cameras," he began.

"Where?" Archive asked.

Protégé and Vaneesh shared a knowing smile. "Everywhere," the computer scientist said, unable to hide the hint of pride seeping into his voice.

"What in heaven's name will you do with all of that data?" the old man asked.

"I've written a script to categorize, sort, and prioritize the video feeds based on some key criteria. Turns out that understanding the mood of the populace really boils down to categorizing the number, size, and entropy level of the crowds that the video cameras detect."

Archive looked puzzled.

"You can think of a crowd's entropy level as its degree of agitation," Vaneesh explained. "The randomness of movement within a crowd, and the energy of that movement, is a good indicator of violence. So good, in fact, that we can consider entropy a proxy for unrest."

"And your script does this automatically for all of the video feeds from all of the street corners in America?"

"Pretty much," Vaneesh said. "I still have a few kinks to work out, but we have enough data over the last day or so to draw some pretty solid conclusions."

"Which are?" Archive asked.

"Protégé and I have seen a steady drop in both the number and agitation level of the crowds in all major metropolitan areas, with a similar trend in the smaller population centers," Vaneesh said. "The upshot is that people are settling down."

Protégé smiled. "It turns out that most of us are pretty rational people."

"There's more," Vaneesh said, expanding the view from a particular video feed to encompass the entire wall of video displays in front of them. "What does this look like?"

Archive studied the feed for a moment. "Is that... barter?"

"It is," Protégé said. "An impromptu open-air market. People meeting each others' needs through trade and enterprise," he said, his voice a little giddy. "What we hoped would happen, is actually happening."

"Not everywhere," cautioned Vaneesh, "but we're seeing more and more of this kind of thing. It's a low-entropy, low-density, long-duration crowd as far as the computer script is concerned, and examples are cropping up all over the place."

Relief was evident on Archive's face. "Thank God. I had hoped that people would get it figured out sooner rather than later, but I was beginning to have my doubts."

"I'm going to unplug your televisions upstairs," Protégé said with a chuckle. "You don't want to become like my dad. He spends his days self-radicalizing with the right-wing news."

Archive smiled, but his mirth was short-lived. "What about the Bitcoin problem?"

A pained look crossed Vaneesh's face. He shook his head. "Catastrophic, I'm afraid."

"Now that we know the digital signature of the virtual theft op," Protégé said, "it's become painfully obvious that we're watching the greatest plunder since Hitler."

A worried expression clouded Archive's features.

"And the stolen virtual currency becomes more and more valuable as dollar-infected fiat currencies continue to lose value," Vaneesh added.

"So the rate of theft hasn't subsided," Archive said, "and the value of the stolen money continues to rise."

"Worse," Protégé said. "The rate of theft has *increased.* There's now another theft operation underway."

"The same thieves?" Archive asked.

"Very similar methodology," Vaneesh said. "It's possible that someone else came up with the same process — hacking into Bitcoin repositories, finding user passwords, and skimming from all of the accounts — but I think it's more probable that the second operation is a clone of the first."

"The second thief is in New Jersey, right?" Archive recalled.

"Not exactly," Protégé answered. "We — Trojan, really — discovered theft activity centered around Seattle, and another locus around a server farm in rural New Jersey. That means that the *servers* used to carry out the thefts are in Seattle and New Jersey. The thieves could be anywhere."

"Any report from Trojan and the feds?" Archive asked.

Protégé nodded. "They're actually en route to Central America right now. They think they have a line on the guy who built the first theft operation. He might have also built the second one, though that's not yet clear."

"It's also not yet clear if the guy was working alone," Vaneesh added.

Archive shook his head, a grave look on his face. "I hadn't foreseen anything like this. Our aim was to end the global oligarchy, not set the stage for an even more consolidated economic power. If we can't reverse the thefts or corral the thieves, all of this effort and sacrifice will have been for nothing. We'll have killed the demon, only to see him replaced by the devil himself."

Chapter 7

Domingo Mondragon, known as Sabot in the small, insular world of computer hackers, was a world away from his element. And he was in a world of shit.

Another vicious deluge of frigid water showered over him, and he felt his teeth rattle as he shivered violently in the cold. His wrist was still chained to the wall. The chain reached low enough to allow him to slump in a heap on the floor, but not so low to allow him to drop his arm below his head. He couldn't feel his hand, and his wrist ached horribly from the shackle digging into his skin and sinew. A trickle of blood snaked its way toward his elbow. But he couldn't stand up to relieve the pain in his arm, because his exhausted legs would not support his weight.

A wave of panic washed over him as his thoughts turned to Angie, what she might be enduring. They hadn't touched him, other than to shackle him beneath the water spigot, but had they shown the same restraint with her?

Or had they taken advantage of her, taken by force the gift of herself that he relished as his alone?

His stomach turned with fear and anger. And something else. Something much, much worse.

Guilt.

Angie was at their mercy, whoever the hell *they* were, because of him. Any harm that came to her was forever on his conscience.

His greed, his recklessness, and his naïveté had brought this down on them.

All of them. Connie, too. Angie's mother wasn't strong or healthy, and if she was being treated in a remotely similar fashion to him, Sabot feared she wouldn't survive the ordeal for more than a few days.

Days? Could it really last that long? Could *he* survive much more of this? He felt himself starting to unravel. Hunger gnawed at his stomach, his muscles ached from the violent, hypothermic shivering, and despair began to overtake his mind. *We're screwed,* the voice inside his head kept saying. *And it's all my fault.*

The pipes rumbled yet again, and the faucet above his head spewed another blast of ice-cold water over his battered body. The water seemed to pour down on him for an eternity. The tears came involuntarily. His torso spasmed, wracked with anguished sobs and shivering uncontrollably. *I'm so screwed,* Sabot thought again.

Finally, the water stopped, and Sabot became aware of another presence in the cell with him. Black boots, green pants, khaki shirt tucked loosely into a black belt. Jet-black Central American hair, dark skin, youngish. The man was sneering at him.

Sabot used his free shoulder to wipe the tears from his face, a useless enterprise given that his entire face was dripping wet from the latest blast of frigid water. The gesture served only to highlight that he'd been crying like a broken man just seconds earlier.

The visitor's sneer turned into a derisive laugh, and Sabot added abject embarrassment to his list of debilitating emotions. *I've got to get my shit together.*

A second man entered the cell, big-boned, muscular, also dressed in khakis, and carrying two wooden chairs. He walked slowly, purposefully toward Sabot, hard eyes boring through Sabot's own, and slammed one of the two chairs down just inches from Sabot's feet. Sabot jumped involuntarily.

"Sit," the large man growled, slamming the second chair across from the first as he strode out of the room, the first guard in tow.

Sabot needed much of his remaining strength to heft himself up from the floor. He sat in the hard wooden chair, his body still shaking uncontrollably. He placed his numb hand in his lap, wincing as the blood began to circulate. He doubled over for warmth, and stared at what appeared to be a blood stain on the grimy concrete floor. The slack chain rattled mockingly with his shivers.

Completely screwed, the voice said again.

He heard boots in the hallway, the clank of a key in his cell door, and the groan of the ancient, rusted hinges as the cell door gave way to a small, slight, severe-looking man with close-cropped white hair, dead eyes, and half a dozen scars on his face.

The man regarded Sabot silently for a long moment, then walked slowly to the chair opposite Sabot's, seated himself, and resumed his dead-eyed stare. Sabot felt himself wither under the hardness of the stranger's gaze. The man looked like death in jackboots, and Sabot couldn't help but notice a bullwhip curled up and fastened to the man's belt. He shivered involuntarily, but not because of the cold.

After a brief eternity, the man spoke. "Domingo Mondragon."

His voice was improbably deep and gravelly. "I am Terencio Manuel Zelaya. I tell you my name so that later, as you endure the atrocities that you are about to suffer, you will know precisely whom to loathe and fear. And, if you are like many other guests before you, you will know whom to beg for your life."

Sabot felt the blood drain from his face. He feared he might faint.

Zelaya studied Sabot for a long moment, as if placing bets inside his head about when and how Sabot would crumble before him, then rose and walked slowly toward the door, extinguishing the light on his way out.

"There are many ways to break a man," Zelaya said, pausing in the dim light of the doorway. He turned to regard Sabot, a small smile creeping onto the corners of his mouth. "But every man breaks."

The door slammed behind Zelaya, leaving Sabot to shiver in the darkness. He heard the pipes rumble, and he braced himself for another frigid onslaught.

* * *

Sabot had no idea how much time had passed since the visit from the diminutive devil when he heard footfalls in the hallway outside his cell. These footfalls were different. Lighter. Feminine. Even a little furtive. The cell door creaked open just enough to emit a shaft of dim light from the dank hallway, illuminating motes of detritus floating in the thick jungle air.

A slight, graceful figure stepped inside the cell. A woman. Dark hair pulled back into a bun, high Central American cheekbones, dark skin. Pretty. The woman peeked back into the hallway before easing the door shut, as if checking whether she'd been spotted or followed.

She padded quietly toward Sabot. He heard her pull the chain attached to the overhead light, and the lonely bulb in the center of his cell came to life, barely filling the dank chamber with feeble light.

Sabot noticed her hands for the first time. They were cradling a tea cup. Steam snaked upward in the gloom. "Drink," she said, *sotto voce*. "For your strength." Her voice was kind, her manner sympathetic.

Exhausted, freezing, and starving, Sabot accepted her kindness without a second thought, brought the tea to his lips with two shaky hands, and sipped greedily. He burned his tongue.

"Careful," the woman said. "It is still hot."

"Who are you?"

"Do not talk. Listen carefully. Soon, they will offer you food. You must not eat it."

Sabot felt his stomach grind with hunger. "That will be tough."

"They will put a drug in your food. Then all will be lost."

"All of what will be lost?"

"Everything," the woman said.

"What are you talking about?"

"Señor Mondragon, you have stumbled into something much bigger than you realize. Not all of Zelaya's prisoners are chained to a wall."

"There were two women with me…" Sabot started to ask.

The woman shook her head gravely. "There is not much time."

"Have they done something to them?"

She looked at him, appearing as if she were weighing something in her mind. A tired, pained expression settled on her face. She nodded slowly.

"What have they done?" Sabot tried to stand up.

The woman put her hands on his shoulders and pressed him firmly back into the chair. "Listen to me," she whispered. "There is still time, but not much. They are alive. But everything depends on you keeping your wits about you."

"Where are they?"

"You cannot help them now."

"Get me out of here! I won't be chained up like a dog while…"

"Lower your voice, Domingo," she hissed. "The guards are armed. You are weak and exhausted. If I unchained you, it would be the end of both of us. You must stay here until the time is right."

"I can't let anything happen to them!"

"There is nothing you can do right now." She took the half-empty cup of tea from his hand, turned off the light, and walked to the door. "Keep your head, Domingo. Be ready when the time is right."

The woman opened the cell door carefully, flinched visibly as the hinges screeched, peered in both directions down the hallway, and slipped away into the dim light.

His cell went dark, and he heard the door lock click into place.

All manner of atrocities flashed before his mind's eye. He pictured Angie, bruised, battered, disfigured, naked. Violated. His breath came in shallow gasps as fear, guilt, and hatred overwhelmed him. His heart pounded in his chest. *I will kill them with my bare hands,* he swore.

You'll die trying, his saner self said. *Be smart. Make a deal. You're not going to fight your way out of this.* Surely there was something these people wanted from him. He was, after all, one of the wealthiest men alive at the moment. That ought to be worth something.

Perhaps it would be compelling enough to save Angie and her mother from what he feared would be an atrocious, brutal end.

But he couldn't wait for his captors to make the first move. Angie's life hung in the balance, thanks to his unbridled avarice.

"Zelaya!" he bellowed. "Come back here!"

His voice echoed off of the damp walls.

"Zelaya!"

No response.

Panic swelled as he imagined Zelaya in Angie's cell at this very moment, doing unspeakable things to her.

Sabot yelled louder, desperation filling his voice. He bellowed himself hoarse, his calls increasingly anguished, shrill. Insane, maybe.

The pipes rattled. Tears welled. He collapsed onto the chair as yet another icy blast crashed down on him from the faucet above his head.

"Zelaya!" The name trailed off, giving way to an abject sob, obscured by freezing water coursing over Sabot's mouth. "You bastard!"

Sabot slumped in his chair, hope draining like exhaled air, tears falling on the wet concrete.

He was already well on his way to broken, he realized, and they hadn't even laid a hand on him.

* * *

In the compound's control room, Bill Fredericks stood next to Terencio Zelaya and smiled in admiration as they watched their quarry melt before their eyes. "You're a true artist," Fredericks said.

Zelaya allowed a small smile. "I should be, after all this time." Then his smile disappeared. "This isn't strictly an Agency effort, is it?" More observation than question.

Fredericks smiled. "After all this time, you should know better than to ask." From a pragmatic standpoint, the problem with a US government agency mucking about in foreign countries — committing crimes, inciting revolutions, assassinating leaders who proved unwilling to play along with Uncle Sam's lustful overtures — was that of plausible deniability. All of the dirty work had to be done via cutouts, using quasi-private funding.

This meant that shill companies, mercenaries, criminals, spies, and — worst of all, in Fredericks' estimation — *lawyers*, formed the backbone of the Central Intelligence Agency's foreign presence. To the men on the pointy end of the unpleasantness, it was often impossible to tell which operations were undertaken at the strong suggestion of the President of the United States, and which operations were merely the bright idea of a rogue CIA agent who had found a fun little opportunity to exploit. They all looked pretty much the same on the ground.

And that was one of the unintended consequences of hiring shady people to do shady work. Abuses weren't a hazard; they were a given. Bill Fredericks certainly had his share of big "wins" for god and country, such as the successful assassination of a recalcitrant Venezuelan president, but he had also indulged himself in many more side ventures that either lined his own pockets or fed his voracious appetite for unacceptably young hookers.

But Zelaya was no stranger to the game, Fredericks knew. Zelaya was one of the last of his era, and in Central America, it was one hell of a brutal era. He wasn't a crusader. Fredericks knew that Zelaya's question — who's behind this particular op? — was far more pragmatic than ideological. Officially sanctioned operations tended to pay much more quickly than the entrepreneurial efforts of opportunistic agents in the field. "We're all concerned about funding, especially now," Fredericks said. "But it won't be a problem for this op."

"Thank you for the pro forma Agency lie," Zelaya said with a smile.

Fredericks chuckled. "I suppose we deserve that," he said. "But this one is better than official."

Zelaya turned. "So I'm working for the United States of Bill Fredericks?"

Fredericks laughed out loud. "Wouldn't that be great? We'd kick some serious ass." He clapped Zelaya on the back. "No, my friend," with an air of condescension not lost on Zelaya, "we're on the Facilitator's dime."

If it was a lie, it was a whopper. Few spoke of the Facilitator directly, or of his right-hand-man, the Intermediary. They were reputed to wield the hammer of the gods, installing presidents, congressmen, and captains of industry in the States, and exerting even greater influence in half of the remaining countries in the world.

More importantly for Zelaya's purposes, they enjoyed a solid reputation for paying on time. Evidently, one didn't become a global crook by acting like a petty crook.

Still, he was skeptical. "Even down here, one hears rumors," he said.

"That so?"

"The Intermediary was arrested, they say."

Fredericks, being a successful CIA case officer, and therefore also being a veteran and inveterate liar, chuckled and shrugged. "Rumors."

But Zelaya wasn't exactly wet behind the ears, and he was astute enough to catch the slight twitch of Fredericks' right eye, which was generally a reliable bullshit indicator, in Zelaya's experience. *Noted.* "As I said, one hears things. But it's tough to know what to believe. We're a long way from Banff, way down here in the jungle."

Fredericks' smile dimmed. *How the hell does this backwater pipe-swinger know about Banff?* Banff was to the Facilitator as Camp David was to the US President, except that no one was supposed to know about the former. The Consultancy clearly had some leaks to shore up.

Zelaya worked hard to repress a smug smile. "You are the

quintessential American bigot, Mr. Fredericks. Your country is richer than most, but you think that makes you smarter than the rest of us. And you conveniently forget that you're standing on the shoulders of your forefathers."

"Yes, yes, the marginalized third-world freedom fighter routine. Aren't we a little beyond that, you and I?"

"You tell me."

Fredericks chuckled. "Look. We've been in this game a long time. It's been forever since I was a true believer. But I've also outgrown my cynicism. I'm on the job. That's it. No songs, no slogans, no bullshit. Fair enough?"

Zelaya considered, smiled a little, nodded. "So we find our interests momentarily aligned."

"Good as it ever gets, my friend."

Zelaya nodded toward the video image of Sabot Mondragon, still doubled over and shivering on the wooden chair in his cell. "This man, he stole something from your employers?"

"Virtual currency."

"I'm confident he'll have a change of heart."

"That would make our employers very happy." A lie. The Facilitator had been extremely clear on the subject. Mondragon was to wake up dead, as soon as possible.

But Fredericks wasn't one to ignore an opportunity, especially one this size. He exhibited poor judgment on occasion, and his dick had often landed the rest of him in deep shit, but he wasn't an idiot. Fredericks had sensed a note of urgency unbecoming a man of the Facilitator's status atop the clandestine global oligarchy. The old man was just a hair too strident during their brief and unpleasant Banff meeting, telltale sign of an involuntarily loosened grip on the reigns.

Fredericks sensed an opening. He had an inkling that the Facilitator's reach wasn't quite what it had been at its peak.

And Fredericks figured there was room enough in his life to play puppeteer for one more asset.

"Broken but alive, please," he instructed Zelaya. "Let's not hobble our new thoroughbred. At least not permanently."

"Consider it done."

Zelaya caught a contemplative look on Fredericks' face. In the past, such a look on the fat man's sweaty mug had almost always been a harbinger of opportunity. Fredericks needed something.

Zelaya let him stew for a moment, then nudged him over the edge. "There is something else I can help you with."

Fredericks nodded. "Know anyone in Costa Rica?"

"Of course." A knowing smile. "But someone at the airport, that is another matter."

"Who said I needed someone at the airport?"

"Nobody. But your friend Mondragon is a popular man. He has important pursuers."

What the hell? Fredericks was taken aback. How could Zelaya — a bit player in a minor fiefdom in the middle of the jungle — have his finger on the pulse of the Department of Homeland Security? They barely had internet down here. How was this guy so dialed in?

Out of the corner of his eye, he detected an unmistakable

smirk on Zelaya's face. "You gringos were always too prideful to keep a secret," Zelaya offered by way of explanation. "And we may be simpletons and shit-farmers, but we learned long ago to look closely to the north for signs of trouble."

Fredericks shook his head. "Balls, Terencio. You got the drop on me."

"Si," Zelaya said. "But it's not really your fault. The redhead's work in Venezuela put her on our map."

"*What* work in Venezuela?" Fredericks bluffed.

Zelaya laughed aloud. "It's not that you're a bad liar," he chided. "It's just that you can't seem to avoid being cornered. You have no subtlety."

Anger flashed across Fredericks' face.

Zelaya's smile broadened. "Relax, Señor Fredericks. The enemy of my customer is also my enemy. I've taken the liberty of making a few phone calls. Not pro bono, of course, but the arrangements will prove useful, I trust."

Chapter 8

"That, folks, is how we do it," the pilot announced, clearly proud of his smooth landing. "Welcome to Costa Rica. Local time is a smidge past midnight. I'm told they've arranged ground transportation and a hotel for us, compliments of the DIS."

Sam rolled her eyes. "We'll be lucky if we aren't all shot on the tarmac." Her view of the Direccion de Inteligencia y Seguridad Nacional, the Costa Rican security apparatus, wasn't complimentary.

Dan chuckled. "You're assuming they can still afford bullets. Besides, I think their primary function is to dig up dirt at election time."

Sam nodded. "Another Agency outpost from the Cold War, hunting snipe and commies."

"No backwater too stagnant for the Silent Service," Brock joked.

The cabin door opened, admitting the loud whine of the passenger jet's auxiliary power unit and a rush of suffocating jungle air. "Like breathing through a sweaty sock," Dan observed.

"With all the charming aftertaste," Sam said, wearily gathering her things from the credenza next to her seat.

Seven thousand minutes later, according to Sam's level of remaining patience, the ground crew finally rolled the ancient stairway up to the US Government VIP jet. The improbable pack of federal agents and federal criminals trudged down the rickety steps and onto Costa Rican soil, where they were met by a wiry chain-smoker with a lubricious, sycophantic air. "I am Juan Rojas," the man said. "On behalf of Señor Solana, President of Costa Rica and the head of the Direccion de Inteligencia y Seguridad Nacional, I would like to welcome you to Costa Rica."

"Thanks," Sam replied, taking the man's outstretched palm and crushing it with her slightly mannish grip. He winced a little, then gestured toward three waiting cars.

"We have taken the liberty of making hotel arrangements for you," Rojas said with a slight bow. "I understand it has been a very long day for you. Your drivers know the way, and the hotel is nearby."

Sam smiled. "That's very kind of you, Señor Rojas. Unfortunately, I'm afraid we have to get directly to work. Would you be able to take us over to the terminal where the Obsidian Air flight disembarked?"

Rojas' smile dimmed, and Sam could have sworn she detected a slight flinch on his face. *Interesting.* Was Rojas just supporting local business, or was something else on the agenda?

Rojas recovered his polish. "Of course, we would be happy to assist you in any way possible, Special Agent Jameson. But if your journey has left you weary, the hotel is much closer."

"Thanks anyway," Sam said.

"Complimentary breakfast, too," Rojas added awkwardly. "And very comfortable accommodations."

"Really, Señor Rojas. We need to get to work," Sam said, a little bit of stop-screwing-with-me in her tone. "If you don't mind, we should really get started."

"Yes, yes, of course. I'll inform our drivers of our new destination," Rojas said.

Come to think of it, where the hell are the embassy people? It was a matter of custom and procedure for federal investigations on foreign soil to have embassy involvement, for obvious reasons. She threw a meaningful glance toward Dan, who was already dialing his phone.

Sam heard two car doors shut, and saw the first black sedan drive off into the darkness of the under-lit tarmac. *Sonuvabitch, something's not right here.* Dan, Brock, herself, and Rojas remained on the ramp, which meant that Trojan and Harv Edwards occupied the first car, its brake lights now receding in the distance.

She looked at Dan, who shook his head. No answer at the embassy. *Not good.* The embassy was supposed to be staffed 24/7. But Sam knew that locals were often hired for receptionist duties in the smaller embassies, a political concession that, the embassy wigs maintained, had no operational significance.

Except when it did.

"Señor Rojas, can you call them back here?" Sam asked. "I'd like us all to stick together."

"No, ma'am," Rojas responded apologetically. "Traveling separately is our strict policy, for safety reasons. It is not always safe for foreigners after dark."

Which was complete bullshit. They were at an international airport. Not to mention that Costa Ricans enjoyed a far more peaceful society than any of their Central American neighbors, largely because the country was the first in the world to abolish its military. Armed teenagers in uniforms, along with the inevitable thuggery, pillage, and abuse committed by soldiers the world over, were simply not found in Costa Rica. "I seem to have left something on the plane," Sam stalled.

Brock, oblivious to the unfolding drama, was halfway inside the second car. Sam spotted him as he began to lower his weight onto the seat. "Brock, can you help me?" It was an unlikely request, given that Brock's thigh was wrapped in a bandage, a painful gunshot wound — remnant of a remarkably shitty weekend — slowing his every step.

He started to protest, but she shot him the kind of glance that was unmistakable between lovers.

"Sure thing," he said, struggling back out of the sedan with a groan.

Sam turned her gaze to Rojas. Confusion crossed his face for the briefest of moments. It lasted but an instant, and Sam saw his eyes harden and his jaw set in a way that she'd seen hundreds of times before.

Professional. He knew she'd sniffed him out.

And she knew the game was on.

She walked with practiced nonchalance back up the stairway to the jet, meeting the pilot and copilot on their way down the stairs. "Get back inside," she commanded. She cut off the pilot's nascent question with a hissed expletive. "Get back on the plane. No time to explain."

Brock hobbled up the stairs behind Sam, and Dan brought up

the rear, phone to his ear.

Sam turned to wave a fake apology to Rojas, taking him in again at a glance. In the intervening seconds, the man's face had darkened noticeably, and his body had morphed. He was no longer the bootlicking chauffeur, with averted eyes and bowed torso. He looked poised, shoulders squared, movements taut. He was the welcoming committee alright, but of a vastly different sort. *Thank goodness for a woman's intuition.*

"What about Trojan and Harv?" Dan asked as they reentered the aircraft cabin.

"Definitely a problem," Sam said.

"What the hell is going on?" Brock asked, lowering himself gingerly into an aircraft seat, bewildered by the strange display.

"Rojas may be here on behalf of the DIS, but he certainly isn't our buddy," Sam explained. "Which leaves us in a little bit of a bind."

Brock looked incredulous. "But you're here on official business as a US federal agent. You really think they'd interfere with you?"

Sam nodded. "Happens all the time. They'll slow-leak the diplomatic channels, and they'll have all the time they need to get whatever they want from us."

"I thought they were our allies," Brock protested.

Dan grimaced. "We're chasing a guy who's many times richer than the Queen right now. There's more than enough money in play to rearrange loyalties for as long as it takes."

"So what now?"

Sam took a deep breath and exhaled slowly. She watched surreptitiously out one of the cabin windows as Rojas and the two remaining drivers huddled on the tarmac below. The drivers wore loose-fitting jackets despite the oppressive heat, perfect for concealing sidearms and other antisocial devices. "Damned good question," she said.

Chapter 9

Domingo Mondragon sat shivering in the semidarkness. He'd regained a bit of his composure, exerted his will over his emotions, and felt far more sanguine about what was otherwise a dogshit situation.

They had him by the gonads, no doubt about it. Leverage was the understatement of the century. He'd very recently become one of the world's richest men, a fact which, if known to his captors, would provide plenty of motivation for them to inflict all sorts of grisly evils on him.

And they had Angie. He imagined her chained in some cell somewhere else in the bowels of the dank dungeon in which he now sat, soaked, freezing, and alone.

But he'd rallied. His moment of weakness had passed, and he was no longer crying like a bitch, or bellowing at his captor, some asshole named Zelaya, like a man possessed.

He grew up in the rough part of Queens, had taken down bastard companies and governments with his hacking skills, and had survived a few years in the federal pen. He hadn't done all of that without having a little bit of sand in his shorts. It was time he started acting like he had a pair of balls, he decided.

But that cold water. It was wearing him out. Fatigue makes cowards of us all, some football coach had said. Sabot believed it. He had to find a way to negotiate that freezing shower out of his life, and soon.

He heard the familiar sound of footsteps approaching. Female again. The door creaked, and the pretty young woman reappeared in the dim light spilling in from the hallway.

She looked furtively in both directions down the hallway before closing the door slowly, wincing as the rusty hinges screeched. He heard her yank the chain, and the dim bulb in the center of the room came to life.

He opened his mouth to greet her, but her finger was already pressed to his lips to silence him. She leaned close, her warm breath on his neck as she whispered in his ear. "They can hear," she said, her lips brushing his earlobe. In spite of himself and his predicament, he felt a zing of excitement, a rush of attraction. He inhaled, and her scent reached his nostrils, warm, clean, and sweet, with a hint of sultry.

"Have you taken any food?" she asked.

He shook his head in reply, started to say that she was the last person he'd seen, and he had no idea how long ago that had been, but her hand pressed to his mouth again. The pressure was firm but feminine, and he felt her curves against his body as she leaned in yet again. "I snuck something for you." She backed away from his body and presented him with a small, hard dinner roll not unlike the kind he'd become accustomed to in prison.

Sabot took it with his free hand, whispered his thanks, and bit hungrily into the roll.

"What's your name?" he asked quietly between bites.

"Marisela."

"What are you doing here?"

"I am assigned here."

"By who?" Sabot asked.

"It's complicated. There is not much time, and you will have to be ready. Soon they will send a doctor, but you must not take the drugs he gives you. And do not eat anything."

Sabot nodded. "What's going on here?" he asked. "What do they want from me?"

"They want everything," she said. "You must be strong."

She kissed him on the neck. Her lips were warm and moist, inciting another rush of excitement.

And then she was gone, padding quietly away down the hallway outside his cell.

What the hell is going on here? He was getting hot and bothered for some strange girl with a dinner roll while Angie, the best thing that ever happened to him, was chained to the wall somewhere? What kind of a man was he?

He was disoriented, incredulous, disappointed in himself. Just when his psyche had recovered from the last wave of despair, another dark cloud had settled over his mind.

But damn, that girl smelled good. And those tits were nice. It was the other voice in his head, the one that came from the reptile brain, concerned chiefly with flexing and fornicating.

He shook his head. *Get a grip, vato.* He needed to focus, to come up with a plan, to figure out some way to get himself and the girls out of this mess. It was, after all, undoubtedly *his* mess, *his* choice, that had landed them all in the middle of the jungle, chained to the concrete.

But it was hard to make a play when you didn't hold any of the cards.

He could barely see the walls of his cell in the darkness, and he certainly couldn't see any way to free himself from the shackle that ground the skin on his wrist to a pulp. He was weak, freezing, exhausted, and, dinner roll notwithstanding, starving his ass off.

He needed to catch a break of some sort. There was some weakness, somewhere, and Sabot resolved to find it. He had spent entire weeks as a hacker scouring servers for vulnerabilities, finally finding the tiniest of holes in his targets' defenses and turning them into a mile-wide security breach. He would do the same thing in this dungeon. There was always a way into any given computer system, a hacker maxim that had defined entire years of his life, and he knew that there must also be a way *out* of this predicament. He made up his mind to figure it out.

* * *

Sabot was still using his tongue to clean his teeth of remnants of the roll that Marisela had brought for him when he heard footsteps down the hall. These were heavy footfalls, more than one set, undoubtedly belonging to a pair of men. Or very, very hefty women.

The footfalls stopped outside his door, and he heard voices conversing in Spanish. He caught only a few words, but it sounded like they were talking about his health.

A now-familiar screech assaulted his ears as his cell door opened. A fat man in a white lab coat stomped into Sabot's cell. A guard stood watch at the door. Sabot wasn't sure, but he thought it was one of the two goons who had paid him a visit earlier.

"Hello, Domingo," Lab Coat said, turning on the overhead light. "I am Doctor Morales. I will examine you."

A doctor? Just like Marisela had predicted. "With all due respect, Doctor, I think I'd really just rather you unchain me and let me be on my way."

"That is obviously not up to me, Domingo." Cold stethoscope on Sabot's chest, faraway look as the doctor timed his pulse.

"Inhale."

Sabot complied.

"Exhale."

"What's going on here, Doc? Why am I here? If they need something from me, all they have to do is ask, you know?"

"Quiet."

"This is bullshit!"

The doctor put down the stethoscope and looked squarely at Sabot. "Señor Mondragon, it is an enduring reminder of my stalled career that I am forced to make calls to this godforsaken place. I want to leave this hellhole only slightly less urgently than you do. Please shut up and let me finish my examination." He produced a tongue depressor. "Stick out your tongue."

"I won't take any drugs," Sabot said.

The doctor shook his head, traces of annoyance on his face. "In that case, I will not offer you any. Open your mouth."

Sabot felt the thin wooden stick flatten his tongue. He felt something else, too. What was that tingling sensation in his mouth?

"Say ahh." The doctor's breath was foul, with traces of stale whiskey and bad teeth. Sabot's head turned away involuntarily.

"Is there a problem?"

"No offense, Doc, but you could knock a buzzard off a shit wagon."

"How would that not be offensive?" He put the used tongue depressor in his pocket, wrapped the stethoscope around his neck, and walked out the door. "Good day, Señor Mondragon. You should drink more water. I'll see you when you get back."

"Get back? From where?" But the door had slammed shut, echoes from receding footsteps once again bouncing off of the concrete walls.

Could this get any stranger? Abducted from inside an airplane, hooded and bound, driven to some hole in the middle of the jungle, chained to a wall, doused with freezing water, visited by a pair of knuckle-dragging guards and a psychopath of an old man, and finally, tended to by a hot Latina and an alcoholic doctor.

And nobody had asked him a single question the entire time.

They knew his name — not hard, since they had his wallet — and they had his girl and her mom. If he understood Marisela correctly, they were being held in similar conditions. If they wanted something else, they sure as hell had a funny way of asking for it.

He suddenly felt lightheaded. Was the fatigue and starvation finally catching up to him? He leaned his head forward in the hard wooden chair. His gyros tumbled crazily, and he thought he might hurl. His pulse pounded, sweat beaded on his brow despite the cold, wet clothes draped over his body, and he felt a fierce bout of vertigo. His eyes snapped crazily back and forth, like after an amusement park ride. *What the hell is going on here?*

And then it passed. He felt fine. Better than fine, as a matter of fact. He felt *right.* Calm, detached, as if he were the observer perched someplace at the periphery of his own consciousness. His shivering stopped, and he felt a warm tingling sensation in his limbs.

He smiled, then giggled a little bit, then laughed. *How funny is this? Chain me to a wall, bitches. Ha!*

Was that his own voice echoing in his cell? He hadn't intended to speak out loud. *Tough to keep track of everything, though.* Seemed to make sense. *Vatos can't always be on top of their shit all the time, yo.* Reversion to ghetto usually only happened when he was pissed off, drunk, or both.

"You crazy vatos, come back here!" He meant to speak this time, but didn't mean to sound quite so insane. "What have you done to me?"

He heard whispering just outside his cell, then cackling, then animal screeches and shouts.

Or was that his own voice making all that noise?

"Bastards!"

The voices stopped, then started again, slowly rising from whispered giggles to horrendous screams and wails.

"Turn it off, goddamn you!" Sabot shouted. At least, that's what he thought he shouted. But he wasn't sure.

The cell door opened. Marisela. Black dress, showing off her curves, hair down around her shoulders, hips swaying as she walked slowly toward him, turning on the light on her way past the pull chain.

"*Damn*, girl, you're fine!" Had he just said that?

She grabbed his free hand, clamped a shackle on it, and chained it to the wall behind him.

"I thought you were on my side!" he yelled. He thought he detected a smile. Her face was too close to his, and he couldn't see her mouth. Then she was kissing him, her tongue wet and searching, her lips soft against his, and what was that pressing against his crotch, her hand? Her pelvis?

He felt a tug at his fly, heard his zipper unfasten, felt both Marisela's hands on his bare ass as she shuffled his wet pants and underwear downward, felt the waiting warmth of her mouth.

This can't be happening. Angie! What's going on?

His eyes closed, and he heard moaning. His own, he realized.

Was that a camera flash?

He opened his eyes, saw only Marisela's dark hair as her head bobbed.

He came, legs cramping with exertion, eyes clamped shut, mouth open, wrists chafing against the shackles.

Another bright flash.

Or had he imagined it?

Had he imagined everything?

Marisela came up, kissed him, caressed him with her hand, nibbled his neck.

And left.

He was alone again in his cell.

Did this really happen?

Moments later, the voices started. Laughing hysterìcàlly. *She's going to find out,* they said. *You dumb sonuvabitch, she's going to find out!*

Angie.

Sabot's heart sank. Tears welled, then flowed, and anguished sobs followed, broken by his own voice. "What have I done?" he wailed, vaguely aware of the pathetic tone and clichéd melodrama bouncing off of the concrete walls.

He sank back down onto the chair, bare ass against the cold, damp wood, and passed out.

* * *

Horrific dreams haunted his fitful slumber. They had the vivid quality of reality, and Sabot's body thrashed about in terror.

He awoke with a crushing headache, wrists shredded by the shackles on both hands, shoulders sore from fighting against the chains mounted to the concrete walls. His pulse pounded in his temples, his mouth was dry and pasty, and his throat was hoarse and sore.

What happened to me? He felt as if he'd stepped in front of a bus.

His mind returned to Marisela. Had she been here? Did she really...? He was naked below the waist, and both wrists were shackled to the wall. *What have I done?* His thoughts turned again to Angie. Had he let someone... *pleasure* him while she was chained in some cell somewhere? He shook his head with guilt and despair.

Then he looked up. Someone had placed a table in front of him in his cell. The overhead bulb illuminated the table's surface, on which were arrayed several photos. Marisela. Him. The back of her head at his waist, his face contorted in ecstasy. Then another, more explicit photo that left no ambiguity.

Guess it was real.

A third photo caught his eye, of a familiar figure. Angie. One hand covered her mouth in shock and agony. The other clutched a photo. Tears streaked down her face.

My god, what have I done?

Sabot exhaled, dejected, alone, ashamed. *Why the hell won't they just talk to me?* There had to be something they wanted, something he could give to them in exchange for ending this nightmare.

But what home would he return to? He'd spend the rest of his days in hiding, looking over his shoulder, waiting for his "employer" — whose identity Sabot still didn't know — to find him and go to work on his kneecaps.

And he would be alone, probably. How could Angie stay after being locked in a cage on account of him, rotting away while he got his rocks off with some nubile young girl? No way would she hang around after this, even if they did manage to survive whatever came next.

He felt hopeless, utterly deflated. His head hurt, and there still seemed to be a veil between him and his own consciousness, some diaphanous layer obscuring his sense and senses.

He heard the pipes rumble. He sputtered and cursed as the frigid water assaulted him yet again. He slumped back into the chair, head down, wits still reeling, awaiting the next indignity that was surely on its way.

Chapter 10

"We can't stay on this plane forever," Dan observed unnecessarily, waiting for someone at the Homeland Security emergency line to answer his call, peering out the window at Juan Rojas and the two driver/thugs conversing on the airport tarmac below.

Voicemail. He shook his head and cursed. There were agents in the field all over the world, and Homeland couldn't find someone to man the emergency line overnight?

Most DHS employees were probably still at home, he realized, defending their families from packs of roving goons who were looting neighborhoods to find food and other necessities in the wake of the societal meltdown over the past few days. Most of the looters were middle-class suburbanites who had made no disaster preparations, and there were a lot of them to fend off.

Sam watched Dan disconnect the call. She shook her head in disgust. They were a little bit screwed, stranded on the tarmac at the airport in Costa Rica, trying to avoid whatever fate the DIS and Juan Rojas had in mind for them. With each passing minute, the distance to Domingo Mondragon and his mountain of virtual currency grew ever greater.

A thought struck. "Can you operate the radios on battery power?" she asked the pilot.

He looked at her as if she had three eyes. "Of course."

"Is there anyone you can talk to on the radio who might know where the Obsidian Air charter flight disembarked earlier tonight?"

"Maybe," the pilot said. Sam handed him a slip of paper with the Obsidian flight's details. He disappeared into the cockpit.

Sam called Harv Edwards' cell phone. A mechanical voice informed her that the subscriber had left the service area. *Jackass.* Evidently, Harv had sat out the cell phone upgrade at Homeland. The old phones only worked in the States.

"Can you reach Trojan?" Sam asked Dan. Harv Edwards and Trojan were in the back of the sedan that had left the tarmac minutes ago, microseconds before the hair had stood up on the back of Sam's neck.

"It goes straight to voicemail," Dan told her after two attempts. "Which is strange, because I know the power is on. I watched him send a text as we taxied in after landing."

"Jammer," Sam said. Standard issue for any self-respecting security apparatus, even in the middle of the jungle. It wouldn't do to have spies and political detainees sending photos of their maltreatment out to the world via cell phone, so the security types invested heavily in signal jammers for cars, safe houses, and interrogation facilities.

The pilot reemerged from the cockpit. "Neither Clearance Delivery nor Ground Control has ever heard of an Obsidian Air charter flight."

"Can you have them search by the aircraft's serial number?" Sam asked. "Maybe they flew down here using a different identifier."

He shook his head. "Tried that. No luck. I also took a peek out the window. They parked us on the charter ramp, and we have a pretty good view of the other jets parked here. I don't see anything from Obsidian."

"Are you sure?" Sam asked.

The pilot nodded. "Their paint scheme is pretty hard to miss. Glossy black, like a spy plane or something."

"Could there be a mistake? There are other airports near San Jose," Dan said. "Maybe we got the wrong airport."

The pilot handed Dan the slip of paper with the Obsidian Air flight information on it. The Obsidian desk clerk's scrawl was unambiguous: Juan Santamaria International, San Jose, Costa Rica. Sam's jaw clenched.

"No worries," Brock said. "This is an international airport. They'll have access to all the flight plans filed to and from the region, and they'll be able to cross reference them by tail number as well." He was speaking from two decades of experience as a fighter pilot. "We should be able to pull up the Obsidian flight plan without too much hassle."

"Unless they falsified the aircraft registration in the flight plan," the transport pilot said.

"Worth a try, though," Sam decided. "Now all we have to do is get them to let us poke around in their system."

"I know just the guy to ask," Dan said, looking out the window at the wiry Costa Rican intelligence officer making his way up the aircraft ladder.

"Balls," Sam said. "Señor Rojas must have run out of

patience."

Her mind raced. She grabbed the pilot by the lapel, whispered quickly into his ear, and released him just as Rojas entered the aircraft cabin.

"Special Agent Jameson," Rojas said, his chauffeur's affectation now fully restored, "I'm afraid we really must be going. Will you and your associates please accompany me to our cars?"

"Sure thing," she said, then bent over as if to pick something up from behind the seat. She waved her left hand in the aisle. The pilot, now sitting back at the aircraft controls in the cockpit, took his cue.

The aircraft went completely dark inside.

There was a flurry of motion, a dull thud, the groan of air escaping a man's lungs, and the heavy thunk of a body hitting the floor.

Sam searched the now-comatose Rojas. Her hand shot inside his pocket, retrieved his DIS credentials, and liberated his service piece from his waist. She also removed a small revolver from the holster around his ankle. "Expect company," she said to Dan. "Don't kill them, please," she added as she zip-tied Rojas' wrists and ankles together.

The aircraft shook as the first of the drivers made his way up the staircase. Dan ducked behind the first bulkhead, crouching low to hide his heft, his arms in a martial artist's attack stance. Even in the darkness, Sam thought he looked a little ridiculous.

The DIS agent stepped inside the aircraft doorway, service pistol drawn and held at low ready. *Amateur,* Sam thought. *Who boards a plane full of hostiles alone these days?*

Dan instantly punished the mistake. His vise-like grip clamped down on the man's shooting hand, and Dan's free hand disassembled the pistol in one smooth motion. Gun parts clattered to the cabin floor, followed shortly thereafter by the crack of bone and a blood-curdling howl. Sam winced as she caught a glimpse of the man's wrecked hand, fingers bent a grotesquely long way backwards.

"Dan!" She yelled, stopping her deputy from delivering a lethal blow to the disabled man's windpipe.

"Sorry," he said, opting instead to knock the man out with a meaty smash to the nose.

"Can't take you anywhere," Sam quipped. "Where's number two?"

Brock's voice came from the back of the cabin. "Crouched down behind his car, with his gun drawn."

"So much for a discreet exit." She turned to the pilot. "Can you get us out of here?"

"And go where?" he asked. "No fuel, no flight plan, and no through-flight inspection. Plus our wheels are chocked."

"I'm officially open to ideas," Sam said.

Dan lay on his stomach in the aircraft aisle, scooted toward the open door until he could train his weapon on the second driver crouched by the car below, and fired a single shot. The .45's report was deafening in the confines of the aircraft cabin.

"Hit," Brock reported. "Got his shooting arm, looks like."

"Not at all what I had in mind," Sam growled. "You get to fill out the paperwork."

"Agreed," Dan said, then charged down the aircraft stairs with his weapon trained on the wounded Costa Rican agent. Sam drew her sidearm and provided cover for Dan from the top of the stairway. The wounded agent offered no further resistance.

Sam and Dan worked quickly, and soon all three DIS men lay inside the US government jet, hands and feet bound.

"Sorry we got off on the wrong foot," Sam said to Juan Rojas, after slapping him in the face a few times to awaken him from her earlier blow to his temple. "Now I'm afraid we'll need a little assistance from you."

All pretense of affability had left Rojas' face, and he was demonstrably upset about the way the evening had turned. "Always the same, you people."

"That's right," Sam said. "Always trying to catch our own criminals without becoming victims in the process. How silly of us."

She waved his identification badge in front of his face. "This says DIS, but let's be honest. You guys are the local branch of the CIA."

Rojas bristled, which told her that she'd struck a nerve. Nobody likes to be anybody's bitch. "Did you get tonight's assignment from the local Agency guy, or from a different asshole?"

Rojas put the chauffeur's sycophantic expression back on his face. "Special Agent Jameson, I am afraid that I don't know what you're talking about," he said with exaggerated deference.

Sam smiled with mock friendliness. "Let me clarify my question." She drew her gun, cocked the hammer, pulled Rojas' head back by his hair, and stuck the gun in Rojas' mouth. "Local Agency asshole, or not?"

Rojas kept his cool remarkably well, Sam thought, his eyes never wavering from hers. So she shoved the barrel of the weapon further down his throat, digging the front sight into the roof of his mouth. Rojas winced in pain and tried to jerk his head free, but Sam tightened her grip on his hair and gave the gun a mean-spirited nudge further down his throat. "I can do this for a long time, Señor Rojas."

He stopped struggling, scowled at her to save a little face, and said something unintelligible. Sam pulled the gun from his mouth and pointed it at his temple. "Not local," Rojas said, still eyeballing Sam. "And not Agency."

"Now we're getting somewhere," she said. It always helped to know the opposition's affiliations. "We'll talk some more about that in a second, but first, you have a phone call to make. I want my two agents delivered back here — untouched — within five minutes."

She pulled Rojas' cell phone from his jacket pocket. "Tell me the number of your third driver. I'll place the call for you." Sam pointed her weapon at the face of the wounded driver, sitting next to Rojas. "What's this guy's name?" she asked Rojas.

"Alejandro," Rojas said.

"No games, Señor Rojas, or you'll be picking Alejandro's brains out of your teeth."

The wiry DIS agent did as Sam instructed. Rojas called his third man at their pre-arranged time, when the cell phone jammers in their vehicles were to be momentarily switched off.

Sam listened carefully to the conversation for any signs of

subterfuge, such as any stilted grammar or out-of-place words that might indicate the use of a code word, but she didn't detect any shenanigans. Rojas had apparently followed her instructions. It made her more nervous, for some reason.

"Why is DIS interfering in a Homeland investigation?" she asked Rojas.

"What makes you certain it's DIS?" Rojas asked.

"Are you moonlighting?"

"Moonlighting?"

"Working on the side. Using your official position to get unofficially paid."

"Aren't we all?"

Sam snorted. "Actually, no. Maybe that makes me the last honest spook. Who's paying you?"

"I don't know the source of the funds."

"I would have been surprised if you did. But you know who you'd shoot if the cash didn't show up, don't you."

"Of course."

"That name will suffice for now."

"Valdez," Rojas said. "He works for the Gray One."

"The who?"

"A foreigner. The Gray One. He has been in the game a long time. Longer than you have been alive, I think."

Which makes him an Agency stooge, Sam realized. Nobody survived in the underworld for that long without CIA blessing. At least, not in the Western Hemisphere.

"Drugs, guns, or girls?" Sam asked. The three toxic offshore cash businesses favored by the Agency to bolster its budget.

Rojas shrugged. "I wouldn't say if I knew."

"I can respect that," Sam said. "How much was your take tonight?"

Rojas scoffed. "Much less than the difficulty demanded," he said.

"Tough times in this corner of the world? You must be running out of enemies."

Rojas chuckled. "Everywhere but in the National Assembly."

"Sounds like you could use a little extra cash. Care to make another phone call?"

Rojas pondered Sam's offer. It wasn't as if the Gray One ran an especially tight ship in Costa Rica. There was probably little danger of blowback, particularly given the paltry sum he and his counterparts had collected for the evening's escapade. "As long as you don't try to pay me with that shit dollar of yours."

Sam laughed out loud. "Fair enough. We could use a friendly introduction at the local flight management office. Thirty seconds of your time."

They settled on a sum, payable in silver bullion, a healthy supply of which Sam had liberated from the Lost Man Lake Ranch's underground storehouse before leaving Colorado several million years earlier in the week. Sam held the phone to Rojas' ear again, and he made the call.

When the call ended, Sam looked at her watch. "One minute, Señor Rojas. Then I become unreasonably upset about my two missing agents."

Chapter 11

Sabot awoke to another viciously cold dousing from the infernal spigot above his head. He didn't remember falling asleep.

His right arm hurt like hell. It was chained to the wall above his head, the shackle furrowing into the flesh of his wrist. He couldn't feel his hand. His head had lolled to the side during his slumber, and his neck ached with every movement.

The events of the preceding few hours came crashing back in on his consciousness: the interlude with Marisela, the photographs, the picture of an anguished Angie viewing the photographic evidence of his betrayal. His heart pounded, and tears welled yet again.

He rubbed his eyes with his left hand.

His *free* left hand.

What the hell? When he was last awake, his left arm had been chained to the wall, along with his right, and the blow-job-induced thrashing had torn both wrists to shreds.

He inspected his left hand. Good as new. Absolutely no evidence that it had ever been chained to the wall. He turned his head upwards to the left, looking for an unused manacle dangling from the wall, but there wasn't one. There was only one chain, the one that restrained his right hand.

Was I hallucinating? It had felt so incredibly real, all of it — the orgasm had been incredibly intense, punctuated by the pain of the shackles on his wrists and the vaguely erotic helplessness of having both hands chained to the wall.

And in the aftermath, when the reality of his betrayal and its effect on his beloved Angie came flooding in, the absolute despair was palpable, crushing, debilitating. *It was goddamned* real, *as real as it ever got.*

And what happened to that table with the pictures on it? But for the two wooden chairs, the cell was entirely empty. *Jesus. What the hell is going on here?*

Another thought struck. Marisela had left him naked below the waist when she walked out of his cell. He had felt the intense, stupefying coldness of that damn shower splashing down on his bare legs after she left. He was certain of it.

He looked down. His pants were on, soaking wet, waistband digging uncomfortably into his midsection as he slumped on the chair.

Am I losing my damned mind?

His thoughts lost focus, and he once again got the feeling that he was an observer inside his own head.

The voices started again, whispering as if they were just outside his cell door, then rising to a screaming, howling crescendo with a single refrain repeating over and over: *You're going to die in here!* He found himself bellowing to drown out their viciousness.

Then it felt as if he were observing himself, his consciousness floating above the small-looking Latino man who was chained to the wall and hollering like a madman.

Another icy shower snapped him back to reality, or at least a reasonable facsimile thereof, and he sputtered and cursed as the water splashed over him.

More footsteps sounded in the hallway beyond the door, too many to count, moving with a purpose toward his cell. They all stopped at his cell door. Could he hear their breathing? Were they whispering to each other?

Sabot stared at the latch in the dim light creeping through the jamb, anticipating their entrance at any moment. He listened, but heard only the ever-present drip of icy water rolling off of his body, and the occasional creaking of the little wooden chair beneath him.

He watched the space between the door and the floor, searching for movement, shadows, any sign of the people who had clearly congregated just beyond the cell door.

The door stayed inexorably, inscrutably, inexplicably closed. There was no sound. No voices, no breathing. No retreating footsteps, retracing their path down the long hallway outside the dungeon. No sign of anyone at all.

The silence was interminable.

It became unbearable. "Open the damned door!" Sabot's voice sounded otherworldly in his ears, like the voice of a madman screaming in the semidarkness, bouncing rudely off of the hard walls, assaulting his eardrums long after he stopped his throat-splitting bellow. "Bastards!" he screeched.

Was that laughter? Did he hear the faint, distant peals of children at play?

Or was he hearing the echoes of the water dripping on the floor?

I'm losing it. I have to get the hell out of here! He rose, stood on his chair, grabbed the chain with both hands, and yanked. His fingers slipped over the wet links. He stumbled backward, misplaced his foot, and fell to the floor, wrenching his leg as he landed awkwardly on the wet concrete.

He climbed up and tried again, this time wrapping the chain around his hands, pulling with all of his might, ignoring the pain in his palms and fingers as the metal dug into his flesh.

Nothing. No movement whatsoever. He thrashed with irrational fury, snapping the chain back and forth to shake it loose from the concrete, barely registering the pain as the links chewed through his fingers. "Bastards!" he howled. "Let me out of here!"

The echoes of his voice receded into the darkness, and the pain in his hands rose to prominence in his consciousness. He released the chain, stepped off of the chair, and sat once again on the hard seat, rubbing his palms together to restore feeling. They felt warm and greasy. Were they bleeding? He couldn't tell in the dim light seeping in from beneath the cell door.

"Domingo."

Had someone said his name? Or had he imagined it?

"Domingo Mondragon."

The disembodied voice sounded deep, gravelly, familiar. It seemed to be coming from everywhere at once, emanating from the far corners of the chamber and bouncing through his skull.

"Domingo," the voice repeated.

"What the hell do you want?" Sabot howled.

Pipes rattled. More cold water. "You sonuvabitch!" It was

equal parts scream and sob.

"You know what we want." The voice was calm, controlled. Maybe even amused.

Sabot slouched in his chair and buried his face in his bloody hands. Exhaustion and panic pounded against what remained of his will.

Yes, he did know what they wanted.

The words sounded small, weak, pathetic, disappearing into the darkness almost as soon they left his mouth: "Then come and take it."

Chapter 12

The old man looked tired, Protégé noted. Archive's trademark arrowhead goatee, normally the picture of perfect symmetry, was off kilter. His white mane was more unruly than Protégé ever remembered having seen it, and the normal sparkle was absent from his eyes. "A little sleep wouldn't kill anyone," Protégé said.

Archive smiled, nodded, but didn't turn away from the wall of monitors in the bunker's computer room. He had been watching representative video feeds, categorized and sorted by Vaneesh's entropy algorithm, and filling pages in his notebook with notes and outlines, for the better part of twelve hours. "I'm expecting a call from General Williamson in a few minutes," he said.

"NORTHCOM?"

Archive nodded. He and the commander of the United States Northern Command, whose area of responsibility included the northern hemisphere of the Americas, were thick as thieves. In fact, Archive had noted sourly while viewing a particularly discouraging episode of violence somewhere in Los Angeles, the two of them might very well hang together. Incumbent powers tended to view radical destabilization dimly, and they tended to use weighty words like "treason" to power the subsequent legal proceedings. Archive's keen interest in society's direction was fueled in no small part by the specter of an unpleasant death at the hands of the government atop the country he loved dearly. And he was no more eager to die than any other average billionaire.

As if on cue, the small red phone rang. Protégé chuckled inwardly at the red phone metaphor — long symbolic of the US president's 24/7 grip on the nuclear enterprise, now ringing in the lair of the eccentric billionaire who might have succeeded in overthrowing The Establishment.

"General, my friend," Archive said with more cheer than he felt. "What's the good word? I've got you on speaker. Our friend Protégé is here."

"Hi, Jack." Sonorous bass tones exuded confidence and authority. "Robert, I trust you're making the old man take care of himself?"

"I'm afraid I'm failing at that task," Protégé said with a smile. "He's overdue for a nap."

"I won't keep him long, in that case," Williamson said. "As you know, the president's martial law order went into effect twelve hours ago."

"And you expected some implementation trouble," Archive said.

"Which has played out about as we expected. A mysteriously high percentage of our Guardsmen seem to be away from their phones at the moment. My notification staff has left a ton of voicemails, and fielded very few return phone calls."

"Nobody's anxious to leave their families in the middle of the chaos in order to report for duty," Protégé observed.

"Right. That's working to our advantage," NORTHCOM said. "The numbers are slightly higher among police and emergency workers, but I'd estimate that only about a third of them are on duty. The rest are probably trying to keep their homes and neighborhoods buttoned down."

"Or they're looting," Archive noted grimly.

"Yes, there have been reports," Williamson said. "Fortunately not very many, though."

"Tell me again why martial law isn't a good thing?" Protégé asked. "It seems like we'd want to demonstrate that there's still law and order, and people can settle down and get back to work."

"That would be a good thing to demonstrate," Williamson said. "Unfortunately, it's not even remotely true. Even if every Guardsman and cop in the country showed up for duty right now, we couldn't possibly restore order. There just simply aren't enough of them."

"It's not a bad thing," Archive said. "We don't live in a police state, after all."

"Right," the four-star agreed. "The martial law construct in America was designed to lock down isolated areas of unrest. It was never intended to canvas the country."

Protégé looked thoughtful. "Will the president use the active duty military forces for more manpower?"

"Already has," Williamson said. "Obviously a higher response rate, given the immediate threat of jail for failure to report for duty, but the numbers are still pretty small. We have less than two million soldiers in the active and reserve components, roughly half that number Stateside at any given time. And truth be told, most of them are clerks and paper-pushers."

"You're not all steely-eyed Rambo clones?" Archive asked with a smile.

Williamson chuckled. "Not even the SEALs."

"So the active duty has been put on domestic police duty, but that won't be enough manpower to lock down the unrest?" Protégé asked.

"It wouldn't be enough to control Southern California. Besides, those kids are trained to blow shit up, not prevent shit from getting blown up. It ain't rocket science. The combination of insufficient numbers and misguided training goes a long way toward explaining our failures in Iraq and Afghanistan, and should tell you a lot about why I vigorously opposed declaring martial law. We're apt to make a much bigger mess."

"You guys didn't tell me this when you recruited me for your little revolution," Protégé said.

"Relax," the general said. "America isn't a time bomb like those other shitholes we invaded. We only have a few religious fanatics, not an army of them, and we haven't been killing each other with pitchforks for the last five centuries. Most Americans want to get along by getting along."

"Maybe so," Protégé said, "but a little bonhomie runs pretty thin when there's no food, water, or power."

"No lie," Williamson said. "Which is why the martial law declaration is potentially disastrous. If we say we're going to restore civic function, then demonstrate that we have no such capacity…"

"People will freak," Protégé finished.

Williamson chuckled. "One way of putting it. 'Open revolt' is another way."

"So we're screwed?" Protégé asked.

"That's one outcome. I'd place the odds at about twenty-five percent for that one, though. The upside of the martial law declaration is that I can turn the crank on the infrastructure, get the power grid up and running at close to capacity, and spend some money to get the fuel supplies running again."

"What money are you spending?" Archive asked. "They can't possibly be so stupid as to print more dollars, can they?"

"I'm afraid so," the general said. "At least, that's what it sounded like at this afternoon's Cabinet meeting. I was a fly on the wall via video teleconference."

Archive exhaled slowly, looking more tired than Protégé had ever seen him. "This is turning into a disaster," he said, his voice low and weak.

"Not yet," the general said. "As usual, when the people wake up and pay attention, they're a lot smarter than the government. Nobody's accepting dollars for anything at the moment. The Fed can print as many new bills as it wants, but that's just paper, and they'll stop printing in no time once they figure out that nobody wants the bills. What really made the world go 'round was the large-scale electronic lending between banks. You gutted that system."

"So the Fed has no real levers to pull," Protégé said.

"Exactly," Archive said, brightening a bit. "It's almost like we designed it that way." The twinkle returned to his eyes for a moment.

"I'm using a combination of bullion from the national reserves and a bit of federally-mined Bitcoin."

"The US government was mining Bitcoins?" Archive asked incredulously.

"Damn right," Williamson said. "In huge quantities. But very quietly, through front corporations."

Protégé whistled. "That changes the equation."

"Not really," Williamson said. "There's not enough in federal coffers to come close to mitigating the banking meltdown."

"So what now?" Protégé asked.

"Finesse," Williamson said. "We let the PLO effect run its course."

"PLO? As in the Palestinian terrorist group?" Protégé asked.

Archive chuckled. "To those of us living in the US, where a pro-Israeli stance is as apple pie as baseball, I suppose the PLO is still considered a terrorist organization. But definitely not in Palestine."

Williamson agreed. "The PLO pulled the rug out from under the incumbent regime by simply being better at providing infrastructure and the rule of law. PLO troops handed out food, provided shelter, and repaired buildings after Israeli attacks. Palestine's titular government was nowhere to be seen. Didn't take long for the people to favor the PLO over the sitting administration."

"So you want a revolution? Overthrow the government?" Protégé looked incredulous.

"Not at all," Williamson said. "But we do want law and order, and the reality is that only the citizens can provide that for themselves. The federal and state governments are stuffed to the gills with bureaucrats, most of whom have no real skill or expertise beyond building PowerPoint presentations."

Archive nodded. "There is still an alarming amount of violence, but we're already seeing strong signs of self-organization."

"By street gangs," Protégé cautioned.

"Among other groups," Williamson said. "Like soccer moms and school boards and professional societies. But I share your concern, which is why I've already started deploying my Spec Ops guys into the cities."

"To take out the criminals?" Protégé asked.

Williamson guffawed. "Hardly! You want complete civil war on your conscience? Their mission is to support productive activity while keeping criminal activity under control. I've told them to be completely agnostic regarding the source of the activity, in either direction. If it's a gang or cartel that's handing out food and picking up the trash, I want them supported. If it's a group of rogue nuns running around looting, I want them stopped."

"Rogue nuns?" Archive laughed.

"You get my meaning," the general said. "Bottom line, there will be skirmishes, and this will not be neat or tidy, but I'm optimistic. My guys know what's at stake."

"So you're not expecting the unrest to last long?" Archive asked.

"I'm expecting it to last as long as it takes to get goods and services flowing again."

"Which takes a viable currency system," Protégé observed. "We need to get that Bitcoin theft operation under control."

"Long-term, absolutely," Williamson said. "If you want my

guess, it's probably some of the usual suspects in the oligarchy game. They didn't get to be as rich as they are — or at least as rich as they were up until a few days ago — by being stupid."

Archive nodded. "Agreed. Trojan is with the federal agents trying to track down the source of the hack right now. And I've got Vaneesh working on things from this end."

"Sounds like a good start. But you need to find where the money trail *ends*," Williamson said. "Those are the people you need to worry about. Unless you get their hands out of the cookie jar, they'll just buy the new government, exactly like they bought the old one."

"And all of this will have been a complete waste," Protégé said.

Archive nodded grimly. "Looks like we've all got our work cut out for us."

"Yep, and I've got to get back to it," the general said. "If we do well, maybe they won't hang us when this is all over."

Archive and Protégé chuckled uneasily. It was an outcome they'd begun to fear in a very real way. Revolutionaries rarely died in bed.

Chapter 13

"Time's up," Sam said. "I'm officially out of patience, Señor Rojas. Where are my agents?"

"Relax, Agent Jameson." Rojas seemed a little too smug, as if her threat of violence no longer seemed credible to him.

It was occasionally necessary to restore a mark's confidence in one's gumption, Sam reflected. "You're not really taking me seriously, are you, Señor Rojas?" She smiled sweetly. "I get this a lot. It's because of my tits, isn't it?"

She placed the muzzle of her .45 against Rojas' thigh and squeezed the trigger. The roar of the big Kimber semiautomatic was like a thunderclap in the confines of the aircraft cabin.

Rojas threw his head back and filled the small space with a howl of agony, eyes closed in pain, veins bulging on his neck.

"Holy shit!" Brock shouted in alarm, surprised both by the noise and by Sam's cold-bloodedness. "What are you doing?"

"This isn't America," Sam said. "The game is different down here. These people will gut you for bus fare."

Brock shook his head, watching Rojas writhe. "Jesus H. You scare the shit out of me sometimes."

Sam chuckled. "I'd hate for you to get bored with me."

She waited for Rojas to settle down. It took many seconds for him to come to grips with his new reality. She hoped her message was clear: the redhead American bitch was crazy, and the situation was a long way out of Rojas' control.

"I trust we now have a deeper understanding of each other, Señor Rojas." Sam's voice was calm and quiet, and she smiled with exaggerated cordiality. "Kidnappings really piss me off."

"She's telling you the truth," Dan said with a chuckle. "Hey, stop bleeding on the carpet." He rolled Rojas over onto his side, wounded leg up, and shoved a cocktail napkin into the wound. Rojas barked in pain.

Sam held the phone to Rojas' ear. "It's ringing. We're calling your friend, the kidnapper. Same rules apply about playing games with me. I'm confident you now have a healthy appreciation for my sincerity."

Rojas clenched his jaw, then spoke rapid-fire Spanish into the phone.

Sam bashed his forehead with the gun barrel. "English!"

"En Inglés, por favor," Rojas told his counterpart on the phone, eyeballing Sam with venom in his gaze.

"There has been a delay." The phone's small speaker crackled with the third driver's voice. He sounded calm, controlled.

"Your amigos are in deep shit," Sam said into the phone. "Two are wounded. One has a mangled hand. I am holding them at gunpoint. I won't tolerate delays."

"There was an accident on the road," the man said. "We are stuck in traffic."

"At this time of night? Bullshit. Hand the phone over to the fat guy."

"Si, señora." Sam heard the rustling of static as the phone

changed hands.

"Hi, Sam." Harv Edwards' familiar smoker's rumble was recognizable despite the speakerphone distortion. "You shot the greasy skinny guy, didn't you?"

Sam chuckled. "How'd you guess?"

"Seemed like your style. Anyway, Pedro here is telling the truth, as far as the traffic goes. There's one lane for both directions, and a guy with a sign to stop and start traffic. But I think our chauffeur is lying about something else."

"Such as?"

"I'm watching planes take off and land," Harv said. "Out the back window of the car."

Sam instantly got his meaning. They were heading away from the airport. *It had that kind of vibe about it.* "So you're going sightseeing?"

"Looks that way. No door handles in this thing, either."

Sonuvabitch. She snapped her fingers at Dan. He nodded his understanding, and was already opening his laptop. He held up three fingers. "I need three minutes," he mouthed. Cell phones were Big Brother's best friend, even in Costa Rica.

"A detour for construction." The driver's voice sounded far away.

"That's funny," Harv's voice said. "Because we haven't made any turns recently. None at all, really, since we left the airport."

Sam shook her head. "Are you guys really that stupid, Rojas?" She pointed the muzzle of her gun at Rojas' buttock and pulled the trigger. He screamed with a renewed agony. Getting shot in the ass was horrifically painful, to both ass and pride.

"Way to show 'em, Sam!" Harv's voice was loud and boisterous. Then, in a quieter voice, "Our man Pedro doesn't look nearly as agitated as I'd expect."

Sam's face registered deep concern. "No worries, Harv," she said, her voice far more nonchalant than her expression. "He probably didn't care much for Rojas either. Just sit tight. I'm sure all of our interests will somehow *intersect.*" She placed heavy emphasis on the last word.

"Will do," Harv said. Then, *sotto voce*, phone held close to his lips, "Looks like Avenue Central and Calle…"

Sam heard a sharp slap, then the call went dead.

Damn. Edwards had almost gotten his location out before the driver took the phone and ended the call.

She looked over at Dan. He shook his head. "Someplace in Alajuela. That's all I was able to get."

"Didn't he give you two street names?" Brock asked.

Sam shook her head. "'Calle' means 'street' in Spanish. He didn't get the name out in time."

"We got one name though. That's something."

Dan called up a map on his laptop. He shook his head. "Avenue Central covers a lot of real estate," he said. "Not much help, honestly."

Sam turned to Rojas, who was moaning softly on the cabin floor. She brought her gun to his face, held it close enough for him to smell the cordite. "I could have sworn we had an understanding."

He flinched. "What do you take me for?" he said. "I am not a fool."

"Yet you interfered with a gaggle of Gringos Federales," Sam said. "Are you new?"

Rojas shook his head. "You heard me tell him to turn around."

"Why didn't he?"

Rojas shrugged. "I do not know him. It was part of the conditions for the job. They said he had to be on the snatch team."

"Who said?"

"I told you already. The Gray One. His people."

"You idiot," Sam said. Rule Numero Uno in the spy business: never work with strangers. Great way to end up dead.

But it's an interesting twist, Sam realized. If the Gray One was a longtime player, he had to have strong Agency ties. Central America was a collection of relic puppet regimes, and while it was true that their spy agencies didn't exactly dance to every CIA tune these days, they sure as hell tapped their feet to the rhythm.

So the Gray One has either gone a little bit rogue, or he hasn't. They were equally probable options, Sam figured. The currency crisis up north probably hadn't done much to extend the Agency's influence down in the equatorial jungle, and there was probably a little more slack in the leash for someone like this Gray One to exploit.

On the other hand, the cash problem up north had left the Agency just as strapped as every other mammoth American bureaucracy. But the CIA was never afraid to dabble in a little entrepreneurship, particularly if it could do so with any degree of plausible deniability. It seemed just as likely that the Gray One was in lock-step with the Agency, which could stand to profit handsomely through a convenient little alliance with whoever was stealing all the Bitcoins. Which, not for the first time, would put the CIA at odds with the Department of Homeland Security.

"So what's your guidance, fearless supervisor?" Dan asked with a sardonic smile.

Sam surveyed the scene. Three DIS agents, in various states of disrepair, were strewn about the aircraft cabin floor. Two of them were leaking blood. None of them wore a happy expression.

Four problems came quickly to mind. First, they had to figure out where the hell Sabot Mondragon's charter flight had disappeared to. Rojas' earlier call to the airport's flight management office would hopefully grease those skids.

Second, Rojas and his fellow goons needed a place to cool their heels. She needed them available to use as leverage, should occasion arise, but she needed them safely out of her hair.

Third, her entourage was missing two members, and they weren't exactly hardened field agents. One was a skinny computer nerd, and the other was a fat academic with poor social skills. She couldn't count on either of them for anything in the way of operational savvy, and she really just hoped they didn't do anything to get themselves shot while she figured out what the hell to do about their kidnapping.

Last, she may or may not be unwittingly working against Agency interests. Or, more likely, against the interests of the local Agency thugs. The only coherent CIA agenda, in her experience, was securing its fair share of the federal budget. Beyond that, all bets were off. There was really nothing to be done about the potential conflict, but it could certainly make life more interesting.

"Just another day at the office," Sam muttered. "Copilot-guy!" Her shout startled everyone in the cabin. The youngish looking copilot peered sheepishly around the corner of the cockpit bulkhead. He clearly wanted nothing to do with the commotion in the passenger compartment, but Sam had other plans for him. "Ever shot a gun?"

He shook his head.

"It's a point-and-click thing," Sam said helpfully. "You're our new prison guard. Keep these three goofballs under control." She gestured toward the disheveled and tied-up DIS agents, racked the slide to chamber a round in Rojas' sidearm, and handed it to the copilot. He took the weapon gingerly.

"Grab it as if you were a male," she said with a good-natured jab to the young man's ribs.

Sam turned to the pilot. "Can you get us ready to get out of here quick?"

"Sure. But I'll need a flight plan, which requires a destination. And we'll have to hope the locals will still take American currency to pay for the fuel and servicing."

"Destination unknown right now, but do everything else, please."

"What about the fuel cost?"

"Surprise me with your ingenuity." She turned to her deputy. "Dan, can you access Zip Line from down here?"

"Strange you should ask," he said, pointing to an open window on his computer screen. "I'll know in a few minutes. Leave me Rojas' cell phone so I can dig out the other guy's number. We'll have some angle problems down here because the satellite is primarily pointed at US territory, but as long as we're still inside the satellite's footprint, Zip Line should be able to ping the phone and get a decent location ellipse."

"Sweet." Sam reached for Brock's hand. "Want to take a stroll, baby? I have a feeling I'm going to need to rely on your experience as a hero fighter pilot. You can impress them with your big wristwatch."

He smiled. "Anything for you, sweet tits."

She pinched his ass on the way down the staircase, and they walked as quickly across the tarmac as Brock's wounded thigh would permit.

"We could use a bit of a break," Sam said as they entered the airport's flight management office, located at the base of the control tower.

Brock nodded his assent. "A little good luck wouldn't kill anybody."

Chapter 14

Zelaya replayed the tape. Fredericks strained his eyes to make out Mondragon's form in the dark cell, and leaned in close to the speaker to hear the mumbled phrase. "What did he say?"

"He said, 'then come and get it,'" Zelaya said.

"So it's done. Nice work. Go get the account information."

Zelaya frowned, wearied yet again by the gringo impatience. "Certainly," Zelaya said. "But you want a new asset, do you not? Not just to steal his lollipop and discard him. That will take a little more time. And a great deal more finesse."

Fredericks nodded, looked at his watch, sighed. The old man had expected Mondragon's death hours ago, and had expected Fredericks to be on a plane back north with the account information. Fredericks wasn't looking forward to the phone call. "Get me someplace near a cell tower," he said.

Zelaya's jaw flexed. Fredericks had the personality of a cheese grater. "Certainly. The lieutenant will take you. I have an appointment with Mr. Mondragon."

* * *

Sabot heard footsteps. "Not again, you bastards!" he yelled. "You're not getting me with that trick again!" *Walk down the hall and then lurk around outside the door. What kind of bullshit is that? Trying to drive me insane.*

His mind still felt heavy, foggy, not quite his own. He was

starving, and food had become an obsession. He dreamt of Fat Joe's Meat Lover's Special, his favorite dish at his favorite Seattle pizzeria. Lots of parmesan and red peppers on top. And he dreamt of Angie's carne asada, some secret family recipe passed down for generations. He was wild about it under normal circumstances, and thinking of the warm, spicy aroma and tender beef nearly drove him to distraction as he sat chained in his cell, freezing, starving, and rapidly losing his wits.

He was beyond surprised when the cell door opened, the rusty hinges screaming their customary protest. In marched two guards. But something was different this time. Was that… Marisela? In a guard's uniform? She stood at attention at one side of the door. A guard Sabot hadn't seen before flanked her on the right.

Sabot stared at her. She was insanely beautiful. Her eyes moved to his. Was it his imagination, or did she wink at him? She shook her head ever so slightly back and forth. *Quiet,* she seemed to be saying. *Our little secret.*

Or maybe he was making it up. He looked at his left wrist. No marks on it at all, as if it had never been chained to the wall, as if he had never torn it up thrashing against the shackles at the height of passion.

He looked up at her again, and this time he swore he caught the vestiges of a surreptitious smile on her lips.

More footsteps, moving quickly. Boot heels pounded in the hallway. A short, crisp, slight figure appeared in the doorway, close-cropped white hair reflected in the dim light. Zelaya.

"Señor Domingo Mondragon," he said, his cool, raspy voice

filling the room. "I am Terencio Manuel Zelaya."

"We've met," Sabot said.

Zelaya arched his eyebrows. "I assure you we have not."

"No, man, we've met," Sabot said. "You said, 'Now you know who to fear,' or some shit like that."

Zelaya studied him for a long moment. "My staff have informed me that you have been experiencing some, shall we say, mental difficulties."

"Really? Let me chain your ass under a cold shower for a week." Sabot waved his shackled hand. "We'll see how long it takes you to lose your shit."

If Zelaya heard him, he gave no indication. "I'll send the physician to examine you."

"That sonuvabitch? He drugged me. I'd swear on my mother's grave."

"Mr. Mondragon, you've not yet met the physician, either."

Sabot was awestruck. "Are you out of your mind, man? Fat bastard, whiskey on his breath, some tingly shit on that tongue stick. He was definitely in here. Right after Marisela came in…"

Shit. Was he supposed to say anything about that? His eyes darted involuntarily to Marisela. She stared straight ahead, ignoring his searching gaze. She never even flinched at the mention of her name. *This is way beyond weird.*

"Mr. Mondragon, I'm afraid I do not know what you're talking about. I do not employ anyone named Marisela at this facility. And I will ask the physician to visit your room to ensure that you are in adequate physical and mental health to begin the legal proceedings."

"Legal proceedings?"

Zelaya looked at him as if he were crazy. "Of course, Mr. Mondragon. Surely you are aware that you will stand trial."

"Trial? For what?" Sabot leapt to his feet. "Man, this is *messed up!*" he bellowed. "We landed at the airport, and you kidnapped us!" He pointed his index finger at Zelaya. "*You.* Kidnapped. *Us*! That's how it went down, and you *know* it!"

"Mr. Mondragon, please calm yourself and be seated." Zelaya's voice was low and even. "You are restrained because you are considered dangerous. You are being held without bond on charges of espionage and murder."

"What the hell?" Sabot stared at Zelaya, open-mouthed and incredulous.

"There is substantial evidence against you," Zelaya continued. "Including a corpse."

"You've got to be out of your mind! I mean, you obviously have me mixed up with someone else!"

Zelaya's expression remained impassive. "If you do not already have an attorney, a public defender will be provided."

"This is crazy! I haven't done anything! And I sure as hell haven't murdered anyone!"

"Mr. Mondragon, in the Honduran justice system, those who confess are treated with greater leniency than those who are convicted. Given the evidence against you, it is an option you should consider."

Sabot's mind reeled. He sat back down in the chair, and tried unsuccessfully to gather himself. Espionage? Murder? Confession?

Honduras?

His eyes snapped to Zelaya's face. "Did you just say Honduras?"

"Of course, Mr. Mondragon. Where else did you expect?"

"Goddamned *Honduras?*"

Zelaya looked at him impassively. "Mr. Mondragon, let us set the games aside. I am neither judge nor jury. It is not me whom you must convince of your insanity."

Sabot shook his head incredulously. "Insanity?" This was a nightmare. They obviously had him confused with someone else. "Can't you see what's happening here?"

Zelaya sighed, tired. "Mr. Mondragon, as I mentioned, I am not the appropriate person for you to be having this conversation with." He produced a typewritten page from a folder and placed it in Sabot's hand. "Please read carefully, make any appropriate changes, and sign."

Sabot looked at the page. He recognized many of the letters, but none of them formed any words. Nothing on the page made any sense.

He thought at first that it might have been written in Spanish or French, but it wasn't even close. Vowels and consonants were jammed together improbably, like in some strange Eastern European language, and some of the letters had odd and seemingly random accent marks. Some didn't look like letters at all. "What the hell is this?"

"Please read carefully," Zelaya said.

Sabot stared at Zelaya, bewilderment on his face, then looked again at the page of gibberish. There were no recognizable words on the paper. Sabot could glean no meaning from the letters. It was written in no language he'd ever encountered. "Is this some sort of a sick joke?"

Zelaya rose. "Mr. Mondragon, I assure you that this is no laughing matter. As you can plainly see, the charges laid out against you on that page are very serious. I will leave you to consider them." He turned to walk out of the room.

"Wait!" Sabot called. Zelaya turned to look at him.

"This is crazy," Sabot said. "I mean, these aren't even words! It's like a child got ahold of your computer."

Zelaya shook his head silently, turned, and walked out of the cell.

Sabot's eyes darted to Marisela. She returned his gaze, but her face was completely impassive. There was no spark of recognition in her eyes, no hint of a connection whatsoever. "Help me," he mouthed.

She looked blankly at him, as if he were an inanimate object. Then she turned and left the room, followed closely by the second guard. The door hinges assaulted his ears with their familiar screech, the lock clicked into place, and Sabot was left alone again.

Am I completely insane?

Espionage? Murder?

Honduras?

He looked once again at the piece of paper in his hand. *There are no goddamned words on this page!*

Oh, no! What about Angie? In his bewilderment, he had

completely forgotten to ask about Angie and Connie. Were they in just as messed-up a situation as he was? Was there anything he could do to help them? Was there any information he could provide that would straighten out this colossal misunderstanding?

He shook his head vigorously, rubbed his eyes, and tried yet again to make sense of the piece of paper that Zelaya had handed him. Hopeless. He balled it up and threw it, then watched it bounce off the far wall and land in a puddle of water near the drain in the floor. "Sonuvabitch!" he screamed.

And then the voices started again. Faint, distant howls, peals of laughter, whispered voices that felt as if they came from inside his skull, admonishments to *confess, Domingo,* delivered in a freakish Darth Vader basso.

Once again, his consciousness disassociated from his body. His sentience suddenly perched itself in the far corner of the room, looking at his body, slumped pathetically in the wooden chair. The feeling of vertigo was almost unbearable. His stomach turned with nausea. He retched bile, his empty gut cramping painfully with each dry heave.

He felt helpless, befuddled, and completely out of control. His hands covered his eyes, and he discovered that he was crying.

Chapter 15

The Facilitator hung up the phone angrily. Just a week ago, he would not have dreamt of tolerating the impertinence of a man like Fredericks. The orders and the timeline were excruciatingly clear, and Fredericks' failure to deliver was entirely unacceptable.

Breaking a man — especially an amateur such as Mondragon, someone completely untrained in interrogation resistance techniques — was a simple matter. It took competent agents just a couple of hours to achieve the required results. Fredericks had so far spent two entire days, and was yet to come through.

"There's some technical stuff that we'll have a hard time replicating," Fredericks had said. "I need him healthy enough to guide me through it. Otherwise, we'll have no idea how to get at the money." Plausible enough, the Facilitator had concluded. But the length of time that had elapsed since Mondragon had been taken was what worried him. Operations that dragged on had a far greater chance of going sideways.

He missed the layer of insulation from operational headaches previously afforded by the Intermediary's presence. And he wasn't such a sociopath that he didn't also miss the Intermediary himself. But mostly, he missed having someone to handle bullshit like this, allowing him to focus almost exclusively at the strategic level.

But his isolation, necessary in order to insulate him from discovery, and to ensure that the man at the center of the

Consultancy remained sufficiently anonymous yet ubiquitously influential, had set the stage for a serious problem. Over the past several days, he had lost three very senior operatives, who themselves accounted for the bulk of the operational expertise and useful contacts he had come to rely on.

He shook his head, and his mouth formed a hard line. It was always a risk, he knew. But the timing couldn't have been worse.

Onward. *There is only this moment.* It demanded action, resolve, clarity. He called out to his steward. "Jordan Mandrake."

"I'll get him on the line for you, sir," the steward replied.

Perception was power. Few understood the concept as thoroughly as Mandrake. One didn't amass the largest single portfolio of media outlets on the planet without having more than just a little savvy regarding the power of public discourse. And no one manipulated it as thoroughly, subtly, and effectively as Mandrake.

People wanted mostly to piss in the wind, Mandrake had once said in an extremely private conversation. They didn't want real choice, real change, or real movement. They had no patience for nuance. They didn't want to choose an outcome; they wanted to choose a side. They had tons of latent anger in search of an enemy. They wanted some small, distant thing to be momentarily outraged about. Then they wanted to get on with their day.

Most of all, Mandrake had said, people didn't want to be responsible.

Obviously, a patently monolithic media stance caused suspicion and reduced credibility. Worse, it was boring. Mandrake cultivated controversy, loved a good cock fight, loved it when people slung epithets and hackneyed labels at each other, and championed a feisty press corps.

But he chose the agenda, carefully picked the impassioned players, and expertly, almost imperceptibly, guided the battles. When oligarchs bought air time, which they did in copious quantities, Mandrake knew exactly how to craft the narrative for maximum impact. He was a king-maker. He delivered riches and ruins, simply by grabbing the herd's attention for a passing moment, thousands of times each day.

"I wondered how long it would take you to call," Mandrake said, the words seeming to come out his nose rather than his mouth, thick and fast and New York all over, bouncing despite the late hour. "Should I be hurt that it's taken this long?"

The Facilitator exhaled, tired, less than amused. "Feel as you wish."

Mandrake cackled. "You're like an ashtray with lips. I love it!"

The Facilitator heard a click. Mandrake had hung up on him.

The old man sighed heavily and handed the phone back to the steward. "Reconnect us, please." He tapped his finger on the leather armrest and gazed out the window at the Canadian Rockies as the steward again navigated the labyrinth of gatekeepers en route to Mandrake. The little magnate was as mercurial as ever, the Facilitator reflected. Undoubtedly a few days into an amphetamine-fueled frenzy.

Unfortunately, Mandrake was more necessary than ever.

It took several more minutes before the steward handed back the receiver. "We must have been disconnected," the Facilitator said flatly.

"It's my thumb," Mandrake said. "It hangs up on the entitled. You should try kissing my ass instead."

"I wouldn't know how to begin."

"'Dear Jordan. Please help me. You are wise and powerful. I'm lost without you.' Try that."

The Facilitator summoned a patience he didn't feel. "Name your price."

"Steeper than usual, for obvious reasons," Mandrake said. "Insurance against all the uncertainty."

"How are your viewership numbers?" the Facilitator asked.

"Better than ever. What did you expect me to tell you?"

"The truth," the Facilitator said coolly.

Mandrake cackled again. "Which one would you like?"

The old man recalled with agitation the same distant conversation with Mandrake. *A new reality is just one headline away.* Arrogant and brazen, but unassailable. Nothing in the human experience existed raw and unfiltered. Observation was an act of creation. The mind made its own truth.

And it was exceptionally susceptible to persuasion. That was precisely why he was putting up with Mandrake's petulant bullshit.

"I would like to purchase several new truths," he finally said. "For immediate dissemination."

Chapter 16

"Si, Señora, we have been expecting you." Sonora, the administrative clerk on the midnight shift at the Dirección General de Aviación Civil office, the Costa Rican counterpart to the Federal Aviation Administration, buzzed Sam and Brock through the door. "Always eager to help our friends at the DIS," the clerk said. Sam wondered whether the flat delivery disguised a sarcastic note.

"Thank you," Sam said. "We'll hopefully be out of your hair in no time at all." She handed over the slip of paper with the details of the flight she was looking for. "It originated at the Pitt Meadows Regional Airport in British Columbia, Canada, and ended up here, maybe a little over an hour ago."

The clerk typed at her terminal. And typed. More typing. "Not a streamlined system," Sam observed.

"Barely a system at all," Sonora said. "Held together by promises from the Assembly. Bigger budget every year, but the money never quite makes it out of the administration building." Her fingers clicked rapidly over the keyboard. She frowned, pounded on the "enter" key with more force than was strictly necessary, and frowned more.

Finally, she shook her head. "No flight from Canada landed here in the last few hours, except for a US government plane," she said.

"That was ours," Brock said. "Can you search by departure

point?"

"Si," Sonora said. More typing.

Sam's weariness returned in force. *How tough can this be? It's the twenty-first century, and there's a robot on Mars right now.* She felt Brock's arm around her waist. He kissed her neck. He had a knack for sensing her tension, and for releasing it.

"No," Sonora said after a few million more mouse clicks. "Several from the States, one from the other side of Canada. Nothing left British Columbia for anywhere further south than Mexico today."

Sonuvabitch. "Can you search by aircraft tail number?"

Sonora checked her watch, and a small sigh escaped. "Si, but then I am off shift."

Sam focused on her breathing while Sonora worked the computer. Moments later, a printer next to Sonora's computer came to life. It spit out a single page. Brock recognized it as a VFR flight plan. Visual Flight Rules plans were almost never used in the commercial aviation business, and definitely not for international travel with paying passengers.

But there it was, clear as day. The Obsidian Air tail number in question was flown VFR to Tucson, Arizona, with six souls on board. The flight plan was opened just a few moments before their own aircraft departed Canada, and it was closed out hours ago.

"The aircraft took off from Pitt Regional in Canada and landed at Tucson International," Sonora summarized.

"We've been screwed." Sam said.

Brock nodded. "Hard."

Then a thought struck. "Can you print a list of everything that left Tucson International in the past, say, eight hours?"

Sonora began to look thoroughly put upon, and glanced pointedly at her watch.

"I'm very sorry," Sam said. "It's just very important that we catch this person. He could be extremely dangerous, and he's doing a great deal of damage to a lot of people right now."

Sonora pursed her lips, then nodded. "I am happy to help you with this one last thing," she said. More sarcasm? Sam wasn't sure.

It took far more time than Sam anticipated, and she began to see why Sonora was none too happy about the request. "Next year, retirement," the clerk said with a sigh. "But I am still younger than this system." She pounded the "enter" key several more times, and the printer began spewing pages.

Sonora collected the papers, stapled them, and handed them to Sam. "It has been my pleasure serving you this morning," she lied.

Morning. Sam looked at her watch. It was definitely three hours past midnight. *I've got to get some sleep at some point.*

"Thank you very much for your help," Brock said. "We really do appreciate it."

They took the report and sat down in the waiting area to study the Tucson departures. They weren't sure what they were looking for, and it was entirely possible that Sabot Mondragon was sleeping peacefully in a Tucson hotel at the moment, or on an overnight flight to Anyplace Else.

Sam's phone rang. "Hi, Dan. Good news, please."

"Sorry, boss. Not much of that right now. There's huge

demand for my favorite satellite."

Balls. The Zip Line system was backed up with requests, and Dan evidently wasn't able to use it to locate the cell phone belonging to the driver who had taken Trojan and Harv.

Something struck her as odd. *Who's pinging cell phones by the hundreds at three in the morning?* "Who has access to the system?" she asked.

"Well, we do, obviously, but I can't imagine anyone at Homeland is burning the midnight oil. Then there's NSA — it's their bird, actually — and the Agency as well. And the Bureau, of course, but they're pretty anal about jumping through all the legal hoops."

"All my favorites," Sam said glumly. "Do you think it would be possible for someone with access to the system to artificially bog it down?"

"On purpose? Sure."

Sam pondered. Perhaps the Agency angle wasn't so implausible after all.

"You're hatching a conspiracy theory, aren't you?" Dan asked.

Sam chuckled. "Dan, there's obviously a conspiracy. I'm just trying to figure out who's playing along."

"Good point. While you do that, I'll go to work on Harv's private cell phone account, and maybe Trojan's. Maybe we'll be able to use the 'locate my phone' function to get a bead on one or both of them."

"You're so much more than just a pretty face," Sam teased. "Someone should give you a raise."

"If only my boss cared about me," Dan quipped before

hanging up.

Sam turned back to the list of departing flights out of Tucson. "Find anything?"

Brock shrugged. "Great big pile of bupkis. I mean, he could be on any of these flights, or none of them. We have no clue where he was headed."

Sam frowned. "Yeah, we're pretty much grabbing at straws here, until we can get our hands on passenger manifests for all of those flights."

"How can you do that?"

Sam smiled. "We are Big Brother. But there's some serious bureaucracy involved and it ain't gonna happen at three in the morning."

"Wait a sec," Brock said, holding up a sheet full of flight plans. "Here's one with a Canadian dip code."

"Dip code?"

"A code identifying the passengers as being under Canadian diplomatic protection. It's supposed to minimize air traffic delays, but mostly it's just there to avoid customs."

"Headed where?"

"Macedonia."

"From Tucson?"

"Via Charlotte, then Heathrow, then Rome, then Zagreb, and winding up in Skopje."

"Sounds terrible."

"Tell me about it. I'd prefer to sleep on gravel than spend that much time in a metal tube." This from the fighter pilot of twenty years.

"How tough would it be to buy yourself a diplomatic code?" Sam asked, mind churning.

"I have no idea. In the third world, probably pretty easy. All you'd probably need is a fat roll of cash. But in Canada?"

Sam nodded. "Probably not terribly corrupt up there."

"Anyway, why would our guy want to go to Macedonia?"

"No extradition treaty with Uncle Sugar."

Brock's eyebrows arched. "Pretty good reason, if you're the guy who just ripped off a few zillion dollars."

"Except that he didn't just steal from US citizens," Sam realized. "Those accounts belonged to people all over the world."

"Hmm." Brock smiled. "I doubt there's any good place to hide."

Sam chuckled. "Some places are better than others. Bring a giant fortune to a poor country, and you could keep the local politicians on your side for a very long time."

"I like his odds in Central America," Brock said.

Sam nodded. "I agree. Let's not race off to Europe just yet."

"But we're kind of dead in the water here."

"And our posse is short by two," Sam reminded him.

"Right. I'd hate to leave that annoying Harv behind."

"Be nice."

Sam's phone dinged with a text message from Dan: "Pay dirt. I love cell phones."

"Looks like Dan located their phones," she said, rising from her seat in the aviation authority's lobby and grabbing Brock's hand.

Brock smiled. "How many assholes have you caught that way?"

"Too many to count," Sam said as they made their way out of the aviation administration building.

"You think people would catch on."

"There are surprisingly few other options," Sam said, supporting Brock's weight as he hobbled on his wounded leg. "I think there are maybe a dozen pay phones left on the planet. The key is keeping your cell number anonymous, and that's actually pretty easy to do by using disposable phones. But once we get ahold of a number, it's pretty much over."

"That's not all bad," Brock said. "I know one guy who's pretty happy about your ability to locate people." He squeezed her arm.

"I know one girl who's very, very happy as well." Sam would never have been able to rescue Brock from his kidnappers without manipulating the cell phone system. She shuddered to think what the outcome of the previous weekend's nightmare might have been without that capability. And without her willingness to abuse it.

"I'm sure Harv and Trojan won't mind your snooping, either," Brock said.

Sam smiled. "Let's not get cocky. Knowing where they are is one thing, but springing them loose from a foreign intelligence agency on its home turf is quite another."

She got out her phone and dialed. It rang four times, then a familiar voice answered. "McClane." It was four a.m. on the East Coast, but it didn't sound to Sam like her boss had been asleep.

"Hi, Mace," Sam said. "Up all night at a rave?" She placed one finger in her other ear to drown out the high-pitched whine of a power cart on the airport ramp.

"Funny. No," Mason McClane said. He'd occupied the Division Chief role for a little over a year. It had taken DHS a while to fill the position, due in no small measure to the fact that McClane's two predecessors had both died violent deaths. Job description: answer email, sit in boring meetings, eat a bullet. Who wouldn't sign up?

"Where are you?" McClane asked.

Sam filled him in on the previous day's fun: her time at the Lost Man Lake Ranch, hideout and de facto headquarters of the conspiracy that had successfully crushed the banking system, and her mad dash to Seattle, Canada, and then Costa Rica in pursuit of the Bitcoin thief Sabot Mondragon.

"Costa Rica?" McClane asked when she finished her update.

"But not for long," Sam said. "Doesn't look like Mondragon ever landed here. So I'd like you to summarily execute the Obsidian Air clerk who lied to me, and get the passenger manifest for every flight that left Tucson International yesterday after four p.m."

McClane chuckled. "The first request would actually be much easier than the second. Could take a while to convince a judge to release all those names. Hell, it could take a while to even *find* a federal judge."

Sam had expected a bit of resistance. "Can you think of a more high-profile fugitive than the richest man in the world?"

"I'll see what I can do."

"And Harv's been kidnapped, I forgot to mention."

"Jesus, Sam."

"And I shot a couple of DIS goons."

Silence.

"I didn't kill them. I'm hoping to exchange prisoners, but I'm not sure how tight their connection might be to the guy who's actually holding Harv." And Trojan, the hacker, who was also a hostage, but Sam didn't want to needlessly complicate the conversation.

"Jesus," McClane said again.

"So, there's going to be a bit of a thing in about thirty minutes. I'll let you know how it goes."

More silence.

"Mace, get some sleep. Normally you'd have some bullshit bureaucratic platitude about being smart and safe, but you're too tired even for that."

"I need to get the op approved, Sam. You're on foreign soil. Stand down until you hear from me."

"Understood." *Not on your life.* "I need something else. A Canadian diplomatic flight left Tucson yesterday afternoon for Skopje, Macedonia. The passenger manifest won't be in the regular system. We need to know who was on that flight."

"I don't see the connection," McClane said.

"There might not be one," Sam said. "Then again, we might just find a lead on whoever is controlling Mondragon."

A long pause. "I'll get our people to work on the manifests."

Sam read him the diplomatic code from the flight plan. McClane read back the code, then added, "I meant what I said, Sam.

You are to stand down awaiting further guidance from myself or the Director. The last thing we need is another gunfight in a friendly country."

"They nabbed our guy, Mace, and nearly had all of us in the bag. How friendly can they be?"

"I need to hear you say it, Sam."

Sam's jaw clenched. "I acknowledge your directive, Mace." Which wasn't the same thing as agreeing to obey, a subtlety she hoped wasn't obvious to McClane in his current sleep-deprived condition.

"Good. You'll hear from me soon," McClane said, confirming Sam's suspicions about his mental state.

"Mace, I need those manifests," Sam said, both to remind McClane and to change the subject.

"Got it. Meantime, find a place to set up a mobile command center and keep your phone charged."

Which was a perfectly asinine process-oriented bureaucratic non-solution, Sam thought. *Meanwhile, here in the real world, two hostages need rescuing.*

* * *

"It was actually pretty easy," Dan explained after Sam and Brock had made their way back to the US government airplane parked across the tarmac at Juan Santamaria International.

"You used the Homeland trapdoor?" Uncle Sugar had thrown his weight around, and the telecommunications industry had done the smart thing: granted permanent access to all users' accounts, with some vague stipulations about warrants, necessity, or the capricious whims of the feds, who were obviously on the side of goodness and truth.

"Actually, even easier. I guessed Harv's password."

"You're kidding," Sam said.

"Nope. Remember that personalized license plate on his penis extender?"

"That giant Super Maxi-Douche diesel truck of his? 'Banger' or something stupid like that?"

"Exactly. I added his birth year to the end. Got right in."

Brock shook his head. "Holy shit. I thought you feds were supposed to be smarter than that."

Dan chuckled. "There isn't a system on the earth that can't be broken into, but most of the time you don't have to break in. People are the biggest security risk by far." He handed a set of handwritten coordinates to Sam. "They're in a warehouse twenty minutes away, and they haven't moved in the last hour."

"How inventive." Sam glanced at the three Costa Rican security service agents tied up and bleeding in the back of the airplane. "How are our guests?"

Dan cocked his head and put a worried expression on his face. "Our two wounded warriors need to get to a hospital. Shock is setting in."

Sam shook her head. "We still need the leverage. Think we can stabilize them?"

"Worth a try. Any luck with the flight manifests?"

"Maybe, but we'll have to wait until the pencil pushers in DC can pull a few strings."

Dan smiled. "I take it you've talked to Mace?"

"Could you tell by the frown on my face?"

"So we're supposed to be smart and play it safe, right?"

Sam smiled. "How'd you guess?"

"I'm glad 'smart' and 'safe' are open to interpretation," Dan said. Sam didn't bother to tell him about the part of the conversation that was clearly not open to interpretation. Dan understood very well that it was a long way from the Beltway to reality, but he had a wife and a kid to think about. Sam didn't want him to worry about getting fired for disobeying orders. That would be all on her.

Dan called up the map of Alajuela. It was a big city, just a bit smaller than San José. Traffic would undoubtedly get heavy after dawn. A blue dot depicted the location of Harv's cell phone. Sam hoped it also depicted the location of Harv's fat self, and the skinny hacker as well.

They conversed briefly about their tactical options, none of which were entirely satisfactory. Then Sam mulled quietly, lips pursed, hands steepled on her chin. Dan resisted the temptation to whistle a game show tune.

After a few moments, Sam had made up her mind. She briefed them on her plan.

When she had finished, Dan shook his head and chuckled. "You've got brass balls, woman," he said.

Sam smiled. "Fortune hates pussies."

"I don't think you quoted it right."

"I'm sure that's what they meant." She turned to the government passenger plane's pilot. "File three different flight plans.

Make sure we're ready to leave on a moment's notice."

"No prob. Where should I file to?" he asked.

She told him.

"You're kidding me, right? You know how much work that will take?"

"No. But feel free to file a union grievance later. Meantime, chop-chop."

She looked at Dan and Brock. "Bullshit flags? Emotional outbursts? Now's the time."

They both shook their heads. "Gutsy plan," Dan said, "and I reserve the right to blame you if it all goes to hell."

Chapter 17

Sabot Mondragon awoke. His head felt clear. He felt comfortable, well-rested, awake, alive. He'd dreamt vivid, strange, disconcerting dreams, but they seemed distant, inconsequential in the warm light of dawn.

He threw back the covers on the bed. High thread count. Expensive and luxurious. Down comforter, also top-end.

He lifted his head from the feather pillow, sat up on the edge of the bed, rubbed the sleep from his eyes, then padded to the bathroom. He relieved himself. He felt and smelled lingering sex on his body. It excited him.

He climbed back in bed, and moved up against Angie's warm, naked body. She was asleep next to him, facing away.

She awoke, stirred, moved her hips against his. He felt her wetness, slipped inside her, sighed, bit her neck. *Angie.* He smelled the familiar perfume, pulled her hair back from her face to kiss her lips.

It wasn't Angie.

"Jesus!" Sabot yelled. He leapt from the bed. "Who the hell are you?"

"Dingo, what's wrong with you?"

Angie called him Dingo. She was the only one who could get away with it.

But this voice didn't belong to Angie. It was lower, huskier.

"Dingo, come back to bed, baby. Are you having one of your nightmares? I'll make it better." Seduction in her voice.

"Where's Angie?" he demanded. "What have you done with her?"

The smile left her eyes, replaced by the beginnings of something else. "Dingo, stop, you're worrying me."

"Goddammit!" he roared. "Where's Angie?"

The woman started to cry. "Dingo, what's happened to you? Tell me how to help you. I'll take you to a doctor."

"The hell you will! Get the hell away from me!"

"Dingo, please…" Her sentence faded into panicked tears.

He charged to the dresser, ripped open a drawer. It was full of Angie's underwear. He picked up her favorite thong, tattered and a bit worn, the seam ripped from *that night.* Definitely Angie's.

He opened the next drawer. Angie's shirts. Even his favorite, the one that said my other boyfriend is rich and handsome. "Where the hell is Angie? What have you done with her?"

The girl cried harder. "Dingo, please, baby! Relax. It's going to be okay. Please!"

He snatched the purse from the nightstand, emptied its contents onto the bed. Angie's phone. Angie's wallet. Pictures of Angie and himself, Angie and Connie, Angie and her coworkers.

Only it wasn't Angie.

"What the hell is going on?" He felt his chest constricting. It was getting harder for him to breathe.

The girl was sobbing on the edge of the bed, covers drawn around her naked body. "Dingo, please baby. It's me!"

He looked again. It *wasn't* her.

Rage. He flew across the room. His hands found her throat. He squeezed, saw the abject fear in her eyes, heard the sickening pop of sinew, saw her face turn red, felt but didn't register the blows of her flailing limbs against his body.

Then it came. Something thick, metallic, unyielding. It crashed into the back of his skull.

Darkness.

Chapter 18

The steward handed the phone to the Facilitator. He put it to his ear, and heard a voice familiar to nearly everyone in the world. It was the voice that had recently declared martial law, the voice that had vowed to throw the might of an entire nation to bring the perpetrators to justice.

"You have a problem," the old man said into the phone without preamble.

"Not me," said the President of the United States. "*We.*"

The Facilitator allowed himself a small smile. The conversation was already going terrifically well. The most powerful man in the world wanted help.

"I've heard an unpleasant rumor. The Journal and the Times are both running a story on the inadequacy of the federal response. Cable news will undoubtedly follow."

"When?" the president asked.

"Tomorrow."

"How long have you known?"

"You are the first person I've spoken with."

"Can you stop it?"

"Of course. But not forever. You're not holding up your end of the deal." Egotistical men were exceptionally easy to manipulate. They feared irrelevance more than anything.

"Martial law," the president said. "I'd say that's a pretty strong move."

"Lip service," the Facilitator chided. "Where are the troops? Where is the law and order? You've got known gang members handing out food to old ladies. Rioting and looting are completely unchecked. Your administration appears absent and impotent. How long do you expect to remain in power under these conditions?"

"These things take time."

"It's a luxury you don't have. They give you trillions every year, and in return they expect at least the illusion of competence in a crisis."

The president snorted. "I have a tenth the troops I need."

"On the contrary," the Facilitator said. "You have all the manpower you need. But only if you find the courage to set an example."

"We've made hundreds of arrests already," the president protested.

"Which have had no appreciable effect."

"What are you suggesting?"

"I am suggesting that you should learn from history," the Facilitator said testily. "The people suspect you're weak. You must demonstrate otherwise."

The president considered. "Violence isn't power."

"No," the Facilitator said. "But the credible threat of violence is certainly a useful proxy. How do you think thousands of Germans herded millions of Jews to their deaths?"

"Jesus. Have you lost your damned mind?"

"Absolutely not. And you should stop letting your emotions

cloud yours. How many more lives will be lost if you let this spin out of control? You'll have open revolt in a week unless you do something to stop this."

The president was silent. The Facilitator let him stew.

Then, the old man gave the president a final nudge. "You must demonstrate that you're worthy of the power at your disposal. Otherwise, it will surely vanish."

Chapter 19

"Señor Rojas, time for another phone call," Sam said as Dan brought the DIS sedan discreetly to a halt in the alley beside the warehouse in downtown Alajuela. She'd have preferred to get the ball rolling much earlier, but where cell phones were concerned, location was everything. It was important that Rojas and his two stooges were in the proper spot on the earth before dialing.

Sam turned around and examined Rojas in the backseat. His breathing was shallow and quick, his skin was clammy, and his pulse was erratic. "I pronounce you screwed," Sam said. She tightened the bandage around his leg and gave him a pat on the shoulder. "But if your guys are any good, this shouldn't take too long."

"You're sure these guys aren't going to screw it up?" Dan asked.

"Not at all. But I still haven't thought of any better ideas."

"We could always do this ourselves, like we're trained to."

Sam shook her head. "Too many unknowns. And we'd have bad guys on both sides of us." She gestured toward the three DIS goons in the back. "Plus Harv and Trojan aren't trained. We'd have our hands more than full if everything went right, and god help us if anything went sideways."

"And just playing devil's advocate here one last time," Dan said. "We're sure we don't want to wait for the cavalry?"

Sam laughed. "I can't imagine how long it's going to take for the suits at Homeland, State, and CIA to even talk to each other, much less hatch and execute a plan. Harv and Trojan will die of old age. Besides, any plan will have to involve the DIS anyway. Why not just sidestep all the bullshit?"

Dan didn't object.

Sam handed the phone to Rojas. "Showtime." She waved her Kimber .45 at him. "Same rules apply. Don't screw with me."

Rojas made the call, played his part to Sam's satisfaction, and handed the phone back to her.

"Ready to make history?" she asked the three DIS agents bound in the backseat of the sedan. They stared blankly back at her. "That was rhetorical, anyway," she muttered to herself, silently opening the door. She took off her shoes, stepped out of the car, and blended into the alley, making her way quickly but quietly toward a side door of the warehouse.

She glanced back at the car. The three DIS knee-cappers appeared well behaved. Dan's pistol, pointed in their vicinity, likely had something to do with that, as did the three gunshot wounds and six pairs of zip-ties between them.

Sam tucked her pistol into her belt, and armed herself with a paperclip and a nail file. Moments later, the lock on the warehouse door yielded. She surveyed the hinges: no visible rust, which was a good sign, but neither were there clear indications of recent lubrication. No guarantee against creaking.

Easy does it, she thought to herself, gently turning the door knob and applying outward pressure. The door didn't move, so she pulled a bit harder, pressing lightly in the opposite direction with her other hand to guard against rapid movement of the door as it passed its sticking point.

Slowly, it moved. Six hours later, or so it seemed, she had enough room to squeeze her body inside the opening and into the darkness of the warehouse.

She crouched low. Her heart pounded in her chest. Her eyes adjusted to the dark. She was in a long hallway that spanned the long side of the warehouse. There were several internal doors along its length. Light emanated from beneath the door at the far end of the hallway.

Slowly, she began to move, her bare feet silent on the hard concrete floor. She stopped at the first door, trying the handle. Locked. She went to work with her nail file and paperclip.

She had moved the first tumbler aside in the door's lock when she heard a sharp, metallic noise at the far end of the hallway. The far door opened, and light spilled out of the room and into the hallway. *Sonuvabitch.* Her heart leapt into her throat, and against all human instincts, she made herself still as stone, hoping she was close enough to the wall to blend into the shadows.

Footsteps. A voice spoke in Spanish. Sam chanced a look: tall, muscular, light on his feet, even in steel-toed boots. The man held a phone to his ear. He was looking straight down the hallway. She could see his eyes. *He doesn't see me, but it won't be long before he does,* Sam thought. It took every ounce of self-control she possessed not to reach for her pistol. The movement would certainly have caught the man's attention. She had no idea how many more men might be in the warehouse, and she wasn't keen to find out the hard way. Especially when she was alone and barefoot.

The man strode quickly and confidently down the hallway. He spoke quietly into the phone. Everything about him exuded control. He looked vastly more capable than the three semi-pro DIS men that were tied up in the backseat of the sedan. *This guy would be a handful all by himself,* she realized.

He wasn't slowing down. She forced herself to take slow, silent breaths.

His phone call ended. He placed the phone in his pocket. He looked right at Sam. She held her breath, and mentally mapped the hand movement required to grab her gun and get a shot off in his direction. She hoped he wouldn't see her until he was close enough to get the drop on him. *Can't catch a damned break,* she thought.

"Pedro!"

The voice boomed from down the hallway. A familiar smoker's rasp with a vaguely northeastern accent. "Señor Pedro, mi amigo." Dogshit Spanish. Obviously not a native speaker.

"Dónde está el baño, muchacho? I'm seeing yellow here." *Harv Edwards!* His voice was loud and obnoxious, even from the other end of the hallway.

The man stopped in the hallway, exhaled, and turned around. He walked back toward the lit room at the far end of the hall. "Pedro! Goddammit, I'm about to piss myself," Harv bellowed.

The agent continued down the hall and disappeared into the lighted room.

Sam breathed a silent sigh of relief, finished picking the locked door in front of her, and peered into the room. Storage closet. Plenty of room for her purposes, she assessed.

She closed the door silently, making sure it remained unlocked, then made her way quickly to the exterior door.

She felt slightly nauseous from the adrenaline pounding through her veins, and her heart rate was up in the low six thousands, or so it felt. She slipped back into the passenger seat of the sedan.

"You look like you've seen a ghost," Dan said.

"Close call." She re-checked her pistol. Nervous habit. "Harv's in there. I don't know about Trojan. One guy for sure, and he's definitely not from around here. We don't want to pick a fight."

Dan nodded. "Any changes to the plan based on what you saw in there?"

"Actually, we caught a bit of a break. Turn right down the hallway, first door on our left is the supply closet. Fifteen paces, total. Piece of cake."

"Famous last words," Dan said.

Sam got out her phone and dialed. Brock answered. "You're on, baby," she said. "Please be careful."

She looked at her watch. "Two minutes."

* * *

Brock hung up his phone, put it in his pocket, and looked once more at the sedan containing Sam, Dan, and the three DIS agents. It was fifty yards away from him, parked along an adjacent side of the warehouse. He was sure they were out of the way.

He looked at his watch. Time to go. He turned the ignition key. The DIS sedan came to life. He suspected it was armored to defend against small arms fire, which would help a great deal for his purposes.

Not that he expected to get shot at.

He lined the car up with the giant warehouse garage door, rolled down the window, engaged the parking brake, and put the automatic transmission in gear.

On the passenger seat next to him was a flat piece of slate they'd liberated from the median a few miles back. He picked it up, opened the car door, and got out of the driver's seat, favoring his wounded leg.

Brock bent down and placed one end of the flat rock on the driver's side floorboard, and rested the top of the rock on the accelerator pedal. The engine revved. Not too much, but just enough.

He quietly shut the car door, then reached in through the open window. His hand found the parking brake lever. He disengaged it, and hobbled out of the way as the the car lurched forward.

* * *

"Go," Sam commanded, watching Brock's driverless sedan accelerate toward the building. She grabbed Alejandro, Rojas' DIS counterpart, and pulled him out of the back of the car. She sliced the zip-tie binding his ankles together, allowing him to walk. With her pistol in the small of his back to encourage cooperative behavior, she pushed him toward the side door of the warehouse.

Dan scooped the wounded Rojas out of the rear of the car. Dan's stocky frame easily handled the skinny DIS agent's weight. He repositioned Rojas over his left shoulder, ignored the groans of pain caused by Rojas' two Sam-inflicted gunshot wounds, grabbed his service pistol in his right hand, and followed Sam in a dash toward the door.

Sam reached the doorknob. A loud crash and the screech of twisting metal announced that Brock's driverless car had found its way inside the warehouse, pounding through the large garage door on the adjacent wall. She registered Brock's limping lope toward their car, where he would keep an eye on the third DIS man imprisoned in the backseat while Dan and Sam took care of business inside the warehouse.

She opened the building's side door, silently cursing the predawn light that now spilled in from a row of high windows, illuminating the hallway. Quickness would have to take priority over quietness. There were no shadows to conceal them.

Sam tugged Alejandro forward into the warehouse. Like a recalcitrant pack animal, he resisted. She backhanded him in the jaw to remind him of their deal: full cooperation would result in full payment, while anything less than enthusiastic participation would be rewarded with permanent scars, at a minimum. Alejandro walked forward, crouching low and staying close to the wall.

An impossibly loud crash assaulted their ears, and the floor shook beneath their feet. Brock's car evidently hadn't stopped once it entered the warehouse, and had found something large and very heavy to collide with.

Shouts came from down the hallway, in the direction of the room that Sam believed to contain Harv Edwards and Trojan. She broke into a run, tugging Alejandro behind her by his lapel.

They quickly covered the ten paces to the supply closet. Sam opened the door without breaking stride, pushed Alejandro to the back of the closet, and held the door open for Dan. He charged inside the small room and deposited Rojas on the floor like a sack of flour. Sam removed Rojas' cell phone from her pocket and tossed it into his lap. "Sit tight," she said. "You're now a hostage. Let's hope your hostage rescue people are worth a shit."

She opened the closet door an inch and peered out into the hallway. It was clear. The calamity on the warehouse floor had attracted attention in the opposite direction, as designed. "Let's go," she whispered to Dan.

Dan grabbed her arm. "Let's just grab Harv and Trojan and be done with it," he said.

She considered his proposal for a fraction of a second. Tempting. The chaos of the car crashing through the warehouse could potentially create a large enough window of opportunity to get their two hostages safely out of the warehouse.

But it could also be a colossal disaster. It would take just a single guard left behind in the room with Harv and Trojan to turn the whole thing plaid. They could instantly find themselves in a firefight against an unknown number of assholes, at least one of whom appeared to be well-trained and highly professional.

Sam shook her head. "Back to the car."

She checked once more for foot traffic in the hallway, then dashed toward the exit. She heard muffled voices shouting in two or three languages.

Sirens blared in the distance. Had the DIS involved the local police in their hastily-hatched operation to rescue their agents? Or did they have their own fleet of urban assault vehicles? *Clowns, either way,* Sam thought, reaching her hand to grasp the exit door. She'd have opted for a stealthy approach.

"Stop!" The voice echoed above the din. *In English. In Costa Rica.* Not a good sign.

Sam's insides clenched, and a fresh flood of adrenaline assaulted her system. She turned to look down the hallway. Her fears were confirmed: it was the pro she had seen earlier, now running in their direction, hand reaching back behind his belt, undoubtedly for a large caliber handgun.

Decision time. Two alternatives: they could have a friendly chat with the fine gentleman reaching for his pistol, for all intents and purposes joining the collection of hostages in the warehouse and hoping that the DIS didn't cock up the rescue operation launched to retrieve Rojas and his fellow stooge. She had already bet Trojan's and Harv's lives on their proficiency. Was she willing to bet her own?

Hell, no.

Which left the second alternative.

"Roll left!" she shouted to Dan, who was two steps behind her en route to the exit and therefore two steps closer to their new friend, who had by now extracted the pistol from his belt and pointed it in their general vicinity.

Dan dove to the concrete and rolled his body toward the far wall, away from Sam. His service pistol roared. A wild miss, but the shot wasn't intended to kill. It was a distraction.

Sam pulled the trigger a fraction of a second later, re-aimed, and fired twice more, hoping like hell at least one of the slugs had found a new home near the agent's center of mass.

The man spun abruptly, right arm flailing, and crashed into the side of the narrow hallway. He fell onto the floor, his body angled, his feet closest to Sam. His flank was exposed, but she couldn't see his gun hand. "Gun down!" she shouted.

No response.

More muffled shouts, and the sound of banging doors in the adjacent rooms. The sirens grew closer. It was officially a party. "Put your gun down!" Sam yelled.

She still couldn't see his gun, but she saw rapid movement from some part of his body, which was more than enough to communicate his intent. She pulled the trigger once more. The side of his abdomen erupted in crimson, and a long, gurgling "hnnnnnnnnnhh" escaped his throat. His back arched, an ancient reflex that reliably indicated death's proximity. The slug had probably snuck beneath his rib cage and pierced his heart, Sam thought.

The sirens drew nearer.

She heard Harv's loud, bellowing voice, cursing at his captors, coming from the room at the far end of the hallway. Some of them must have returned to the room from the warehouse floor, undoubtedly alarmed by the gunfire. *This is turning into a completely disaster.*

She fired a fourth shot into the supine agent, whose writhing had presented her with a head shot. It struck home, scattering the man's thoughts all over the floor.

"Cover!" she shouted to Dan, then sprinted to the dead agent's corpse. She wasn't expecting to find a photo ID, written outline of the nefarious plot, or map to a secret hideout — she was still convinced he was a pro, despite the quick end to the engagement — but she had seen him with a cell phone earlier. *Jacket pocket,* she recalled as she skidded to a stop in front of his body, floor slick with the sweet, metallic fluid still pouring out in rhythmic gushes. The rest of his body evidently wasn't finished dying.

She shoved her hand inside his pocket, fished around until her hand grasped the phone, and jerked it free just as the hallway became bathed in fluorescent light. Someone had turned the lights on, and it probably wasn't Dan. She turned, still crouched, and started toward the exit door.

Her foot slipped in the dead man's gore, and she fell forward onto the concrete. Her hands pounded the floor painfully. *Sonuvabitch.* Her handgun crushed the fingers on her right hand, and the confiscated cell phone shattered in her left.

Another deafening roar filled the small hallway. Dan had fired again. Sam rolled onto her back and raised her pistol in the direction of the far room, and her eyes focused just in time to watch another wounded man fall to the floor. Dan's shot had found its mark.

She felt a vise-like grip on her left arm. Before she could protest, she felt herself being dragged backwards across the concrete toward the exit. She glanced upward to see Dan's thick legs pumping, his pistol raised and pointed down the hallway.

Her ears were ringing horribly from the gun blasts in the confined space, but she could plainly hear the sirens converging on the warehouse building. She scrambled to her feet, shoved what remained of the dead man's crushed cell phone into her pocket, and followed Dan out the side door of the warehouse.

Brock had the engine running. Dan dove into the backseat, forcibly moving their remaining DIS prisoner over to the far side of the car, and Sam rode shotgun. "Away from the sirens, please," Sam said, out of breath.

Brock threw the car into reverse and backed out of the narrow alleyway, spinning the wheel to right the car in the direction of the one-way traffic at the alley's exit. "I figured the gunshots meant a slight change in plans," Brock deadpanned, accelerating into traffic and maneuvering to take the first available turn away from the downtown district.

"We no longer want to have a conversation with the locals," Sam said. "At least not while they can take evidence from us."

"What about Harv and Trojan?" Brock asked.

Sam looked out the back window. No followers that she could detect. "They're still at the top of our agenda. But we still have to trust the DIS hostage team to get them out safely, along with Rojas and Alejandro."

"So hope is our course of action," Brock observed, cutting off traffic to turn south, eliciting an angry honk in the process.

"Always was," Sam said, suddenly annoyed. "We had to hope that the suits in DC could put a decent plan together, or hope that Dan and I could shoot our way through a warehouse full of assholes, or hope that the DIS hostage rescue team has a good day. The last option seemed like the best of the shitty odds."

"You don't have to sell us," Dan said with a smile. "We've

already rolled our dice."

Sam exhaled. She allowed a small smile. "Thanks for playing along. But there's a lot more gambling left, I'm afraid."

She pointed her finger out the window. "Take the next left."

Brock complied. He rounded the corner at a moderately unreasonable speed. "Earlier, you asked Rojas if he was ready to make history. What did you mean?"

"Far as I know," Sam said, "this was the only time anyone has ever broken into a hostage situation to *add* hostages."

Brock chuckled. "Nice." He changed lanes to dodge a beat-up pickup truck that pulled out into traffic.

"There." Sam pointed to a gas station. "Pull in, if you can."

Brock screeched the tires and made an abrupt turn into the gas station parking lot.

"Pull up next to the men's room entrance, on the side of the building," Sam said.

Brock brought the DIS sedan to a halt, its passenger door adjacent to the outdoor entrance of the restroom.

Sam handed her pistol to Brock. "I'm sorry, baby, but I need you to babysit our goon."

Brock had almost forgotten about the third DIS agent, still sitting glumly in the back of the car with his arms and legs bound together. "You're shitting me."

"No, but you're on the right track. I need you to lock yourselves in the bathroom until we get back."

Brock looked at the dilapidated, disgusting restroom. "I love you," he said. "But no way."

"Unless you have a DHS badge that I don't know about, you can't be part of our little charade. And I'm not ready to give up the leverage by setting him loose."

Brock gritted his teeth.

Sam rubbed his leg. "I'll make it up to you in spades."

He smiled. "Deal. But why did you hand me your gun? Won't you need it?"

"It shot some bullets that are lodged in a dead guy they're about to discover. I'd prefer that nobody in the Costa Rican government has a chance to run any forensics on it."

"Won't you need one for yourself?" he asked.

Sam lifted her right pants leg, exposing a holster. She pulled out her reserve pistol, chambered a round, and set the safety. "I'll just use this one."

She put her hand into her pocket and collected all the shards of the dead man's cell phone, then handed them to Brock. "Please hang onto this, too. Best that we keep all the details of our first visit to the warehouse just between us."

They removed Rojas' compatriot from the sedan and perched him on the toilet in the restroom. Brock locked the door from the inside after Sam and Dan left the small latrine, and Sam ensured the bathroom was inaccessible from the outside.

They climbed back into the car, and Sam chirped the tires as she drove away. "I hope the whole thing isn't over already," she said, rounding the corner and heading back north toward the warehouse they'd left just minutes before.

"I doubt it," Dan said. "The hostage team is probably still

getting their bearings."

Sam ran a red light, angered a few Costa Ricans, and nearly clipped the curb as she turned left onto the thoroughfare that ran in front of the warehouse. "Except that someone probably reported the gunshots from earlier."

"Good point. That will probably expedite the proceedings."

Sam pulled to a stop in front of the warehouse next to a black DIS sedan with police lights embedded in its grille. Four police cruisers were also on the scene, and a crowd of gawkers had gathered.

She opened the door before the car had fully stopped, her Homeland badge held high. She jumped out of the car and walked quickly to the first official-looking guy she could find, Dan in tow. "Special Agent Sam Jameson," she said. "I heard that two of my people might be hostages. How can we help?"

Chapter 20

Sabot's head pounded. The pain was intense, unrelenting. Nausea struck. He rolled over in bed, kicked the covers aside, and retched. There was nothing in his stomach, and his innards cramped in a painful contraction. The exertion amplified the pain in his head. He curled into a ball, used the bedcovers to wipe the snot, bile, and tears from his face, and moaned in quiet misery.

He closed his eyes, but the feeling of vertigo became overpowering. He opened them again to stop the room from spinning. It was if he was suffering the combined effects of a hangover and a blow to the skull.

He gingerly touched the back of his head, and winced to discover a golf-ball-sized knot, complete with a bloody gash where the blow had broken the skin.

So at least one of the crazy dreams had been true. Someone had clocked him in the back of his gourd.

How about the other dreams? He looked at his wrists. One was chafed, bloody. The other was normal. Had he really been chained to a wall and doused with freezing water? Seemed probable.

Had he really had oral sex with the fetching guard, Marisela? Seemed less likely, given the way he remembered the episode — both hands chained against the wall, both wrists bloody afterward.

He looked around. Was he in a hotel? Nondescript quasi-art on the walls, clean white linens on the bed, television bolted to the dresser. A doorway led to what looked like a bathroom. Light spilled in from behind paisley curtains. *Where the hell am I?*

Sabot marshaled his strength. Gritting his teeth, he sat upright. A fresh wave of pain shot through his battered head, and his stomach threatened further jihad. *Breathe.* He hoisted himself upright, leaning on the night table. Through the fog of his pain and nausea, he vaguely registered that there was no telephone beside the bed.

He staggered to the bathroom. Used towels were strewn on the floor. A woman's cosmetics bag sat perched on the edge of the bathroom countertop, and various items were strewn about. Whose stuff was this?

Sabot turned on the faucet. Cold water poured out. He cupped his hands beneath the stream, leaned forward with his elbows on the counter for support, and splashed the cold water on his face. Washing his face this way had always felt like clarity to him, like a re-acquaintance with cold, hard reality in a no-bullshit way. The starkness was refreshing, and his pain and nausea momentarily abated.

But there was no clarity, and he deemed any and all of his notions regarding reality as highly tenuous until proven otherwise. There were simply too many strange images floating around in his head. It felt as if he had existed in a dreamlike state for the better part of a week, and a part of his psyche wondered whether he would be able to fully participate in the real world again, after things got back to normal.

What things? And how were they going to get back to normal? The question led him full-circle: *where the hell am I, and what am I doing here?*

Sabot dried his face on a hand towel. It was damp, as if it had already been used. *And who the hell is here with me?*

He heard a door open, then shut, and heard footsteps. Something else, too. The creaking of a pushcart, its wheels in need of grease.

"Who's there?" His voice was much softer than he had intended, yet the exertion sent a flash of searing pain through his aching skull. He became fully aware for the first time that he was completely naked. He grabbed a towel and wrapped it around himself.

The cart creaked closer. "Who's there?" Sabot repeated.

"Señor Mondragon." The voice was deep, gravelly, and familiar. Dread settled like lead in Sabot's stomach, and adrenaline surged. He walked gingerly from the bathroom, one hand securing the towel around his waist, the other pressed against the wall to steady himself.

Sabot peered across the bedroom. A man stood in the doorway. He was small and slight, had close-cropped, ghost-white hair, and wore a button-down shirt, slacks, and a physician's smock. Sabot's eyes focused on the man's face. *Sonuvabitch, this can't be happening.*

"I am Doctor Terencio Manuel Zelaya," the man said. "You have been assigned as my patient. I am here to check up on you."

Panic struck. Sabot looked around, frantically searching for anything he could use as a weapon. "You're no goddamned doctor!" His heart raced.

"Señor Mondragon, you are not well," Zelaya said. "I am indeed a doctor, and I am here to help you."

Sabot's head swum. Reality seemed to be receding again. He found it hard to focus. *Get out of here,* urged a voice inside his head.

His hand gripped a table lamp. He brandished it, yanking the cord from the wall and knocking over a plastic vase full of fake flowers. "Where's Angie? What the hell have you done with her?"

"Señor Mondragon, please relax. May I call you Domingo? I am here to help you feel more settled and less anxious."

"The hell you are! Last time you were trying to get me to sign a confession. And the time before that you told me how you planned to torture me."

Zelaya smiled sympathetically. "Your medications have unfortunately worn off. Your anxiety has returned. It is accompanied by psychotic episodes and occasional paranoia with hallucinations. These things happen from time to time. Now, if you'll kindly set the lamp down, I would be happy to administer the appropriate dosage to set your mind at ease again."

Can this be true? He was certainly having some crazy dreams. Sabot looked again at the short, slight man in physician's garb. The man looked distinguished, educated, confident, all common attributes in the medical profession. And Sabot's confidence in his own sense of reality was shaky at best.

"That's right, Domingo. Just take it easy," Zelaya said, his voice remarkably soothing. "We'll have you back to normal in no time." The man reached into the pocket of his lab coat and produced a syringe.

The motion — the man's hand reaching into the pocket of the lab coat — struck a chord of recognition deep in Sabot's mind. He didn't know how or why he knew it, but he suddenly knew that his life was in danger.

Sabot charged Zelaya, lamp swinging wildly, feral yell spilling from his hoarse throat.

With uncommon quickness, Zelaya reached into the medicinal cart, then raised his hand up toward Sabot. As Sabot's wobbly legs closed the distance between them, he recognized a dark, sinister shape in the old man's hand. *Gun. He's going to shoot me.*

Sabot leaped the remaining distance, hurling the lamp at Zelaya.

Zelaya raised his free arm in time to deflect the flying lamp from hitting his face. He recovered his balance and raised the pistol again.

But Sabot was on him, arms and legs flailing wildly. Zelaya backed away to gain fighting separation, but Sabot kept coming, all fists and kneecaps, somehow preventing Zelaya from firing the gun.

One of Sabot's wild swings connected with Zelaya's sternum. The blow resounded like a bass drum, and Sabot heard the wind escape the small white-haired man's chest.

Sabot took advantage of his good fortune. He brought his fist down on Zelaya's arm, sending the pistol clattering to the floor.

Zelaya lunged for the pistol on the floor. Sabot raised his knee violently. It struck Zelaya in the face. The white-haired man collapsed in a heap on the floor, his mouth a bloody mess. *Lights out, you sonuvabitch.*

Sabot's head swum, his legs wobbled beneath him, and his breath came in gasps and spasms.

But he wasn't done.

He grabbed the pistol from the floor, looped his finger through the trigger guard, brought the sights to his eye, and filled the aiming reticle with Zelaya's chest.

"For Angie," he said. He squeezed the trigger.

Chapter 21

Against his better judgment, and against Protégé's stern advice, Archive watched the presidential address broadcast on television. It was filled with the usual bullshit rhetoric — we will hunt down the terrorists who have perpetrated these crimes against our way of life, who are envious of our freedom and therefore hate us for it, who have committed these cowardly acts of violence that have robbed us of the fruits of our labors, and so forth.

Robbery? Who had really been robbed? What the president didn't mention was the obvious: if the banking system had been destroyed, all of the debts of individual Americans had effectively been erased. It was as if they had never existed. Sure, those mortgage banks whose databases survived the cyber attack might still send mortgage bills. But the bills were payable in a worthless currency, and the scale of the default would be too massive to enforce any consequences for nonpayment.

Unless…

"As you know," the president intoned, "I have called on the men and women of our National Guard to help restore peace and order. Tonight, it is my duty to announce that I have instituted a zero tolerance policy for looting, violence against persons and property, and non-payment of lawful debts."

Protégé looked incredulous. "Lawful debts? What the hell?"

A dark cloud fell over Archive's face. "The banks have found a way to buy the government again."

"Law enforcement officials and our National Guardsmen," the president continued, "are authorized to use all measures necessary, including lethal force, in the enforcement of these important measures. Our nation, and indeed our way of life, faces a test unlike any before in our history. We must band together, call on the great strength within us that made America the greatest nation in history, and, most of all, we must obey the rule of law. It is our calm obedience that keeps civilized society from descending into barbarism."

Protégé shook his head. "How are they going to enforce the debt collection measure?"

Archive was already dialing his phone. "Archive for General Williamson, please," he said when the general's secretary answered. "Yes, that's right. Tell him Archive is calling. He may choose to adjust his schedule."

She placed him on hold. A few moments later, the deep voice of NORTHCOM, the commander of the military's Northern Command, resounded in Archive's ear. "I know what you're thinking," the general said. "Please keep in mind that what the president says on television is a different thing than the orders my troops receive in the field."

"Understood, General, and never for a second did I doubt your levelheadedness or commitment to a peaceful outcome. I just wanted to know what we can expect in the way of enforcement. I'd like to help keep the wheels from falling off."

"My orders against looting and violence actually won't change at all in light of the president's announcement. Lethal force has been authorized from the beginning."

"But the debts?" Archive asked.

The general was silent for a moment. "It's obvious to me that special interest has gotten the president's attention, to the detriment of the greater good. There is no way in hell I'm going to let loan officers at some bank finger citizens for incarceration, or worse. It's just not going to happen."

"So you're going to disobey the president's orders?"

"I'm not stupid. There's a long line of ambitious assholes behind me who would enthusiastically enforce that executive order in exchange for a chance to sit in my chair," the general said. "I'm going to make use of the most powerful foot-dragging tool ever invented by mankind. I'm going to form a committee."

Archive smiled. "Aren't you afraid they'll see right through you?"

"Not at all," the general said. "I'm not going to call it a committee. I'm going to call it a Tiger Team."

Protégé laughed out loud. He was very familiar with the term. It implied a reduction in bureaucratic red tape, but in reality, tiger teams generally produced little more than lengthy reports that nobody read.

"I'm thinking thirty people, from law enforcement, military, and banking communities. The first meeting will be an emergency organizational meeting. It will all sound very urgent."

Archive chuckled. "And the even number gives you the opportunity for gridlock."

"Absolutely," Williamson said. "I'll actually invite thirty-one, but ensure that someone is called away at the last moment."

"You're an expert bureaucrat," Protégé teased.

"Not at all," Williamson said. "I have no time for pencil pushers. But I've learned a thing or two along the way about how to use the system against itself, when necessary."

"How can we help?" Archive asked.

The general thought a moment. "Maybe it's time for your Monopoly Man to make another appearance." NORTHCOM was referring to the series of cartoon videos that Archive's group had produced in the immediate aftermath of the cyber attack, which playfully urged citizens to use their heads, to ask themselves what, if anything, had really changed, and to take a circumspect approach to the short-term chaos. If Vaneesh's assessment of the downward trend in society's apparent angst was an accurate indication, the videos seemed to have had a positive effect.

"An excellent idea," Archive said. "We'll get busy."

"And I'll get busy pretending to be busy," Williamson said.

Archive chuckled. "I hope you do a good job of it. It would be crippling, perhaps catastrophic, if you were to be replaced."

NORTHCOM agreed. "I have very, very few trusted agents in my command," he said. "And most of them are too junior to really make an impact if I were to be canned."

"You're really hoping the masses behave," Protégé observed. "You've basically cast yourself on the mercy of man's better nature."

"We all have, son," Williamson said with a chuckle. "We all

have."

* * *

Archive's relative calm was short-lived. Less than half an hour later, a breaking news alert flashed across the screen. "We warn you," the talking head said gravely, face stern in a look of practiced concern, "this footage is graphic, and some viewers may find it disturbing."

The broadcast cut to grainy video, obviously taken by a smart phone. Hollers and screams were audible just beneath the shouted commands of a bullhorn-wielding soldier. The soldier's counterpart carried an M-4 carbine slung across his shoulder, muzzle pointed toward the ground.

The screams and shouts of the crowd grew louder. "I say again," Megaphone called, urgency in his voice, "stop what you're doing and lay face-down on the ground!"

Carbine raised his weapon to low ready.

The crowd's intensity grew. Alarmed shouts drowned out Megaphone's next amplified demand.

Carbine aimed. Women screamed, men shouted. The center of the crowd melted to the side, split by Carbine's aim.

But the edges of the crowd closed in around the soldiers, who were vastly outnumbered. And, evident even in the grainy video footage, vastly afraid.

A crushing sadness descended over Archive as he watched the inevitable tragedy unfold. There was only one possible outcome.

Megaphone's final warning was lost in the din of the agitated crowd.

The shots rang loud, clear, devastating.

Bedlam.

Horrified citizens sprinted for cover. Enraged alpha males charged the soldiers, hurling rocks, brandishing sticks and baseball bats.

Several men were chopped down by a maelstrom of 5.56 rounds from Carbine's weapon. They were dead before their faces shattered on the pavement.

But the crowd was too close, and there were too many of them, and they were too far gone, utterly consumed by righteous outrage. The soldiers didn't stand a chance.

The news broadcast cut to a still photo of the aftermath. A half dozen civilians lay dead, their blood darkening the street and sidewalk. The soldiers' bodies were battered and broken, limbs bound at disgusting angles. The uniformed men were suspended by their necks from the overhanging arm of a street light. They'd been lynched.

"My God, it looks like fucking Baghdad," Protégé said, mouth agape.

He looked at Archive, and saw tears welling in the old man's eyes.

The words didn't need to be spoken. Their worst fears had materialized before their eyes. *We've started a civil war.*

Chapter 22

The DIS hostage rescue team member gave Sam a decidedly frosty look. It wasn't entirely unexpected. She and Dan had just arrived at the scene of a warehouse standoff, complete with reports of hostages and gunfire. Unwanted help always tended to show up at inopportune times, especially in a relatively sleepy town with little violence, and Sam understood the unfriendly glare on the DIS man's face. She also understood why he tried to get her to wait behind the police perimeter.

But she didn't have any time for it. She flashed her DHS badge, stepped confidently across the police line, and reiterated that a credible report had placed two American hostages inside the building.

"You must wait here," the DIS agent commanded.

"You must point out the agent in charge," Sam retorted, striding past the armed agent.

"I'm afraid your American credentials don't entitle you to access to this scene," the agent said, placing his hand on her arm to restrain her from moving closer to the warehouse.

Sam glared. "Two of those hostages are my people," she said, shaking her arm free. "So unless you're the agent in charge, which would be a big surprise given that you're obviously on traffic duty, I'm afraid you and I are done talking."

Dan shrugged an apology to the agent as he followed Sam

toward the front of the warehouse.

"Who is the agent in charge?" Sam asked loudly, badge held high, her voice cutting through the noise of radio chatter and background conversations.

Half a dozen faces turned to look at her, then most of them turned to gauge the reaction of one particular agent. Sam deduced that the individual whose facial expression was of such interest to the rest of them must be the honcho. She held her hand out in greeting and announced her name.

"Javier Mercado," the agent replied. He carried a handheld radio and wore slightly-too-tight slacks and a light tan sport coat with dark stitching. An unfashionably large mustache adorned his pockmarked face. He looked like a character out of a 1980's cop show, a caricature of himself, like mariachi music personified.

"Pleasure, Javier. What's the plan?"

Mercado eyed her warily. Gringo interference, even in sleepy Costa Rica, was nothing new. But there was a protocol, an established hierarchy of gringo meddlers, and the buxom redhead was nowhere on the list of the usual holier-than-thou "advisors" who showed up to provide condescension disguised as expertise. "I am securing a perimeter around the building and assessing our options," Mercado said.

A bureaucrat's answer, Sam thought. But there was something in his eyes that triggered her bullshit detector. "There are reports of gunfire," she said. "And have you seen the far wall? It's already breached, by a car I'm guessing."

Mercado's radio crackled. He turned the volume down quickly

and stuck the radio to his ear. It was clear he didn't want Sam to overhear. He spoke quietly into the radio. Sam read his lips: *tres minutos*. Three minutes. They had a plan after all, and they were going to execute the plan in three minutes' time. Sam felt relieved that the DIS hostage rescue guys weren't nearly as incompetent as Mercado's original answer had implied.

He turned his attention back to her. "I'm afraid you must leave," he said.

"I'm afraid I'm not going anywhere. There are two Americans hostages in that warehouse, and I'm going to make sure they get out alive."

"This is not America, Agent Jameson," Mercado said. "And I have a job to do."

"I'll stay out of your way," Sam said. "But I'm not leaving."

Mercado shook his head, and motioned back toward the perimeter. "You may not be inside the perimeter. I cannot assure your safety."

"I'd never ask you to," she replied. Sam was tempted to secure Mercado's permission to stay at the scene by divulging that she had intimate knowledge of the interior of the warehouse, and that she had a solid understanding of the kind of people they were facing, but she thought better of it. It would create far more complication than it solved.

Instead, she dug out her phone and dialed the embassy. When the operator answered, she asked for a particular individual, Joel Griffin. Officially, Griffin was a mid-level functionary on the embassy staff. Unofficially, Sam knew, Griffin was the CIA station chief. He dispensed the bribes upon which the DIS's underpaid agents had come to depend, and made the local puppets dance when he desired.

Before Griffin answered the operator's page, Mercado got the message. "That is not necessary, Agent Jameson," he said, looking tired and put-upon. "You may stay. But you must remain back here. I cannot tolerate anyone placing my agents in jeopardy."

"I wouldn't dream of it," Sam started to say, but she was interrupted by shouts from the crowd of agents.

"Fuego!" they cried. Fire.

Sam turned to look at the warehouse. The flicker of flames was clearly visible through the row of windows high above street level. It wasn't a small fire by any stretch. It appeared to be coming from the large loading bay, the same place Brock had aimed his driverless sedan to create the diversion that had allowed her and Dan access to the warehouse just minutes earlier.

There was no time to lose. The DIS hostage team had to storm the building, or risk losing everyone inside.

Sam turned to prod Mercado to action, but he was already on the radio: "Go," he commanded.

Sam heard the distinctive sound of flash-bangs exploding inside the warehouse, devices that created a blinding flash and a deafening noise. Even if occupants were prepared for the assault on their eyes and ears, it was difficult not to wind up incapacitated for a few critical seconds.

DIS agents charged the building on three sides, using battering rams to break through doors. Sam knew that at least one of the doors was unlocked, because she had picked the lock herself, but she kept quiet and observed the assault from behind Mercado's car.

Three shots rang out above the din of crashing doors and shouting DIS agents. Then three more. Sam instinctively drew her pistol and crouched behind the nearest car.

Smoke began to billow from open windows in the warehouse bay, and more gunshots came from inside the building. Seconds later, two DIS agents charged from the building, carrying a corpulent middle-aged bald man. Harv. He appeared to be fine.

A third agent emerged from the building and dashed for the cover of the row of cars, with Trojan thrown over his shoulder like a sack of potatoes. The agent ducked behind the car adjacent to Sam, and set Trojan down on the pavement. The skinny hacker also appeared unharmed. Sam breathed a sigh of relief.

A burst of gunfire came from behind them. Sam whirled to see a DIS agent on the roof of the building across the street, firing carbine bursts into the evolving fray in the warehouse.

The line of agents taking cover behind their autos also opened up on the warehouse, and it didn't take long to figure out why. The fire had driven a suspect out of the burning building. He had emerged with his gun leveled at the line of officers, which earned him several dozen bullet holes.

Motion caught Sam's eye, toward the side of the warehouse. She saw three DIS men hustling Rojas and Alejandro out the side door, the same door through which she and Dan had hustled them *into* the warehouse moments before the hostage team's arrival.

Rojas and Alejandro appeared little worse off than when she

and Dan had deposited them in the supply closet. She was relieved that they had made it out alive. She wasn't particularly fond of the men who had tried to kidnap her team at the airport, but she certainly wouldn't have relished being responsible for their deaths.

A final burst of gunfire sounded from within the warehouse, then relative calm, with only the noise of the flames crackling in the warehouse bay reaching Sam's ears. Three DIS agents hustled out of the front door, accompanied by a chorus of "Hold fire, hold fire!" commands.

It was over.

After several seconds, Mercado ordered his team to check in. All agents were accounted for, and all hostages had been rescued. One DIS agent was wounded, shot in the thigh and in the ass. Already the jokes began, and Sam had to suppress a laugh. The only casualty was Rojas, and the bullets in his skinny body were from her weapon.

Sam released her grip on her pistol, clicked on the safety, and holstered her weapon. *Be quick but not too quick,* she thought. She needed to take advantage of the relative chaos, but not act so hastily as to arouse undue suspicion. "Congratulations, Agent Mercado," she said, shaking his hand. "Your team did an outstanding job in a very dicey situation. You should be very proud of them."

Mercado smiled and thanked her for the sentiment. He offered no resistance as Sam grabbed Trojan's hand and ushered him quickly toward the car. Dan grabbed Harv Edwards, and seconds later, the four of them were strapped in and ready to leave the scene. "I've got to get these guys to the embassy," she lied to Mercado in answer to his askew glance. "Otherwise, the ambassador will have me shot at noon."

If Mercado recognized the car as one of the DIS fleet, he certainly gave no indication, and while it was clear to Sam that Mercado knew instinctively that something wasn't right — hostage victims as a matter of course first went by ambulance to the hospital, and when deemed sufficiently healthy, were made immediately available for hours of questioning and form-filling by various functionaries — Mercado allowed Sam to whisk her two former hostages away without anything more than a quizzical and slightly disapproving expression.

Sam didn't look a gift horse in the mouth, and the Costa Rican DIS sedan full of Americans soon sped away from the scene, back toward the gas station to pick up Brock and their own DIS hostage, along the way passing an ambulance and a fire truck heading the opposite direction toward the burning warehouse.

* * *

Sam climbed the steps to the US government jet's cabin, and turned to watch the DIS sedan drive away. She hadn't even bothered to ask the third DIS agent's name. She had held him hostage as insurance, in case a little leverage became necessary to nudge the DIS in the proper direction.

Fortunately, it hadn't, and Sam had given the DIS man all of the money — in the form of silver bullion taken from the Lost Man Lake Ranch in Colorado earlier in the week — she had promised to Rojas for his cooperation. Without Rojas' phone performances over the past few hours, her investigation would still be dead in the water, and her two compatriots would still be hostages. Sure, the two bullets she'd lodged in Rojas' mortal coil had certainly ushered things along, but money was still a powerful inducement.

As insurance against a double-cross, Sam had used her phone to send a text message to Rojas, indicating the exact weight of silver she'd given to his counterpart. Then she commandeered the DIS guy's phone and sent Rojas another text message: I have received fifty ounces of silver.

With that bit of business settled, and with her entire entourage safely aboard the airplane, it was time to get back to the real business at hand: figuring out who the hell was stealing tens of thousands of Bitcoins every hour, and how to stop them.

The pilot met her at the door. "Can you have us ready to roll in five?" she asked.

"Only if I know where we're going," he replied.

Good point. *Where the hell* are *we going?* She remembered the remnants of the cell phone she had removed from the dead thug's jacket after her pre-dawn shootout in the warehouse. She'd given them to Brock for safekeeping, just in case the encounter with the DIS hostage rescue team went sour.

Brock still had the shattered phone, which he handed carefully to Dan for analysis.

"Let's hope this thing gives us some clue about what to do next," Sam said. "I'm ready to get the hell out of this country."

Chapter 23

Sabot Mondragon was confused. He had expected an explosion and a mighty kick after he pulled the trigger, but he had gotten nothing of the sort. It sounded like a puff, and a little hiss, and the gun barely jerked at all. Had it misfired?

He aimed again, filling the gun sight with Terencio Zelaya's chest from just a few feet away, far too close to miss. He squeezed the trigger again.

Again, the gun puffed and hissed, like a soft drink machine at a fast food restaurant. *What the hell is this?*

Then he looked closer at Zelaya's chest. Two darts protruded, stuck in the man's torso, their small stabilizer fins visible in relief against the white physician's coat that Zelaya wore. It was a tranquilizer gun, Sabot realized.

Sabot pulled the trigger twice more, wondering whether he'd just given Zelaya a lethal overdose of tranquilizer, then wondering on the other hand whether he'd given Zelaya enough to keep the man from waking up anytime soon.

Sabot stared at the small, slight, unconscious man who had wreaked such havoc on his psyche over the past… How long had it been? Days? Weeks? Sabot had no idea how long he had been held captive, and still had no clear idea of what they wanted from him.

He looked down at his hands, flexed them, considered wrapping them around Zelaya's neck and squeezing with all of his might, thought about what it might feel like to watch the life drain from his captor, wondered how it would feel to kill a man with his bare hands.

He shuddered at the thought. Zelaya was undoubtedly a bastard, and he might even deserve to die. But killing another human, one who was unconscious and defenseless... That was a darkness into which Sabot lacked the will to plunge.

So he settled for tying Zelaya's hands behind his back using the lamp cord, and using Zelaya's shoelaces to bind his ankles together.

Time to find Angie and Connie and get the hell out of here.

But where was *here*? He went to the window, and carefully parted the curtains a fraction of an inch, then peered through the opening. He saw diffuse light, but no sharp features beyond the window.

He threw the curtains back. *Sonuvabitch.* The window wasn't normal glass. It was made of those thick glass squares that people put in their bathroom windows. Light came in, but Sabot couldn't see out.

He started toward the door, but realized after two steps that he was still stark naked. He changed course and headed for the closet. Sabot discovered his clothes, cleaned and neatly pressed, hung inside the closet. Who had washed them? And when? Hadn't he been wearing them while he was chained to the wall, underneath that freezing shower?

Or had he dreamt all of that? Sabot still had no inkling of how he came to be in the room with the soft bed and the beautiful woman whose body he'd briefly been inside, until he'd made the shocking discovery that it wasn't Angie's slippery warmth he was enjoying.

Was *that* real? Had he really woken up next to some girl he didn't know? A memory came crashing on his consciousness, a recollection of his own uncontrolled rage, his own hands tightening around the girl's neck, the way her sinew popped as he squeezed, the way panicked tears rolled down her cheeks, then a metallic smell in his nostrils and a blinding light inside his head as someone knocked him out from behind.

Had *that* really happened? He reached his hand to the back of his head. *Ouch.* A painful knot greeted his touch. It certainly felt real enough.

He looked again at Zelaya, lying comatose on the floor, tranquilizer darts protruding from his chest. Sabot's head swum. Everything felt surreal. *This can't possibly be happening.* The objects in the room seemed a long way away from him. His legs shook, his stomach threatened further revolt, and his breath came in shallow gasps. He felt as if he might faint.

Sabot sat heavily on the edge of the bed. He rested his head in his hands, and became aware of the throbbing of his pulse in his temples, and the throbbing pain in the back of his head. The pain was certainly not a figment of his imagination. He was in terrible shape.

He took several deep breaths, steeled himself, and rose to his feet. He put a hand against the wall to steady himself against a wave of dizziness, and breathed through another sickening surge of nausea. *They screwed me up good,* he thought.

He dressed, pausing for breath between clothing articles. It felt as though he'd been in bed for months. His body lacked strength, and he wondered how he had possibly overcome Zelaya in a fistfight just moments earlier.

I've got to get out of here. They're killing me. He took the tranquilizer pistol and tucked it into the back of his pants, like he'd seen people do in the movies. He had no real experience with physical violence, having instead chosen to commit his crimes using a computer keyboard, and he felt decidedly vulnerable. He needed to use his head, to stay out of situations that would require him to use his body. He couldn't rely on his physical skills in the best of circumstances, and certainly not when his head felt six feet thick.

Sabot stepped over Zelaya's body, lying inert in the doorway to the foyer, and made his way through an anteroom full of dated Dick Van Dyke furniture to what appeared to be the exit.

There's no goddamned doorknob.

Just a key slot greeted him. He pushed against the door, but it didn't budge. He knelt down and slipped his fingers between the floor and the door, and used friction to tug inward on the door, but it didn't move. It was locked.

Sonuvabitch!

Sabot paced, gritting his teeth and clenching his fists. No windows and no doorknob. The place was built by kidnappers. How the hell would he get out?

His eyes returned to Zelaya's body. *Of course.* He walked over and knelt next to Zelaya, and searched the comatose man's pockets. It didn't take long to find a key ring full of two dozen identical-looking keys, each differentiated only by a stenciled number.

Sabot returned to the door and tried each key in sequence. It seemed to take forever. He went through all of the keys without success. He felt despair and panic creep into the edges of his consciousness. How was it that none of the damned keys worked in this damned lock?

He cursed his stupidity. He had tried all of the keys with the jagged part facing down. He hadn't even thought to try any of them the other way. *You gotta get your mind right, vato,* he chided himself. He started again.

A half-dozen keys into his second attempt, he found the right one. It slipped easily into the slot, and Sabot heard the lock click as he turned the key clockwise.

Adrenaline surged through his veins, and his heart pounded anew. He pulled slowly on the key, opening the door just a crack, subconsciously holding his breath as he looked out the door and listened for any signs of movement.

It looked like a hotel hallway. He saw ugly carpet on the floors, grossly outdated wallpaper and pseudo-art on the walls, and half a dozen identical doors, each with a number but no doorknob.

He watched and waited, breathing as quietly as he could. No motion caught his eye, and no sounds alerted his ears. He pushed the door open wider, and peered around the doorjamb in the opposite direction down the hall. He saw a single door at the end of the hall, again with only a key slot and no other opening mechanism.

Sabot took a deep breath and tiptoed out into the hallway. Were Connie and Angie in one of these rooms?

He glanced at the number on the front of his door: 427. It corresponded to the number stenciled on the key that had liberated him. He found key 428, and quietly opened the door to the room next to his.

Sabot snuck inside the room. It was nearly identical to the room he'd just left, except this room showed no signs of recent habitation. No clothes hung in the closet, all of the bathroom towels were fresh, and the bed was made.

He crept carefully out of the room and snuck one door further down the hall, repeating the process of quietly inserting the key, turning it slowly, applying slight pressure to silently move the door away from the jamb, and carefully peeking inside the room before stepping through the door.

Empty.

Same for room number 430. And 431. His heart sank. His hopes of finding Angie and her mother were fading fast.

There was but a single room left in the hallway, number 426. He inserted the key, turned the lock, and snuck in.

This room felt different. The chairs in the kitchenette were pulled away from the table, as if used and not replaced. Sabot's heart rate surged. *Angie?*

He crept through the anteroom toward the bedroom. He heard the shower running through the wall. His hopes soared. Had he found the girls? *God, I hope so.* There was so much to discuss, so much he wanted — needed — to tell Angie. Time was short and life was precious, and he hadn't properly expressed the way she had changed his life for the better, the way he wanted to be part of her life until they were old and wrinkled.

He caught sight of the bed. It had been slept in. *Someone's definitely here.* The closet doors were open, but he couldn't see any clothes inside.

Sabot crept toward the bathroom, felt the steam from the shower warm his face as he rounded the corner. Someone was in the shower, washing.

Eager anticipation took over, and he abandoned caution. "Angie?" he called. "Angie, is that you?" He walked across the tile floor to the shower curtain, raised his hand to draw it back so he could lay eyes on his Angie for the first time in a horrific eternity.

The shower curtain flew open. A deep voice yelled.

Sabot leapt back in shock.

The man nearly lost his balance in the shower, gripping a handhold at the last second to avoid a painful fall on the hard, wet tile. "What the hell!" he hollered.

Sabot backed away from the shower, his hands raised in a conciliatory gesture. He regarded the wet, naked abomination of a body in the shower. The man was fat, balding, his jowly face draped by the longest flap of comb-over hair Sabot had ever seen.

Familiar.

"Hey, I know you!" the man said. "Are *you* behind all this bullshit?" He scrambled to turn off the water and throw a towel around his waist. "Wait till I get out of this shower. I'm going to kick your ass, you sonuvabitch!"

Why did the man look familiar to Sabot? Had they met before? "Do I know you?" Sabot asked.

The fat, naked man huffed. "Knew I shouldn't have trusted a complete stranger," he said as he dried off. "You just wait, buddy, I'm going to hand you your ass." He wagged a finger at Sabot. "Lock me up like a damn criminal, you're gonna find out what happens…"

The airplane. This was the guy who had begged Sabot to share the charter flight from Canada to Costa Rica. "Wait a minute," Sabot said. "They locked you up, too?"

"I'm in this goddamned cage, aren't I?"

He had a point. There wasn't a doorknob to get out of this room, either, Sabot reflected.

"Tell me your name again," Sabot said.

The man stopped drying off, and used his hand to whip his comb-over into place. "Fredericks," he said. "Bill Fredericks."

Chapter 24

"Slobodan Radosz," Dan said. "He turned up in the Interpol database." Dan had lifted three distinct sets of prints from the smooth plastic face of the dead spy's cell phone, the one that Sam had shattered as she slipped in a pool of the man's blood and fell hard on the cement floor of the warehouse.

Two sets of prints had returned a match. One of them belonged to Sam. As a federal agent, Sam's prints were in the database, and she had obviously handled the phone.

The second set apparently belonged to Radosz, a small-time Serbian criminal who had been jailed briefly in Macedonia for agitation, just before the war broke out in Kosovo, but had subsequently worked his way onto the Interpol watch list as a potential terror suspect.

The system hadn't found a match for the third set of prints.

"Thanks, Dan," Sam said. "I'm betting the dead guy isn't Radosz."

Dan nodded his agreement. "He looked pretty professional. Too professional to have a record." It wouldn't make any sense for a clandestine organization of any standing to go to the trouble of training a field agent who had an arrest history. All of the agent's biometrics would be in police computer systems all over the planet. It would just be too hard for him to hide, and too easy for him to leave damning evidence behind.

But nothing said that Radosz couldn't be the wet man's handler. "Radosz is probably middle management," Sam said.

Dan agreed. "But it's a weird scenario," he said. "A Macedonian Serb's fingerprints on a dead pro's burner in Costa Rica?"

"Right." A pro they'd shot while trying to orchestrate a hostage rescue, a scenario that had unfolded as they were trying to track a cyber criminal who had recently fled North America from a Canadian airport. It made Sam's head hurt. "This one's kicking my ass," she admitted. "Anything on the SIM card?"

Dan inserted the electronic chip from the disposable phone into a USB device, which he stuck into the side of his laptop. He clicked a few keys, then frowned. "It's a DC area code."

"Of course it is," Sam said with a sardonic smile. "Recognize the number?"

Dan shook his head. "No. But I'll check the registration. Maybe we'll get lucky." Odds were high that the call to the dead agent's phone would have originated from another disposable cell phone, but it paid to check anyway.

"Holy shit," Dan said, eyebrows arched in surprise. "It's a registered number."

"Cell?" Sam asked.

"No, residential. One of those bundled internet and phone deals."

"People still have those?"

Dan chuckled. "Apparently. Looks like it's registered to…" He frowned again. "Seriously?"

"What?" Sam prodded.

"It's registered to John Q. Public. No shit."

Sam shook her head. *Very funny.* "Is it a real address?"

Dan called up a high-resolution street map. "Sure looks like it. One of those new apartment buildings in Shirlington."

A memory flashed in Sam's mind, images of the Shirlington apartment that contained the bloody remains of a friend and colleague. *I'm getting tired of all of this,* she thought. "Any other information?"

Dan nodded. "Apartment 1236. Looks like it's on the top floor of the building. Let me ping it to be sure." More keystrokes sent an electronic ping from the massive computer server in the basement of the Homeland building in DC to the telephone number they had discovered in the phone's SIM card. Seconds later, a confirmatory window popped open on Dan's laptop. "Positive. It's a real phone number in a real place," he said.

Sam's face registered surprise. "Who sends instructions to a field goon from a phone with a physical address?" It didn't make any sense. It was just too easy to trace phone calls.

"Red herring?" Dan asked.

"Feels like it," Sam said. But then she had second thoughts. "Although it's not always possible to hide communications to and from agents in the field with a cut-out layer protecting both ends. Sometimes you have to take a risk."

Dan nodded. "Maybe they were in a bind."

Brock piped up. "We just flew down here last night," he said. "It isn't like we planned the trip weeks in advance. Maybe they were scrambling to put our welcoming committee together."

"Good point," Sam agreed. "Maybe they didn't have time to do it clean. We probably have to investigate the lead."

"There's another call in the SIM card's registry," Dan said. "This one's an outbound call. It's to a foreign number. I don't recognize the country code."

"Let's try to Zip Line it," Sam said. She was referring to the top secret payload on a few government satellites that allowed Big Brother to find virtually any cell phone on any network within the satellite network's footprint.

Dan navigated to the Zip Line client on his laptop. "Shit. Still completely backlogged."

He called the agents-only hotline at Homeland. Someone answered this time, and Dan asked the operator to patch him through to the National Technical Means department. The phone rang a dozen times before the operator picked back up. "I've tried paging them as well," the operator said, "but nobody answers."

"Damned cubicle zombies," Dan groused.

Sam frowned. "Time to ask dad for the keys," she said, choosing a familiar contact in her cell phone and pressing the "call" button.

As her phone rang, the pilot walked up the stairway, his preflight inspection complete. "We're ready to roll," he said, "but I still need to know where we're going."

"Working on it," Sam said, phone pressed to her ear.

The call connected on the fifth ring. Mason McClane sounded terrible. "Have you slept yet, boss?" she asked.

"For a couple of hours, on my couch," he said. "It's been pretty nonstop here."

"Nonstop what?"

"Meetings, phone calls, emails. The Executive Branch has worked itself into a lather."

"Treacherous," Sam said.

Her sarcasm wasn't lost on McClane. "Not all of us get to play cops and robbers. Update me, please."

Sam told him about how the DIS hostage team rescued Trojan, Harv Edwards, and two Costa Rican agents. She left out the part about the shootout inside the warehouse that she and Dan had experienced just moments before the DIS team arrived. It had been a direct violation of McClane's earlier orders, and she wasn't in the mood for one of *those* conversations.

"I'm glad they're safe. We really owe our DIS counterparts a big thank-you," McClane said. *Like they gave us a bouquet of roses or something,* Sam thought. McClane was a nice guy and he meant well, but half the time he talked like a douchebag bureaucrat.

"Yeah. Anyway, Mace, I need that passenger manifest for all the outbound flights from Tucson yesterday afternoon. And for the diplomatic flight from Canada to Skopje."

She heard computer keys clicking. "I saw that in my inbox, I think. Hold on." A moment passed, during which Sam chewed her fingernails. "There it is," McClane said. "Coming your way. I'll copy it to Dan as well."

Sam thanked him. A few moments later, Dan gave her the thumb's up. "We got the manifests," she told McClane. "We need something else, too," Sam said. "Your Zip Line access code."

McClane was silent for a moment on the other end of the line. "Can't do it, Sam. You know that's a security violation."

"Do you know how to use it?" she asked, knowing the answer.

"Why don't you talk me through it," McClane said. *Figures,* Sam thought. McClane probably hadn't done anything with any direct operational application in his entire tenure at Homeland. He was too wrapped up in meetings and memos to notice anything that happened outside the building.

Sam gave him the cell phone number they were searching for, and walked him through the application's interface. "It says here that the system is experiencing a backlog due to extreme demand," McClane said after a few minutes of back-and-forth.

Sam's jaw clenched. "That's why we need your access code, Mace. You're one of twenty humans with the power to jump to the top of the list."

"I am?"

"Mace, you're completely worthless sometimes."

"I don't appreciate your insubordination," McClane warned.

"And I don't appreciate your operational incompetence," Sam said, knowing instantly that she'd pushed too far. Some things couldn't be un-said.

A long moment of silence passed, after which Sam apologized.

Mace quietly accepted her apology, but she knew that she'd crossed a line with him. *Another burned bridge?* She really had to watch her mouth when she was tired and pissed off.

"Tell me where to type the access code," McClane said

quietly. Sam told him. She heard computer keys clicking in the background.

"Rome," McClane said after a moment.

Sam didn't think she'd heard him right. "Rome? As in New York?"

"No. As in Italy," McClane said. "That cell phone is in Italy right now."

How's that for a wrench in the works? There were suddenly jurisdictional problems that an army of pencil-pushers might not be able to solve. McClane would want to ask the Homeland chief for permission to pursue the Rome lead; Homeland's boss would want to ask the DCI, who would want to involve the CIA, after which everything would get screwed up beyond recovery.

"Damn," Sam finally said.

"Listen, Sam, get everyone home," McClane said. "Your financial crime investigation was hugely important two days ago, but the demand signal from the senior leadership in the Executive Branch is now very heavily focused on the foreign terror threat."

More bullshit bureaucrat non-speak, Sam thought. But she held her tongue as McClane continued. "There have been several incidents involving National Guardsmen and citizens, and shots were fired this morning. There's fear of a widespread uprising."

Sam shook her head, suddenly feeling extremely tired. "That's not good."

"Not at all," McClane said. "DCI is afraid that foreign interests will use the unrest to their advantage, and launch an attack on US soil."

"Did you explain to him that there's already a serious attack underway?" Sam asked, an edge returning to her voice.

McClane sighed. "I relayed my serious concerns about the severity of the cyber currency theft. He was unmoved."

"Did you tell him that the thieves already have enough money to buy themselves a new government?" Sam pressed.

"Sam, I did my best to convince him. You and I know the case you're working is important. But give me some plausible deniability here, please, and come home."

Sam considered. There was no way they'd receive permission to use a US government jet to chase a cell phone hit in freaking Italy. It would require State Department coordination that wasn't likely to happen in her lifetime.

And there was that apartment in DC, the one with a telephone that someone had used to call the goon in Costa Rica just before the drama had unfolded. It was a lead that had to be run to ground, and it didn't sound like Homeland had any spare resources for her Bitcoin theft case at the moment.

"Okay, Mace," she finally said. "I appreciate your going to bat for us. We'll see you in a few hours."

She hung up the phone and walked forward to the cockpit. "Home, James," she told the pilot. "Reagan International."

The pilot nodded. It was one of the three destinations Sam had told him to plan for, so he was prepared to go right away. He and the copilot got busy as Sam and the other passengers strapped themselves in.

The airplane began to taxi, and Sam's eyes grew heavy with

the rhythmic motion of the plane's wheels crossing the concrete slabs on the tarmac, bouncing gently up and down. She was asleep by the time the jet reached the end of the runway.

As the engines spooled up for takeoff, Dan reached across the aisle and nudged her awake. She looked at him with groggy annoyance.

"Sorry," he said, "but they figured out who was on the Canadian diplomatic flight through Tucson to Skopje. Apparently there are still peace talks going on, something about the Muslim situation in the Balkans. Some senator from Arizona apparently hitched a ride with a minister from Canada. Good looking lady. Anyway, aside from the boy-girl angle, it looks legit."

Sam nodded groggily.

"But you need to see this," Dan said. He handed his laptop to her.

It took her a moment to figure out that she was looking at the airline passenger manifests McClane had sent via email just a few minutes earlier.

Dan placed his thick, stubby thumb at a particular spot on the screen, right beneath one of the names on one of the passenger lists.

Slobodan Radosz.

Destination: Rome.

Chapter 25

Sabot sat on the bedroom writing desk and gathered his wits. In the bathroom mirror, he was reluctant witness to Bill Fredericks toweling himself off. Fredericks' fat, hairy ass looked like used bubble gum rolled in dust bunnies. Sabot cringed.

Fredericks was talking. He hadn't stopped talking since Sabot had walked in on his shower. "They've really been screwing with me, man," Fredericks was saying. "I mean, how long have we been in here? It must be weeks. And they chained me up under a cold shower for days. I thought I was going to die of hypothermia." Sabot unwittingly caught sight of another ass shot in the mirror. He felt violated.

"And those chicks," Fredericks continued. "I mean, no offense, I know they were traveling with you and all—"

Sabot sat up. "Chicks? Women?"

"Yeah, women. You know any other kind of chicks?"

"Angie and Connie?"

"Yeah, man," Fredericks said, toweling off his ridiculous hair, leaving the rest of his eyesore physique uncovered. "I like them just fine, don't get me wrong, but all that screaming…"

"Screaming?" Sabot stood, fists clenching subconsciously.

"Bloody murder, man," Fredericks said. "I thought someone was slaughtering pigs in there."

"In where?" Sabot's agitation grew.

"Right next door. Felt like right inside my ear, though, man. I mean, really, they have a pair of lungs on them."

Sonuvabitch. If anything had happened to Angie and Connie... "Where are they now?"

"What do I look like, man? Clairvoyant? I been locked up in this shithole for who knows how long."

"Dammit, Fredericks, did you *hear* anything? Did anybody *say* anything when they took Angie and Connie away? Like, anything about what they were going to do with them?"

Fredericks winced a little. "Yeah, man, now that you mention it. That mean little cocksucker, Terencio What's-his-nuts."

"Zelaya," Sabot spat.

Fredericks nodded. "That's right. Zelaya. He was saying something about how they'll fetch a nice price."

"A price?"

Fredericks shook his head. "You're a little dense, aren't you, man? Price. The oldest profession. They were going to put the chicks to work. Sell them off."

Sabot's jaw was agape. "To a pimp?"

"Sorry, man."

Dread overcame Sabot. "You're fucking with me," he said quietly, tears welling.

Fredericks shook his head and grimaced. "Wish I was," he said.

Sabot's heart pounded. He sat heavily on the edge of the bed, fists clinching, his feet blurred by the tears in his eyes. *What the hell have I gotten us into? And how do I get us out of it?* His mind raced.

He imagined horrific scenarios, saw visions of Angie lying naked, drugged and chained to a bed in a brothel, sweaty men having their way with her.

And he imagined beating that smug bastard Zelaya to death with his bare hands.

He knew what to do. He would start with Zelaya. He rose from the bed, jaw set at a determined angle, wiping his eyes on his shirtsleeve.

A corpulent paw shoved him back down. Fredericks stood over him. "You need a plan," Fredericks said. His face had changed. The usual, slightly stupid expression was replaced by something else. Something hard, efficient, and cold.

"Zelaya," Sabot said through clinched teeth, voice shaky with emotion.

"That's not a plan," Fredericks said. "That's a target."

Sabot bristled. "What the hell do you know? Fat piece of shit."

Fredericks laughed. "You're right, *ese*. I don't know anything about anything. Knock yourself out." He returned to buttoning his shirt. "But before you get your skinny beaner ass capped, I want you to tell me how you got out of your room and into mine. I have no plans to rot in this godforsaken place." The yokel affectation was now entirely gone. Fredericks sounded… professional.

Sabot stood, suddenly angry. "When you begged me for a spot on the plane," he said, pointing at Fredericks' chest, "you said you were running from something. What have you done?"

"None of your business, *vato*," Fredericks said, all vestiges of joviality gone.

"Damn right it's my business," Sabot said. "What if we're all in this goddamned place because of something *you* did?"

Fredericks snorted. "I don't think so, tough guy. I mean, if that were the case, why have they asked me a thousand questions about you?"

"About me?" The piss and vinegar left Sabot's voice and face. He looked at Fredericks. The fat man nodded pointedly.

Maybe this is all my fault after all, Sabot thought.

"Yep," Fredericks said. "That prick Zelaya kept asking me for passwords. 'Give me the passwords, or I'll electrocute your nuts.'" Fredericks looked hard at Sabot. "I assume you know what he was talking about. I sure as hell don't."

Sabot's stomach turned, and his face flushed. *This whole mess is on me.* There was no longer any doubt about it. "Is that all they asked?" His voice sounded weak, deflated.

"And account numbers," Fredericks said. He glared at Sabot again. "You stole something, didn't you?"

Sabot nodded.

"And you still have it, don't you?"

Sabot's hesitation was confirmation enough for Fredericks. "Thought so," he said, jowls jiggling. "Thanks for nothing, you little asshole. Plenty of pain and suffering on account of your skinny beaner ass." He bent down to tie his shoes, the strain of his considerable mass causing obvious distress for his knees. "Least you can do is get me out of here," he said.

Sabot sighed, then nodded. He reached into his pocket, retrieved the key ring he'd taken from Zelaya, and jingled the keys.

Fredericks whistled. "How did you manage to get your hands on those?"

Sabot told him about his most recent meeting with Zelaya, and about the altercation that ensued.

"You left him alive?" Fredericks asked, incredulous.

Sabot nodded.

Fredericks shook his head. "We really need to get out of here. I want to be on a different continent when that bastard wakes up."

Chapter 26

Vaneesh sat in the semi-dark room in the basement of the main house on the Lost Man Lake Ranch compound. The rooms above him afforded staggering views of some of the most spectacular scenery on the planet, but Vaneesh hadn't seen the Rocky Mountains, or daylight for that matter, for nearly two days.

Like many in his rather rarified peer group, the kind of talented computer programmers that made the modern world go 'round, Vaneesh had been vigorously recruited by the National Security Agency. His thesis had raised eyebrows around the world. His graduate work had been in the field of pseudo-quantum decryption, a technology that used a normal computer to mimic a quantum computer's uncanny ability to find factors of very large numbers. It was an arcane and esoteric discipline, at least until one considered that finding factors for very large numbers was *the* key to breaking cryptographic codes.

Passwords, for example. Like the kind protecting the US banking system. Rather, the kind that *used to* protect the banks, until last Tuesday, when Vaneesh's handy little algorithm had made minced meat of their state-of-the-art security infrastructure.

He shook his head. He still couldn't believe what he'd taken part in. Really, the whole thing couldn't have worked without his contribution. His was the crushing blow.

He looked at the computer screens, the graphs he had created to help the old man understand what all the data meant, and he found himself deeply worried.

Had he cast his lot with the wrong crowd? After grad school, he had eschewed Big Brother's advances, which were long on dogma and short on payola, and had opted instead for the more lucrative private sector.

He was chagrined to discover almost immediately, however, that the private sector wasn't entirely private, and he had worked out that Pro-Tek, the sleepy little computer security firm with the staggeringly attractive compensation package, was little more than a front company for the NSA.

So the feds had gotten him after all. And he was working on some seriously dangerous shit, the kind of code that could, realistically and with no melodramatic hyperbole, subjugate millions of people. Maybe even billions.

He had somehow found himself working on the modern computer equivalent of the Manhattan Project. It had freaked him out. He wasn't a hippie peace freak, but neither was he a fascist, and he didn't trust the government — any government — to act responsibly when it held the passwords to everyone's pocketbooks in its hands. It was simply too much power, and too much temptation.

And it was wrong. Illegal. Unconstitutional. A violation of any number of international treaties.

But there was another set of laws that prevented him from doing anything about it. He was legally bound, on pain of lengthy incarceration or even death, not to disclose *any* information the government considered classified. Even if the classified information revealed criminal activity. *Especially* if that criminal activity was officially sanctioned, ordered, in fact, by the very government he served.

Dilemma.

So, after a couple of years of soul-searching, and a concomitant ulcer, he had ultimately concluded that it was necessary to do what was right, even if it meant doing what was illegal.

That conclusion had set in motion the chain reaction that led to his presence in the basement, really a bunker carved into the side of a Colorado mountain, at Archive's Lost Man Lake Ranch. His code had devastated the banking system, and was largely responsible for the chaos that seemed to be gaining momentum again.

He looked back at the computer screens, felt the familiar weary angst settle over him once again, took a deep breath, and picked up the phone. "Sorry to wake you," he said to Archive. "But I think you need to see this."

* * *

Archive arrived in the computer server room, housed underneath thousands of tons of Rocky Mountain granite. Large purple bags hung beneath his eyes. He hadn't slept much since their plan had unfolded several days earlier. The aftermath was tearing him up.

"I'm afraid the news isn't going to make you feel any better," Vaneesh said. He pointed to a graph displayed on one of the large computer screens in front of him. "Crowd entropy," he said.

Archive nodded. "Analogous to the level of civic unrest."

"Right. You'll notice the trend isn't good."

Archive studied the graph. It showed the chronology of the unrest, at least since Vaneesh had produced the algorithm that measured how many crowds were gathered in view of traffic cameras throughout the country, and how unruly those crowds were. The graph had started out fairly high, as looting and chaos threatened to take root, but had settled down rapidly as people began to cooperate and work together, just as they had done before the banks were disabled.

But the graph had risen sharply in the past twelve hours. In fact, it was at its highest level, and it appeared to still be on the rise.

People were pissed off. They were gathering in crowds, and those crowds looked mean, if Vaneesh's estimates were correct.

"Martial law," Archive said, shaking his head.

"I'd say so," Vaneesh agreed. "There's more."

Archive steeled himself for more bad news. "The Bitcoin theft operation appears to be accelerating as well," Vaneesh said, pointing to another graph on a different computer screen.

"What am I looking at?" Archive asked.

"I have a bot following all of the transactions that have happened subsequent to the thefts from our Bitcoin accounts a couple of days ago," Vaneesh explained. "I've seen a pattern develop: rapid transactions, with the money staying in a single account for only a couple of seconds before being sent on to a brand new 'wallet.'"

Archive nodded. "It's the continuous laundering operation we discovered earlier."

"Right. I've learned how to identify those kinds of transactions in the global Bitcoin market, and I've built a graphical representation of all of this type of activity."

Archive studied the chart. It increased linearly at first, which made sense to him. As the thieves stole more money, they had to use more accounts to launder the money by keeping it in constant motion.

But in the past day, the graph began to increase at an exponential rate. "What does this mean?" he asked.

"There are vastly more accounts involved in the laundering operation today than yesterday," Vaneesh said. "But the transaction sizes are roughly the same as before. They're still moving very small fractions of a Bitcoin in each transaction, but there are many more transactions going on every second."

"That means there's more money in play today than yesterday," Archive concluded.

Vaneesh nodded. "Exactly. They've grown their operation."

Archive sighed heavily. "I was afraid of that. Is the operation still centered in New Jersey and Seattle?"

The computer ninja shook his head. "That's a bigger worry," he said. "Before, they were using just a couple of computers and an address-masking program. They used the IP mask to make it look like a bunch of computers were involved in the theft, but the timing of each transaction made it clear to us that there were just a couple."

"And now?" Archive asked.

"Transactions are distributed evenly with population."

Archive blinked a couple of times, not grasping the significance.

"They must've found a way to package the Bitcoin theft program in a virus," Vaneesh explained. "My guess is that it has infected thousands of computers already, and is spreading fast. That's why the amount of stolen money in constant motion has increased so rapidly over the past day."

Archive's eyes betrayed the weight he felt. "They've created an army of computerized thieves."

Vaneesh nodded. "Essentially, yes. And that army is growing by the second."

Archive was silent for a moment, his eyes moving between the bad news and worse news depicted on Vaneesh's computer screens. A sickening thought struck. "How much market share do the thieves have?"

"Market share?"

"I mean, can you estimate what percentage of the total global Bitcoin market these guys have stolen?"

Vaneesh pondered a moment, then turned to operate the mouse and keyboard. "I can do better than that," he said. "The total number of Bitcoins on the global market is public information. And I'll just add up the total value of all of those rapid Bitcoin transactions…"

It was a remarkably simple script, and it took Vaneesh less than a minute to produce the answer. "Thirteen percent."

"Jesus," Archive said.

"Up from six percent yesterday."

Archive grimaced. "We're in trouble," he said. "When one group wields that much economic power…"

Vaneesh smiled darkly. "You get the Fed."

Archive nodded gravely. "The thieves already have enough to buy half of Europe."

"Or all of America."

Archive laughed in spite of himself. "Quite so," he said. The dollar was now more valuable as wallpaper than as currency. It was exactly as he and his group of co-conspirators had designed.

But they hadn't counted on such a devastating upstart arriving on the scene so quickly. "We've enabled this situation," the old man said. "We must do something to reverse it."

Vaneesh nodded. "I started working on a destructive code snippet to disable the theft algorithm," he said.

Archive brightened. "You can stop the thefts?"

Vaneesh shook his head. "No. Not yet, anyway. It might not even be possible, depending on how the theft algorithm is constructed."

"But there's a chance?" Archive asked.

Vaneesh held his thumb and forefinger close together. "About that big. And that's just to get one computer to stop stealing Bitcoins. Now there are thousands."

Archive mulled. "You'd need to construct a virus."

Vaneesh nodded. "And it would have to spread exceptionally quickly. I mean, it would have to be the highest infection rate since…"

"Last Tuesday?" Archive's eyes twinkled.

Vaneesh caught on immediately. "Holy shit! Why didn't I think of that?" Vaneesh's pseudo-quantum code-breaking algorithm had been the payload inside Trojan's computer virus. In an irony that

Vaneesh found utterly delicious, the virus had spread along the communications infrastructure that the NSA had built to spy on the world's internet and email traffic. Two hundred million computers were infected within a day. The infected computers devastated the banking system and destroyed the dollar.

"Hidden in plain sight," Archive said, still smiling. "Have you heard from Trojan lately?"

"Dialing now," Vaneesh said, phone in hand.

Protégé walked in, interrupting Archive's response. "Monopoly Man is ready," he said. "And I need to talk to you."

Archive nodded and followed Protégé out of the computer room and down the hallway to the bunker's media room. "Let's get the video distributed as quickly as possible," he said. "All the usual outlets."

"Of course," Protégé said. "They haven't discovered the trapdoor, so we still have complete access." Archive and his group had hijacked television broadcast media on a number of occasions since last Tuesday's plot unfolded, and had used the pirated airtime to broadcast cartoon videos of Monopoly Man, the chapeau-wearing mascot of the popular board game.

The cartoons urged patience and cooperation, and emphasized that while it seemed like everything had changed in the aftermath of the financial crisis, in reality all that had changed was the agreement between people. Dollars used to lubricate commerce, Monopoly Man suggested, but dollars had become corrupted. So it was time for the people to find a new agreement, one that was free of manipulation and exploitation by the Establishment. That was the message, and that was also the heartfelt belief held by Archive and his band of barons-turned-revolutionaries.

"We're ready to broadcast," Protégé said, holding the door open for Archive. He followed the old man into the media room.

"But first, you should see this," Protégé said. He pointed a remote control at the wall of televisions and pressed play.

Archive sighed. Protégé had earlier urged him to watch less television, as the reports of gloom and doom were sensationalized and largely inaccurate. He wondered what could have changed Protégé's mind.

He didn't wonder for long. Adjacent to a familiar talking head was pasted the headline "Administration Castrated by Crisis." With a grave expression, the announcer relayed that Americans were rapidly losing confidence in their government, which had so far proven itself incapable of restoring order, and had recently resorted to violence to control crowds.

The broadcast cut to a senator representing the opposition party, who demanded the president be impeached. "His negligence is criminal, and that alone should be sufficient cause to remove him from the most important office on this earth," the agitated Southern senator said. "But the President's fascist crackdown against peaceful citizens is an absolute abomination," he went on. "It's a cowardly abdication of all that it means to be American."

Meanwhile, the talking head explained, Americans were taking matters into their own hands, organizing grass-roots militias to restore law and order, and installing barter systems to transact goods and services. "According to federal law, however, such activities are illegal," the announcer said. "Federal troops have been dispatched to enforce these and similar laws, and have been given authority to use lethal force, if they deem it necessary."

Archive shook his head. He was chagrined but not surprised.

"One thing is clear," the announcer concluded. "Conflict appears inevitable."

Protégé stopped the playback. "This kind of stuff is on all the major news outlets."

Archive nodded. "That's not surprising. The media seems to move en masse."

Protégé chuckled. "You're surprised? They're all owned by the same guy."

"I need to talk to General Williamson," Archive said. "He has got to stop his goddamn soldiers from shooting civilians. Otherwise, we'll have ten thousand casualties by Saturday."

"Two steps ahead of you, boss," Protégé said. "I talked to him while you were catching up on some sleep."

Archive arched his eyebrows.

"He says they've run facial recognition software on all of the soldiers who were caught on camera committing violent acts against the civilian populace," Protégé said.

"And?"

"They're not in anybody's biometrics database."

"Meaning?"

"The Defense Department stores biometrics on all of its people, including Guard and Reserves," Protégé explained. "These guys — the ones shooting civilians — aren't in any biometrics database, anywhere."

Archive looked incredulous. "What are you saying?"

"They're not American soldiers," Protégé said.

Chapter 27

Daylight waned as the Facilitator boarded his Gulfstream. It was outfitted with all the usual trappings, and then some. It was as much necessity as luxury. Security demanded constant motion. He remained anonymous by remaining on the move.

Through various straw men and shill corporations, he owned luxury properties on five continents. Many of them earned money on the rental market, part of the elaborate cover story that had become so practiced, so routine, that it was virtually indistinguishable in his head from the real story. Most properties were fully staffed, and all were exquisitely maintained.

He often stayed as a guest in his own properties, the management agency and staff never knowing that the real owner was in their midst. He could be anyone that the exigency of security demanded, could tell any tale that convenience allowed, as long as the clues he left behind in people's minds pointed anywhere but true.

He was completely unknown in all but the smallest of circles, and those were not terribly social circles.

It was the way of things. The world's most powerful men were, almost without exception, also its loneliest.

He sat heavily in the plush leather seat and dutifully strapped himself in. One of the stewards handed him a martini. Gin, up, olive. The first sip burned a little on the way down, not unpleasantly.

A second steward handed him a folded slip of paper. The

Facilitator took it wordlessly, barely acknowledging the steward's existence. He read the message: *LIMITED successful. WIDESPREAD now underway.*

His expression softened, but only slightly. It was what passed for satisfaction on the Facilitator's face. Not everything was up in the air. The most important thing was right on track, and right on schedule.

Twenty-five percent, the models said. He'd need no more than a quarter of the world's Bitcoin to secure the kind of reach and influence that, heretofore, the Consultancy had only dreamt of. Undoubtedly, they already swung the hammer of the gods — quietly, of course, as pomp and circumstance were the domain of amateurs. Real power moved unperceived, and remained imperceptible to everyone but the illuminati. But the Facilitator had seized the opportunity of the millennium, and by week's end, he reflected, the few will have established unprecedented control over the many.

Two more days, at most. The infection rate of the theft virus was high enough that they would have to be very careful not to overwhelm the market. It would do him no good to steal every last Bitcoin on the planet, because then there would be no functioning market to dominate. He would be the undisputed king, but he would rule a kingdom of one. In order to exercise his will and exert his authority, he needed regular market activity. Everyday commerce was necessary, ironically, to facilitate his absolute dominion over the political and financial system.

Twenty-five percent. It was a big number, to be sure. Big enough to shift the world on its axis.

But small enough to be in his pocket before the weekend.

He pressed a button on the arm of his aircraft seat, and the television screen mounted to the front bulkhead came to life. He hadn't tuned to any station other than the Continuous News Network in years. But he'd rarely seen news reports as thoroughly satisfying as the ones he now witnessed.

They *should* be satisfying, he mused. They'd cost him enough. But Mandrake, that mercurial little media magnate, had come through in spades. Impeachment, even. Such a nice touch. The Facilitator hadn't even needed to hint at it. Mandrake was so thoroughly devious that it occurred to him simply as a matter of course. The man was truly a genius. In addition to being a pompous prick.

Speaking of pricks. He hadn't heard from the fat bastard he'd sent to Honduras to take care of the entrepreneurial hacker. How tough could it be? One little hacker. It was a thirty-minute job, but it was coming up on the third day since the Facilitator had dispatched the sweaty oaf to Central America.

And he'd yet to hear about the little soiree with the entourage of Homeland agents. They were well off track, from what he understood. In the wrong damned country, even. But things were in a fragile state, and one couldn't be too careful. The job needed to be completed. The absence of a progress report was disconcerting. Sloppy. He'd never have stood for it.

But he'd long ago learned never to launch Plan A without Plans B and C waiting in the wings. The Homeland agent would be taken care of, one way or the other.

How much can change in a week, he thought as he typed a text message into this week's burner phone. He'd gone from riches to rags and back again in a matter of days. And now he stood on the verge of something truly extraordinary. Far too extraordinary to allow a rogue arm of an otherwise impotent federal agency to screw things up.

He sighed. It was obvious that he had some housecleaning to do. The past week had been rough on his roster, and he lacked confidence in his remaining talent. It would take time to rebuild.

But there would be plenty of time for that, he reflected as he pressed the send button. He would begin as soon as the big pieces had settled themselves.

The jet's engines spooled to life, and the pilot announced that they would be taxiing momentarily.

The Facilitator looked at his watch, fished a sedative and a blood thinner from his jacket pocket, and washed the pills down with a healthy swig of gin. With any luck, he'd sleep all the way to Rome.

Chapter 28

Sabot peered cautiously around the doorjamb and into the hallway, holding his breath and listening carefully for any signs of his captors. Finding none, he stepped quietly out of Fredericks' cell, the fat, balding man following closely behind. Sabot ducked into the next room, the place he'd awakened earlier with a splitting pain and all sorts of crazy images in his head.

Zelaya still lay comatose on the floor, tranq darts protruding from his chest, a bluish pallor to his pockmarked face. Sabot stepped over his limp form and examined the medicine cart's contents.

It contained bandages, scissors, surgical tape, stitching, and hook-shaped needles in the top drawer. The next drawer contained pharmaceuticals. "Diazapem," Sabot read. "Paramescaline-B. Any idea what these are?"

"Hell if I know. Do I look like a doctor?"

"Maybe we can sell them," Sabot said. He pocketed a few of the vials, and grabbed a handful of hypodermic needles, but thought better of placing them in his pocket. Instead, he grabbed a pillow from the bed, liberated the pillowcase, and stashed the drugs and needles inside, taking care to tie shut the opening.

"I thought you said you left him alive," Fredericks said, kneeling over Zelaya's body with his fingers pressed against the comatose man's neck.

Sabot turned white, and felt a surge of fear and dread. *I killed him?* He'd never killed anyone in his life.

"Just kidding," Fredericks said, amused at Sabot's reaction. "He's alive. But aren't you quite the tough guy!" Fredericks barked a loud, insulting laugh.

"What, you're some kind of ninja assassin yourself?" Sabot shot back.

Sabot caught a momentary smirk on Fredericks' face. It made him wonder. "What exactly did you say you did, again?"

"Private security," Fredericks replied.

Sabot snorted. "You're a night watchman?" He looked over at Fredericks, who was patting down Zelaya's body.

Fredericks found something near Zelaya's ankle, and raised the comatose man's pant leg to reveal a holster and small pistol. "Hardly," he replied, unstrapping the holster from Zelaya's leg and fastening it to his own. "Personal security." He removed the gun from the holster, checked the clip, chambered a round, and set the safety. "Corporate CEOs, visiting dignitaries. That sort of thing."

Sabot didn't quite believe him. *If this guy ever had to haul ass, it would take two trips.* He imagined Fredericks waddling after some bad guy. *Stop, or I'll eat another donut.* He smiled for the first time in what seemed like forever.

He looked up and saw Fredericks watching him. "Let's get out of here," Sabot said, his smile fading. "Time's wasting."

They returned to the hallway and made their way to the doorway at the end. It didn't have a room number on the door, but neither did it have a doorknob. Sabot searched Zelaya's key ring for an unmarked key. There were half a dozen of them, and he tried them sequentially in the lock, this time remembering to try them both directions before moving on to the next key.

Each attempt rattled the door and the lock. Sabot's heart pounded, and his hands began to shake. *What will they do if they catch us?* He couldn't help but wonder about the atrocities they'd inflict on him if they caught him trying to escape.

The lock yielded to the fourth key. Sabot pulled on the door, but it wouldn't budge. He pulled harder, feeling panic start to swell. *What if this is another cruel trick? What if this door doesn't open?*

Fredericks nudged Sabot aside with a pudgy paw, then pushed on the door. It opened easily. Fredericks shook his head and smirked. Sabot felt sheepish.

He followed Fredericks into a low, dank, dark hallway. It was concrete on all four sides. It was poorly lit, but Sabot could see that the hallway made the shape of an L.

Their footfalls echoed. Sabot walked on his tiptoes, cursing Fredericks for his girth and clumsy gait. "Be quiet," he hissed. "You're going to get us caught."

Fredericks walked slower, but wasn't appreciably quieter. Sabot's anxiety grew as they neared a doorway on the left side of the hallway. He could see a small window cut into the door, with a metal flap covering it. The door had a number on it.

Fredericks paused, crouched beneath the window, and moved his ear near the door to listen. He tried the handle. Locked.

Sabot searched Zelaya's key ring for the matching number, cursing every metallic *ting* that echoed in the concrete hallway as the keys jostled against each other. His hands shook. His nerves were shot.

He produced the key, tried it in the lock, and opened the door.

He shuddered. The room was familiar. It smelled musty, damp, and moldy. The bare concrete floor had small pools of stagnant water. The room contained nothing but a pair of wooden chairs, two chains attached to the wall, and a shower head. *Jesus, maybe I didn't imagine all of this.*

He turned to leave the room, more anxious than ever to find his way out, heart thumping loudly in his ears, legs shaky.

Fredericks turned suddenly. He threw a large hand against Sabot's sternum, shoving the smaller man violently backward. Sabot's breath left his lungs in a whoosh. He stumbled backward into the cell, a look of shock and fear on his face. He opened his mouth to protest, but Fredericks clamped a hand around Sabot's face, twisted his slight frame, and wrapped a large, fat arm around his torso. Sabot twisted and kicked, but Fredericks' grip was just too strong.

Sabot vaguely registered Fredericks closing the door to the cell, stopping the door's travel just shy of the latch. "Stop," Fredericks whispered into Sabot's ear. "Stop struggling."

Then Sabot heard them. Footsteps, echoing from around the bend in the hallway. Guards.

Sabot tried to relax. He held his breath and waited, certain that his pounding heart was audible for miles, feeling anxiety and dread build with each echoed footfall just beyond the door to the dank cell.

Fredericks loosened his grip on Sabot's mouth, but held the smaller man firmly against his chest.

The footsteps slowed as they approached the door.

Balls. All the other doors are completely closed. This one isn't.

Fredericks had the same thought. He clamped his hand tight against Sabot's mouth again, tightened his second hand around Sabot's torso, and hoisted the diminutive hacker off of the ground. An involuntary grunt threatened to escape Sabot's windpipe, but Fredericks' fat hand completely blocked his mouth and nose.

The big man stepped to his left and whirled, Sabot's legs flaying outward. Sabot saw the door begin to open, then felt Fredericks' body halt abruptly as the big man flattened himself against the wall, just to the side of the doorway. Sabot's feet dangled, suspended above the floor, as light from the hallway spilled through the now-open cell door. The guard's deep, gruff voice said something in Spanish.

We're screwed. Sabot fought panic, fought the urge to charge, to fight, to go down swinging, at least. Fredericks' arms clamped tighter around his body, and Sabot felt Fredericks' hand smash harder into his face.

More gruff Spanish. Out of the corner of his eye, Sabot saw a boot and part of a khaki-clad leg step into the cell from the hallway.

He thought he might piss himself. *I can't do this any more. I can't take any more bullshit.* No more freezing faucets and illegible confessions and vicious blows to the head. No more guards' footsteps on wet concrete, no more howling voices, no more messed up dreams, no more Zelaya. He was exhausted, done, scared witless, but ready to die fighting rather than subject himself to more prolonged abuse.

He felt his body trembling, felt Fredericks' grasp clamp down even tighter, felt his body's overpowering urge to *breathe*, saw twinkling stars in his eyes as his brain exhausted its short supply of oxygen.

Sabot's vision closed in, and he could no longer see the guard's leg. *Jesus, is he inside the cell?* He fought the nearly uncontrollable urge to shake himself free of Fredericks' grasp. He was going to pass out.

A deafening noise rang in his ears. His body jerked, and his legs kicked. He expected sharp pain, something horrible.

But no pain came.

It was the cell door slamming shut, he realized.

Footfalls retreated down the long hallway.

They hadn't been caught.

Fredericks' grip on his face and body loosened. Sabot's feet touched the concrete again, but his legs threatened not to support his body. Fredericks steadied him. "*Who's* going to get us caught?" Fredericks whispered angrily as Sabot caught his breath and steadied himself against the wall. "You froze up. You gotta keep your head, man."

The fat man was right. Sabot had to keep his wits about him, or he'd never find Angie, never get the hell out of here.

Wherever *here* was.

"You good now?" Fredericks asked after a few moments.

Sabot nodded. "I'll follow you," he said.

"Damn right you will. *I'm* not getting caught again," Fredericks said. "Open the door and let's get out of here."

Sabot unlocked the cell door from the inside using Zelaya's key. Fredericks led them out into the hallway.

"We gotta check for the girls," Sabot whispered as they approached the next cell door.

Fredericks shook his head. "They're gone, man."

"What if they're not?" Sabot unlocked the cell and peered inside. Empty.

He checked every chamber as they made their way down the L-shaped hallway, ignoring Fredericks' growing impatience.

The cells were all empty. Sabot's heart sank.

The last door on the left wasn't a holding cell. It was a supply closet. Fredericks shoved Sabot inside, followed him in, and shut the door after him. "Look for anything useful," he whispered, switching on the light.

Sabot searched the shelves. There were dozens of plastic bottles. Bleach, muriatic acid, antifreeze. Sabot shuddered. *What the hell do these animals use this stuff for?*

Fredericks found a crowbar and a box cutter. Sabot winced as the crowbar scraped on the shelf, metal on metal.

Something caught Sabot's eye on the shelf below. Something soft, out of place. Clothing.

Women's clothing.

Angie's clothing.

His heart leapt to his throat. He snatched the shirt, held it open, held it to his nostrils. The scent spoke directly to the ancient part of his brain. *Angie.* There was no doubt. It was hers. Her pants were there too. And her underwear, bra, socks, and shoes. Tears streaked his cheeks. *What have they done to you? So help me God, I will kill them with my bare hands.*

Sabot felt a hand on his shoulder, turning him. Fredericks. The look on the big man's face said he understood. "There's nothing we can do here," he whispered. "This is their house. It's no help to her if we're chained to the wall."

Sabot nodded, numb, shaking with helpless rage.

Fredericks led them out of the storage closet and back into the hallway. They arrived at the final door. Sabot found the right key. The door opened.

What the hell? Was his mind playing tricks on him again? Was he dreaming? The door opened to yet another concrete cell. Shackles, chairs, and that damn shower faucet.

"How do we get out of here?" They'd opened every door, found nothing but holding cells and a janitor's closet.

Sabot's hands clinched. He felt adrenaline surge through his system yet again. *What kind of a place has no exit? Where did those guards come from? How did I get in here in the first place?*

Fredericks looked flummoxed. The big man's jowls jiggled as he looked around the cell, looking for anything resembling an exit or an opening. There was nothing of the sort. It was all solid concrete.

They backed out into the hallway, scanning for any doors they'd missed earlier. Sabot looked at the numbers on each cell door. He was certain they'd searched them all.

He opened his mouth to speak, but Fredericks silenced him.

Sabot heard the footsteps a second later. The guards were returning from the other end of the hallway. His ass clenched in fear.

With surprising agility, Fredericks ducked back into the supply closet. Sabot followed. He shut the door behind him, twisting the handle to prevent the latch from clicking.

Darkness. The closet door muffled the sounds of gruff voices and clicking boot heels. They were getting louder, closer.

Sabot felt a whoosh of air. It was warm, damp. The sickly sweet smell of decomposing vegetation assaulted his nostrils. He swooned. *I've got to be dreaming again.*

Fredericks' hand clamped down on Sabot's arm and dragged him forward. Sabot's foot kicked hard against the bottom of the metal shelf. The metal scraped over the top of his toes, undoubtedly peeling a toenail backwards, his tennis shoes offering little protection. The pain was intense, but he made no sound.

Fredericks pulled him harder, faster. He followed blindly, his eyes not yet adjusted to the dark. He took short, halting steps, afraid of stubbing his toes again.

"Come *on,*" Fredericks hissed, still pulling him forward into the darkness.

Shouldn't they have reached the far end of the closet by now?

The smell of vegetation was stronger, more pungent. The air was hot and muggy. The floor finally came into focus as Sabot's pupils dilated in the dim light. It was dirt. So were the walls.

A hallway. More like a mineshaft. Thick wooden beams held up the ceiling, held back the earth. Tree roots protruded from the floor and walls, threatening to trip him.

The gruff Spanish conversation sounded behind them. The guards were following them.

Fredericks tightened his grip on Sabot's arm, pulling him forward into the earthen passageway. *Can this be happening?* The now-familiar feeling of surreality came again, and Sabot felt far away from himself, as if he were watching himself stumble forward into the darkness. *We walked through a storage closet into a mineshaft?*

He began to feel claustrophobic, and his breathing became rapid and shallow. Panic welled up again. He slowed his pace.

Fredericks pulled him harder. Sabot stumbled forward. His injured foot caught on a root poking up from the floor. A groan of pain escaped his lips.

The guards behind them stopped their conversation.

They heard me. He had no idea how far back the guards were. And he had no idea how far he and Fredericks had walked.

Suddenly, Fredericks jerked him hard to the right. He stumbled again, and Fredericks caught him. Sabot felt a hand on his head, pushing downward. "Duck," Fredericks whispered. "Hands and knees. Follow me."

He crawled behind Fredericks. His head scraped against the roof of the tunnel. It was some sort of side shaft, only a few feet tall, branching off from the main earthen causeway.

The guards' footsteps grew louder. They were too close. Sabot stopped moving. The noise would give them away. He grabbed Fredericks' foot in front of him, squeezing. Fredericks stopped crawling as well.

They held their breath in the darkness. The guards drew closer.

A flashlight beam played over the floor of the causeway,

dancing toward him.

The light reached Sabot. It stopped, lingering on his body.

He felt abject fear. His bowels threatened to vacate. He felt trapped, completely vulnerable. How far was it to the mouth of the side tunnel? Could he make a dash for it?

There was no way. He was going to be caught. He would end up back in one of those damned cages, chained underneath the cold water again.

Hold it together. His pulse pounded in his head. Claustrophobia assaulted him, and he felt the walls crushing in around him.

The footsteps grew quicker, louder, closer. The flashlight beam washed up his leg and settled on his chest, inches from his face.

It was over. They'd found him. He was certain of it.

An eternal moment passed. Sabot's heart pounded, his muscles tensed, but he willed absolute stillness into his body. If he moved, he was dead. Hell, he was probably dead anyway.

Then, the impossible happened. The light moved on. The footsteps receded into the distance. The gruff conversation returned, fading off into the distance, voices echoing through the small space.

Sabot lay motionless, sweat pouring from his face, heart pounding. He felt nauseous.

After a while, Fredericks crawled forward.

Sabot followed. His body shook with the aftereffects of gallons of adrenaline slamming through his system.

They crawled forever. His hands and knees sunk into the soft, fertile soil. Rotting vegetation stuck to him. He knocked his knee painfully against a protruding root.

Then Fredericks stopped. Sabot heard him grunt, as if struggling against something. A metallic clang echoed through the small tunnel, and the creak of rusted hinges. Fredericks moved forward again, grunting, repositioning his fat body.

Sabot crawled forward. He felt the air change above his head. He was out of the low tunnel.

He looked up. Fredericks was standing over him, a fat hand held down to help Sabot up to his feet. Sabot took Fredericks' hand, rose shakily, dusted himself off. He smelled gasoline.

"Pay dirt," Fredericks said, pointing.

Sabot's gaze followed Fredericks' pudgy arm. He saw tires and handlebars.

A motorcycle.

Chapter 29

Sam awoke to the sound of the pilot's voice announcing their imminent landing at DC's Reagan International. Her neck was stiff, and she felt dried drool in the corner of her mouth. She ran her hand through her hair and grimaced, chagrined by how greasy and dirty she felt.

How many days had it been since she'd slept in her own bed, or had a shower? She wasn't sure. It felt like it had been a single, exceptionally long day since she'd chased down the giant wolf of a man who had broken into their house, shot and kidnapped Brock, and put her in the crosshairs of one of the world's biggest assholes. They hadn't even left the hospital after Brock's harrowing rescue when the world's economy shat itself, letting loose society's nascent knuckleheads, necessitating Sam's nonstop attention to find and stop the bastard du jour. *Sabot Mondragon, God help you when I find you. You have seriously fucked up my week.*

Sam pulled the hair out of her face and looked out the aircraft window as they taxied from the runway. Airline traffic had resumed, but the passenger load was a tiny fraction of its pre-crisis level. She hadn't seen the airport this quiet since 9/11.

The jet taxied to a stop, the door opened, and an addled-looking junior DHS officer walked onto the plane. Sam recognized his face, but couldn't conjure his name. "There's a helicopter waiting for you," he said.

"For us?" Sam was incredulous. "Since when did I rate a helicopter?"

"Since traffic is impassable, but more because the Director wants to see you."

"Shit." Sam realized where she'd seen the guy. He was the DHS boss' executive assistant. Fluffer, as Sam called him.

"Right this way, please," Fluffer said.

* * *

Sam's entourage barely fit inside the cramped helicopter. They lifted off from the executive ramp at Reagan, circled out over the Potomac, then headed west-northwest toward the Homeland edifice. Sam felt her stomach tighten. Why did she feel less anxious about chasing dangerous people in foreign countries than she felt about returning to the office?

Maybe time for a change, she mused. She wasn't exactly a team player at heart. Not that she had any subversive tendencies. She just never could force herself to drink the Kool-Aid.

She looked at the streets. *Sweet Jesus.* DC's major arteries were jammed with people. Crowds milled about at the periphery of town, but as they approached DC's capitol region, Sam sensed a growing purposefulness. People weren't standing around. They were marching. "What's going on?" she asked Fluffer.

"Demonstrations. They've been growing more intense for the past twelve hours."

"Why?"

"There have been a couple of incidents. You haven't seen them on TV?"

Sam chuckled. "Haven't had much leisure time lately."

"Violence. Some fatalities. The President has ordered a crackdown."

"Lethal force?"

Fluffer nodded.

Sam shook her head. *Because that's been so effective everywhere else on the planet we've tried it.* Why was it that those in the position to make history were never its students? "Silly citizens. I don't know why they'd mind their government shooting them in the streets."

Fluffer's expression grew pained.

True believer, Sam thought. She'd have to watch her step around this guy. Made sense, though — one didn't usually get the "opportunity" to pucker up for the Director on a daily basis without demonstrating the proper political sensibilities.

She sighed. Yet another indication that she and her employer were on divergent vectors, working toward different ends. She wanted to get rid of the world's bastards. That was tough to do when there were a gaggle of them in her chain of command. She'd have to seriously reconsider her employment status. She'd already felt a little bit like she worked for a pre-fascist state, and that feeling had hit her long before the recent crisis and the nationwide crackdown that was apparently underway.

The helicopter landed atop the Homeland building. Sam felt the weariness in her legs as she disembarked. She wasn't in the mood for the Director, or McClane for that matter. They had a way of gobbling her time. Best to keep the rest of her team busy and working toward figuring out who the hell was redistributing the world's wealth at breakneck pace.

She motioned to Dan, and he leaned in. She cupped her hand over his ear and raised her voice to be heard over the whine of the helicopter engines. "Get Trojan out of sight. I don't want the bureaucrats throwing the book at him yet. Maybe let him help you."

Dan nodded. "I'll have him check in with the rest of his crowd at that mountain lodge. They seemed pretty plugged in — maybe they've learned something helpful."

Sam agreed. They parted ways. She followed Fluffer toward the executive suite, while Dan, Trojan, and Brock made their way down toward Dan's office on the worker-bee level.

* * *

"Mace tells me you've had quite an interesting week." Homeland Director Henry Blankenship was fifty-something, tallish, with smart eyes, a soft midsection, but a firm handshake. He smiled mostly with his eyes, the reverse of the normal megawatt-powered fakeness endemic in the kinds of guys who usually found themselves in positions as lofty as his. In another life, Sam had often mused, Blankenship might even have been worth a shit.

Sam smiled. "That's one way of putting it."

"Thanks for returning on such short notice."

"No sweat, sir," Sam said. "It's not like we were vacationing down there."

"I'll need a full report, of course," the Director said. His face lost a little of its practiced joviality. "I'll be interested to see how it compares with the tense conversation I had with my Costa Rican counterpart this morning."

Aha. Mystery solved. The Director hadn't summoned Sam for a strategy session. More for a dressing-down. "I'll be sure to include all the details," she said.

"Please do. There were some interesting, shall we say, *tidbits* that my counterpart shared with me. They've requested some help with a few forensics *anomalies* at the scene of the event." The Director's eyes twinkled a bit.

Sam felt a bit of the blood drain from her face, and fought to keep her expression as neutral as possible. This wasn't an unexpected development. She and Dan had fired a few rounds, and one of them was lodged in the ass of a DIS agent. But Sam was still caught a little bit off guard by the Director's veiled accusation. She hoped her surprise didn't show. *I need some sleep,* she realized for the fiftieth time.

The Director put on a tired smile. "But all's well that ends well," he said. "And we have bigger fish to fry." He nodded to Mace McClane, who pulled out a paper printout of a PowerPoint briefing. The President's executive seal was on the top of the presentation. The briefing had been prepared by White House staffers.

"As you undoubtedly saw on your way from the airport," McClane began, "there's cause for concern about what many are considering to be an uprising."

Sam had definite ideas about what might have contributed to the unrest, but she held her tongue. This wasn't an audience that appreciated out-of-school thinking.

"The President has reason to believe," McClane went on, "that there are foreign agitators at work within our borders, inciting unrest and escalating violent situations. He's asked us to find and neutralize these cells."

Sam nodded, trying to keep the weariness out of her expression. Done well, these kinds of efforts consumed a great deal of time and money to produce marginal results. Done poorly, they turned into witch hunts.

"I'm pulling you off of the financial crime case," the Director said.

Sam's jaw clenched. "This isn't your average financial crimes thing," she protested. "These people are stealing enough money to buy themselves a continent."

"Yes," the Director said, "and while I share your view that such things shouldn't be allowed to continue, the current civil crisis has a higher priority in the President's mind. He simply cannot allow a foreign influence to destabilize American society."

That's rich, Sam mused. How many countries had the Agency destabilized in the past fifty years? Too many to count. But she had to admit that things took on a different flavor when they happened on one's home turf. "So you want my team to join the search?"

The Director nodded. "You have my full support." A wry smile crossed his face. "At least until the Costa Ricans call for your extradition."

Sam chuckled with a mirth she didn't feel. She followed her boss out of the Director's suite, and they walked back toward McClane's office. "I happen to share your opinion," McClane said.

"About?"

"The seriousness of the crypto currency theft case you're working." McClane turned to look at her. "And also about your assessment of my operational skills."

Sam flushed, embarrassed. "I'm sorry, Mace. I'm a little strung out, and I don't always think before I open my mouth..."

"It's okay," McClane said. "I focus too much energy on the administration and too little on the reason we exist. I appreciate your pointing it out to me."

"Really, Mace, I'm sorry about the things I said."

He sighed. "You didn't pull any punches, that's for sure. But I accept your apology, and appreciate your honesty. Anyway, we need to figure out how we're going to tackle this new directive."

Sam smiled. She'd already thought of an angle. "Foreign fighters on US turf need funding, don't they?"

Mace stopped and turned to face Sam. "What are you suggesting?"

"Maybe we'll kill two birds with one stone."

"You think there's a relationship between the Bitcoin thefts and the destabilization op the President's concerned about?"

Sam shook her head. "No. But I think there certainly *could* be. And there's only one way to find out for sure. Plus, nine times out of ten, it's the money trail that leads us to the assholes."

McClane looked thoughtful. He smiled. "I like it. Press on."

"Thanks, Mace. And again, I'm really sorry—"

McClane cut her off with a wave of his hand. "I needed to hear it." He smiled. "But you could certainly work on your bedside manner."

He handed the White House briefing pages to Sam. "Keep me posted, please. Use whatever resources you need. But be sure to leave me some plausible deniability."

"Always," Sam lied.

* * *

Sam found Dan, Brock, and Trojan slouched in various chairs around her office. "Green light," she announced.

"You're not on notice?" Dan asked with a knowing smile.

"I wouldn't go that far," Sam said. "The Director's already had a phone call from down south. But for the moment, we're good."

"Trojan has some news for us," Brock said.

The skinny hacker nodded. "I called back to Lost Man Lake Ranch, and I talked to Vaneesh and Protégé. I'm afraid the news isn't great."

"I'd be surprised if it was," Sam said.

"Looks like the thieves have stolen around fifteen percent of the global supply of Bitcoins," Trojan said. "And it also looks like they've found a way to vectorize the theft algorithm."

"Meaning?" Sam asked.

"It's in a computer virus that's spreading rapidly," Dan translated.

"So they're co-opting other people's computers to steal more Bitcoins for them," Sam said. "And there's no way to accelerate mining operations to dilute their share of the market?"

Trojan shook his head. "Not without a huge investment in mining hardware. In fact, that's the beauty of the system. It is inherently resistant to the kinds of manipulations that doomed the dollar."

"Which is why you tubed the greenback," Brock said.

Trojan nodded. "It had become hopelessly watered down and over-leveraged, which made it an instrument of theft."

Sam waved her hand. She'd heard all of this before, at the ranch in the mountains, from the old man himself. "We'll save the philosophizing for another time," she said. "For now, I'm mostly interested in stopping these guys."

"Not to toot my own horn," Trojan said, "but I have some experience with these kinds of things."

"Economic meltdowns?" Sam asked.

Trojan shook his head. "Computer virus attacks."

Realization dawned on Sam. "That's right. You're the guy, aren't you?" In the chaos of the past night, she'd forgotten that Trojan had built the virus responsible for hacking into all twelve Federal Reserve bank branches and erasing all the account data. Which, she reflected, had to be the world's most devastating cyber attack, by a wide margin.

Trojan nodded, a strange mixture of pride and sheepishness on his face.

"So you can build a virus to stop these thefts?"

"Probably," Trojan answered. "But it'll take a while to spread, unless I can launch it from the NSA pipes again."

"Do you still have your guy inside NSA?" Dan asked.

Trojan shook his head. "He's long gone. Tropical island somewhere, with a new name, if he has half a brain."

Sam nodded her understanding. Nobody could ruin your life

like an angry Uncle Sugar. He had a way of coming after you with relentless abandon. "Other options?"

"I thought maybe you government types could let us in from the inside," Trojan said.

Dan raised his eyebrows. "Hmm. I hadn't thought of that. Sam?"

She pondered, then shook her head. "I'll ask. But I don't have high hopes. They're pretty pissed off right now. And it'll have to go to the DNI's level."

"DNI?" Trojan asked.

"Director of National Intelligence," Dan translated. "Chief spook."

"More apparatchik than spook," Sam said. She looked at Trojan. "Would it be possible to sneak in to NSA's network?"

Trojan nodded. "Anything's possible. Those pipes are massive. They're making a copy of every byte of internet, email, and telecomm traffic. It's just a matter of taking the time to find a vulnerability."

Sam thought for a moment. "We need to find a place for you to work, without fear of some low-level fed molesting you."

"Can you get me back to Colorado?" Trojan asked. "I have everything I need there, and then some. And I'll need Vaneesh's help on the algorithm."

Harv Edwards piped up. "I could travel with him. NORTHCOM headquarters is out there in Colorado Springs. I'll lend a hand with the counter-terrorism effort."

Sam nodded. "Sounds good. We've been given the keys to the

kingdom. I'll have a DHS jet take you guys out west." She looked at Trojan. "You work on sneaking the virus into NSA's pipes, and I'll start working on the bureaucratic angle. Maybe one of us will break through."

Trojan nodded his agreement, and Sam turned to Dan. "We should probably chase down that John Q. Public lead before it goes stale on us."

Dan nodded, then looked out the window. "We'll never get there by car, and I don't know if the metro is running."

"No worries," Sam said. "We'll travel like rock stars." She dialed McClane's office and filled him in on her plan.

Moments later, they made their way to the roof of the DHS building and boarded the helicopter.

They made two stops, first dropping Trojan and Harv off at the executive ramp at Reagan International to climb back aboard the government VIP jet for their trip to Colorado, and then at Sam and Brock's brownstone in Alexandria. They hadn't been home since the crisis struck, and they feared the worst.

Their fears weren't unfounded. Looters had broken in. It looked as if they'd stolen the flat screen television and all of the food in the refrigerator and pantry. Everything else was untouched. "At least they were polite about it," Sam said.

Brock nodded. "The food would have spoiled anyway."

They made their way to the secure room in the basement. It was a vault, protected by a heavy steel door and disguised by room decor. It contained everything they'd need to either hole up for a couple of weeks, or grab a hit-and-run kit full of money, ammo, passports, and other sundries for a quick getaway.

The video feed from a dozen security cameras positioned around the house was also stored on a large-capacity hard drive in the vault. The surveillance footage was how she'd begun tracking down the werewolf-looking freak of nature who'd kidnapped Brock the previous weekend. She was tempted to search through the video to find footage of the looters breaking in, but realized it would be a pointless exercise. The looters would be long gone, and who would care enough to catch them?

Instead, they prepared for the unknown. They packed overnight bags. Brock grabbed his handgun from its case in the vault, a Kimber .45 that matched Sam's beloved sidearm (his-and-hers Valentine's Day gifts to themselves a few years back), and Sam restocked their supply of ammunition. Then they took turns in the shower and dressed in clean clothes.

They also donned ballistic vests. The world had turned uglier in the past two days, and it was best not to tempt fate.

Half an hour later, the helicopter lifted off from the park across the street from Sam's house and veered southwest toward John Q. Public's address in the trendy Shirlington neighborhood.

* * *

The Homeland chopper landed on the empty rooftop section of the Shirlington parking garage adjacent to John Q. Public's address. Sam and Dan disembarked, while Brock remained behind. His leg wound was still painfully sore, for one thing. For another, in case anyone ever got back around to caring about due process, having a citizen participating in the official search of another citizen wasn't even close to kosher.

Thanks to the President's declaration of martial law, and several provisions in the USA Patriot Act, Sam didn't need a warrant to search the apartment. She and Dan stopped by the apartment super's office, hoping to have an electronic key programmed for Mr. Public's door, and hoping to discover the name of the person who really lived in the apartment.

They found the super's office vacant. "No sweat," Dan said, producing a key card with a USB attachment from his laptop bag. "We'll let ourselves in."

They took the elevator to the twelfth floor and followed the signs to apartment 1236. Sam knocked. "Federal agents," she announced in her most fear-inspiring voice. "Please open the door."

Her request was met with silence. A nosey neighbor peeked through the doorway of an adjacent apartment. Dan shooed the old woman away with his hand.

Sam repeated the knock and announcement, waited a few seconds in silence, then nodded to Dan. He inserted the key card device into the apartment's electronic lock, plugged the USB attachment into his laptop, and flipped open the computer. A few clicks later, the lock yielded.

"Scary," Sam said, still awed by how far technology had come during her tenure at Homeland. "We'd have bashed the door in five years ago," she said, drawing her weapon and releasing the safety.

She and Dan followed standard two-person forced-entry procedures to clear the apartment. No one was home.

But she was surprised, because the apartment was obviously

someone's home. There were pictures of friends and family on shelves and desks, bad bachelor art hung on the walls, dirty dishes rotted in the sink, and the bed was unmade. "This isn't a safe house," she said.

Dan nodded, searching for the cable modem. He found a modem and wireless router sitting atop a dusty printer in a corner of the room, and attached his laptop to the USB port. "Let's see what's up," he said, mostly to himself.

Sam continued to search the apartment while Dan conducted an electronic search of the modem and wireless router. His laptop contained a Homeland-issued application that bypassed the password protection on most personal computing devices, but Dan didn't need to invoke it. Username: admin. Password: password. "Sixty percent of the time, it works every time," he murmured with a smile, quoting a favorite low-brow comedy flick.

He frowned as he dug through the modem's information. "Interesting," he said after a moment. "This is a ComQuest modem, and it's billed to a Jeffrey Santos." He chuckled. Mr. Santos had paid eleven bucks every month for the past two years to rent a modem he could have bought for $90. Another victory by smart companies over stupid consumers.

"What happened to 'John Q. Public?'" Sam asked.

"Exactly." Dan searched through the modem's cache. It didn't have much memory, but it gave Dan a flavor of the recent activity. He found searches for internet porn, video game cheats, and a query on how to beat a parking ticket. "I don't see anything out of the ordinary, and there's no trace of anything related to John Q. Public.

No phone calls in or out, either, but the cache only goes back about twelve hours."

Sam pondered. Had they been duped? Was it possible to have internet service at one address but billed at another? Certainly, she realized, but the service address would be plainly listed, which meant that they would have seen a different physical address when they looked up the telephone number they found in the dead spy's cell phone.

Something else nagged at her. "What was Mr. Public's internet company?"

"It was a Horizon account," Dan said. "This modem is ComQuest."

"Horizon is a satellite company, right?"

"Think so," Dan said. "But don't quote me. I don't have any time for TV because my boss works me too hard."

Sam chuckled. "That bitch." She went to the balcony. Sure enough, a Horizon satellite dish sat perched atop the ledge, pointed south and up. Her eyes followed the cable at the base of the dish. It went into the exterior wall just beside the sliding glass door, but Sam didn't see where it came out inside the apartment.

On a hunch, she grabbed a chair from the kitchenette, scooted it over to the wall adjacent to balcony door, and stood on the chair. She moved aside a ceiling tile. "Bingo," she said. "Bring your geekinator. I found another modem."

"John Q. Public," Dan announced moments later. "This is our modem. Gimme a sec while I pull up the activity history." He tried the admin/password combination, but was surprised to discover that whoever owned this particular modem had changed the password to something slightly more secure. Dan invoked Homeland's intrusion software.

He and Sam scanned the modem's recent activity history. "Looks like two phone calls in the past day, and nothing else," Dan said. "The first call is weird. Looks like this modem acted as a go-between."

"So they laundered the call's origin?"

"That's what it looks like. It originated from the 403 area code." He did a quick internet search. "Banff, Canada," he announced.

"Strange. Where did the call connect?"

Dan pointed his finger at a telephone number. It was a familiar number. "Is that...?"

"Yep. The dead guy in the warehouse."

They were on the right track, but if anything, the picture was even muddier. Why would someone in Canada call a goon in Costa Rica, but take pains to route the call through an electronic cutout in DC? "You said there was a second phone call?" Sam asked.

Dan nodded. "To another familiar number."

Holy shit. It was the number that Sam had asked McClane to locate using his Zip Line credentials. It belonged to a cell phone currently located in Rome.

Sam shook her head. "This is turning into a yarn ball."

"Don't they all?"

"So what does our friend Jeffrey Santos have to do with it?" By Sam's reckoning, the odds were very low that Santos didn't know something about the satellite internet service billed to his address. After all, the dish stared him in the face every time he looked out the balcony door.

They decided to wait around for a friendly conversation with Mr. Santos. They filled the time with a thorough search of Santos' apartment.

* * *

They didn't have to wait long. Half an hour later, they heard the click of the lock on the front door. In walked a muscular twenty-something, attractive, hair gelled in a gravity-defying configuration, black tee shirt half a size too small, a cologne cloud nearly thick enough to see. Did he wax his eyebrows? Sam thought they looked a little too perfect.

"Hello, Mr. Santos," Sam said in the overly friendly tone that Dan recognized instantly as dangerous. "We appreciate your hospitality." They flashed tin, and watched Santos blanch just a little.

"Got a warrant?" Santos asked, puffing his chest out a little further.

"Don't need one," Sam said. "Martial law, plus a serious national security concern, means we get to waltz right in like we own the place. Have a seat."

Santos remained standing.

"Really, Jeff. Have a seat." Sam pointed to an overstuffed chaise lounge. "We're not going away anytime soon."

Santos complied, and Sam continued. "So here's the way this works. We're in what the bureaucrats call a national security situation," she said. "It essentially means that you don't enjoy all of your usual rights as a US citizen, if you get my drift."

Santos' eyes narrowed. "I want a lawyer."

"Sure thing, Jeff. But I'm not sure how many days you'll have to spend in the tank before we find a public defender for you. Things are a bit of a mess right now, as you may have noticed."

"You're taking me to jail?" Santos stood up, arms held back, chest puffed out, neck forward in an aggressive stance. *Mr. Testosterone here,* Sam thought, rolling her eyes a little.

"Not really jail, per se," Sam said, her tone still friendly. She leaned back in the chair and crossed her legs. "That implies a lot more due process than we'll need to apply in your case. Think more along the lines of Guantanamo."

Santos' face lost color. Sam smiled inwardly as she watched most of the bluster leave his expression, replaced by fear. Then outrage. "This is bullshit! I haven't done anything!"

She smiled. "Then this will be easy. Have a seat."

Santos sat back down, and Sam got right to the point. "You have two internet services here. One is in your name, and the other is registered to John Q. Public. We're interested in the second one."

She watched the wheels turn inside Santos' head. His eyes darted about. He was clearly struggling to conjure a plausible story, Sam surmised.

Sam leaned toward Dan and cupped her hand over her mouth. "He's going to tell a lie, isn't he?" she asked in an exaggerated stage whisper. "Maybe we should ask him about his bank receipts."

Dan unfolded a half dozen pieces of paper from his jacket

pocket. "I found these in a file marked 'bank statements' in the other room," he said.

Santos' face flushed and his pupils dilated. *Bingo.*

"Nothing really looked unusual," Dan said, "until I noticed that someone seems to be giving you two hundred bucks on the fifth of every month." He waved the bank sheets for emphasis. "Tell us about that."

Santos considered. He seemed to deflate. A worried frown settled on his brow.

"You've been naughty," Sam said. "Haven't you, Jeff?"

Santos bristled at Sam's prod, recovering some of his swagger. "I wouldn't say that," he said. "They rent a spot on my balcony. What's the big deal?"

"Do you know what these guys are involved in?" Sam asked.

Santos shook his head. "No way. I don't know anything about their business."

"You didn't ask any questions?" Sam asked. "That's a little strange, don't you think?"

Santos shook his head again. "I didn't *want* to know. Besides, that's part of the deal. No questions. I'm not involved at all, whatever it is."

"Unfortunately," Dan said, "that's not going to be much of a defense. As far as the law is concerned, you're a full partner."

"And these guys are into some very bad stuff," Sam added. "Hence our interest. So who's your contact?"

Santos shook his head. "I have no idea. The money shows up in my gym locker every month."

"Cash?"

Santos nodded.

"How did this little deal get set up in the first place?" Sam asked.

"I was out drinking," Santos said. "I met up with some friends, and this guy was a friend of a friend."

"What guy?"

"They called him 'Slow'."

"As in not fast?" Sam asked.

"Right," Santos said. "Some Russian guy or something. Had a funny accent. Real tough guy, though. You can tell."

So Slow was short for Slobodan. "Go on."

Santos eyed her uneasily, but continued talking. "So we go out drinking a few times, a group of us, and one thing leads to another. Next thing you know, Slow hands me five hundo, cash. He promises me two more Benjies every month."

"In return for what?" Sam asked.

"For leaving my door unlocked one day, and then for not asking any questions after that."

"Sounds too good to be true."

"Maybe," Santos said. "But that was real money. I mean, it used to be. Can't buy shit for two hundred bucks any more, though."

"You have Slow's phone number? For emergencies?" Dan asked.

Santos shook his head. But Sam caught something in his eyes. She and Dan shared a glance.

"You have no way at all to get in contact with him?" Sam

asked, disbelief in her voice. "Like in case the satellite dish blows off the balcony in a storm?"

"No. Nothin' at all. That was part of the deal, right? No contact."

"Okay then," she said, rising to leave. "Don't go anywhere. And definitely don't try to leave the country. You're under the eye, and a guy we call Knuckles will have you bent over for a cavity search faster than you can imagine."

They left Santos' apartment and walked down the hallway to the elevator lobby. "Knuckles," Dan said, shaking his head and laughing. "I almost pissed myself."

Sam smiled. "I might have stretched the truth a wee bit."

"I think he definitely got the message," Dan said, opening his laptop. "Okay, we're still connected to his Wi-Fi. Any bets on how long it takes before he calls someone?"

Sam didn't have time to make a guess. Santos' modem became active almost immediately. "He's dialing," Dan said.

They both recognized the telephone number.

"Guess we should pack our bags," Sam said.

Dan smirked. "Apparently, all roads lead to Rome."

Sam groaned. "I don't know how your wife puts up with you."

"I'm not sure she does," Dan said, punching the elevator button.

Part 2

Chapter 1

Sabot looked around. They were in some sort of earthen chamber. The floor was the same wet, loamy soil they'd just crawled over, through some low side tunnel that branched from a larger cave — a cave they'd accessed through a hidden doorway inside a broom closet. *Am I hallucinating?* He once again had that strange, faraway feeling, as if he were outside of himself.

Fredericks' body odor hit him like a freight train. *I don't think I'm imagining that,* Sabot thought. Fredericks had showered less than an hour earlier, but the man already smelled like a goat.

Fredericks was bent over the motorcycle, inspecting it. "I think it runs," he said. "Still warm."

They followed the tracks left by the dirt bike's knobby tires in the soft, damp soil, moving slowly in the dim light cast by bare bulbs hanging from wires above their heads.

Sabot felt the earth angle upwards beneath his feet, and he soon had to lean forward for balance. The walls of the chamber narrowed, and he felt the need to duck his head, though the roof of the cave was still several feet above his height.

He heard Fredericks' heavy footfalls behind him, and the fat man's heavy, gasping breaths. Fredericks seemed every bit a liability, and Sabot resolved to ditch him as soon as it became practical.

The upslope steepened. Sabot's feet slipped in the soft earth, and he put his hand forward to catch his fall.

"Easy, surefoot," Fredericks said between gasps, nearly stepping on him.

Several steps further, Sabot encountered a set of double doors. They were made out of wood planks, reinforced by a zigzag frame, secured by a latch and padlock.

He tugged on the doors. They wiggled ever so slightly, but showed no signs of allowing passage. "Shit," Sabot said.

"Try your keys," Fredericks suggested. *Of course.* How had Sabot forgotten about the key ring he'd stolen from Zelaya? *I've got to get my mind right,* he thought for the thousandth time. *I'm never going to survive this otherwise.*

He held the keys up to the dim light. They were all large keys. None was small enough to fit in the padlock's slot.

Sabot's heart sank. They'd come such a long way. Their captors would undoubtedly be searching for them by now. They didn't have time to waste. Sabot didn't want to spend another second in one of those cells. He had to escape, to get the hell out of this godforsaken place, to find Angie and Connie. They'd figure the rest of it out after that. He just had to get out of this hellhole.

He pulled on the door handles. The doors had just enough play to make an ungodly racket in the otherwise silent chamber. But there was no chance of getting through without doing something about the padlock.

"We're stuck," he said, dejected.

"No we're not," Fredericks said. He was wielding a pickaxe.

"Where'd you find that?" Sabot asked.

"You should look around, notice things," Fredericks said, slipping the narrow end of the pickaxe through the latch. "Amazing what you'll find sometimes."

Fredericks put the butt of the axe against the doors, creating a lever. He pushed down against the axe handle. The latch groaned. He put more of his mass into the effort. The latch didn't stand a chance. The metal pins securing the latch to the door yielded with a god-awful screech that echoed forever down the chasm. The mechanism fell to the earth with a clank.

And the doors opened. Sweet, muggy air filled Sabot's lungs as he walked further up the sloping path. He heard insect sounds, and the earth became spongy with decomposing vegetation. They were definitely in the jungle someplace. There was almost no light. It was nighttime, ink black. The jungle canopy exaggerated the darkness, letting no starlight through.

Sabot's heart pounded. Were they really about to break free? He could hardly believe it.

He heard Fredericks' footsteps retreating back down into the tunnel. "Come on," Fredericks said. "We won't get far on foot."

They hustled back into the underground chamber, back to the motorcycle. "You ever ride?" Fredericks asked. Sabot shook his head.

Fredericks swung a fat leg over the dirt bike. He pulled the motorcycle upright, and stowed the kickstand. "Get on."

Sabot did as instructed, doing his best not to rub his body against the walrus-sized human in front of him. But there was no avoiding physical contact with the sweaty fat man. There simply wasn't enough space on the bike seat for the appropriate amount of man-clearance.

They heard a loud creaking sound from the far end of the chamber. A door opening? "Hurry up," Sabot whispered.

Boot steps, and voices.

Fredericks jumped on the kick-starter. The bike's suspension groaned in protest beneath Fredericks' tonnage. The engine lubbed.

But it didn't turn over.

Someone called out loudly in Spanish.

Jesus, they sound close. Sabot felt a rush of panicked adrenaline hit, and his bowels clamped. "Go!" he hissed in Fredericks' ear.

Fredericks jumped on the starter lever again.

The engine grumbled again, but didn't start. Fredericks cursed.

Sabot heard a click from the far end of the chamber. Halogen lights flickered to life above his head. More shouted Spanish assaulted his ears.

And the unmistakable sound of a round being chambered. "Goddamn it, *go!*" Sabot yelled.

Fredericks tried a third time to start the dirt bike. It still didn't start.

Sabot panicked. He turned to look back down the chamber. The halogen lights were now near full strength. He saw a guard stop, raise his pistol, click off the safety.

Fear blinded him. He ducked, eyes closed, curling his body into Fredericks' bulk on the bike seat in front of him.

The guard fired. The gunshot was incredibly loud in the small chamber. Sabot pissed himself a little. *Am I hit?* It didn't feel like it. "Gawhhh!" he shouted nonsensically, his terrified reptilian brain overpowering all logic.

Fredericks futzed with something near the gas tank.

Sabot jabbed the fat man's ribs. "Goddammit!" he yelled. "Go!"

Another gunshot deafened him. The slug splintered the wooden support above their heads. *We're going to die here.*

Fredericks' body heaved for a fourth time. The motorcycle engine sputtered, complained, clanked.

Then it started.

Sabot heard the engine rev as Fredericks twisted the accelerator on the right handle. He felt Fredericks' left foot jam the bike into gear.

Fredericks popped the clutch. The front tire jumped off the ground even as the back tire spun in the soft earth. Sabot nearly fell off the back of the bike. He threw his arms around Fredericks' pudgy girth and squeezed for all he was worth as the bike lunged forward and upwards.

Another gunshot assaulted his ears. He felt a sharp, stinging pain in the back of his left arm. *I'm hit!* He lost his grip on Fredericks' midsection. He felt his body sliding off the back of the bike. His arms flailed involuntarily.

His right hand brushed against something fabric. Fredericks' shirt. He clamped his hand closed and held on with all of his might, torso hanging precariously over the back tire, left arm flailing.

He felt Fredericks' body heave backwards. *Sonuvabitch, we're both going to fall off of this thing.*

Fredericks let off the gas and tapped the rear brake. The forces shifted. The front tire slammed back to the earth. Sabot's body lunged forward. His face smashed against Fredericks' sweaty back. The bike accelerated.

And then they were gone, weaving wildly up the narrow earthen passage, flying by the still-open gate, into the heavy, humid jungle air.

Chapter 2

Maurizio Turcoe rose as the sun peeked over the Adriatic Sea. He was a sailor, and had been his entire life. He got his sea legs in the Italian Navy, then cut his managerial teeth as a mate on a freighter.

He loved the nothingness, the haze gray, the sameness as far as his eye could see in all directions. Underway, Turcoe felt in his proper place, a mote, adrift on a speck, bobbing in an unfathomably large ocean.

Then came a wife, and kids, and his heart became a house divided, his love for the sea at odds with his love for family. Cruises were the answer, short jaunts to and fro. Not on those gigantic floating bacteria farms full of human livestock, where he'd be just another underpaid footman, with little chance of advancing to Captain. Maurizio opted to be a bigger fish in a smaller pond. Private cruises, on private yachts worth as much as small cities. He knew a guy who knew a guy, and the rest was history. He paid his dues, but his expertise was soon impossible to hide, and he found himself climbing the ranks rapidly.

And, in time, the day arrived. He was Captain of the *Anzio,* one of the largest private yachts ever assembled. At long last, he was *the guy.* Sure, the pay was better on the big ships, the supertankers and the cruise liners, but he really liked being in charge.

And truth be told, only the *official* pay was better on bigger ships. The *unofficial* pay he enjoyed as captain of the *Anzio*, on the other hand, was a compelling perk. In exchange for mountains of under-the-table cash, Maurizio greeted the *Anzio's* exceptionally distinguished and fanatically private guests with a smile, sailed at a medium pace between Italy and Croatia, avoided rough seas, and kept his mouth zipped about who had been onboard his vessel and what they might have discussed. It wasn't terribly exciting work, but Maurizio and his family lived very, very well.

He crept out of bed, dressed silently, and left, opting to let his wife of fifteen years get a few more hours of sleep rather than waking her for a goodbye kiss. It was going to be a short trip, less than a full day, and he planned to be back for dinner.

Maurizio drove toward the shipyard, checking his phone as he rounded the corner. Sure enough, there was a text message.

Maurizio didn't much care for the man handling the details for this particular client. Maurizio never asked for his clients' full names, and his clients never offered, so Maurizio knew the administrative man only as Bojan. Bojan had a buzz cut, and his lips seemed to be in a permanent snarl. Maurizio had instantly placed the man's name and accent as Balkan, though he'd never bothered to learn how to distinguish between the various ethnic groups that had scattered like cockroaches when the wars broke out in the Nineties. Italy had soaked up far more refugees than her fragile economy could absorb, and things had never fully recovered. Maurizio had no real reason for the bitterness he harbored, as his cup had certainly run over, but he nonetheless looked down his nose at people like Bojan.

And Bojan, with his imperiousness and air of thuggery, did nothing to endear Maurizio. Bojan's text message said, "Hurry. We want to leave right away."

Maurizio was accustomed to indefinite scheduling. It came with the territory. Anonymity often demanded strange hours. But he was also accustomed to a little more courtesy. He let the wave of anger pass before he typed a suitably courteous and subservient response.

It had the makings of a long day. But the pay would certainly put a smile on his face.

Chapter 3

"Fall in Canada is like winter in Wisconsin," Dan protested.

"Pack warm," Sam said. Despite Dan's earlier attempt at humor, all roads did not, in fact, lead to Rome. A couple of them led to Banff, Canada, as that was the apparent origin of two of the important phone calls they'd recently traced. Sam thought it would be best to send someone up there to poke around in person.

Sam was in a foul mood. Her request to allow Trojan access to the NSA's data pipes in order to unleash another virus — this one designed to use its digital powers for good rather than evil — hadn't made it past the Homeland Director's office. McClane insisted he had represented Sam's perspective to Director Blankenship as vigorously as possible, which in McClane's case meant not very vigorously at all, Sam thought darkly, undoubtedly why the request was summarily denied.

But she wasn't surprised. It was a tall order under any circumstance, but it would have required a miracle for the NSA to agree to a *second* infiltration by the same crowd who, days earlier, had piggybacked on NSA's snooping infrastructure to destroy the banking system. In fact, NSA was pushing for vigorous prosecution, staved off only by Homeland's insistence that Archive and his group were cooperating fully in an ongoing investigation with enormous national security implications, and couldn't be interfered with at the moment. The tenuous truce between DHS and NSA undoubtedly made Director Blankenship extremely reluctant to upset things with a difficult request, Sam figured.

"Be sure to stop by Tourism before you leave," Sam reminded Dan. "You're not visiting our neighbors in an official capacity." Homeland's Travel Agency, or Tourism for short, made anonymized travel arrangements and provided false travel documents for Homeland agents whose investigations took them abroad under nonstandard and sometimes questionable circumstances. While Sam had visited Tourism's office in the basement of the gigantic Homeland building on many occasions, the office didn't officially exist.

Brock spent the next three minutes convincing Sam to let him accompany her to Rome. She objected, citing the inherent danger and his wounded leg, but he pointed out that their home wasn't entirely safe, either. He had been shot last weekend, he reminded her unnecessarily, in front of their bedroom door. "Statistically speaking," Brock said, "our home is the most dangerous place I've ever been. Besides, I'm a grown man, and you can't stop me from going to Rome if I damn well please. Plus, I want to have sex with you in Italy, which I have never done before."

"You're so romantic," she teased. But she ultimately relented, and after stopping at Tourism themselves, they made their way to the rooftop helipad.

The Homeland chopper deposited them on the private tarmac at Reagan International, which was conveniently located adjacent to long-term airport parking. They exited the helicopter, nodded to the bovine TSA agent barely sustaining consciousness in the guard shack at the ramp's exit, walked across the parking lot, and caught the shuttle bus to the airport's passenger entrance. Taking the government jet to Italy was out of the question — it was simply too high profile for what she had in mind — so they gritted their teeth and stood in the security line.

Their fake passports wouldn't fool anyone with access to the ubiquitous facial recognition software run by all but the world's dinkiest governments. But the false documents would add a layer of obfuscation that might come in handy.

The airport wasn't crowded. The airline industry was still taking a beating as a result of the currency meltdown. Domestic flights now cost an outrageous number of dollars, and relatively few Americans had any other form of money in sufficient abundance to be spending it on air travel. And most people were worried about food, water, and shelter at the moment.

It wasn't difficult to spot their tails. There were three of them. Sam knew what to look for, and while their practiced nonchalance might have fooled someone with less experience, Sam immediately noticed the way they intensely ignored her. And they couldn't hide the hardness in their eyes.

She'd lost track of the number of times she'd spotted a tail in the Reagan airport. It was almost a joke by now. But she wondered who might be interested enough in her and Brock to go to the trouble of having them watched.

And she wondered what else they might have in mind.

There was a tall Asian man in baggy jeans, a concert tee, and a loose-fitting rain jacket; his apparel said 'computer geek,' but his eyes said something different entirely. She also saw a dumpy-looking middle-aged guy in a ridiculously oversized sport coat pretending to flip through a magazine outside a book store just inside the security screening area. The third tail was an athletic-looking guy with a short haircut and a decidedly crooked nose who seemed overly interested in the talk show playing on the television in the restaurant across the way.

She grabbed Brock and gave him a long, wet kiss, after which she whispered in his ear: "Heads up. We have three watchers." He started to look around, but she brought her hands up to his face to restrain him. She kissed him again, then said, "Play it cool, please." He nodded.

After security, they moseyed toward their gate. Sam used the reflection off the plastic information kiosk to check behind them as she and Brock walked slowly past the shops lining the walkway. They were definitely being followed.

"Let's overpay for shitty pre-fab food," Sam said as they passed a restaurant. "I'm starving." She couldn't remember the last time she'd eaten a proper meal.

The airport meal they endured was anything but proper, but it was nourishment, and sitting down at the restaurant afforded her the chance to see the way the three goons deployed to watch her and Brock as they ate.

They finished their food and continued toward their gate. Sam tried on a pair of sunglasses at a kiosk, using the mirror to watch the nearest tail. It was the big guy in the frumpy suit. He'd do just fine.

Sam reached into her purse, felt for the ceramic blade hidden in the side of the bag, and casually slipped the knife into her front pocket. She led them past a men's room. Five paces later, she stopped abruptly and whirled around.

The guy in the frumpy suit was caught off-guard. A real pro would have continued walking past, but this guy ducked into the men's room. Sam smiled. "Be right back," she told Brock.

She waited a few seconds, then charged into the men's room. The guy was standing at a urinal, dick in hand, trying to make it look as if he really was just a random guy in need of a pit stop.

She strode up behind him, grabbed his non-pissing hand, and wrenched it behind his back. He groaned, and tried to whirl to relieve the torque on his arm, but Sam pinned him up against the urinal divider. "No sudden movements," she said. "You'll spoil your aim."

She wrapped her free arm around his neck, twisted harder on his wrist, and pulled him into the handicapped stall. She locked the door behind her.

The man had stopped urinating, but his junk was still exposed. Sam let go of his arm, grabbed the ceramic blade from her pocket, and placed the knife against the man's stubby penis. "Good behavior is in your best interest," she said. "You don't want this thing getting any shorter."

The man twisted in her grip, as if to break free. She clamped down on his windpipe with one hand, and dug the blade a few millimeters across the man's penis with the other, drawing blood. His pained howl didn't make it past Sam's choke hold. "I'm not screwing around," she said. "I will not hesitate to slice your dick off." She felt his body tense, and she tightened her grip on his neck. "I'm going to ask you a couple of questions. I'm going to loosen my grip on your throat to let you answer. If you yell one time, or try anything stupid, you'll be fishing your tiny little soldier out of the toilet."

The man nodded. Sam felt his body relax. "Who hired you?" she asked.

He shook his head. "I don't know."

"Wrong answer." She dug the blade into his johnson a bit deeper to express her displeasure.

"I'm serious," he said. "I'm local. This guy was an out-of-towner, Chicago or something. Cash up front kind of thing."

"What'd he hire you for?"

He shook his head. "You're not going to like the answer."

"Will you like your new life as a eunuch?"

"Capture or kill," the man said.

"Who?"

"You."

This just got real.

Again.

"Why?" she asked.

The man shook his head again. "Lady, I really don't know."

"Who's running your little team here today? Is it you, or the tall Asian guy, or the guy with the messed-up nose?"

The man hesitated. He was clearly surprised that she'd found all three of them.

"I'm going to figure it out one way or another," Sam said.

"The question you need to ask yourself is whether you still want to have your gonads attached to your body when I do."

"The Asian guy."

"Thanks," Sam said. "You've been very helpful." She moved the crux of her elbow in front of the man's windpipe, then applied pressure on both sides of his neck. This particular choke hold cut off the flow of blood through his carotid artery, which induced a much faster loss of consciousness than achieved by constricting a person's windpipe.

He was comatose in seconds. She released her grip. She didn't want to fill out the paperwork that accompanied a fresh corpse on American turf.

She twisted his slack body as gravity took over, plopping him on the toilet seat. She pulled off his jacket, took the cell phone and car keys from his pockets, then used the jacket's arms to tie the man's hands to the plumbing behind his back. *Ladies and gentlemen, amateur number one.*

Sam picked up her ceramic blade, rinsed it off in the sink, straightened herself out in the mirror, and smiled at the dumbstruck older man who had just wandered in to use the facilities.

Then she strolled back out onto the concourse and took Brock's hand. "What was that all about?" he asked.

"Nothing big," she said, chuckling at her own joke. "Let's get an ice cream cone."

They walked into the ice cream shop and ordered, then sat at a table. Sam enjoyed a few licks as she waited for the other two goons to catch up. She didn't have to wait long, as the guy with the crooked nose took up a position next to the sunglasses kiosk, and the Asian guy sat down at the restaurant across the concourse.

Sam pulled out the cell phone she'd taken from the guy in the bathroom. She checked the phone's history, highlighted the most recent phone number, and pushed the call button.

Then she watched the Asian guy fish the vibrating phone out of his pocket and answer. "Where the hell did you go?" the Asian man asked.

"Hi sweetie," Sam said. "Your guy had a small problem in the restroom." The Asian man's eyes snapped to hers. She waved and smiled. "You should really hire better talent," she said, getting to her feet. "Have the guy with the funny nose join us at your table." She hung up.

She motioned for Brock to accompany her as she walked slowly across the concourse to the restaurant where the Asian man sat. Then she dialed 911, asked for the airport security people, and identified herself to the airport security operator. "I'm at the pizza restaurant in the International terminal. I need you to send a security team right away."

She smiled and waved as she and Brock entered the restaurant. The Asian man rose from his chair, but Sam put her hand on his shoulder and pushed him back down into his seat. "Please, don't get up on my account," she said.

She brushed up against him as she sat down next to him. "Is this your first day on the job?" she asked sweetly. "Because you guys are really not very good."

"Go to hell," he hissed.

"I think not," Sam said. She saw the security team approaching, radios held to their ears. "Over here, guys," she said, waving her arm.

The uniformed officers approached. "I saw this guy put some sort of a knife in his pocket," she said.

"That's a lie!" the Asian man said, his face contorting with anger.

But then he put his hand in his pocket and felt the knife she had planted on him. A knowing look settled on his face. "You bitch," he said quietly, submitting to the police frisking. Sam watched, a small smile on her face.

She showed her Homeland badge to the policemen, and announced her intention to take part in the interrogation. They agreed without hesitation.

* * *

"Won't we miss our flight?" Brock asked as they made their way to the detainment center, walking behind the two policemen and the slack-jawed Asian guy in the cops' custody.

"We will," Sam said. "But that's a good thing. Someone's obviously onto us. Best not to stick to our itinerary."

They entered the interrogation room. Sam watched as the policemen strip-searched the Asian man. He glared at her, uncomfortable with his nakedness in front of her. "Nothing I haven't seen before, buddy," she said.

The search produced a wallet, a cell phone, a slip of paper, and Sam's knife. She didn't bother to mention to the uniformed officers that the knife belonged to her, and that she'd planted it in the Asian man's pocket as she sat down at his table. The detainee accused her of as much, but his accusations fell on deaf ears. What good was the truth, when your opposition wielded a badge?

Sam examined the wallet. The driver's license said Henry Feng, of Alexandria, Virginia. The wallet had several hundred dollars in cash. "Going to a strip club later?" Sam asked. Feng didn't answer.

"And what kind of a two-bit amateur brings his wallet on the job with him?" Sam asked, shaking her head.

Feng glared at her, but said nothing.

She looked at the slip of paper from Feng's pocket. It was a receipt. Wu's Dry Cleaning and Alterations, located in the underground mall at Pentagon City. "Henry, is this your guy?" she asked Feng.

He didn't answer, but his eyes betrayed him.

"Come on, love," she said to Brock. "I think we need to change our plans a bit."

Chapter 4

The door to the computer center beneath the Lost Man Lake Ranch house slid open. Vaneesh looked up from his screens and smiled. "Holy shit, we thought you were a goner!"

Trojan laughed as he stepped into the room. "You're not the only one. It felt like we were in deep kimchi."

"So you won't be returning to Costa Rica in the near future, eh?"

"Never might be too soon," the skinny hacker said as he plopped down next to Vaneesh. "How are things?"

Vaneesh shook his head. "Not good. People were calming down, but there are some people posing as US soldiers who are shooting civilians. Shit's about to hit the fan."

Vaneesh also filled him in on his efforts to stop the spread of the Bitcoin theft virus that was infecting people's personal devices and using hijacked computing power to break into Bitcoin accounts.

"I would think it would be pretty easy to shut the script down," Trojan surmised.

Vaneesh nodded his agreement. "But then the thieves know it's happening," he said. "I don't want them to change tactics on us right away. I'd like them to think things are still going well."

"Much more difficult," Trojan said. "Are you thinking of going after the laundering script?" Bitcoin transactions didn't take place without a computer and a "wallet," or an application that issued Bitcoin transfers to other accounts, so the thieves' technique of keeping the digital currency in continuous movement to new, randomly generated accounts was dependent on several computers operating around the clock to generate the new accounts and transfer orders.

"I'd like to shanghai the laundering script," Vaneesh said. "But I don't want to shut it down completely, for the same reason. The thieves will know they've been squashed."

"But you'll have won," Trojan said. If the money ever stopped moving, it could be traced to the accounts in which it rested, which was why the thieves kept it in constant flux. "We'll be able to find them and steal it all back from them."

Vaneesh shook his head. "Ideally, yes. But I think there's too much money in play for these guys not to have an alternate plan. I'd rather be more subtle about it, so they still think their system is working."

"So you just want to tweak it," Trojan said. "You need to target the computers that are already infected, and maybe siphon off some of the money that's being moved around."

"I'd like to siphon off *most* of the stolen money. Like ninety-nine percent. Maybe just keep a small amount moving around in their laundering operation."

"You won't buy much time that way," Trojan said. "I'm sure they're keeping tabs on how much money they're moving."

Vaneesh nodded. "I thought about that, too. But I don't think it'll be a big concern. I'm sure they're running a script to tally the number of Bitcoins in play."

"So you'll just tweak the counting script a little," Trojan said.

"Right. I'll have the laundering program siphon money into accounts that we create and control, but I'll make their tallying script count the money as if it were still in their possession."

Trojan smiled. "You're a devious one. We should get together — maybe we could do something big."

They shared a hearty laugh at Trojan's joke. More than any two other people on the planet, the pair of computer geniuses in the basement bunker in the Colorado mountains were responsible for ushering in the new world order.

"So what about distribution?" Vaneesh asked.

Trojan shrugged. "I'd love to use the NSA data pipes again."

Vaneesh laughed. "Who wouldn't?"

Trojan smiled. "Right? Sam Jameson actually asked for official permission, but I got a text saying it wasn't going to happen."

"Shocking," Vaneesh said. "That would kind of be rubbing their noses in it."

Trojan nodded. "I agree. But instead of rubbing their noses in it by asking for their permission, I'm going to shove it up their asses by hacking in."

Chapter 5

Sam and Brock walked hand-in-hand through the concourse, quietly discussing their options. Their investigation of the global-scale Bitcoin theft operation propelled them toward Rome, Italy. But the three clowns sent to "kill or capture" them at the airport had derailed those plans. They'd missed their flight to Zurich, and there was no way they'd find another flight arriving in time to make the connection to Rome.

The pipe-swingers at the airport — led by one Henry Feng, who, it turned out, had no priors but half a dozen dropped assault charges — had rearranged their priorities a bit. It was a disconcerting development that someone was able to assemble and deploy a snatch team to Reagan International fewer than two hours after they'd made their flight reservations.

And they'd made those reservations under false names.

It was highly unlikely that the goons had tailed them from the DHS headquarters building, because Sam and Brock had departed by helicopter from the rooftop helipad.

All of that implied that the muscle squad — such as it was — had inside help. If so, it wouldn't be Sam's first experience with a double agent working inside Homeland. In fact, she had once been dead for a short time, due in no small part to a Homeland mole.

The thought of another compromised agent running amok within DHS made her suddenly feel exceedingly tired. Life was very difficult in the field when you couldn't trust the home office. And with the global economy in free fall, and capturing an emerging economic hegemon on the top of her to-do list, things were plenty tough already, thank you very little.

"I feel like we need to figure out who's got us under the crosshairs here," Brock said. "I mean, if we don't chase this down, nothing stops them from sending more assholes after us."

Sam nodded. "I tend to agree. We're not going to catch anyone in Rome if we get jammed up here."

The immediate problem was one of transportation, however. The Homeland chopper had dropped them off and left, and Sam was loathe to call them for a ride to the Pentagon City mall to investigate Wu's Dry Cleaning and Alterations due to the possibility of a Homeland security breach.

But even by DC standards, traffic was impossible. The demonstrators marching in the streets had turned the Beltway into one giant snarl, and the Metro system was still running at partial capacity — and horribly behind schedule — due to the dollar's collapse.

Walking might have been an option, except Brock's thigh was still recovering from the gunshot wound he suffered over the weekend. It would have taken them an hour and a half to make the trek, assuming they ran into no trouble with the angry crowds marching around the city.

"Let's take bikes," Brock finally said.

"That's a great idea," Sam said. "You're so much more than just a big dick and a pretty face." She pinched his ass and winked.

Who rides bicycles through airports? Cops do. Sam was able to commandeer one young police officer's bicycle on the strength of her Homeland badge. The second officer they encountered was far more reticent, until Sam produced a couple of ounces of silver. "Oops, I dropped these," she said to the bike cop, "and you found them. Damn the luck."

He handed over the bike.

"Glad to see the crisis has brought out the best in you," Sam said with a wicked smile. "Your nation thanks you."

It took several minutes of slow pedaling for Brock's injured leg to loosen up, but he was finally able to complete a full rotation of the pedals without grimacing, and they set off to the Pentagon City mall.

* * *

Wu's Dry Cleaning and Alterations was closed when they arrived. The door was locked and the shop was dark, but Sam saw a patch of light coming from the back of the store. It looked as if there was a partition separating the main shop from an office area. The wall defining the office area didn't reach the shop's ceiling, and the light spilled over the top of the office wall.

Sam felt uneasy and naked without her piece. Their weapons were in their checked baggage, probably thirty thousand feet over the Atlantic on the airplane that they were supposed to have been on. She'd briefly considered returning to DHS to pick up a service pistol, but quickly dismissed the thought. Homeland was located in the thick of the protestors, and it would have taken a week to fight their way through the horde. There were no pawn shops nearby, either, so they'd ultimately decided to take their chances.

Sam banged on the glass door at the entrance to the dry cleaners. There was no reply after a few seconds, so she banged again, harder. She saw a tuft of black hair peer around the edge of the office in the back of the shop. "We close!" a small Asian man hollered. He made a shooing motion with his hand, then disappeared behind the makeshift wall.

Persuasion was clearly necessary. Sam pondered using her badge, but thought of a better idea. She fished an ounce of silver from her pocket, and pounded the fleshy part of her fist against the glass door.

The shopkeeper emerged from the office and walked toward the entrance of the shop. "We close, no service, you come back tomorrow," he repeated, but the sight of the shiny metal in Sam's hand brought him up short. Curiosity and avarice replaced annoyance on his face. He twisted the lock and opened the door. "What you want?"

"I'm really in a bind, and I need to pick up my dry cleaning," Sam said, still holding the silver bullion in view.

The shopkeeper nodded and opened the door for them. Once inside, Sam produced the receipt she'd found in Henry Feng's pocket at the airport and handed it to the shopkeeper.

He peered at the receipt, and a strange expression came over his face. "One minute," he said. He turned and retreated quickly to the office.

Sam and Brock waited at the customer counter near the entrance. They heard the sounds of rummaging in the office area, and then a metallic sound that Sam knew all too well. "Get down," she told Brock, just as the barrel of a semiautomatic pistol protruded from behind the office wall.

He looked at her in confusion. "Down!" she yelled. She shoved him toward the fake plant in the corner, then lunged toward the forest of clothing hanging from the dry cleaning shop's conveyor system. The gun barked, a diminutive report by handgun standards, loud but nothing like 45 auto. *He's got a 9mm or a .40,* Sam thought, not that the knowledge made any difference. She was unarmed, and a bullet wound of any size would unfavorably alter the course of her day.

She heard another shot, then the sound of breaking glass. The bullet had shattered the glass case that served as the checkout counter, right in front of where she'd just shoved Brock.

Jesus, I just threw him into that one. "You okay?" she shouted.

"Fine," Brock said. He started to say something else, but was interrupted by another blast from the shopkeeper's pistol.

The slug ripped through the clothing hanging from the conveyor system, way too close for comfort. Sam dropped to the floor and wedged herself between the clothes and the long wall leading to the back of the shop.

The shopkeeper fired again. A freight train slammed into her chest. All of the breath left her lungs, and a searing pain assaulted her senses. Her hand snapped to her chest by reflex.

She'd half expected to find a pool of blood and innards, but instead her fingers found the spot on her ballistic vest that had trapped the slug. *They don't tell you how much it hurts,* she thought, and not for the first time.

She took a few deep breaths, calming herself down, regaining her composure.

Time to change the game up, she decided. She scrambled backwards toward the front of the shop, interrupting the line of sight between the shopkeeper's office and her pink body. "Can you turn on the conveyor?" she yelled over to Brock.

"The what?"

"There's a switch hanging from the ceiling above the counter. Hit the green button."

She saw Brock rise to a crouch and peer above the shattered counter toward the back of the shop. Another shot rang out, this one passing over Brock's head and through the plate glass window at the front of the shop. He flattened himself against the floor again.

Sam reached up and shook the clothes hanging above her head. Her diversion was rewarded with another gunshot in her direction, away from Brock, the bullet ricocheting in her vicinity. It missed everything important in her life. "Now!" she shouted to Brock.

She saw his hand flash above the counter, flounder for an eternal second, then slam against the electrical box suspended from the ceiling.

The machinery grumbled and creaked, then clattered to life. The clothing began its parade around the interior of the shop.

Sam waited for a woman's gown to make its way to her position. As it passed, she rose and followed it around the track, keeping the long garment between herself and the pissed-off Asian man with a gun, hoping that its length hid the motion of her feet. *So far, so good,* she thought, pulse hammering, now halfway along the side wall and making steady progress toward the office area.

"Over here, asshole!" Brock shouted from the front of the shop.

Sam cringed. *Don't be a hero, baby.*

Another gunshot rang out, and the sound of more shattering glass came from near the entrance. *Gotta stop this before Brock gets himself plugged again,* Sam thought to herself as she hustled toward the back of the shop, no longer bothering to keep pace with the long dress hanging from the conveyor that had hidden her movement.

She dove forward onto the floor and slid to a stop in front of the makeshift wall defining the office area. She rolled herself into as small a space as possible, feeling horribly exposed. The shopkeeper needed only to peer around the corner, and it would be all over for her.

Sam smelled cordite from the gun blasts. Her ears were ringing, and her heart threatened to beat its way out of her chest. She heard Brock shout at the shopkeeper again, and flinched as another shot rang out. How many was that? She cursed herself for losing count. The gun retreated back around the corner of the partition.

Now or never, Sam decided. In one motion, she rose, twirled to face the drywall partition, leapt, and grabbed the two-by-four framing at the top of the wall. Then she scaled the wall, swung her feet atop the frame, hefted herself up to a low crouch on top of the narrow wall, and grabbed a ceiling joist above her head.

She walked carefully atop the narrow frame, hands gripping the ceiling structure, moving toward the corner the gunman was using as a firing position.

She peered over the edge of the doorframe. The shopkeeper was crouched low, gun pointed toward the shop entrance. *Don't screw this up. Probably won't get a mulligan.*

Sam lunged forward and away from the wall frame, out over the shop floor. Her hands hooked the ceiling joist directly over the shopkeeper. Her legs swung out, around, and forward. She kept her eyes on the gunman's head, flattened her right foot, and kicked with all of her might, adding the force of her leg muscles to the momentum of her body.

The gunman caught the motion out of the top of his vision. He looked up. The timing couldn't have been better.

Sam heard a sickening, wet crunch, felt the bones of his face give way beneath her blow, heard the crack of his skull against the concrete as he fell to the floor.

She let go of the rafter and jumped down to the floor. Her foot hurt like hell. She wondered if she'd broken a bone. "Party's over," she yelled to Brock.

She kicked the gun away from the comatose shopkeeper's grip, and turned his head to make sure he was still breathing. His nose was destroyed, shoved halfway into his skull and splattered wide across his face. His jaw hung at a grotesque angle, and there was blood everywhere.

"Holy shit," Brock said, hobbling to a stop at Sam's side. "You messed him *up.*"

Sam couldn't find a pulse.

The little guy suddenly looked pathetic — small, slight, old, face smashed to hell, kicked straight to the afterlife by her own boot. She began to shake a little, a byproduct of the stale adrenaline and a sudden, random wave of remorse at the way she'd just ended a man's life.

Her eyes teared up. Sure, the guy had tried to kill both of them just a moment ago, and she knew she shouldn't really feel too badly about the way things turned out, but it wasn't a rational reaction she was having. Sometimes the craziness of it all, and the finality, got to her in a place she tried hard to protect.

Brock grabbed her in a tight embrace.

"I'm sorry," she said after a moment, straightening herself up. "Sometimes it just hits me."

Brock kissed her forehead. "I'd worry if it didn't, baby." He brushed the hair back from her face. "That's how I know you're still human," he said with a smile.

She returned his smile, exhaled, and then put her game face back on. "Would you mind grabbing his gun and standing guard? I'll search the office."

"What about fingerprints?" Brock asked.

"I don't think there'll be a functioning justice system in this town for a long time," Sam replied. "Besides, taking the gun is a perfectly reasonable reaction when someone tries to grease you."

Brock nodded, picked up the pistol, and positioned himself with a view toward both the front entrance and the back exit of the shop.

Sam looked around in the office. A distinctive smell permeated the small area. Her nostrils were assaulted by a powerful punch of garlic and fermented cabbage. Kimchi. *A Korean guy running a Chinese dry cleaner's shop?* That almost never happened, in Sam's experience. It implied that laundry wasn't the primary business of the dry cleaning shop, and the guy calling the shots at Wu's Dry Cleaning and Alterations probably wasn't anyone named Wu. "Starting to smell an awful lot like a front," she muttered as she searched through the desk.

"Whatever led you to that insight?"

"I'm not in the mood," she said. There was another pistol in the center drawer of the desk. She cleared it, checked it, chambered a round, and tucked it in the back of her pants, pulling the tail of her blouse out to conceal its shape.

"Hurry," Brock said, eyeballing the growing crowd of people gathering around the shattered glass at the front of the shop. "Gawkers."

"I don't see anything weird," she said, leafing through the accounting book.

"We need to get out of here soon, I think," Brock said.

Sam felt frustration mounting. They needed to catch a break, and her search of the office wasn't yielding anything helpful. It looked like a dingy little office in a dingy little dry cleaner's shop, complete with a shitty old television, stinky Korean food, and a stack of barely-legible receipts on the desk.

She absently pawed at the yellow slips of paper, picking one up for examination. She turned it over a couple of times, frowned, then picked up several more receipts. Then a half dozen more.

Brock peered through the opening. "Babe? May we please get

the hell out of here?"

She rushed out the office doorway, brushing past Brock, and knelt at the dead shopkeeper's body. She shoved her hands into his pockets, finding the usual — keys, an old cell phone, a money clip... and Henry Feng's receipt, the item that had prompted the earlier festivities.

"Bingo," she said. There was a small red checkmark on the back of the receipt. She rushed back to the pile of receipts on the desk and leafed through them one by one, setting aside those with red check marks on them. There were easily fifty receipts, but only four had the red mark. She shoved them in her pocket along with the shopkeeper's cell phone, grabbed Brock's hand, and dashed out the back door of the shop.

They emerged in an underground alleyway, the delivery entrance for all of the underground shops in that section of the Pentagon City mall. "Hide your gun," she told Brock as they hustled around the corner into the main portion of the mall and joined the crowd of onlookers attracted by the commotion at the dry cleaner's shop.

As nonchalantly as they could manage, they elbowed their way to the front of the crowd and retrieved the two police bicycles still leaning up against the wall next to the shop entrance.

They mounted the police bikes. A few people in the crowd stared, pointed, whispered.

"Call housekeeping," Sam said to no one in particular. "Something should be done about this mess."

* * *

Sam and Brock kept their eyes moving as they pedaled back toward Reagan International. The crowd was growing in numbers, and, Sam felt, growing more truculent as the day wore on. "We need to get through here before something goes down," she told Brock, pointing to the police insignia on their commandeered bicycles. "These people don't have a police-friendly vibe about them."

"I think the shootings might have something to do with that."

Sam nodded. She mulled their next move. The Rome lead wasn't going to chase itself down, but she needed someone to grind through all the new investigative work that had arisen as a result of their little laundromat foray. She badly wanted to know about the four people whose receipts the crooked laundromat shopkeeper had marked with a red check. She also wanted to know more about Henry Feng and his two friends, the semi-pro muscle she'd rolled up in the airport an hour or so earlier.

She'd normally turn to Dan for help, but he was winging his way to Banff to investigate the origin of a couple of those phone calls. One of those calls had snaked its way through Jeffrey Santos' DC apartment on its way down to Central America, finally connecting with the phone that bore Slobodan Radosz' fingerprints. It was the same phone she pulled from the body of the guy who tried to kill her in the warehouse in Costa Rica, which accounted for her greater-than-usual curiosity regarding the particular phone in question.

After Dan, there was an extremely short list of people whom Sam implicitly trusted in the Department of Homeland Security. The list was so short, in fact, that there were no names on it.

She thought again about how quickly the team of three knuckle draggers had found her and Brock. They'd barely had time to get their shit together and make it to the airport themselves. She was even more convinced now that no one could have assembled a snatch op that quickly without inside help. Which meant that there was no way in hell she was going to risk calling anyone at DHS to help her investigate the laundry shop leads.

But one name did pop into her head. Special Agent Alfonse Archer, a buttoned-down Bureau guy. She'd leaned on him pretty heavily over the past weekend. They'd met at the grisly scene of a parking-garage incident that had left a US senator's driver extremely dead, and Big A, as she'd come to know him, had come through in a big way to help her retrieve Brock from the assholes who'd shot and kidnapped him. And, like Brock, Big A was recovering from a bullet wound. She called his cell phone, slowing down her pedaling to catch her breath a bit.

He picked up on the third ring. "I told myself I was never gonna answer another phone call from you," he said, only half joking.

Sam laughed. "Big A, how's life in the crime fighting business?"

"Lots of dull moments this week," Archer said. "I'm stuck in the office while my arm heals."

"You're actually at work? Everyone else is out stealing their neighbors' TVs."

"Don't get it twisted," Archer said with a laugh. "I definitely thought about augmenting my pay, especially after taking a bullet in the line of duty."

Sam chuckled. She filled Archer in on the situation, gave him Feng's name, and read the names from the four dry cleaning receipts with the red check marks on them. "And just for giggles," she said, "maybe see what you can dig up on a guy named Slobodan Radosz."

"Sounds like a name that would stand out nicely in our database, if we had a reason to know of him," Archer said.

"That's what I was thinking."

"I'll get back with you as soon as I can."

Sam thanked Archer for his help and hung up.

She had another problem to solve, a very important one. She dialed her cousin. "I need a favor," she said, after brief pleasantries.

Chapter 6

The Facilitator's head hurt, the annoying aftereffects of too much gin, a sedative, and his trip halfway around the globe. After the refueling stop in Rome, his private jet made the relatively short trip to Pescara, on the coast of the Adriatic Sea. As the engines spooled to a stop, he had exited his plane and climbed aboard a waiting helicopter for the brief trip out to sea.

His was, by design, the last arrival on the *Anzio*. The super-yacht was full of European dignitaries, both the public-facing figureheads occupying political office, and the real power brokers, the ones at the helm of the big banks, big corporations, and big lobbies.

In attendance were also an impressive number of obscenely wealthy private individuals, most of whom functioned in the same fashion as the bankers and captains of industry: to dictate pan-European fiscal and social policy. *Sub rosa*, of course, leaving little surface indication that the various political systems were anything other than what they claimed to be. Power brokers only remained powerful as long as the groundlings remained docile.

"Signore, please accept my warmest welcome to the *Anzio*," Captain Maurizio Turcoe said nearly as soon as the Facilitator stepped from the helicopter onto the yacht's helipad. "It is my pleasure to serve as this beautiful vessel's captain. I trust that you'll find all arrangements to your satisfaction, but should you need anything, however insignificant, it would be our pleasure to provide it for you."

The Facilitator nodded and grunted without making eye contact. He turned to the sour-faced Serb on the captain's left. "Everyone is here," Bojan said, "except the parliament president's chief of staff. He had a… sudden illness."

The Facilitator smiled knowingly. "Let us hope he recovers." But not too quickly. Parliamentary politics frequently impeded the sort of progress the Facilitator was after.

It was exceptionally rare for the Facilitator to attend meetings such as this one, though he'd called the meeting, massaged its attendee list, and, of course, authored the script. Though no one on board knew it, the yacht belonged to him. Accounts under his control had made the appropriately sized donations necessary to rent the various politicians for the afternoon. And the meeting's keynote speaker was a longtime member of the Consultancy, all of which was usually more than good enough to faithfully serve the Facilitator's interests.

But this time, much more was at stake. It was in his best interest to be a fly on the wall, to witness both context and subtext, to watch for askew glances between attendees, to hear the questions in person, the ones that were asked and the ones that were merely implied.

Many of the people in attendance would recognize him, but only two would recognize him for who he was. He possessed little of the usual megalomania that accompanied the kind of weight he threw around. Consequently, he possessed little of the attendant yearning for the spotlight that those in power frequently felt. Such a yen would be exceptionally hazardous. Anonymity was absolutely essential.

Bojan accompanied him to the yacht's ballroom. The Facilitator took a seat in the back of the room, and Bojan watched the door. Johann Froehlich, the current president of the European Central Bank, and the Facilitator's highly-placed shill, spoke from behind the podium.

"The American situation requires some difficult choices," Froehlich said, his Austrian accent leaving sharp edges on the words. "My staff and I no longer view the US dollar as a viable reserve currency, which places many of us in an awkward situation, given the size of our long positions in the dollar."

The Facilitator paid more attention to the crowd than to Froehlich. He had approved Froehlich's message, so he was intimately familiar with its contents. He was much more interested in the audience's receptivity to what came next.

"Naturally, this raises the issue of conversion from the dollar to a more suitable reserve currency," Froehlich continued. The Facilitator noted nods from the distinguished audience, a positive sign. "From an optical perspective, it seems most appropriate for us to hold the Euro in exclusive reserve at the dawn of what many of us believe to be the post-dollar era. The Euro is, after all, the currency of the land."

"Not mine!" announced a voice with a Londoner's accent. "Pound Sterling or nothing at all, my good man." All heads turned to witness a sardonic smile on the British banker's face.

Froehlich smiled. "As our English friend has humorously pointed out, some of us have made the Euro switch in all but the name. But we're all equally exposed to what has become just as leveraged a currency as the US dollar was, which brings me to the topic of our purpose here today: determining the right currency for us to invest in now."

The audience murmured. The politics behind the Euro provoked strong feelings on both sides of the argument. But the crowd was hand-picked, and the Facilitator was confident that everyone in attendance understood the degree to which the Euro was just as vulnerable to a crisis of confidence as the dollar had proven to be.

What only a few people understood was that *every* currency was subject to a similar crisis. Even gold, Libertarian squeals about some monumental but indiscernible difference between "money" and "currency" notwithstanding. Money couldn't be eaten, didn't keep one warm at night, didn't provide shelter from the elements. It was therefore only valuable as a marker, a shorthand for the relative value of the things that provided the necessities of life, and as such, all money was equally vulnerable to the shifting tides of circumstance and popular opinion.

Sure, humans had valued shiny gold pieces for eons, which made gold, empirically speaking at least, a more durable trade lubricant than anything before or since. But it was still just a proxy.

As the Facilitator had recently come into possession of an ungodly amount of a different kind of proxy — the kind that existed as a string of ones and zeroes inside of the world's computers — he stood to gain a great deal if this august coterie of European heavies chose to cast their fortunes with Bitcoin.

"There are two major advantages," Froehlich intoned in his precise Austrian-accented English, "to a digital currency. First, none of the digital currencies under consideration are yet leveraged. They are not susceptible to multiple claims against the same unit of denomination, which is the major problem that every other fiat currency has today. We will, of course, maintain the mechanisms that allow borrowing against the currency of choice, even if we elect to adopt a particular digital currency. This ability to earn leveraged gains will still provide for the kind of profitable inflation that our various institutions have come to rely upon, and that our consumers have come to crave as well, but at a sufficiently slow pace to ensure stability."

The Facilitator watched as the crowd digested Froehlich's last statement. The Brit raised his hand and was recognized. "So we throw out the poisoned currency, and set about poisoning the new one, then?"

Froehlich smiled indulgently. "One might regard it that way. Or, if one happens to enjoy the institutional profits that inflationary borrowing permits, one might view the change as a move to greener, more fertile fields, ripe for planting."

The audience laughed, the Brit right along with them. "Right, then," he said. "Sign us up. Only, why don't we just go back to the gold standard?"

Another voice piped up, this one with a Swiss-German accent. "You know how to gain access to the Americans' vaults?"

The Facilitator smiled. Of course not. Even if the US government somehow agreed to let the Europeans have back all the gold that the American vaults had "safeguarded" on the Europeans' behalf over the past half-century, there was no way that *he,* the Facilitator, would allow the transfer to take place.

Froehlich fielded the delicate question expertly. "There is an access issue," he said. "Not all of us are in physical possession of the gold to which we have a claim, and there are security concerns associated with transporting large quantities of precious metals in the current, chaotic environment. So returning to a gold-based currency system, at this moment, would likely create an unfavorable situation for most of us. Hence, my belief, and that of many of my colleagues, is that investment in one or more digital cryptographic currencies would provide an attractive combination of opportunity and security."

The Facilitator noted nods of assent from many in the audience. A good sign. Froehlich had appealed to the crowd's lust for more wealth, and had played on their fear of losing the wealth they currently had. It was the oldest and most effective one-two punch in salesmanship, and it appeared to have been well-received by the crowd of European luminaries.

"But there is a further question that requires our consideration," Froehlich went on. "The matter of *which,* or which *combination,* of the dozens of virtual currencies in existence is most suitable for our purposes."

"Are we sure this currency can be safeguarded?" The speaker was a Swiss banker, caretaker of several of the Facilitator's own accounts. "I have read of thefts."

"Anything can be stolen," Froehlich said. "For years, we've all dealt in cash, which is the most-stolen item in the world. And the digital systems our banks have employed for years are also vulnerable to exploitation."

The crowd murmured, but Froehlich continued. "But digital money can be stored on small memory devices, which can be physically and electronically isolated from any computer system until they're needed for a particular transaction. And since it's nothing more than an account number and an associated passkey, it can also be stored on a slip of paper and locked away in a safe. So just like the currencies we currently employ, it is simply our own diligence that is necessary to safeguard our assets from misappropriation."

"But there are two dozen of these currencies out there," said a man with a thick Irish brogue. "Half will be gone in five years. So where will that leave us if ours disappears?"

"It's a concern. But it's no less and no more a problem than we face today with our existing systems," Froehlich said. "Let us not forget that we are here today because the US dollar has just disappeared from beneath our feet, for all practical purposes."

The Facilitator detected uncertainty in the crowd. They had arrived at the crux, the decision point. He looked back at Froehlich, who was already delivering the coup de grace.

"But by virtue of our collective participation in one or several of these digital currency markets," Froehlich said quietly, his calm voice assuaging uneasiness as effectively as his words, "the currency or currencies we choose to adopt will enjoy a substantial boost in legitimacy and consumer confidence. We will, by our mere presence in the market, create the market strength that we require."

Heads nodded. The Facilitator smiled. He exchanged a congratulatory glance with Froehlich, who nodded a discreet acknowledgement. It was all down to the details now. They had carried the day. The Facilitator's mountain of stolen Bitcoin was about to triple in value, maybe more.

Before week's end, his position would be solidified. He would remain damn near the most powerful man on the planet; that was never much in question. But he would soon wield reach and influence on a scale he'd never before imagined possible. What he had just accomplished was a hair shy of overt global dictatorship.

The meeting adjourned, and the Facilitator made a quick exit. He had another item to attend to. He nodded to the dour Serb on his way out of the yacht's enormous conference room.

Bojan followed the old man to the captain's quarters belowdeck. The Facilitator rapped three times on the door. Maurizio Turcoe opened the door, an obsequious smile on his face, but the Facilitator walked past the captain, into the captain's own private chamber, as if Turcoe did not exist.

A familiar face greeted him inside the captain's quarters, reclining behind Turcoe's desk. Fyodor Alexandrov had aged considerably since last they spoke in person, the Facilitator noted. His skin was pale, almost translucent, and dark purple rings encircled his eyes. But Alexandrov's high Russian cheeks, square jaw, and piercing eyes made for as intimidating a presence as ever.

He was equal parts feral thug and calculating statesman, characteristics that undoubtedly accelerated his rise to the top of the KGB, the most feared intelligence service on the planet. Until the Soviet Union disintegrated in disgrace, that is, and Alexandrov was forced to channel his vision, will, and absolute lack of human empathy in a more entrepreneurial direction.

"My friend," the old Cold War spymaster said, rising to shake the Facilitator's hand. "Thank you for your business. I trust things are proceeding to your satisfaction?"

"Quite so," the Facilitator said. "I have need of further services, as well."

Chapter 7

Sabot was drenched, but sweat was only part of the problem. It was more that the wet, sweet, heavy air of the jungle condensed on his face and body as the small motorcycle, struggling under the combined weight of Sabot and his corpulent companion, cut through the pre-dawn darkness. The air was impossibly thick, and Sabot felt a wheeze in his chest with every breath.

His neck was sore. He'd craned it around hundreds of times since leaving the strange underground garage buried deep in the jungle, searching behind them for signs of anyone following them. To his utter amazement, he'd seen nothing. Had they really gotten away from that god-awful nightmare of a place?

His arms were wrapped reluctantly around Fredericks' sweaty hulk, gripping the pudgy mass only as tightly as necessary to keep from toppling off the back of the motorcycle. The odor was intense, and the combination of the loamy jungle air and Fredericks' foul funk was enough to turn Sabot's stomach. "Can you go any faster?" he asked.

"Not unless you want to get decapitated by a tree branch," Fredericks called over his shoulder in reply. "In case you haven't noticed, it's still dark out here."

Sabot grunted. His arm stung. Technically, he'd been shot while Fredericks tried to start the motorcycle, but it had turned out to be such a glancing hit that the slug had done little more than shave the outer layers of skin from a spot on his upper arm. But it still hurt, especially as his salty sweat found its way into the wound.

Fredericks was still talking. "And we could always plow into a tree trunk. That'd be fun, don't you think? Maybe have some injuries to deal with while we're waiting for those assholes to nab us again?"

Sabot grunted again.

"And we could always—"

"Okay!" Sabot yelled, suddenly fed up. "For fuck's sake, shut up!"

Fredericks bristled. "You wanna walk? Little ingrate beaner. We'll see how far you get..."

Sabot tuned the fat man out. He had bigger things to worry about. Like Angie and Connie, tied up somewhere, under duress, maybe forced to do unspeakable things, all on account of Sabot's decision to skim a little slice of the Bitcoin action.

He frowned, trying for the thousandth time to work out a way to find Angie and Connie. He had no clue where to begin.

And his head hurt, something awful. It felt like a hangover, but he had no recollection of drinking alcohol since the charter flight.

Jesus, how long ago was that? It felt like an epoch ago when he, Angie, Connie, and fat Fredericks had boarded the airplane in Canada. He had no real idea of how long ago that had been, but it had certainly been a world away from where he now found himself.

A warm orange glow peeked through occasional bald spots in the dense canopy. Sunrise provided a welcome distraction, moving Sabot's consciousness ever so slightly away from his private misery. With the sun's orange glow came possibility, maybe even hope.

But with the sun also came rising temperature, which added vigor to Fredericks' already eye-watering stench. Sabot tried to further loosen his grip on his fat compatriot's torso, but the rough jungle trail required frequent and stomach-turning embraces to keep him from toppling ass over teakettle off the back of the dirt bike.

The rough trail mercifully gave way to a two-rut jeep trail, which itself eventually ended at a T intersection with a perpendicular-running dirt road. A sign made it clear that, should one be interested in reaching a place called Tegucigalpa, left was the way to go. Was that a town in Costa Rica? Sabot had no idea. And he still really had no idea where he was, due in no small part to the mindscrew Zelaya had laid on him over the past few days. Or months. He wondered yet again how long it had been since he and the girls had made their hasty exit from Seattle.

Fredericks followed the sign, turning left onto the dirt road. Sabot was tempted to question the decision, but restrained himself. Fredericks had only recently shut up, and Sabot had no desire to provide an excuse for more asinine blather shouted over the ragged sound of the motorcycle's overworked engine.

Plus, upon reflection, it probably made sense. It wasn't as if they had their choice between booming urban centers. The sign pointing toward Tegucigalpa was the only harbinger of civilization they'd yet encountered, and it made sense that if Zelaya and the other bastards had indeed attempted to sell Angie and Connie into the oldest profession, a city was the most likely place to find them.

A stabbing, clawing pain suddenly assaulted his innards. It was as if he'd swallowed something jagged, which was now working its way through his system.

Come to think of it, he *had* swallowed something jagged, something his body wasn't designed to process. Perhaps the heart-shaped USB drive he'd hurriedly slammed down his throat during his abduction at the airport was about to reenter his life in a meaningful way. Giving ass-birth to that damn thing promised to be an eye-watering experience. He sincerely hoped the digestion process had left unmolested the ones and zeroes living in the USB drive's innards. They now represented one of the most sizable fortunes on the planet.

The dirt road wasn't smooth by any stretch of the imagination, but it was a damn sight less atrocious than the jungle trail, and Sabot was able to hazard some separation between himself and his disgusting traveling companion. It reduced his misery a fraction.

Soon, dirt gave way to pavement, and jungle sounds slowly gave way to traffic noises. They stopped for gas at a dilapidated filling station on the edge of a town called El Chimbo. The cheap. *Hell of a name for a town,* Sabot thought.

He surveyed the ramshackle village as Fredericks went in to pay. Everything was dilapidated, falling apart, every block looking like a redneck's backyard. *Hell of a town.* He decided the name fit perfectly.

Fredericks returned, a brown bag in his hand and a jaunty bounce to his step. "Got us some libations to celebrate our escape."

"Because my head's not screwed up enough already," Sabot said, unsmiling.

Fredericks snorted. "Suit yourself, esé."

Something struck Sabot as odd. "Where'd you get the money to pay for the gas?"

"Stole it from Zelaya," Fredericks said.

Sabot frowned. He remembered Fredericks searching Zelaya's comatose form, but he didn't recall seeing the fat man take any cash.

And Sabot himself had searched Zelaya, moments after he'd fired several tranquilizer darts into the small, slight man's chest. Could he have missed the cash? More to the point, could he have missed finding the cash himself, *and* failed to notice Fredericks finding money on Zelaya? Those seemed like unlikely odds. His hackles rose, and he eyeballed Fredericks askance. Was there something going on here that he'd missed?

It was entirely possible. He wasn't exactly at the sharpest he'd ever been in his life. He had a golf ball-sized knot at the base of his skull, a throbbing headache, and a seriously shaky sense of reality. Upon reflection, quite a few things could have escaped his notice.

Still, the cash thing was strange.

And it was also strange that Fredericks had found the opening in the back of the janitor's closet leading to the earthen tunnel, and it was extremely weird that the fat man had discovered the smaller ventilation shaft, if that's what it was, that led them to the underground garage.

Fredericks was certainly more than he first appeared. But Sabot wasn't sure what that knowledge might imply.

"You coming?" Fredericks' voice interrupted Sabot's rumination.

Sabot shook his head as if to clear the cobwebs. Fredericks

started the motorcycle, and Sabot reluctantly climbed back on. "Where to?" he asked.

"Someplace with Wi-Fi," Fredericks said, gunning the engine and heading into town.

"Wi-Fi? What are you talking about?" Sabot asked over the motorcycle engine noise, incredulous. "We've got to find Angie and Connie. God knows what's happened to them. We don't have any time to waste."

Fredericks shook his head. "What makes you think you have the slightest idea how to find those two women?" he asked.

"I *don't* have any idea," Sabot said, his voice raised over the sound of the motorcycle. "But I know it doesn't involve Wi-Fi."

Fredericks laughed. "You're a smart beaner," he yelled over his shoulder. "You're right. Wi-Fi isn't going to find them."

"Then what the hell are we going to do with Wi-Fi?"

"Not *we*, vato," Fredericks said. "*You.*"

"Bullshit!" Sabot protested. "I'm going to find those girls!"

"We've already established that you don't have the first clue how to do that. But I do."

"Then I'm going with you," Sabot declared.

Fredericks shook his head again. "No, little buddy, you're not going with me."

"You're going to find them? By yourself?"

Fredericks nodded. He braked and leaned right, turning into a dirt parking lot. Casa Mejia, a sign declared, its bright, hopeful lettering long faded into tired resignation.

"No way, man," Sabot said. "I'm not waiting in this dump

while you blunder around looking for Angie and Connie."

Fredericks turned off the engine and dropped the kickstand. "Get off," he said.

Sabot didn't move. "Look, man, I really just need to find Angie and her mom before anything really messed up happens."

Fredericks swung his corpulent leg, shoving Sabot's slight frame off the back of the motorcycle. Sabot stumbled sideways for several steps before regaining his balance, cursing as he did so.

When he'd recovered, he saw Fredericks walking toward the motel's dilapidated office. "Fredericks!" Sabot yelled. He ran, grabbed the fat man's arm, and turned Fredericks around. "I have got to find those girls, dammit!"

"Lower your voice," Fredericks said, resuming his march to the office. "And relax. You do computers. This is what I do."

"You said you were in private security," Sabot said.

"That's mostly true."

"Mostly?"

Fredericks turned abruptly. "Yes, you little sonuvabitch, *mostly*. But I do other things too. Useful things. Like finding people who need to be found, for instance. And I sometimes find people who don't even *want* to be found." He turned again toward the office.

"What are you going to do when you find them?"

"Depends."

"On what?"

"On what I think is best." Fredericks pushed Sabot to a stop with a meaty palm in the smaller man's chest. "Wait here and watch the bike."

Sabot's protest went unheard as Fredericks disappeared into the motel office. The big man reemerged moments later with two keys in his hands. "This way," he said, pointing toward the end of the building furthest from the road.

Fredericks unlocked and searched the first room while Sabot waited outside. It was empty, and Fredericks searched the second room with the same result. "Now the hard part," he told Sabot, dangling a room key in front of his face. "You wait."

"And do what?" Sabot protested.

"I don't know. Maybe jerk off to lingerie ads. Whatever. But keep your skinny brown ass inside that room, don't make any noise, and don't open the door for anyone in the world but me. Got it?"

"Fuck you, Fredericks. I'm not sitting on my ass all day and—"

Fredericks cut him off with a wave of a hand. "You're right. You're not going to be sitting around all day. You're going to be very busy when I get back."

A quizzical look crossed Sabot's face.

"Quid pro quo, little man," Fredericks said. "I'm going to find those two women for you. But I'm going to need something from you in return. Now get inside that room."

There was a sudden hardness to Fredericks' face, a bare-knuckled competency mixed with a healthy dash of meanness, and the change in Fredericks' mien caught Sabot off guard. It was the second time that Fredericks had morphed right in front of his eyes.

Sabot shut up and did as he was told.

* * *

Two hours later, Sabot sat restless and awash in the stench of
mildew and stale cigarettes, the gloom of his dirty room in the Casa
Mejia motel in greater downtown El Chimbo doing little to calm his
angst or lift his depression. The carpet was nothing short of vile, and
the curtains looked like they had seen better decades.

But there was a hot shower, of which Sabot had availed
himself. It felt good to be clean, to wash away the residual stench of
Fredericks' sweaty disgustingness that lingered from their lengthy
motorcycle ride out of the jungle.

And there was Wi-Fi, which was evidently important to
Fredericks for an as yet unannounced reason.

He glanced at the hotel's guest folder. The tattered cover bore
coffee and food stains. Bienvenue á Casa Mejia, it said. El Chimbo,
Honduras.

Honduras.

Which was a different place entirely than Costa Rica,
important because Sabot had chartered a flight from Canada to Costa
Rica, and definitely *not* from Canada to Honduras.

Honduras.

Fredericks had shared that flight. Did Fredericks think they
were in Costa Rica? Or did he know they were in Honduras?

A chill came over him. Zelaya, that sadistic little bastard
who'd wreaked so much havoc on Sabot's mind and body since he'd
awakened in that dungeon in the jungle, had mentioned something
about Honduras. He also vaguely recalled Zelaya saying something
about crimes against the Honduran government that Sabot had

supposedly committed.

Sabot felt panic rising, the feeling that he really had no idea what was real and what was a figment of his imagination. Or maybe he felt panic because there was the possibility that it was *all* real. His betrayal with that beautiful guard, Marisela, and Angie's heartbroken reaction when she learned of it... the woman in the bed with him in that fake hotel room, the one who'd had all of Angie's clothes, and who he'd briefly slipped inside, but who definitely wasn't Angie... Had all of that really happened? Was it as real as the fact that he was in Honduras, and not Costa Rica?

My mind is messed up in a big way, he thought to himself. He needed some air, and to hell with Fredericks' admonishment to remain hidden inside the room. He arose and walked to the door, his legs feeling distant and shaky.

He put his hand on the lock and twisted, but a thought stopped him from opening the door. What if Zelaya was telling the truth? What if Sabot *was* guilty of some crime? What if the Honduran government *was* interested in prosecuting him?

He sat back down, heart suddenly pounding, his breath shallow and unsteady. *Get it together, esé.* He had to get this situation figured out, pronto. How would he possibly get Angie and Connie home if he was a wanted man himself? Assuming he could find them in the first place, and then rescue them from whatever fate they were currently suffering.

What fate *were* they suffering? He began imagining atrocities, indignities, violations, Angie and Connie in horrific situations, at the mercy of truly evil men, and the thoughts filled him with overwhelming worry. Rage and guilt also swirled, and his eyes teared up with un-channeled, unproductive emotion. Fredericks was right about one thing: waiting was awful.

Sabot turned on the television. It was tuned to a local news station. Sunday, it said.

When had they left Seattle? Was it Thursday? Friday? Just a few days ago? How could that be possible? It seemed a lifetime away. So much had happened — the endless hours chained to a wall, the days — was it days? — spent in a fake hotel room, all of the interrogations with Zelaya, the doctor's visit, Marisela, the unlikely escape from the prison in the jungle. Could that have all taken place in just a few days?

Or had he been imprisoned for a week? Two? It seemed far more likely than just a couple of days. Try as he might, he couldn't remember the date when he, Angie, and Connie had packed up their car and left Connie's place in the Seattle suburbs. Regardless of what the calendar said, it was ages ago.

His own mind felt alien to him, like a foreign entity that he needed to understand, but couldn't figure out. He didn't trust his recent memories. But he desperately needed them, because he desperately needed to understand his situation.

Someone pounded on the door to his motel room.

Adrenaline surged. Sabot crept to the peephole.

It was Fredericks. Sabot opened the door.

"You look like shit," Fredericks announced without preamble, plastic bags in his hand. "Eat something," he said, handing one of the bags to Sabot. "Sorry, but this is what passes for a burrito in this shithole," Fredericks said.

Sabot examined the food wrapper. *Baleadas,* it said. Inside, he found a flour tortilla with an insufficient supply of refried beans, a hard white cheese of some sort, and scrambled egg. He devoured it hungrily.

In spite of himself, he was glad for Fredericks' company, distasteful as it was. Sabot knew that he was starting to go a little bat-shit crazy, sitting in that room by himself.

"Ready to earn your keep?" Fredericks asked when Sabot had finished his food.

The question was evidently rhetorical, as Fredericks produced a laptop computer from another plastic bag and handed it to Sabot. The laptop was a bit beat up, but looked to be in decent working condition. "Where'd you get this?" Sabot asked.

"Don't worry about it. I get things," Fredericks said, shoving a piece of paper in Sabot's direction.

"What's this?"

"Your homework," Fredericks said, rising.

Sabot opened the folded paper. On it were written four lengthy strings of letters and numbers, with colons interspersed. Sabot recognized the strings as IP addresses. They were the virtual addresses of four computerized devices of some sort. "What do you want me to do with these?"

"Do what comes natural." Fredericks opened the door and walked out.

"Wait!" Sabot shouted, before Fredericks could shut the door. "What about the girls?" Sabot asked.

Fredericks turned, fished around in his pocket, and produced a photo.

Sabot leapt to his feet and charged at Fredericks, ripping the photo from his hand. His eyes filled with tears as he studied its details.

Angie was dressed in a negligee. Her eyes were glassy, vacant. She reclined provocatively on a red velvet couch. Drug paraphernalia littered the glass table in front of the couch. Drunk, leering men flanked her on both sides. One of them had his hand on Angie's thigh. Up high, on the *inside* of her thigh.

Sabot's body shook. Tears streaked his cheeks, his jaw clenched until it hurt, and rage threatened to erupt. Then he felt Fredericks' thick hand squeeze his shoulder, hard, and he looked up to find Fredericks looking intently at him. "You need to trust me," Fredericks said, swiping Sabot's room key from atop the desk where it sat and shoving it into his pocket. "I promise you. I will take care of this. Now get to work."

And then Sabot was alone inside the disgusting hotel room, opening the laptop with shaking fingers, finding the Wi-Fi network, opening a search window, doing what came naturally.

Chapter 8

"You have a cousin in Baltimore?" Brock asked Sam.

"Is that so strange?"

"It's forty minutes from our house. Why didn't you ever introduce us?"

"Because she's hot and promiscuous and has no respect," Sam said, "and I didn't want to worry about her throwing the kitty at you."

Brock laughed. "Seriously?"

"Seriously." Sam didn't laugh.

"She's hot, you say?" Brock asked. "Maybe we'd all get along."

Sam elbowed him a bit too hard in the ribs. "Maybe you'll wait in the car." They'd commandeered a luxury sedan from the valet at an upscale condo complex near Crystal City. The board full of keys was left completely unattended, and the valet was nowhere in sight, so Sam wrote Mason McClane's name on a yellow sticky, along with a 1-800 number that rang deep in the bowels of the Homeland building, and pasted the note on the vacant spot on the keyboard where the Mercedes' keys were hung.

It had taken them the better part of an hour to get out of DC, but the decidedly run-down section of highway corresponding to Maryland's sub-par stewardship was pleasantly untrafficked, and they made good time to the appropriate Baltimore exit.

"Her name is really Sheena?"

"Yes," Sam said, parking in front of an apartment complex that didn't look entirely safe. "And I wasn't kidding. You're really staying in the car. I don't want her batting her eyes at you. Or humping your leg."

Brock chuckled. Sam ran inside the apartment.

She returned moments later with a passport and driver's license in her hands. Sheena's, evidently. Brock snatched the passport and flipped it open to view the picture. The woman looked quite a bit like Sam, though with a more vacant look in her eyes and a few more crow's feet.

"I'd do her," he announced, then braced for another elbow.

* * *

The Baltimore-Washington International Airport wasn't crowded. It barely looked open for business.

The familial resemblance was strong enough that Sam passed herself off as Sheena Wade without a second glance from either the ticket clerk or the more-bored-than-usual TSA guy.

Sam paid for the tickets in silver. It was illegal to use anything other than dollars for business transactions in America, but that law was passed with the kind of hubris that never foresaw the dollar's disintegration, and people had adapted in the few days since the economic meltdown.

Sam's nerves were on edge after the earlier encounters at Reagan International and at Wu's dry cleaning. Everyone in the airport looked suspicious and conspiratorial, she thought, but she and Brock boarded their first flight — nonstop to Atlanta — without further incident.

They detoured to the second concourse in Atlanta to enjoy a real meal of southern fried chicken, made on location right there in the concourse, a throwback arrangement that flew in the face of the trend toward the shrink-wrapped pseudo-food that most other airport restaurants served. The meal was deeply satisfying, and the Atlanta airport was much more crowded, which gave it a much less sinister vibe than BWI.

Sam pulled her phone from her bag. Alfonse Archer had left a message. So had her deputy, Dan Gable. She called Archer first.

"Big A," Sam said when the FBI agent answered. "Talk to me."

Archer gave her an update. Henry Feng, the ringleader of the muscle squad that she'd upended in the DC airport, apparently had ties to the Triad. "The Chinese gang?" Sam asked.

"Yep."

"Was he moonlighting? I mean, I've had nothing to do with any counter-gang ops at Homeland. How do they know about me?"

"A solid question," Archer said. "Moonlighting, maybe, or possibly something else. Like maybe the guy who's got a hard-on for you rolls deep enough to buy services from a few different sets of people."

"A few different *sets*?"

"Yeah," Archer said. "Because the shopkeeper was Korean. It'd be less weird for my black ass to marry a white supremacist's daughter than for a Korean to be eyeballs deep in a Triad deal."

Sam chuckled.

"And," Archer went on, "two of the four names you gave to me are known gang-bangers."

"Street gangs? Like, black gangs in DC?"

"Yep."

Sam pondered. Three ethnic underworlds, all doing business happily together through one shill company? "Is this some kind of a joke? Those people hate each other."

"It's a new thing the street crimes guys have been talking about. It's like a little market economy. Some groups are better at some stuff than others, so they buy services from each other."

Sam shook her head. "Unbelievable."

"It gets better," Archer said. "The other two names on the list you gave me are into some seriously weird stuff. I'm still confused as hell, and I have more digging to do, but get this: one guy's home address is one that I'm familiar with."

"How so?"

"It's an FBI safe house."

Sam whistled. "That freaks me out a little bit."

"Tell me about it. And as it turns out, I spent some time in that same safe house last weekend, babysitting that Senator people kept trying to kill."

"Small world," Sam said with a mirthless chuckle. She had a sinking feeling. Was the strange FBI safe house connection related somehow to the apparent information breach at Homeland? She shuddered at the thought. A trust problem at her own behemoth of a federal agency was bad enough. Another one at the Bureau might prove insurmountable. Together, those two agencies had enough reach to ruin just about anyone's life.

"I'll keep digging and let you know what I find," Archer said.

Sam thanked him and hung up.

Shit. She had a sickening realization. Her lengthy conversation with Archer had been on her work cell. If the leak at Homeland was electronic, she might have just placed herself — and Archer — in substantial risk. She cursed, shaking her head. She was tired and strung out, and through her inattention and carelessness, she'd just committed a cardinal sin.

She grabbed a pencil and paper from her bag and jotted down several phone numbers from her cell phone directory. When she had finished, she shoved the paper into her pocket, grabbed Brock's hand, and walked quickly to a mobile electronics store. She paid silver for a new laptop and two pre-paid cell phones, "burners" as they were called by spies and cheating spouses.

They found a Wi-Fi hot spot, and Sam logged onto a very retro-looking message board with the humorous moniker "Screw Big Brother." Her username was Curvy Red Bizzo.

She opened one of the burners, turned it on, and found its phone number. Using the letter F as the starting point, she used a standard alphabetic offset codex to encode the burner number. She typed the encoded phone number into the message board, and the message became part of the ongoing conversation about spooks, conspiracies, and true lies.

Then she used her work cell phone to dial Dan Gable. "Go to the SBB site," she told him, "and contact me using our standard precautions."

She heard Dan's gears turning through the silence on the other end of the phone. "Not this shit again," he finally said.

"Afraid so," Sam said. "And hurry — Brock and I are about to board."

Sam hung up. She led Brock to the line at a coffee shop. As they made small talk, Sam surreptitiously dropped her work cell into the handbag of the customer in front of her in line, a large black lady. If the assholes were indeed tracking her cell phone, it was best to disassociate herself from it. She was briefly worried about the safety of the person to whom she'd just given her phone, but decided that given the large differences in bodyweight and skin color, there was little probability of mistaken identity.

They did their best to relax as they sipped their lattes and waited for Dan to decipher her burner number.

It took just shy of fifteen minutes. She answered her burner on the second ring. "Talk to me," she said.

"After you tell me why all the cloak and dagger," Dan replied.

She told him about the incidents at Reagan and the dry cleaning shop. "You're trouble, you know that?" Dan said after she'd finished.

"So I'm told. Anyway, what have you learned up north?"

Dan had located the source of the telephone call that had been routed through the hidden modem in Jeffrey Santos' DC apartment and answered by the dead spy whose cell phone Sam had liberated in the Costa Rican warehouse. "That number rings at the concierge desk of an extremely upscale condo building in Banff," Dan said.

"Hmm. So was the concierge just doing his job, or earning a

little on the side?"

"I can easily envision a rich guy handing a slip of paper to the concierge and asking him to make a phone call. But I could also easily envision a crooked concierge, so I looked at the phone record again. It was a long call, so they were definitely having a conversation."

"With one party standing at the concierge desk," Sam said, finishing Dan's thought.

"Right. That's the angle I played when I talked to the concierge on duty. But he pointed out that a dozen residents use that phone every day, to order everything from pizza to prostitutes."

"Yeah, I imagine," Sam said.

"But I took a chance and mentioned the name Slobodan Radosz. Maybe it was just indigestion, but the guy definitely got a weird look on his face. So I'm going to do some digging into his background while I'm waiting for his shift to end, and then I'm going to have another conversation with him."

"Sounds good," Sam said. "Listen, Brock and I have to catch our flight to Rome. Let's use the FBB bulletin board to initiate contact. Don't use a burner more than once, and for God's sake, don't call back to Homeland."

Dan agreed. "I was just thinking as you were talking," he added. "We're looking for people with enough computer savvy to steal zillions in electronic currency. Maybe they don't actually have anyone on the inside at Homeland. Maybe they've just found a back door into the computer network."

Sam nodded. "I thought of that. Either way, it's the same result for us. We have to behave as if everything is compromised."

"What about McClane? He told us to keep him in the loop."

"I've got it," Sam said.

"I'm sure you do," Dan said with a knowing smile in his voice. "I don't know how you haven't been fired yet."

"Because of my tits," Sam said. "I'm demographically useful."

Dan laughed, they said their goodbyes, and Sam and Brock took a seat in the waiting area for their flight. It was scheduled to last nine hours, and traverse fifty-six hundred miles of the earth's surface. Sam hoped it also afforded them a little bit of rest. She had the feeling that they would need it.

She and Brock glanced up at the television at the same time. "Monopoly Man is back," Brock said.

The cartoon character, lifted from the cover of the world's most popular board game, danced in an affected style, rolling his top hat across his shoulders and clicking his heels together. Sam had first seen the cartoon character several days earlier on the television in General Mike Hajek's office, when she first began her investigation into the banking collapse, and she'd seen several new videos since that first one. She had subsequently discovered that Archive's team had put the videos together to calm the human herd, and had found a way to hijack air time to broadcast the videos on just about every satellite and terrestrial station.

"You're being naughty again," the cartoon character said, pointing a gloved index finger at the camera. "Hurting each other and breaking things. Tsk tsk." He waved his finger in the air. "You must know that you only win this fight by not fighting. Not fighting at all." The cartoon character placed his hands on his hips. "They may have guns, but have you forgotten who has the power?" The last word repeated in a dramatic echo. "You!" Monopoly Man pointed at the camera again. "*You* have the power! So start acting like it. Be calm. Trade with each other. Make new agreements. Smile." He spread his arms wide. "Does that sound so hard?"

The character danced around again, twirling his hat on his finger. "Be good, my friends. Make it a nice day!" And then he was gone.

Brock chuckled. "I'm not much for propaganda of any flavor, but the cartoon guy makes a solid point."

"Oh, shit," Sam said. "I just had a troubling thought." She pulled her burner from her pocket and dialed.

Chapter 9

Trojan and Vaneesh clicked away at adjacent terminals in the dark computer room in the basement bunker at the Lost Man Lake Ranch. Except to use the restroom and load up on coffee, neither had moved in what felt like eons. Their eyes were red and bleary, but they wore looks of deep concentration. Neither had spoken in over half an hour.

Trojan's cell phone rang. Sam Jameson. "You sound awful," she said. "You haven't slept in a while, have you?"

"Occupational hazard," Trojan said.

"You wouldn't happen to have access to a burner phone, would you?"

Trojan laughed. "Who do you think you're talking to? Of course I have a burner. I'll call you back."

He did so. When Sam picked up, Trojan put her on speaker, and the two computer ninjas filled her in on their progress to date. Vaneesh spoke of his plan to make it appear as though the thieves' algorithms were still functioning properly, and to merely re-appropriate the funds into friendly accounts.

"Prepare for some serious federal oversight," Sam said. "I can't imagine we'll let you out of our sight after you gain control of that much stolen money."

"Understood," Vaneesh said. "It's not a done deal yet, anyway."

"How long?" Sam wanted to know.

"I can't really give you an estimate. The old hacker saying is that the code doesn't work until it starts working, and it's impossible to predict that breakthrough moment. Could be hours or days."

"How about the virus delivery?"

Trojan piped up. "Slow going. NSA is pretty damn good. But I've found a few weaknesses that might be exploitable, and I have a few trial versions floating around, probing NSA's system."

"How are you doing that, if Vaneesh isn't done with his part yet?" Sam asked. "The virus isn't complete, is it?"

"You're right," Trojan said. "It's not. But the virus will instruct the host computer to run the file transfer protocol in the background to download a script at a particular IP address. When Vaneesh is done with his algorithm, he'll upload the script to the specified IP address, and we'll be in business. The virus will just download the executable code onto the host computers, and they'll start stealing the Bitcoin back."

"Very clever. You have a bright future," Sam said. "Listen, I have a hunch that things might have become a little more urgent. Is the old man around?"

* * *

Archive took the phone from Trojan's hand and pulled his eyes away from the carnage on the television screens in front of him. "I need some good news, Special Agent Jameson," he said into the phone.

"I'm afraid I don't have any," Sam said. She explained the events that led her to believe there was an information breach at

Homeland. "The snatch squad was on us at Reagan incredibly quickly. They had to have mobilized within an hour of our flight reservations."

"That's disconcerting," Archive, "but please forgive me. I don't see the connection to our operation here in Colorado."

"Trojan took a Homeland transport flight from DC to Aspen."

Archive felt the color drain from his face.

"Also," Sam went on, "we have to assume that they'll be smart enough to trace the origin of the virus that Trojan and Vaneesh are getting ready to release. When you steal the money back, my hunch is that you'll find yourself in the middle of a serious shit storm."

Archive mulled. He mentally inventoried the provisions at the ranch. Though it ran counter to his politics and sensibilities, he'd reluctantly agreed that an armory was a necessary evil. He now wondered whether it was sufficiently provisioned to hold off a coordinated attack of any size.

He also thought of the two dozen people holed up at the ranch house. Very few had any military experience, and none were seasoned combat troops. Most had never even fired a gun before.

"Can you send reinforcements?" he asked.

"I'd send them if I had them," Sam said. "And given the strong probability of a security breach at DHS, it would be a bad move for me to request anything through the home office. Brock and I are going to be out of the country for a while, so we won't be much help to you, either. I'm afraid you're on your own for physical security at your enclave."

Archive bristled a bit at Sam's terminology — in his mind,

'enclave' connoted a cult hideout or polygamist colony — but he got her message loud and clear. "We'll do what we can. How can I get in touch with you if I need to?"

"I'm getting rid of this phone as soon as we're done here. I'm afraid you're going to have to wait for me to get in touch with you via Trojan's burner."

"I understand," Archive said. "Thank you for the warning, and please travel safely."

He ended the call, then immediately picked up his land line. He speed-dialed the NORTHCOM commander. General Williamson picked up on the fourth ring. "I don't have much time," the tired-sounding general said in lieu of hello.

"I understand. I'll get to the point. The ranch is about to become the next Fort Knox, and I'm going to need some help defending it. There's been a security breach of some sort at Homeland, and our position might already be compromised."

It took the sleep-deprived four-star a moment to process what Archive said. "Fort Knox?" he asked.

Archive explained their plan to stop the ongoing theft of digital currency, and explained that his computer experts were about to have an enormous sum of Bitcoin under their control. Williamson understood Archive's security concern immediately. "It's clearly a significant national security issue," Williamson said. "I don't have anyone to spare, but I'll find a way to reinforce your ranch. My forces will have to take it out of hide somehow."

"I'd be grateful," Archive said. "And you know I'd never ask anything like that for personal reasons."

"It goes without saying," Williamson said. "By the way, thank you for your Monopoly Man video. Every little bit helps."

"I hope it has some impact. Are you seeing progress?"

"Anything but," Williamson said, his voice weary. "I'm aware of twenty thousand casualties in Los Angeles alone, with proportionate numbers in other urban areas. And I've had nearly a dozen of my embedded special operators summarily executed by the militia groups they infiltrated."

"But they were helping!"

"But thanks to the impostors wearing US uniforms, people are having a hard time trusting anyone associated with the US government, particularly anyone in the military. I've pulled my forces back to play defense, mostly around landmarks and big federal targets. I just can't afford to have flare-ups. The people have figured out that we lack the force size to keep things under control on every city block. And I refuse to resort to using firepower. I've told the President that no matter how bad things get, there is no way in hell that I will ever mow down my fellow citizens, or order anyone else to do so."

Archive was momentarily at a loss. He was sickened by the violent turn things had taken. *We were so close to a bloodless devolution,* he thought. But things had gone to hell, and more rapidly than he'd ever imagined possible. "How did the President react?"

"He's not as hawkish as his TV appearances have made him sound. My impression is that he's even more squeamish about the use of force against American citizens than I am."

"Any idea who the agitators were? I'd love to get my hands on them."

"You're not the only one. It's really disconcerting. None of them were American soldiers, and most of them weren't even Americans."

Archive whistled. Had a foreign government or organization created unrest in the US? "Who's behind it?"

"Most of the ones we've identified have been from Russia or from satellite states of the former Soviet Union. If I didn't know better, I'd be tempted to blame it on the KGB."

What an unbelievable mess, Archive thought, his mood at its darkest since the unrest began.

"I have to go," Williamson said. "You'll be hearing from me or someone on my staff regarding reinforcements at your ranch." With that, he signed off, and Archive was left alone with his worries, the television screens in front of him playing loop after loop of violent clashes in the streets of iconic American cities.

Chapter 10

Sabot sat alone in the shitty motel room, his head throbbing, his nostrils inured by now to the permanent stench of mildew and cigarette smoke, his torso hunched over the aged laptop that Fredericks had somehow procured in the dilapidated Honduran town. He was grateful to have something to occupy his mind, other than his worry over Angie.

The picture haunted him: his Angie sat tarted up and stoned, with dim-witted mooks pawing her. His rage was murderous.

But he forced himself to focus. Fredericks had somehow found her in less than a morning's work, which was a damn sight better than Sabot could have done for himself. It was against his nature and his hacker ethos to place much trust in other people, and something about Fredericks sat very wrong with Sabot, but Fredericks had won his confidence. At least as far as the fat man's tactical prowess was concerned. About everything else regarding Fredericks, Sabot had his doubts.

It was still excruciatingly difficult for Sabot not to be directly involved in the search for Angie and her mom. But Sabot recognized the signs of a pro at work, and contented himself to stay out of Fredericks' way. For the moment, anyway.

His mind returned to the computer as his login credentials were accepted by the high-end anonymizing service he'd retained for his earlier work on the Bitcoin theft operation. Any affiliation was a risk, of course, so he'd used a false identity, complete with its own PayPal account, to provide a layer of protection. It was a thin layer, as the Internet and the millions of computers that comprised it were a forensic investigator's wet dream, and Sabot knew he was on borrowed time.

He typed in the first IP address from the list that Fredericks had given him. An extremely fast computer lived at this address, Sabot realized at once. It was hidden behind a firewall, but that couldn't disguise the blazing speed with which it was sending and receiving messages. And while it was upscale, expensive, and customized, the firewall itself offered Sabot little challenge. He breached it within minutes, and began rooting around the computer's root directory.

Sabot saw many standard applications running on the computer he'd just raided. Some he recognized right away. Others had filenames that looked vaguely familiar; he opened them to discover that they were, indeed, mundane housekeeping programs that ran in the background on most personal computers and mainframes.

But a couple of the applications stood out. Their filenames were strings of letters and numbers that didn't make much sense to Sabot, so he opened them in a text editor to view their source code.

His blood ran cold. It was a Bitcoin operation of some sort.

Jesus, is this a coincidence? Was Fredericks familiar with crypto currency, too? Where had he gotten the IP addresses?

Sabot looked closely at the code. It was very elegantly written. Russian? They were the most fastidious coders he'd ever encountered, and the precision of the routine in front of him seemed to have a characteristically Russian flavor.

The code used two kinds of inputs: the name of a Bitcoin wallet, which it retrieved from an IP address, and the password associated with that wallet, which it retrieved from a separate IP address.

With those two inputs, the program seemed to be running a single loop over and over again. First, it created one or two new Bitcoin wallets, using a random string of up to thirty characters as passkeys. Then, it transferred all of the Bitcoins out of the "old" wallet and into the "new" ones it had just created. Finally, it sent the name of the new accounts to one IP address, and the corresponding passkey to a separate IP address. Sabot checked these addresses against the list Fredericks had handed him. They both matched.

The script ran through its loop several hundred times every second.

It took Sabot a while to understand what was really happening. The script was apparently designed to keep money in constant movement. *But what good is money if all you do is move it around all the time?*

The computer script also kept a running archive of the wallets it created, and passed it along to two other computers on Fredericks' list. The reason was fairly obvious: misplacing a Bitcoin wallet's name or passkey was exactly the same as misplacing a wallet full of cash. If you couldn't find it, there was no backup. It was gone.

It was this second aspect of the computer script, the continuous archiving of the randomly generated accounts and passwords, that finally led Sabot to understand what was happening. Whoever was running this computer script was trying to keep their money safe by keeping it in constant motion, to prevent someone from stealing it.

But there was another possibility as well. *What if they're trying to hide the money?* Every Bitcoin transaction was a public event — in fact, there were websites dedicated to nothing but listing all of the thousands of Bitcoin transactions occurring every hour of every day — and it was alarmingly easy to figure out exactly how much money was in each and every Bitcoin wallet in the world. Unlike cash, Bitcoin transactions were infinitely traceable. But if someone's money spent only a few seconds inside any given wallet before it was shuffled off to another account, there was effectively no way to figure out where it sat at any given moment.

Unless, of course, you could read the script directly, just as Sabot had done moments before. Then, it would be an extremely simple matter to liberate every last fraction of every last Bitcoin. You'd simply insert a line of code that sent the money into your own account, and send fake account information to the two recipient addresses specified in the original code.

In fact, Sabot felt an exceptionally strong temptation to do just that. It would be like swiping candy from a kid. He wondered how much money might be in play, how many Bitcoins these algorithms were throwing around every second.

He spent the next half hour investigating the computers behind the rest of the IP addresses Fredericks had given him. He also called up the public transaction record to see how much money was moving around with each of the transactions created by the code he'd just examined, and he used a spreadsheet to estimate the totals.

The numbers were staggering. This operation dwarfed what he'd stolen. And he'd stolen a truckload of money. He sensed opportunity on a scale he'd never encountered.

Oh, shit. A disconcerting realization hit him. *Why didn't I think of this before?* All of the Bitcoin he'd stolen was instantly traceable to static accounts. Sure, his theft operation had created a ton of new accounts, and he'd only swiped a small amount of Bitcoin from each victim. But the money was just sitting there for all the world to see. Every person he'd stolen from could very easily use the public ledger to find the wallet containing the money that Sabot had taken from them.

He made a copy of the perpetual account motion program and saved it to the tired laptop's hard drive. He saved another copy on the server he rented, located in New Jersey. As soon as humanly feasible, he needed to get the laundering algorithm working to preserve the fortune he'd stolen over the past few days.

Sabot was suddenly very eager for his alimentary canal to pass that infernal USB drive. It contained the key to ungodly riches, which might, even at this moment, be under attack by angry victims.

Or by someone else, someone with sufficient resources and vision. Like, perhaps, the people who had created the computer script he'd just examined.

He got a sinking feeling in his gut. *Where did they get all this Bitcoin?*

And who the hell were they?

Because to Sabot's knowledge, the only Bitcoin theft operation in existence with the scope to produce numbers that staggering, was the theft operation he'd created.

Balzzack011. That was the moniker of the person who'd directed Sabot to set things up. But Sabot had never even spoken with him. Or her. Sabot had no idea who Balzzack011 really was. But he suddenly felt confident that the IP addresses Fredericks had asked him to investigate either belonged to Balzzack011, or belonged to Balzzack's employers.

So how the hell did Fredericks get his hands on those IP addresses? Did he rip off a private security customer? Or was Fredericks more directly involved? Had Fredericks stolen from Balzzack himself? Or Balzzack's employer?

An even more disturbing possibility occurred to Sabot. Were Fredericks and Balzzack the same person? *Holy shit, that would be the mindscrew of the century.*

He rose and paced the room, recounting the unaccountably weird incidents that had rocked his world, searching for some piece, some clue, that allowed him to wrap a unifying theory around all of the seriously messed up happenings.

He'd chartered a flight from Canada to Costa Rica, but somehow ended up in Honduras.

Fredericks, that fat, smelly bastard with the ridiculous comb-over, begged a ride on the charter flight, spent time in the same dungeon in the jungle, pulled three rabbits out of his hat to help them escape, and then handed Sabot a list of IP addresses that could very well be linked to the Bitcoin operation that he, Sabot, had set up in the first place. *That's hardly screwed up at all,* Sabot thought sarcastically, shaking his head.

And then there was Zelaya, the slight, graying man with eyes like iron who had claimed to be Sabot's torturer, then a court administrator, and finally a doctor. What was that all about?

And then there was that *other* doctor, the one who had visited Sabot while he was still chained beneath the freezing shower. Sabot recalled the guy in a doctor's lab coat with booze on his breath and the strange-tasting tongue depressor...

The tongue depressor.

Sabot slapped his pockets, searching for the drugs he'd stolen from Zelaya's medicine cart moments after shooting the little bastard with the tranquilizer gun. The drugs were nowhere to be found, of course. He'd obviously lost them at some point, possibly during their search of the dungeon, or during their long crawl through the earthen tunnel, or as he and Fredericks had bounced along the jungle trail on the rickety motorcycle.

What did the label say? Metha-something? *Para*-metha-something? With the suffix "-B". He was sure of the suffix.

He ran to the laptop and typed "Paramethalin-B" into the internet search engine.

"Did you mean *paramescaline-B?*" responded the most intelligent organism on earth.

That's it. Paramescaline-B. Sabot clicked on the Wikipedia article that topped the search engine results. A caution informed Sabot that more citations were required, and that the article contained unsubstantiated information, blah blah. Sabot read it anyway.

His jaw dropped. Paramescaline-B was apparently a derivative of mescaline, a psychedelic drug. The article claimed that Paramescaline-B had been synthesized in a long-running CIA experiment that was never acknowledged by the US government.

The secret drug induced dramatic temporal distortion and exceptionally vivid hallucinations, but it did not cause the tripped-out feeling that other psychedelics caused, and there was no synesthesia, which was the phenomenon that made users of psychedelic drugs see sounds and taste colors. Paramescaline-B's milder peripheral symptoms made it very difficult for test subjects to know whether they'd received the drug or a placebo.

The drug was exceptionally useful in interrogations, the article claimed, because interrogation subjects had trouble differentiating between real and imagined events. The CIA denied all allegations of psychedelic experiments, including paramescaline-B, the article said.

The drug's side effects included a nearly debilitating headache as it cleared the subject's system.

Sabot's head pounded like a drum with each heartbeat. "My God," he said aloud. "What have they done to me?"

The door swung open, and light suddenly filled the musty room. A fat figure stood silhouetted. "Hi, esé," Fredericks said.

Chapter 11

Sam splashed water on her face and rubbed the sleep from her eyes. The flight had been an exceptionally welcome relief. Brock's gimpy leg had earned them an upgrade to first class. She and Brock had enjoyed a toe-curling carnal encounter in the first-class lavatory, and then they'd slept like the dead for the remainder of the flight. It felt like she'd been living one exceptionally long day for the past two weeks, and the seven hours of sleep she managed to steal during the flight was a lifesaver.

She exited the ladies' room in Rome's Leonardo DaVinci International airport and found Brock waiting for her. He was moving much better now, the pain from the gunshot wound in his thigh finally letting up somewhat. "Where to?" Brock asked. "Colosseum? The Forum? Pantheon?"

Sam smiled. "Maybe next time." She bought a new burner and dialed Alfonse Archer's number.

"Can you call me back on a fresh burner?" she asked as soon as he answered.

"Why?"

"Telling you right now would defeat the purpose, wouldn't it?"

"Right. Sorry."

Ten minutes later, Archer called back using a disposable cell phone. Sam filled him in on her suspicions regarding the leak at

Homeland.

"Not this again," he said.

"You're not the first person to have that reaction," Sam said with a chuckle. "Anyway, I just wanted to see if you'd uncovered anything else from our list of laundromat names."

"Actually, I do have some news," Archer said. "The guy on your list from the laundromat? He's ex-KGB."

"The guy who listed his address as the FBI safe house?"

"Right. He's an old school Cold Warrior, evidently. He knew of the Bureau safe house because he switched teams at some point in the Eighties."

"A KGB defector?" Sam asked, incredulous. "Selling thug services through a Chinese laundromat?"

"Times must be tough," Archer said.

"Guess so," Sam said. That was one hell of a curveball. It had been a while since anyone had mentioned the KGB. The wall had fallen, what, twenty-five years ago? After that, the KGB had officially ceased to exist, but in reality, it just got a new set of initials: FSB. Same goons, different letterhead.

"I don't really know what to make of the KGB angle," she said, after mulling things over for a short while.

"Me neither, but I would be damn careful if I were you. They're still bad hombres. There were crazy stories of those dudes having their fingernails and teeth pulled out during training, just to toughen them up."

Sam shuddered. "Thanks, we'll keep an eye out," she said. "Listen, would you mind running a Zip Line query on a number I've got?"

Archer was silent for a moment on the other end of the line. "Sam, this is an open line," he finally said.

Sam nodded. "I was afraid you were going to say something like that." Zip Line was an unacknowledged program. It was used to eavesdrop on folks, including US citizens. There was often a warrant involved, but often not, which Sam guessed was a big reason for the secrecy. Domestic espionage tended to piss people off. "We're sightseers until we get a lead of some sort. So I'm going to text you a phone number, and if you happen to text any information back to me, that will be between us and the fates."

"Uh…" Sam could hear the indecision in Archer's voice. He was a straight-laced Bureau guy, and Sam's request wasn't exactly by-the-book. Or, according to some interpretations, legal.

"If it's any help," Sam said, "my supervisor at Homeland did the honors for us last time. I'm just not confident there's a way to contact him without our conversation being broadcast to the other team."

Archer considered for a moment longer. "All right, Sam. Then you have to promise me you're going to burn the burner afterwards."

"Please," Sam said. "What am I, a rookie?"

Archer snorted. "If memory serves, you're the same girl who spilled her guts using her work cell phone, last time we talked."

"Touché," Sam said. She hung up, dug from her pocket the slip of paper containing the phone numbers relevant to the case, and typed in the cell number that they'd earlier traced to Rome. She sent the number as a text message to Archer's burner.

Then they busied themselves looking at tourist trinkets in the airport. There weren't many American tourists buzzing around the globe since the dollar shat itself, but acting like tourists would give them a chance to spot a tail before they left the airport.

She felt her burner vibrate with an incoming text message from Big A. *Hotel Bellariva, Pescara, Italy.*

We're in the right country, at least, Sam thought. She replied with a query: "How latent?" Meaning, how recently had the cell phone been active and tracked by the satellite?

Archer's reply came quickly: *3 hrs.* Sam was elated to be chasing a live lead.

She thanked Big A for his help, removed the SIM card from the burner, and flushed it down the toilet in a nearby women's room. Then she wiped the handset clean of her fingerprints and dropped it in a sanitary napkin receptacle in the stall.

Now, where the hell is Pescara?

She rejoined Brock on the concourse, and they walked slowly, searching for a map of some sort. Their first notion was that Pescara might be the name of a district in Rome, but finding nothing resembling a map, they stepped into a trinket shop and asked the shopkeeper.

"Pescara is a quaint fishing village and tourist destination on the Adriatic coast," the shopkeeper replied in practiced English.

"Which coast?" Sam asked, her geographic ignorance not feigned.

"East. East coast. Adriatic Sea." The shopkeeper produced a map and pointed. Pescara was on the far side of the boot.

"How long to drive?" Sam asked.

The shopkeeper laughed. "Maybe a week, maybe two. Depends on your thirst. We serve vino in big pitchers here in Italia."

"What if we're in a hurry?" Brock asked.

"Then you should relax," the shopkeeper advised. "You're on vacation, no?"

"Right. But just the same," Sam said, "what's the quickest way to get there?"

The shopkeeper put on a disdainful look and shook her head. "Then fly. Three hundred Euro." She pointed across the concourse to a sign advertising the services of a regional air carrier.

"Grazie," Sam said.

"Prego," the shopkeeper replied.

"I sure hope not," Brock said as they walked toward the charter service. "Pretty sure I pulled out in time."

Chapter 12

"Holy buckets," Trojan said, looking at his monitor. "I think a few of these guys are working!"

Vaneesh looked up from his own computer screen. "Which guys?"

"I sent out a dozen different trial versions to probe the NSA data acquisition system. Looks like three of them have pinged our download site."

"So they worked? We're in?"

"That's what I'm saying. It looks that way. For the moment anyway." Trojan clicked a few more keys. "Yep, they've definitely pinged our server, looking to download the payload file."

Vaneesh's expression soured. "I just got this damn thing to compile ten minutes ago. Now I have to test it for functionality. Could be a few hours before it's ready to roll."

Trojan frowned. "We may not have that much time. The virus is coded to start replicating, and it will eventually draw attention. I'd hate to get shut down before we even deliver the executables." Meaning, there was a possibility that the NSA would discover and remove the virus from its data pipes before Vaneesh had a chance to finish the code that would allow the virus to intercept the Bitcoin laundering operation.

"No pressure," Vaneesh said. "It's just the fate of the free world."

Just then, the door to the computer room burst open. Two men wearing camouflage fatigues and kevlar helmets strode in, assault rifles in their hands.

Trojan leapt to his feet.

"Jesus!" Vaneesh shouted. He nearly fell out of his chair.

"You can just call me Captain Gilmore," one of the uniformed men said with an amused chuckle.

Archive stepped through the doorway. "Sorry for the commotion," he said. "But our friends from NORTHCOM are here. This might become a very popular place once you two get your magic working, and I thought a little professional help might be appropriate."

"You scared the living shit out of me," Trojan said.

"Guilty conscience?" Gilmore asked with a chuckle. "Anyway, we're the cavalry. Custer's last stand, they said, so I thought I'd better get acquainted with the place we're supposed to be protecting."

"How many did you bring with you?" Vaneesh asked.

"Two dozen."

"Let's hope that's enough," Archive said.

"I can't imagine it wouldn't be," Gilmore said, puffing his chest a bit.

"I bet you can't," Archive said to the uniformed man. "And I hope you're right. Let's allow these two gentlemen to get back to work, shall we? At the risk of melodrama, I daresay their task is of existential importance to what's left of the nation."

Chapter 13

"Hello, Balzzack011," Sabot said, a snarl in his voice.

Fredericks smiled. "Look at the brain on our little Domingo."

"You sonuvabitch," Sabot said, rising to his feet, jaw and chest jutting forward. "What did you do to the girls?"

"Relax, vato," Fredericks said. "They're fine. Absolutely peachy. Maybe better than ever."

"Why all this?"

"All what?"

"This whole goddamned charade. The dungeon in the jungle. The bullshit about running from your employer."

Fredericks laughed. "You're a rube, aren't you. You've done federal time, and you've even shoveled manure as a Bureau stooge, but you still don't see it, do you?"

"I see you clear enough now, you lying sack of shit."

Fredericks' smile hardened. "What makes you think I'm lying?"

The question stopped Sabot short. What if Fredericks *wasn't* lying? That would imply...

"So you really *are* in some sort of a bind, aren't you?"

Fredericks snorted. "No, I'm just fond of your company, and the great smell here in the rectum of Central America," he said. "*Of course* I need your help. That's why I didn't slit your throat. But I also needed a little plausible deniability to avoid getting crossways with the guy who's paying me."

Sabot shook his head. "Who is it? Who's pulling your strings?"

Fredericks laughed derisively. "Do you think you'd recognize the name if I told you?"

Sabot's anger swelled anew. "Why take Angie? What kind of a sadistic bastard messes with a man's woman?"

"Insurance, little buddy." Fredericks tossed another photograph at Sabot. Angie and Connie, both barely dressed, both glassy-eyed, both laughing heartily at some joke told by a greasy-looking asshole shoving a needle into his arm. "Those ladies know how to par-tay," Fredericks said. "Like escaped nuns or something."

Sabot charged, fists flying.

And then he was flat on his face, one arm wrenched behind his back and stretched an impossibly long way toward the nape of his neck, Fredericks' considerable weight pressing Sabot's chest into the disgusting carpet.

"I don't blame you, little man," Fredericks said, crushing Sabot with his weight. "I'd be pretty pissed off myself. But ask yourself if you'd rather be dead. Because that's what you would have been if I gave a damn about following my orders. You'd never even have made it to Central America. That sedative on the plane, the one that made your skinny beaner ass sleep right through the stop in Tucson? That would have been cyanide instead. And I will kill you, in two seconds or less, unless you get your head on straight *right now*."

Fredericks shifted his weight and pressed his knee into the

back of Sabot's neck, jamming Sabot's face into the unpadded carpet. The pain was excruciating, and Sabot worried his neck would break.

"How much pressure do you think it would take to snap your little spine?" Fredericks asked. "Do you think I weigh enough to make that happen? I did eat two of those greasy little burrito things for lunch today. My money's on me, vato." Fredericks wiggled his knee for additional emphasis, wrenching the skin behind Sabot's ear and sending a stabbing pain through Sabot's vertebrae.

Sabot struggled for breath, his windpipe also constricted by Fredericks' ponderous heft. "Okay," he wheezed.

Fredericks stood up, clasped Sabot's armpits, and effortlessly lifted the smaller man to his feet. "That's a good man!" Fredericks said with mock bonhomie. He made a show of straightening Sabot's shirt and dusting off his shoulders. Fredericks extended his hand. "No hard feelings."

Sabot eyeballed him, angry, embarrassed, and confused. Who did this fat bastard think he was?

Then he reluctantly took Fredericks' hand, his own skinny computer hacker's paw instantly lost in Fredericks' crushing grip. The whole thing seemed a little surreal, like the end of a playground dust-up.

"Partner," Fredericks said, pumping Sabot's hand, wearing an exaggerated smile, clapping Sabot on the shoulder with his free hand.

Sabot glared, pride and body both hurt by Fredericks' surprising agility and strength.

"Aw, c'mon now," Fredericks chided. "Buck up little camper." He put on an artificially bright smile. "This is going to be a very, very lucrative partnership. It's going to make all those digi-dollars you stole before look like chickenfeed."

Jesus. He knows. Sabot pondered the implications. Had he gone from frying pan to fire?

"What about Angie?" Sabot asked after a moment.

"First things first, beaner buddy. You have work to do."

It didn't take much imagination to figure out what Fredericks wanted. Hell, it was what *Sabot* wanted, too.

He didn't resist. If he played his cards right, Sabot realized, there was a decent chance he could wind up in pretty good shape. It would take some careful manipulation, maybe a little misdirection, but it was certainly possible.

And it wasn't like he had any better alternatives.

He got to work.

Chapter 14

Off duty foot soldiers tended to drink. Especially foot soldiers in crime organizations. Their daily reality was sufficiently unpleasant that attaining an altered state was often more necessity than desire. Many of them had done unspeakable things, and guilt strengthened the compulsion to gain some psychological distance from themselves. No matter where you go, there you are, unless you're drunk out of your mind.

Sam was betting that the foot soldier who owned the cell phone they'd traced to Pescara wouldn't be much different. She and Brock arrived at the Hotel Bellariva without a clue where to begin searching for the phone's owner, so she figured the hotel bar and restaurant was as good a place as any to start. There was always the possibility that their mark preferred getting pasted alone in his hotel room, or that he was a teetotaler, but in the absence of any better ideas, Sam and Brock bellied up to the bar.

The familiar scents of booze and bar nuts hit her nostrils, and for the briefest of moments, Sam was tempted to indulge. Her stomach was empty, and the burn of a vodka, neat, no twist, would feel pretty damn amazing right now, she thought.

But moderation wasn't a gift she possessed and her sobriety was too hard-won, so she sighed and ordered a club soda for herself and a beer for Brock.

The hotel was nearly empty. Europe's holiday season was long over, and the hotel had let its hair down a bit. The bartender sipped occasionally from a tall glass of wine, and the wait staff seemed more interested in the Italian reality show on TV than in the customers.

Of which there were half a dozen. There was an old man in his sixties, sharing a table with a fading glory in her forties. She clearly wasn't what she once was, but she still looked like a catch for a codger. Neither looked like the person Sam was looking for; not because of their age or dress, but because of their eyes. Hard people had hard eyes, and a steely gaze transcended just about any disguise.

There was also a pair of attractive girls sharing an appetizer who looked to be of college age. They might prove useful later in the evening. Sam hoped they stayed.

Sam also noted some sort of business meeting taking place at a table for two. The middle-aged men were poring over documents spread out atop the table, voices rising occasionally as they jousted for verbal dominance in that annoyingly male fashion. They didn't have the look, either. Their hands and midsections were a little too soft, in addition to lacking the permanently distracted gaze that muscle squad members almost universally developed over time.

Sam sighed. "Hungry?"

"I could eat your shoe," Brock replied.

As the town's name implied, seafood was *de rigueur* in Pescara. They ordered, sipped their drinks while the kitchen prepared their food, and discussed the predicament in low tones.

It was beginning to have the vibe of a snipe hunt, Sam decided. The lead that had brought them to Italy was a solid one, and the Zip Line hit that Alfonse Archer had dug up earlier in the day gave them definitive evidence that the cell phone in question had been at this address as recently as just a few hours ago, but they were beginning to feel the sort of frustrated ennui that usually preceded arriving at a dead end.

The meal was delicious, prepared with the famous Italian fervor that seemed incongruous with the mid-priced hotel atmosphere, and Sam and Brock ate in silence at the bar, a gauche Americanism that drew curious stares from the other patrons.

But there was a method to their madness, and it paid off just a few moments later when a tall, athletic man seated himself two places over from Sam's position at the bar. His face had Slavic features and a prominent scar beneath one eye. His eyes were several steps beyond cold, and his mouth had a bit of a permanently etched sneer. *Strong candidate,* Sam decided.

She leaned over toward the stranger, covered one side of her mouth conspiratorially, and whispered, "Save me."

The man regarded her, a quizzical look on his face.

"Save me," Sam repeated. "This guy keeps hitting on me." She gestured surreptitiously toward Brock, who was trying somewhat unsuccessfully to wear a nonchalant expression.

"You want me to tell him to get lost?" The man's accent was tough for Sam to place. Eastern European? Baltic? Not quite Russian, but not quite non-Russian, either.

"I don't want to hurt his feelings," Sam said. "We work together."

The man eyeballed Brock menacingly. "Can I buy you a

drink?" he asked Sam.

"Please do."

The man motioned to the bartender. He ordered a vodka. *Man after my own heart,* Sam thought. Sam just asked for "another one," and the bartender brought her another club soda.

"I'm Sheena," she said, extending her hand. She had paperwork to back up the alias, so she went with it.

"Sheena?"

"Yeah," Sam said. "I'll never forgive my mother. I'm in interior decorating. My horny friend and I are here to research coastal Italian decor for a client with more money than sense."

The man smiled. The hardness in his features diminished, but didn't entirely vanish. "Bo," he said.

"Like Bo Jackson?" Sam asked.

He chuckled and shook his head. "Bojan."

"Is that a Russian name?"

Irritation flashed across Bojan's face. It was short-lived, but Sam caught it nonetheless. "Thankfully not, though the Russians still think they own us."

"Own who?"

"The Serbs." His chin lifted slightly as he pronounced the word.

"When did the Russians own the Serbs?" Sam asked.

"Ever hear of the Cold War?"

"Ahh," Sam said, nodding, making sure her cleavage was visible. "Right. I always confuse Russians and Soviets." Not true, but it was best not to seem too intimidating. She wanted Bojan thinking about her boobs rather than her brains.

Bojan shook his head and smiled. "Me too. There's a surprising number of Soviets still around," he said, his high Slavic cheeks scrunching with his smile.

"Will you excuse me a moment?" Sam asked. "I just need to go freshen up a bit." Bojan smiled at her. She caught the glimmer of hope in his eyes, and she also caught his micro-gaze down her shirt. She gave him a slightly naughty smile, and made a show of wiggling her ass a little bit more than normal on her way to the restroom, giving Brock a surreptitious wink over her shoulder when Bojan turned back to face the bar.

She didn't go to the women's room. Instead, she dug a fresh burner from her purse, powered it on, and dialed the number of the cell phone Big A had traced to this location earlier in the day. She needed to know whether she was wasting her time with Bojan, or whether they'd hit the jackpot. She pressed the call button and peered around the corner.

Sure enough. Bojan patted his jacket pocket, pulled out his phone, examined the number, and answered. "Bojan," he said.

Bingo. His voice was gruff and unfriendly in her ear. She hung up without uttering a word, hustled to the women's room, and disassembled and disposed of the burner, flushing yet another SIM card down yet another toilet. She touched up her makeup to add realism to her trip, then returned to the bar.

She gave Brock a nearly imperceptible nod as she sat back on her barstool. He took the cue. He finished his drink and retired to their room.

* * *

Over the course of half a dozen more rounds, Bojan's tough guy exterior melted away to reveal a tough guy interior.

But even tough guys liked to have sex, a fact that Sam exploited expertly. She made it apparent to Bojan that she was in heat. She obliquely mentioned that the previous night, she'd felt lonely in the big hotel room, her eyes throwing the kind of come-hither glance that had encoded itself in the female genome about a trillion years ago.

Bojan and the bulge in his pants followed eagerly back to her room.

He had been inside Sam's room for less than a second before she had him on the floor, his limbs tied up like a pretzel. At first, he thought it was a sexual thing, a little girl power with pain and bondage thrown in, some fun with a tough-looking stranger, but Brock's appearance from around the corner stopped the blood flow to Bojan's little brain, and redirected it to his business brain. "You have no idea who you're fucking with," Bojan said.

"Why don't you enlighten me," Sam said, dragging him to the center of the room, his limbs now expertly zip-tied together. "You got a call from Canada the other day. I'd like you to tell me about it."

There was the usual bluster and posturing. Sam feigned a yawn, produced a razor blade, and pulled Bojan's pants and underwear down around his knees. Brock held his torso, and Sam sat on his legs. She positioned the razor near his scrotum. *Testicular torture is getting to be a thing with me,* she thought absently. *Should*

I see somebody about this?

Bojan struggled, but was bound fast. "What's the matter, Bo?" Sam asked mockingly. "Suddenly shy? A minute ago, you couldn't wait to show me your prong."

He glared at her.

She put on a bored look. "People really bleed for a long time," she said in a disinterested tone of voice. "You hear of rape suspects getting castrated by the fathers of their victims. A surprising number of those men die from all the blood loss. It's really a dangerous thing," she said.

She gave Bojan's skin a little slice for emphasis. The man's body bucked, and he screamed obscenities. But Sam and Brock's combined weight, along with the disadvantaged position Bojan's arms and legs were bound in, left him mostly helpless. She gave him another little slice, this time where his scrotum met his abdomen. "You're going to run out of fight long before I lose interest," Sam said.

She could tell from his eyes that Bojan believed her.

"Nobody would fault you for talking," she said, her voice quiet and controlled. "I mean, who in his right mind would lose his schwanz to keep a secret?"

Bojan glared. "Bitch," he spat.

Sam shrugged. "If the shoe fits…"

"You have no idea who you're fucking with."

"You keep saying that. You're obviously in the kneecapping business. Despite falling for the honey trap like a complete amateur, you've got a tiny bit on the ball, so maybe you're moving up the ladder. But you're not old enough to be running the show. So you're mid-level muscle. For whom?"

Bojan's facial expression changed.

"Did I *expose* you just now, Bo?" Sam said. Brock chuckled at the pun.

"You were also pretty insulted about being called a Russian."

Bojan's eyes narrowed.

"I'm guessing you're either in competition with the Russkies," Sam said, "or you're on their payroll, pissed about being a Serb ass kisser in a Russian world."

"Go to hell," Bojan hissed.

"Just a name and number," Sam said. "Or contact instructions. That's all you'd need to give me. We'll pass it off like I'm looking to hire you guys. Nothing blows back in your face."

"Why should I trust you?" Bojan asked, anger and hatred in his eyes.

"Maybe you shouldn't," Sam said, smiling sweetly. "But I will tell you that I won't hesitate to turn you into a soprano." She cupped her hand around his reproductive gear, stretched the parts to one side, and positioned the razor for a healthy slice.

"Okay," Bojan said quickly.

* * *

"Why am I not surprised that Slobodan Radosz' name came up again?" Sam asked.

"I'm shocked that you got that information out of him inside of five minutes," Brock said.

Sam laughed. "Can you think of one secret you'd be willing to lose your manhood over?"

"Not a damn one," Brock said, shuddering. "We're seriously going to Moscow?"

"It isn't likely that Radosz will come to us."

"And you think he's really there?"

Sam shrugged. "Sounds like he's the point man for the Serb contingent. He'll have to make occasional trips to the home office to stay relevant and keep his guys employed."

"You talk like the Russian leg-breakers are a political organization," Brock said with a chuckle.

"Politics are an outgrowth of human nature," Sam said. "It is what it is, regardless of your profession."

"Somebody paid attention in Sociology 101," Brock chuckled. "I was busy trying to get lucky with the blonde in the third row."

"Too bad I didn't know you then," she said. "I'd have ruined you for anyone else."

"Better late than never," Brock said with a smile.

They packed their bags, left the semi-naked Serb tied up in the bathroom, and went downstairs to the internet cafe, where Sam logged in to the "Fight The Power" bulletin board. Dan had left her an encrypted phone number where she could reach him. She decoded the digits, then used her last virgin burner to dial the number.

"What's up, eh?" Dan said in a shitty imitation of a Canadian accent.

"Hi Dan. What's the news?"

"I followed the concierge home after his shift," Dan said.

"Did he offer you a drink?"

"Funny. But he was talkative, after we established the right environment. He has a fairly large digital footprint, which is how I figured out that he's sleeping with the building owner's trophy wife."

"I imagine that helped you put him in the right frame of mind," Sam said.

"It did. So here's the deal. Our guy is a regular at this upscale condo place, like we figured out earlier. He has this thing with his clothes. He's obsessed with looking neat, and he has to get his clothes pressed every night before he wears them the next day."

"Radosz, or the concierge?"

"Radosz. Pay attention."

"Is this going somewhere?"

"Yes. So one day, the dry cleaner brings a fistful of Limpura to the concierge."

"Limpura." Sam frowned. "Isn't that a small marsupial?"

"No," Dan said. "It's the national currency of Honduras. Radosz left it in his jacket. So the laundry guy gives it to our friend the concierge, who takes it up to Radosz' room."

"Really, Dan, we have to catch a plane," Sam said. "Can you speed it up a bit?"

"I'm getting there. So the concierge knocks on Radosz' door. Turns out that Radosz is very busy, beating the shit out of a prostitute. The concierge hears the noise, so he knocks harder. Radosz finally opens the door, all pissed off at the interruption. Anyway, this half-naked girl runs out of the room, bloody and beat to hell."

"Dan, you're killing me. Get to the point, please."

"So the concierge freaks out a little bit. But Radosz pays him a grand to keep his mouth shut about the assault."

"Man of the year," Sam said, tapping her foot impatiently.

"Seriously. But now, Radosz figures the concierge works for *him*. He starts expecting the guy to fetch hookers, drugs, cash, whatnot."

"I'm not interested yet."

"And then Radosz asks him to fetch computer hackers."

Sam raised her eyebrows. "Maybe I'm interested now. When was this?"

"Last week. Roughly the time the dollar went to shit. Turns out, the concierge has a kid brother who's home on break from college in Vancouver. Computer science major, but with a juvie prior for hacking into a government website and defacing it with titty pictures. Anyway, the concierge turns his kid brother on to Radosz. Short term job opportunity kind of thing."

"You're thinking this is connected with the Bitcoin theft operation?"

"I am. The concierge's brother had an interview with a group of five Russian programmers."

"Russians?"

"Russians. Evidently, they're some of the best coders in the world. Something about not having much computer time, so they had to learn how to write clean code that works without a bunch of debugging. The kid brother started to work the next morning, and the concierge hasn't seen him since."

Sam mulled. The universe was full of coincidences, and she was certain that Russian computer hackers were busy hacking all kinds of things at any given moment. But what if they *were* working on the Bitcoin theft operation?

"Hey," Dan said. "You said you were catching a flight. Where to?"

"Moscow," Sam said. "Slobodan Radosz is supposedly on his way there now. We're hoping for a chat. But I need some dirt on him, if you can dig any up. And maybe a way to find him. We got contact instructions from our new friend Bojan, but I always like a backup plan."

"Shouldn't be too hard. Sounds like the concierge has him on speed dial these days."

"And find out who those hackers are. We're going to need a little leverage, I think."

"I'm on it, boss," Dan said.

Chapter 15

"Boo-yah!" Vaneesh exclaimed.

Trojan looked sideways at him. "Does anyone say that anymore?"

"Hot damn!"

"It's working?"

"Like a champ!" Vaneesh rose from his chair and raised his arms above his head in victory.

"Hang it on the download site," Trojan exhorted. "I've already got close to three thousand pings."

"You've infected three thousand computers already?" Vaneesh asked, incredulous.

"Haven't you been listening?"

"Apparently not," Vaneesh said. "I'll upload the code, and you tell Archive that we're live."

Trojan walked down the hallway in the subterranean bunker. He was a veteran hacker with serious street credibility, but even he was somewhat amazed by what they'd been able to accomplish. He had invented a family of viruses capable of penetrating the NSA's data pipes and distributing themselves to thousands of personal computers linked via the internet, and Vaneesh had somehow found a way to engineer an application that re-stole Bitcoin from computers already infected by the thieves' virus.

But they were not out of the woods yet. It wasn't enough to

infect thousands of computers with their code, or even millions of computers. They had to infect *the same* computers that had been co-opted into stealing Bitcoins for the thieves. They couldn't identify those computers directly, so they had to use the old fashioned method: brute force. Trojan's virus had to infect enormous numbers of computers in order to have a reasonable certainty that they'd infected enough of the *right* computers.

It wouldn't take long, all things considered. There was a reason they'd gone to all the trouble of breaking into the NSA's data-sucking system. No wired device on the planet was more than a few nodes removed from the NSA's tentacles. Just like with the virus they'd used to castrate the banking system, this one would find happy homes on several hundred million computers by morning.

Trojan smiled as he walked into the media room and spied Archive's white mane protruding from the top of a plush leather chair. It was nice to bear good news for a change.

Chapter 16

"You're done?" Fredericks' mouth was agape.

"It wasn't brain surgery," Sabot said. "It's pretty simple code."

"How long till the money's all transferred?"

"Done."

"Already?"

Sabot nodded, a bemused smile stretching across his face. "You don't know much about this stuff, do you?"

Fredericks huffed. "I know enough."

"To be dangerous," Sabot finished. "It's over. All of the money moves at least once every second. So it took less than a second to funnel it all into our accounts."

"And you set us up with that perpetual motion-thingy, too?"

"Wouldn't do any good otherwise," Sabot said. "I'm guessing it'd take them half a day to steal it all back from us if we left it all in static accounts." Which reminded him that he needed to get that USB drive out of his digestive tract as quickly as possible in order to protect the gaudy fortune he'd already stolen.

"And you covered your tracks?" Fredericks asked.

"Naw, I left a nice big Thank You message," Sabot quipped. "Of course I covered my tracks."

Mostly, he didn't add. There was no such thing as permanently deleting a file once it had been saved on a data drive. But as much as was feasible to accomplish remotely, Sabot had removed all traces of his hack, and had restored the original scripts to their proper function. He had even created false entries in the computer's root logs, making it virtually impossible for all but the most accomplished computer security experts to trace his foray into the computer's innards.

Fredericks' face erupted into a huge grin. "Damn. Nice work, partner!" Sabot saw the jaded pipe-swinger turn giddy with greed.

Then Fredericks' smile disappeared. "Give me the files," he said.

Sabot laughed. "Look who's out of his league now! You think I'm going to just hand it all over to you and hope for the best?"

"That was our deal. You hand over the accounts, I hand over the women."

"Right. I hand you your cut, and then you shoot me and take mine. I don't think so."

Fredericks sneered. "You think I couldn't do that right now anyway?"

"You'd never get your money, fat boy."

"You spent the last three days spilling your guts, singing like a jaybird, you little beaner bastard."

It was *you all along, you fat bastard.* Fredericks' angry slip-up had confirmed Sabot's inchoate suspicions: Fredericks was much more than a hapless hanger-on in Sabot's little adventure over the past several days. Fredericks was at least involved, and potentially behind the whole damned thing.

Sabot saw Fredericks' face change. It was clear the fat man realized his mistake. He had revealed a little more than he had intended.

But it didn't change anything, Sabot knew. He suspected Fredericks knew it, too.

"You're a pencil-neck computer geek," Fredericks said, derision in his voice. "What makes you think you could withhold a few passwords from me?"

Sabot laughed. "Passwords? Ha! Who's the rube now?"

Fredericks' look turned confused, disconcerted.

"Sure, you could take the files," Sabot said. "You could torture and kill me. But you'd never have access to your money. You need me for that. Every day of your miserable life."

"What the hell are you talking about?"

"Biometrics, big guy." Sabot wiggled his fingers and winked. "Fingerprints and a retina scan. *My* fingerprints and *my* retina. That's what unlocks your money and mine. Every time you want to move your money? You go through me."

Fredericks seethed. "What makes you think I won't rip your eyeballs right out of their sockets? Slice your goddamned fingers off?"

"You could do that," Sabot said, "but you'd be throwing away every penny. Your accounts are only unlocked by a biometric report from *my* workstation at the FBI office in Seattle. And the time stamp has to be inside of fifteen minutes of when you log in. Otherwise, no access."

Fredericks advanced menacingly, eager to do bodily harm.

"Think it over, fat man. Do you think you're going to break into the Bureau office with my eyeballs in your pockets?" He laughed. "Besides, even if you could, my retinal signature becomes unrecognizable after the blood vessels stop feeding my eyes."

Sabot let it sink in. "You said you were in private security," he said after a long moment. "Well, now your new full-time job is making sure I stay safe and sound."

Fredericks' jaw and fists clenched.

"And if you piss me off?" Sabot said, eyebrows raised, "I cut you off. No questions asked. Not a thing you could do about it, either."

Sabot sat back in his chair, a satisfied smile on his face. "I believe that's what you call *insurance.*"

Fredericks paced, his mind churning through possibilities. "Bullshit," he finally said. "No way you did all of this in an hour. With me watching you the whole time."

Sabot chuckled. "You were a pig staring at a wristwatch. You had no clue what I was doing. But it wasn't hard." A sardonic smile settled on his face. "Everything's easy when you know how."

Fredericks shook his head. "Unfuckingbelievable."

"Look on the bright side, *vato,*" Sabot said after a while, placing sarcastic emphasis on the Latino euphemism, as Fredericks was fond of doing. "As of right now, you're one of the richest men in the world. You could buy a small continent. So I've thrown in a minor inconvenience to get at your money. Big deal. I think it's a small price to pay."

Fredericks sat heavily atop the desk, shoulders slumped, shaking his head. "You damned nerds have taken over," he said. "This world has gone to shit."

Sabot smiled. Then his face turned serious. "Listen, *partner,*" he said. "Now it's your turn to get to work. I want Angie and Connie back with me, safe and sound, *right now.* Harm a hair on their heads, and it's over. You'll never see a dime."

Fredericks glared, angry but defeated. He left the room without a word.

Sabot smiled, satisfied, listening to Fredericks' heavy footfalls retreating down the walkway in front of the motel. "Who's the bitch now, bitch?"

Chapter 17

It was surreal. Sam sat in the window of a darkened hotel room, the scope of her high-powered rifle trained on Brock's figure seated several hundred yards away on a snowy park bench.

In Gorkiy Park. In Moscow. In fucking *Russia*. The storied, iconic center of all things cloak-and-dagger, in what remained of one of the world's most paranoid states.

It had been an easy decision. Brock had to be the one to place the strip of bark atop the snow-covered retaining wall and await further contact. Sam was simply too recognizable.

But she felt helpless, warm and protected inside the fifth floor hotel room while Brock braved the cold and the contact with what she was certain was a ruthless and brutal organized crime syndicate. She was also pretty certain the group had official state sanctioning. Russia had been the Wild West since the Berlin Wall had fallen a quarter century ago, and the oligarchs that ran things now were little more than thugs in expensive suits.

Her uneasiness grew as each second passed. She rechecked the rifle, idly fondling the safety. It had been easy to acquire the military sniper rifle on Moscow's famous black market, and for that she was grateful. But not every conceivable problem was solvable with a slug from four hundred yards. And she wasn't that confident in her marksmanship at this distance.

The crux of the issue was this: Had Bojan, the boorish Serb

they'd met in Pescara, given them legitimate instructions to initiate contact? Or had he told them how to sign their own death warrants? She'd coerced contact instructions out of him, but there was no way to tell whether the procedures he'd specified, and that they'd followed religiously, would garner the introductions they sought. It was equally likely they'd earn Sam and Brock a painful death at the hands of a Russian gang.

Sam heard a chirp from the laptop computer perched on the table to her left. Someone had posted a new message on the Screw Big Brother site. Her heart leapt when she saw who: DynoDaniel469. Dan Gable. She quickly decoded the phone number embedded in the message, whipped out a new burner, and dialed as fast as her fingers would move. She held the phone to her ear, and returned her eye to the rifle's scope. She was relieved to see Brock still sitting alone in the cold.

"Reader's digest version, please," Sam said as soon as Dan answered. "We're eyeballs deep right now."

"Right. I'll get right to it. The concierge's little brother got hired to hack by Slobodan Radosz' group. Turns out, they whisked him away to the US. Their security wasn't as tight as it needed to be, I think because these guys were hackers and not spies, and Big A was able to get a make on them."

"Big A?" Sam asked, still surveying Brock's position through the sniper rifle's scope.

"Yeah, he's been a godsend. Two Canadians, five Russians on the team. They made a bunch of phone calls from the same cell phones, before someone wised them up on how to stay under the radar. Guess where three of those calls went."

Sam rolled her eyes. "You know I hate the guessing game."

"Moscow," Dan said.

"Jesus."

"Lubyanka, in fact."

Sonuvabitch. Lubyanka was the former headquarters of the KGB, and was widely rumored to be the hub of quasi-criminal, quasi-state-sanctioned heavies. "Got any names?"

"Yep," Dan said. "And those initial seven people networked with a half dozen more before they tightened up their security procedures. If we had any manpower, we'd be able to roll up a huge foreign operation on US soil."

Sam whistled. She had Dan spell the names for her, and she wrote them on a sheet of paper torn from the hotel notepad, being careful not to leave indentations on the nightstand that could be traced later.

"And there's one name of particular interest," Dan said. "The guy in Moscow. Make sure you're sitting down."

Dan told her the name.

"Oh, no," Sam said, incredulous. "Are you sure?"

"Sure as the day is long."

"You're *absolutely positive?*"

"Yes, Sam."

"Dan, this is extremely important. You have no doubt whatsoever it's him?"

"Sam, Big A says it's a hundred percent legit. No question about it."

This changes everything.

Electric fear spread through her body. Her fingers felt numb. "I have to go," she said.

She hung up and dialed Brock's burner, panic rising.

It rang. "Answer, dammit!" she said aloud, phone pressed to her ear, eye peering at Brock through the scope.

Finally, she saw him unzip his coat and retrieve his cell phone.

"Get out! We're in deep shit!" Sam shouted as soon as he answered.

"What's going on?" Brock asked.

"Just stand up and walk away!" Sam heard the note of hysteria in her own voice.

Brock wasn't moving. "Baby, please, get the hell out of there. Don't stop for anything. Come straight back here. Hurry!"

She saw Brock stand and turn toward the hotel. He moved haltingly. His gunshot wound had tightened up in the cold Moscow air. "Hurry, baby," Sam exhorted.

"This is as fast as I can walk right now," he said, an edge to his voice. "Will you tell me what's going on?"

"You just have to trust me right now." She swept the rifle's sights around Brock, checking for pursuers.

Motion caught her eye, at the far edge of the scope's field of view. *Oh, shit.* Her focus settled on man dressed in black, moving with a purpose, thirty paces behind Brock, his eyes focused intently on Brock's back.

Her heart thudded against her ribs. "Walk across the street, baby," she said. "Now! Fast! You have a tail."

Brock checked for crossing traffic and stepped out into Krimsky Val, urgency now evident in his gait.

His pursuer followed suit, closing the distance with each step.

"Faster, baby," she said into the phone, panic in her voice. "He's gaining!"

She settled her sights on the man behind Brock and moved her finger to the safety. *I can't believe this is happening,* Sam thought, clicking off the safety. *Breathe,* she commanded herself, willing her skyrocketing heart rate to settle back down enough to give her a fighting chance at hitting her target.

Another pursuer came into her field of view, moving parallel to Krimsky Val on the opposite side of the street, on course to intercept Brock easily. *Sonuvabitch!* "Turn back!" she yelled into the phone. "Go back to the other side of the street!"

She heard Brock's panting as he speed-walked with the phone pressed to his ear. "Shit, I see him," Brock said, but Sam had dropped the phone to line up her shot. She saw Brock's limp turn into a lop-sided gallop.

Sam re-centered her sights on the nearer of Brock's pursuers. *I can't believe this is happening.* She squeezed her index finger. The rifle slammed into her shoulder as the heavy slug left the silenced barrel. It traveled through the hotel room window in front of her, leaving just a half-inch hole in the glass.

Her target spun and fell on his face in the middle of Krimsky Val. He didn't move.

Sam worked the rifle's bolt, ejecting the spent cartridge and chambering another round, fighting the adrenaline that robbed her hands of the precision she desperately needed.

She moved the scope, searching for the second pursuer, forcing herself to breathe.

Her movement was erratic, and the scope passed twice over the dark-clad man now crossing from the opposite side of the street toward Brock. *Relax,* she coached herself, first finding the target with her naked eye, then moving the scope until she centered the death dot on his chest. She inhaled, held her breath, refined the rifle's position, and added pressure to the trigger.

The rifle jerked. She vaguely registered the pain of its kick in her shoulder.

She saw sparks fly from the pavement behind the second pursuer. *Sonuvabitch.* She'd missed.

She worked the bolt a second time. The pursuer was just a few paces behind Brock, and gaining fast. Sam fought panic, fought the urgency that she knew was the enemy of accuracy.

Breathe.

It had to be now. The man would be on Brock in seconds. She wasn't going to get another clean shot.

She lined up the sights, feeling her pulse pound in her temples, willing smoothness into her motions, doing her best to shut out the fear for Brock's safety that threatened to launch her into hysterics.

She squeezed.

Blood erupted from the pursuer's back. The bullet's momentum threw him onto the pavement. Sam was sure he was dead before he hit the street.

She pulled the phone to her ear. "Brock, baby, can you hear

me?"

"Jesus, Sam, what's going on?" he panted.

"Don't come back to the room," she said, her voice breaking with adrenaline and fear, her eyes scanning the area around Brock for any additional pursuers. "I'll meet you in the lobby. We'll exit through the service entrance in back. Hurry!"

She wiped the gun clean of her fingerprints, grabbed the list of names she'd written during her conversation with Dan, and ran from the hotel room.

Chapter 18

"Oh, no." Vaneesh got a sinking feeling in his chest. Had he made a mistake?

"What's wrong?" Trojan asked.

"Oh, no," Vaneesh repeated.

"Dude, let me look." Trojan peered over his shoulder at the computer monitor. The virus and its embedded payload code were both reporting all kinds of activity, which should only happen if the virus had successfully found and diverted funds from the Bitcoin accounts involved in the giant theft operation.

But there was no money flowing into the new accounts.

"What's going on?" Trojan asked.

"I'm stepping through the debugger again now," Vaneesh said. He clicked frantically, watching each line of code as it executed, and watching the effect the code had on the Bitcoin accounts created to receive the recovered funds. "Disaster," he said after a while. "I did not see this coming at all."

Trojan's virus and Vaneesh's algorithm were working perfectly.

But someone had swiped the money out from underneath them.

Chapter 19

Sabot waited in the wreck of an automobile he'd purchased five hours and two hundred miles ago. His nerves were frazzled. He eyeballed the titty bar with growing uneasiness.

He'd already paid half the fee to the local gang. It was enough to keep the average Honduran family financially comfortable for roughly seventeen thousand years. The other half of the fee was due upon delivery.

The appointed hour came and went. There was no sign of motion from inside the bar. There were no cars parked outside, at least not that he could see. Nobody came or went.

He wondered whether Fredericks had double-crossed him. If so, it would be an easy fix. Sabot would simply take every last zillionth of a Bitcoin from every one of Fredericks' accounts.

And then he would hire someone to pull Fredericks' limbs off.

Sabot handled the pistol he'd bought, surprised again at its heft. Despite his upbringing in a rough corner of Queens, he had no experience with firearms. He was pretty sure he'd lose any kind of a shootout, but he still felt marginally better with a gun in his hand. This kind of thing could be dicey.

He toyed with the idea of walking into the bar. The instructions were explicit — under no circumstances was he to get out of his car — but Sabot was beginning to come unraveled as the minutes ticked away.

Where the hell are they?

A van pulled up. It was white, beat up, with no windows. A classic kidnapper's van. *Jesus,* Sabot breathed to himself, imagining the kinds of horrors that could go on in the back of a van like that. He didn't know what he would do if anything had happened to those girls.

The back doors opened. The angle was wrong, so he couldn't see inside the van. But he saw a foot touch the ground. A woman's foot.

Then another.

The woman turned around, helping someone else out of the van. Sabot still couldn't see anything but her feet.

Then he saw another pair of shoes emerge from the van, familiar shoes this time, and then it was hard for him to see anything at all, because his eyes filled with tears.

Hand in hand, Angie and Connie ran toward the car, and Sabot didn't try to stop the sobs of relief and joy that erupted at the sight of them.

Chapter 20

Sam was still shaking as she exited the subway station, Brock's hand clasped firmly in her own. They'd found no additional muscle tailing them, but it was only a matter of time before more trouble appeared.

"This is insane," Brock said. "We're going to die here."

Sam quickened her pace, walking toward the giant rectangular edifice that had inspired fear and loathing in the hearts of millions. "Not without a fight," she said.

Brock pulled her back. "Sam, we can't win this. I don't want to die today."

She saw real fear in his eyes, the same fear that had coursed through her veins and made a mess of her nervous system since Dan Gable had told her the name of the Russian at the top of the conspiracy she and Brock now stood poised to attack.

She caressed Brock's cheek and looked into his eyes, her heart full of the love she felt for him, that she had always felt for him. He was the one. She felt sadness at the danger that faced them, and silently cursed the shitty odds. Her throat constricted and her eyes misted at the thought that the future they planned together might never happen.

"We have to do this," she said, her voice choked. "We know who's behind this. We know they will find us. We're on their home turf. We'll never make it out of the city if we don't handle this now."

He exhaled, weariness settling over his face, resignation in his eyes. He nodded slowly.

They turned, grasped each other's hands, and walked into Moscow's Lubyanka Prison.

* * *

"It is said that this is the tallest building in Russia," the short, gruff man said, his feet propped on his desk, his impossibly blue eyes blazing with a disconcerting intensity. "From the basement, you can see all the way to Siberia." He laughed a hearty Russian laugh.

Sam caught the humor, but it seemed far less than funny under the circumstances. She and Brock were keenly aware of the building's history. Lubyanka had temporarily housed tens of thousands of prisoners, political and otherwise, during the Cold War years. Many of those prisoners were sent to the Siberian Gulags, where they were worked to death.

The luckier ones had their brains splattered onto the concrete wall in the courtyard.

It was hard for Brock and Sam not to imagine a similar fate for themselves.

"Mr. Alexandrov," Sam began.

The old Cold Warrior cut her off with a wave of his hand. "You are a beautiful woman, and I would much prefer if you called me Fyodor."

Sam shuddered. *Fyodor fucking Alexandrov.* She still couldn't believe she was sitting across the table from one of the most feared men in the history of the clandestine services, in *any* nation. Alexandrov had ruled the KGB with an iron fist. Loyalty wasn't necessary in Alexandrov's organization, defectors joked, because agents never lasted long enough to betray the Motherland.

The hardness in the man's eyes was frightening, and his attempt at charm had made her skin crawl.

She felt exceptionally vulnerable. She had but one card to play. There was no guarantee it would prove compelling. There was no guarantee that Alexandrov would even find it remotely interesting. He was still very much the puppet master, having opted to continue wielding real power after the Soviet Union crumbled, rather than pursuing a career as a phony politician, as so many of his counterparts had done.

As a result, Sam knew, he owned just about everyone. He was Russia's equivalent of J. Edgar Hoover, minus the homosexuality, and even more devoid of any degree of moral compunction. He was a prime mover. People had long ago lost count of the deaths on Alexandrov's ledger.

Sam cleared her throat. "I have a business proposition."

Alexandrov's blazing blue eyes turned to ice. "I am sure that you do." He lit a filterless cigarette and took a healthy swallow from his tumbler of vodka. "You should know that I move slowly in business matters."

Sam forced a smile. *Here we go.* "Your reputation says otherwise." She reached into her purse. "And I'm afraid this is a one-time offer," she said, handing a crumpled piece of paper to Russia's most powerful thug.

Alexandrov puffed his cigarette and studied the handwritten page. Then he looked back at Sam, his baleful eyes boring into her.

Her heart raced. She struggled to control her breathing. She feared he was going to shoot them on the spot.

After an interminable moment, Alexandrov sat back in his chair, and turned to look out the window. "You look like a beautiful woman," he said after a puff on his cigarette. "But I think you're hiding testicles in your pants."

"I've been accused of that before," Sam said.

"She's one hundred percent woman," Brock said with a protective look on his face.

Alexandrov regarded Brock with knowing admiration. "I am envious."

The smile left Alexandrov's face, and he sighed heavily. "And I am disappointed. It has become so difficult to find skilled personnel, and the world has changed in so many unexpected ways."

Sam nodded. Had the danger passed? She didn't know. "It's not our game any longer, is it?"

Alexandrov snorted. "*Our* game? What would you know about it? You hadn't yet opened your legs for your first man when I took over this building, guardian of everything that it stood for." He had venom in his eyes.

She held his gaze, wondering what was churning inside his head. Was he contemplating the specifics of their demise? Pondering which wall to stand them against while he took aim? Wondering which of them to shoot first? Her heart pounded anew, and she hoped that the vein in her temple wasn't throbbing with her pulse, betraying how truly afraid she was.

Sam inhaled. The situation demanded poise, confidence,

aplomb. She felt none of those things. But she decided to fake it. "I wouldn't be so sure," she finally said, the beginnings of a smile curling the corners of her mouth. "I was pretty young when I started taking advantage of horny young men."

Alexandrov studied her, his eyes intense, his jaw working.

Then his booming Russian laugh filled the room. "Started young," he repeated, laughing harder. "Indeed!"

Sam and Brock laughed, uneasily at first, then with more vigor, far more out of relief than mirth.

Alexandrov's laughter diminished to a lingering smile, and he took another healthy swallow of vodka. He returned his gaze to Sam. His eyes still blazed a stellar blue, but the venom was now gone from them, replaced with something Sam thought might be kinship, maybe even reluctant admiration. "I'm listening," he finally said.

* * *

They sat at the Aeroflot terminal at Moscow's Sheremtyevo Airport. Despite Alexandrov's assurances, Sam and Brock were still on edge.

The old Cold Warrior had accepted their terms, no questions asked. That either meant that the terms were agreeable, or that he was about to have their throats slit. Only time would tell, but Sam saw nobody who aroused her suspicion as they waited for their direct flight back to Washington, DC.

"Alexandrov was right, you know," Brock said, breaking the tense silence.

Sam looked at him quizzically.

Brock smiled. "You do have brass balls."

She shook her head, chuckling. "Lubyanka was a slightly outrageous gamble," she admitted. "But in retrospect, I think Alexandrov is in a tough spot. If he balks, we roll up his entire operation. If he's bluffing... we roll up his entire operation."

Brock shook his head. "No way. We couldn't find a dozen cops on the job right now to go arrest them."

"Probably true," Sam said. "But Alexandrov doesn't necessarily know that."

"So you trust him? That horse shit about some deep roller on a yacht in the Adriatic, and Mondragon in the jungle in Honduras?"

Sam sighed. "Of course not. But my calendar is suddenly pretty open, and I have nothing better to do than give him the benefit of the doubt. And his clock is ticking." Two days, they'd given him. It would be plenty of time to hold up his end of the bargain.

The loudspeaker announced the flight, and the passengers arose and got in line. "Besides," Sam said. "I've been hearing rumors about some ultra-deep power player for years now. It would be interesting to see if there's anything to them."

Chapter 21

Captain Maurizio Turcoe bowed deeply, extending his hand. "Welcome back to the Anzio," he said.

The Facilitator grunted his reply and strode past. He barely noticed that there was a new security guy in place of the dour-faced Serb who'd pulled guard duty during his last visit, just three days earlier.

That particular meeting had gone extremely well, and the Facilitator had spent the intervening time in the French Riviera, planning ways to consolidate his fortune and restore his organization to its former glory.

Turcoe led the Facilitator to his quarters. If the ship's captain had any inkling of what was about to happen, he didn't let on.

The Facilitator strode through the door that Captain Turcoe held open for him. Shock registered on the old man's face. He had expected a follow-up strategy meeting with Johann Froehlich, the head of the European Central Bank.

Fyodor Alexandrov was the last person he expected to find on his yacht.

The Facilitator recovered his composure. "Fyodor," he said, taking the seat adjacent to Alexandrov's. "Have we left an open matter that I'm not aware of?"

Alexandrov smiled. "Old friend. Must every visit have a reason?"

The color drained from the Facilitator's face.

"Yes, comrade, I'm afraid you're right," Alexandrov said, noting the change in the Facilitator's visage. "There will be unpleasantness."

Alexandrov rose. "You were a worthy friend, mentor, and confidant, and this is not an easy thing." He produced a silenced pistol.

The Facilitator shook his head. He felt weight, sadness, the sting of unrealized ambition. He hadn't expected the end to come this way. But enemies rarely killed powerful men. Usually, it was a friend. Just as it would be for him.

Alexandrov set his jaw, his face grim. "It is time," he said. He pointed the gun at the Facilitator's chest. "Goodbye, old friend."

He pulled the trigger.

Chapter 22

Three days had passed since their return from Moscow. Sam and Brock had slept in their own bed for two nights in a row, something that hadn't happened since Brock was kidnapped from their home two weekends earlier.

Homeland had indeed been breached. But it didn't appear to be an inside job. Alexandrov's Russians, partially in response to the Facilitator's wishes as Alexandrov's client and partially due to their own entrepreneurial brand of trade craft, had pulled a page from the NSA's playbook. One of the hackers had revealed — bragged, really, while Dan and Sam questioned him in an unofficial capacity, so as not to violate their agreement with Alexandrov — that they had strapped an inductive shunt onto the data cable leaving Homeland's building. The upshot was that the computer whiz kids hired by the Facilitator to take over the Bitcoin theft operation after Domingo Mondragon's hasty departure had been reading Homeland's email and listening to phone conversations for nearly the entirety of Sam's investigation.

It was a lot of data to sift through, but they were smart guys, and they built automatic filters to help them keep tabs on Sam's investigation. Those filters instantly showed them everything that had anything to do with Special Agent Sam Jameson. The whole thing creeped her out, but she was thankful to be at the bottom of the mystery surrounding how Alexandrov's men had deployed a team of heavies to Reagan International so soon after she and Brock had made their travel reservations to Rome. It was a damn good thing she'd gotten off the grid when she did. There was no telling when her luck would have run out.

Fyodor Alexandrov, by all indications, was a man of his word. He faxed a photo of a dead man, someone whom Sam didn't recognize, but whose death had caused hushed whispers all the way up to the Office of the President. If the rumors were to be believed, the balance of power — the *real* power — had just undergone a monumental shift. At the bottom of the photo, in bold Slavic scrawl, Alexandrov had written the words *RIP Facilitator.*

Sam's interest in the man Alexandrov had called the Facilitator extended only to his role in the redistribution of roughly a quarter of the world's crypto currency wealth, and in any role he might have played in the civil destabilization operation on American soil. However, now that the Facilitator's final photo had been circulated through the corridors of power, there was prevalent talk that the ugly old bastard had been involved in much, much more.

Was it bullshit? Sam had no idea. There was no shortage of conspiracy theories in DC, and, in Sam's experience, there was also no shortage of conspiracies. She wasn't inclined to believe the rumors that this particular conspiracy was all that important.

On the other hand, perhaps it was. She wouldn't be all that surprised if it turned out to be true. Either way, though, she was pretty sure she'd never know for certain.

She also had mixed feelings about her deal with Alexandrov. The deal had undoubtedly kept her and Brock alive, and, judging by the dispersal of the Russian hacker operation and the end of the agitation caused by Russians posing as US soldiers, it had also put a stop to a significant threat to US national security.

For the moment, anyway. She'd been forced to leave the organization intact, which certainly meant that they'd cause further trouble at some point down the line.

The deal had also cost a man his life. And it had made Sam a partner with one of the most evil men on the planet.

She shook her head. Truth was a damn sight stranger than fiction, and nothing ever really ended cleanly.

And now, Belize. There was a gigantic loose end remaining. The money was still missing. Trojan's virus had evidently succeeded in breaking into the electronic equivalent of an empty vault. The theft operation had ceased to be an operation, but the digital money was nowhere to be found.

Sabot, you crafty little bastard.

The flight to Belize had been smooth. She had taken the Homeland jet, and had even consented to having it filled with Homeland field agents. The coordination with the authorities in Belize had been remarkably painless, and McClane, to his credit, had cleared away mountains of red tape on the American side.

It was time to bring in Sabot Mondragon.

"Alpha ready," Sam's radio earpiece crackled. She gripped her pistol, thumbed the safety to the off position, and nervously felt her ballistic vest with her left hand. It was getting close to show time.

A few seconds passed. The top floor hallway in the luxury beachside hotel was completely silent. The hotel was almost entirely deserted. It hadn't been terribly difficult to find the one guy with cash to burn after the global economic meltdown. Mondragon hadn't left the hotel in days, apparently, but he wasn't exactly laying low.

She heard "Bravo ready" in her earpiece. Then, "Charlie Team is all set."

She took a deep breath, clicked the transmit button, and whispered "go."

It was over in an instant. Mondragon and his girlfriend were taking a siesta, and had no stomach for a struggle.

The girl's mother was sunbathing down at the pool. The arresting officer said she actually looked *relieved* to have been arrested by an American agent.

* * *

Forty-five minutes later, the Homeland VIP transport plane nosed skyward. Sam unbuckled and walked back to Mondragon's seat.

He was strapped in and handcuffed, and he looked tired and strung out. "You've had one hell of a week," Sam said.

"I was coerced," he said.

Sam nodded. "I know." She looked at him and felt pity. He was a convicted felon, but he had been on the straight-and-narrow until a little over a week ago. Hell, he was even working for the Bureau. He couldn't have gone crooked if he tried, at least until that phone call.

She suspected that Sabot was the Facilitator's Plan A — if, as Alexandrov had intimated, the Facilitator was behind Mondragon's recruitment into the Bitcoin theft operation — but that Mondragon had worn out his utility when he started skimming.

Sam shook her head. "You had to put your hand in the cookie jar, didn't you?"

Sabot snorted. "What would you have done?"

"Honestly? I don't know. It turned into a lot of money, and fast, didn't it?"

Sabot nodded, sadness in his eyes. "I didn't know how else to get out of the situation. Guys like that don't exactly offer a 401k."

Sam smiled. "Guys like that don't usually leave guys like you alive to talk about it. You were lucky."

"The feds will say I violated my parole," Sabot said. "They're going to throw away the key. Sometimes I wish those Honduran bastards had killed me."

Sam shook her head. "That's actually what I wanted to talk to you about. I think sending you back to prison would be a tragic waste of talent."

Sabot looked confused.

"I've talked this over with the US Attorney at length," Sam said. "He agrees that if you and I can come to an agreement, that's good enough for him."

Sabot looked incredulous. "What?"

"Yeah," Sam said. "You're a regular hero. You shut down the biggest theft operation in human history. At least, that's what the story will be." She looked pointedly at Sabot. "After you give back every last nickel you stole."

Sabot took a deep breath, exhaled, and nodded. There was a part of him that hadn't really expected to ever live long enough to spend that money. And if he did happen to survive the adventure, keeping the money had always felt like a long shot.

"Why are you doing this for me?" he asked.

Sam smiled. "I'm doing it for me," she said. "I think you did what most people would have done in your situation, which was a shitty situation, so I'm not anxious to ruin your life." She smiled. "And as my new Russian friend pointed out just a few days ago, the world has changed quite a bit in the past few years."

"I don't understand," Sabot said.

Sam chuckled. "I want a guy like you to owe me a favor so big that it can never be repaid." She patted him on the shoulder, turned, and walked back toward her seat.

Halfway there, she stopped and wheeled back around. "Almost forgot to mention," she said, leaning conspiratorially close to Sabot's ear, "that a very bad person has just died. He was also a very rich person. So rich, in fact, that it will take an extremely long time for the federal government to inventory his assets, much less seize them."

Sabot looked confused again.

"I'm saying that there's a large pile of uncounted assets. If the ownership of some of those assets was to change hands before we got around to accounting for it, that would probably fall in the moral category of a victimless crime, and in the practical category of a non-event. A tree falling in the forest, as they say."

She winked and returned to her seat. She felt good about helping Mondragon out. He seemed like a good kid at heart.

She sighed heavily. Her next task was going to suck.

Sam lifted the receiver of the in-flight telephone next to her seat, typed in her Homeland badge number to access the satellite phone system, and dialed a number she had copied down in the BWI airport concourse several days earlier.

Trojan answered. "Thanks for all of your work on that virus," Sam said. "But I think we finally have the Bitcoin issue wrapped up."

"You got the thief?"

"We did."

She asked to talk to Archive.

Moments later, she heard the jovial voice of the wizened old mastermind behind the conspiracy that had thrown the entire globe into fiscal chaos. "How is everyone at the ranch?" Sam asked.

"Fine, fine, thank you very much for asking," came Archive's reply.

"Are the federal officers still protecting you?"

Archive answered in the affirmative.

"Is there any sign that you're about to be attacked by anyone?"

"There's no one within fifty miles," Archive said. "It's gotten cold up here, and people are afraid to come up to the mountains now."

"Good," Sam said. "Who appears to be in charge of the federal contingent?"

"A young man called Captain Gilmore," Archive said. "Would you like to speak with him?"

"I would."

Sam heard the rustle of the phone changing hands, then

Gilmore announced himself.

Sam identified herself as the agent in charge of the investigation into the suspicious failure of the US dollar and the collapse of US banking system.

She hesitated, momentarily uncertain of her decision, but decided to carry on. It had to be done.

"Captain Gilmore," she said, "I would like you to please arrest every last person at the ranch. Take them to the Denver office of the Department of Homeland Security. I'll meet you there tomorrow morning."

She hung up, feeling the pang of sadness that she had fully expected to feel. She had grown fond of the old man, the skinny hacker, even the cocky young executive they called Protégé.

She even figured that, once the dust had settled, the world would be a better place. What the old man and his menagerie of exceptional malcontents had accomplished wasn't, at the end of the day, all that bad an idea. In fact, it had probably saved countless thousands of lives, at least compared to what might have happened if the runaway economic inequality had been allowed to grow unabated until the masses revolted of their own accord. The French Revolution would have looked like a game of patty-cake by comparison, Sam figured.

But you don't get to make up the rules for everybody else, she had ultimately concluded. *Even if you're right.*

She shook her head. There was no telling how the judicial system would handle them. She suspected it would be anything but pleasant.

Assuming a functioning judicial system still existed, she thought.

She flipped on the television in front of her and tuned it to a news station. Time to figure out what the hell was going on in the world. The unrest had died down somewhat, but it still seemed like it could go either way. *Could be an interesting week. Again.*

She grabbed Brock's hand and brought it to her lips for a kiss. He smiled at her, that boyish twinkle in his eyes. It made her heart beat faster, just like always.

Sam exhaled and closed her eyes. A smile settled on her face. An unprovoked sense of wellbeing filled her mind. In that tiny moment, on the razor's edge of now, unencumbered by fabricated notions of future or past, life was pretty damn good.

Epilogue

A shadow fell over the small, slight man with ghost-white hair. A large shadow. It blocked his sunlight, which annoyed him. He was sunning himself the late afternoon glow. It bathed the pristine Croatian beach in a gorgeous, golden warmth.

He looked up. In front of him stood a very large figure. A monstrosity, really, a travesty in a bathing suit. With the world's most ridiculous comb-over.

"Terencio Manuel Zelaya," the fat man said, extending a drink. "You are one magnificent bastard."

Zelaya smiled. "Señor Fredericks," he said, his words slurred after a long session of day-drinking that had begun with breakfast, "I am one magnificent *retired* bastard."

Bill Fredericks smiled. "I'll drink to that," he said, his finger idly fondling the key to his sprawling new villa, tangible evidence that, at least as far as Sabot Mondragon was concerned, honor still mattered among thieves.

A smug smile settled on Fredericks' face. *Matter of fact,* he decided, *I'm going to drink to that for a very, very long time.*

Ready for more?

Get Lars' **#1 Bestselling noir thriller,**

DESCENT

What readers say:

"**The best writing in decades. Move over, Lee Child.**"

"**Some of the best action and spy thriller fiction you will ever read.**"

"**Right up there with Patterson, Baldacci, Forsyth, and DeMille.**"

"**The best thriller I've ever read.**"

"**LOVE LOVE LOVE this series!**"

Become part of Lars Emmerich's book launch team

WANT TO GET A **free** advanced copy of every new thriller Amazon #1 Bestselling Author Lars Emmerich releases?

Just click here to join Lars' Book Launch Team

Books by Amazon #1 Bestselling Author Lars Emmerich

The Incident: Inferno Rising

The Incident: Reckoning

Fallout

Descent

Devolution

Meltdown

Mindscrew

Blowback

Excerpt from #1 Bestseller DESCENT

Chapter 1

It was three a.m., but Evelyn Paulson wouldn't have been able to sleep if she had tried. She wore a space suit. None of her flesh was exposed, and she wore a mask over her entire head, like the kind that hazardous materials response teams wore. Hospital monitors beeped. There was the omnipresent cyclical whooshing of the respirator that breathed life into her nine-year-old daughter, Sarah.

This can't be happening, Evelyn thought for the thousandth time. Two weeks ago, Sarah had been active, athletic, beautiful. She'd fallen on the playground and broken her ankle. It was an unlucky break, the doctor said, and it required surgery to set the bones properly. Otherwise, if the break wasn't set right, it would heal wrong and interfere with her growth. She'd walk with a limp.

It had been an easy decision at the time. What parent wants their daughter to walk with a limp? Fears of infections and hospital-borne diseases were the furthest thing from Evelyn's mind as the orderlies wheeled Sarah away. Her ankle will be good as new in a few months, the doctor said.

Now, Sarah had no ankle. She had no leg below the femur. They had amputated just below her hip in a futile attempt to stop the bacterial infection, a gram negative bacteria, a term which meant nothing to Evelyn two weeks ago, but now meant that her daughter hung to life by the thinnest of threads while a toxic bug multiplied inside her little body.

They'd tried antibiotics, of course. Those were given for everything. Scratch your finger? Antibiotic ointment, coming right up. Can't risk infection. Persistent cough? Here's a six-day course of antibiotics. Be sure to take them all.

But antibiotics had done absolutely nothing against the bacteria ravaging Sarah's body. The infection had spread through her system. It pounded her lungs, and threatened to stop her heart. A machine cleaned and oxygenated her blood, because her little body was no longer fully capable of performing those tasks on its own.

Evelyn recalled the hushed, concerned conversations between doctors, and then the clinical, terse, pained exchanges they'd had with her: we've worked our way through nearly every known antibiotic and combination of antibiotics in our arsenal, but the infection just keeps advancing.

For the first week, there was always another drug to try, and Evelyn had felt certain they would find one that worked. But they hadn't. They'd airlifted Sarah to New York, to the National Institute of Health, the vanguard research hospital in the western medical world. Just ask them, Evelyn thought. They'd be happy to tell you how incredibly good they are.

And yesterday, after flying in some exotic and highly toxic antibiotic therapy, which hadn't worked, hadn't even slowed the infection down an iota, they told her that they were out of options. It was down to Sarah's innate strength, her will to live.

There had to be *something* else to try, Evelyn had protested. It's the twenty-first century, there's a rover running around on Mars, and people in jungle villages have cell phone service. How can the

NIH have run out of antibiotic drugs to give to a little girl? To save her life?

Because in all the world, there isn't a drug capable of killing *this* bacteria, the doctors told her. At least, not one that won't also kill Sarah in the process. We've tried every last antibiotic drug in the human medical arsenal, they said. But Sarah's infection was pandrug resistant. It was completely unfazed by every known pharmaceutical concoction.

It was a superbug, they told her.

Evelyn had asked where it came from, how Sarah could possibly have been exposed to such a horrific disease, and the doctors had exchanged furtive glances with each other. "We can't say for sure," Sarah's lead physician had said.

Superbug? It was also going to be a super lawsuit, Evelyn had decided in that moment. It didn't take a rocket scientist to figure things out. Evelyn wasn't a biologist, but she was a college graduate, for pete's sake. Bacteria became drug resistant through evolution. Most of them reproduced at least a dozen times every day. Some bacteria reproduced more than a hundred times a day. Each new generation brought the possibility of genetic variations that made the little bastards resistant to the antibiotics in their environment.

The *hospital* environment. Evelyn knew it in her bones. The hospital had bred this nightmare bug that had left her daughter's body in ruins, had left her little angel clinging desperately to life.

Maybe not on purpose, not maliciously, but where else could such a bug possibly evolve? Certainly not on the playground where Sarah had fallen.

The nurses' attitude had changed after the discovery that Sarah's disease was pandrug resistant. They were sympathetic, and they were doing their best for Sarah, and they offered more than just good care for her, but anytime Evelyn brought up the possibility that inadequate hospital procedures were responsible for harboring — no, for *developing,* and *then* harboring — such a terrible affliction, the nurses clammed up immediately. None of them wanted to say anything that got the hospital sued. None of them wanted to lose their job. Evelyn's rage grew, festered, rotted her insides just as surely as the superbug was devouring Sarah's.

The doctors gave Sarah a ten percent chance of surviving.

One in ten. Bile boiled in Evelyn's gut. She couldn't stop being outraged, because then the heartbreak would overtake her, and she knew that once it started, it would consume her.

Anger displaced despair and worry, and Evelyn became extremely angry. She had to be. For Sarah's sake. Sarah needed her to be strong, to be there, a pillar. Evelyn couldn't let her own emotions overwhelm her.

The infernal beeping continued. Evelyn heard another sound, the now-familiar whoosh of air that announced that someone had opened the outer airlock. There were negative-pressure pumps whirring 24/7 in Sarah's room, creating a slight vacuum that would prevent any air from escaping, and with it, any airborne bacteria. It was surreal, like Sarah was some sort of biological weapon. Which, Evelyn reflected grimly, she had certainly become. Sarah harbored a disease with a ninety percent mortality rate.

Jesus, this can't be happening, she thought again.

The inner airlock door opened, and Evelyn twisted her torso to bring the doorway into her field of vision. A large man entered. The baggy white biohazard suit and respirator looked small on his muscular frame. His face looked fit and handsome, at least what she could see of it through the biohazard suit. He carried a cooler. "Good morning, Ms. Paulson," he said. "I just need to collect a sample. This won't take long at all."

Evelyn didn't recognize the man. Was he a doctor? Nurse? Evelyn thought of asking his name and position, just to be sure, but the security around this wing of the NIH hospital was otherworldly. She wasn't sure the Crown Jewels were protected so thoroughly. There wasn't much chance that the guy didn't belong.

The man poked a syringe into an existing needle that had been in Sarah's arm since she arrived at NIH several days earlier. Evelyn watched the dark crimson liquid fill the tube in spurts. When he'd collected enough, the man sealed the sample tube, rinsed it under the sink, then sprayed a sterilizer around the outside. Then he wrapped the sample in foam and placed it on the ice inside the cooler he'd brought with him.

"It's best if you get some rest," the man said on his way out of Sarah's room.

Easy for you to say, asshole, Evelyn thought. How could she sleep when her daughter was fighting for her life just inches away?

On the other hand, it was three in the morning, and Evelyn hadn't left Sarah's room for the better part of eleven hours.

Three a.m. Why were they taking samples at this time of the morning? They hadn't done that before. And Evelyn was pretty sure she knew everyone on the hospital staff by now, at least in the infectious diseases wing. But she didn't recognize that guy.

She shrugged. Doctors kept weird hours. And maybe that particular doctor had been on vacation during Sarah's first week at NIH, which is why she hadn't met him before.

Evelyn turned to look again at Sarah, willing her to heal, wishing there were some way to lend Sarah some strength, just for a few days, just until she rounded the corner and started to beat back the deadly disease that was eating her alive.

The ventilator continued its inexorable pace. The monitors beeped. Tears formed in Evelyn's eyes. Exhaustion and fear overcame her, and Evelyn's shoulders shuddered with her quiet, desperate sobs.

Chapter 2

Viktor Kohlhaas' driver shut the rear door to the Mercedes. It closed with a solid *chunk*, reminding Kohlhaas that the door was twice as heavy as the average car door, on account of its armor and bulletproof glass.

The car was both perk and necessity. In fact, there were several cars, all identical, all taking different routes through the city, all traveling at slightly different times throughout the day. It was like he was a head of state, rather than the CEO of what was, by industry standards, a minuscule concern.

His company was located in the outskirts of Paris. World-class cosmopolitanism notwithstanding, Paris was a backwater in his line of work. Nobody had a plant there, nobody was doing research, and there was no community synergy upon which to draw for inspiration. Perhaps that was the genius of the location. Even if you knew what you were looking for, you'd never think to look in Paris.

But that didn't mean the security wasn't necessary. It very much was. Kohlhaas' life had been threatened on a number of occasions in the past year. Some of the threats had been veiled, while some were more overt, but the message was clear each time: play ball, asshole, or we're coming after you.

But they hadn't come after him. At least not seriously, anyway. Not yet. And Kohlhaas' work had to continue, because it was important work. Which was to say, the work that Kohlhaas' *employees* did was meaningful, useful work. *He* didn't do much of that kind of thing, and in fact he had very little background in the biochemical sciences. His role was to sit through meetings, allocate resources, and, occasionally, when it couldn't be avoided, to make a decision.

And his role also apparently included absorbing the threats of grievous bodily injury.

He had been tempted to cave in to them, as any sane man would have been tempted. But, so far, he had persevered, and had done what was necessary.

Viktor Kohlhaas was not a crusader. He wasn't an idealist, or a starry-eyed dreamer, or a philanthropist. He wasn't even a particularly nice guy. His family didn't care much for him, and truth be told, he didn't much care for them either. Degenerate sons, an aloof china doll of a wife, a daughter wrapped tightly in her own righteous anger over something Kohlhaas barely remembered, nephews popping out of the woodwork all the time with their hands out; it didn't make for a terribly satisfying home life, despite the ridiculously elegant flat he and his wife shared in the St. Germain-de-pres, or 7th Arrondissement.

So Kohlhaas worked. Weekends, too. He drove his people hard, but he drove himself even harder. His flight from New York had landed but a few brief hours earlier, and yet there he was, on his way to work on a Friday morning with scarcely more than five hours' sleep after a whirlwind trip across the Atlantic.

More than anything, Viktor Kohlhaas gravitated toward opportunity. He had an eye for it, could spot it where others passed right by, and pursued it with a ruthless, dogged single-mindedness that left others struck dumb by his intensity and tenacity. It was undoubtedly this element of his personality that had propelled him to the stratospheric ranks of the rock star CEOs.

People were surprised when he had taken his current position. It was a private company, which meant that there were fewer shares of preferred stock with which to pad his compensation package, and fewer options on that stock. But Kohlhaas had nevertheless negotiated a favorable equity position in addition to a very healthy cash signing bonus and monthly paycheck, all of which had left him exposed to very little downside risk, should he fail to guide Pharma Synergique to the exceptionally bright future that the board envisioned. And the equity position left him poised to reap incredible rewards if he succeeded.

Kohlhaas looked out the window, annoyed at the duration of the car ride from his flat into the office. Each day, Kohlhaas selected a driver at random from among the four that showed up at his flat, a bit of subterfuge that would make the US Secret Service proud. And each day, the drivers took a different route to the nondescript warehouse on the southern periphery of Paris, far from the landmarks, romantic cafes, and world-renowned masterpieces of fine art for which the city was famous. Today's route seemed about thirty percent longer than normal.

Remaining unpredictable was the first and most important security measure, Franklin Barnes had told Kohlhaas a year ago. Kohlhaas had hired Barnes to head up Pharma Synergique's security department. Before Barnes, there was no security department. They had locks on their doors, and that was about it.

But things had changed. Paris was still a backwater, but one little leak had put Synergique on almost everyone's map. They'd had to move offices. In fact, they'd had to gut an entire building and rebuild its insides around a high-security vault in the center, designed to keep the right people in and the wrong people out.

The heavy Mercedes pulled to a stop in front of a door marked only with a street number. There was no parking on the street, and the employees had to park a block away in a public lot, but Kohlhaas rated doorstop service. The driver opened the car door, Kohlhaas stepped out, walked to the building, and inserted his magnetic key card into the card reader adjacent to the door handle. He typed his twelve-digit identification number, received a beep and a green light in response, and waited for the latch to release with its characteristic *clack.*

He pulled the door open, stepped inside, and waited for his eyes to adjust to the darkness of the anteroom, then placed his left eye over the retinal scanner affixed next to the second door. It beeped its approval and let him through to the third layer of external security, a slightly larger room filled with a full-body microwave scanner, just like the kind the US government had bought by the thousands in the wake of the 9/11 debacle. Kohlhaas had reluctantly authorized the ridiculous expense, and he had wondered every day whether the cost had been justified.

Three armed men manned the scanner. "Morning, Mr. Kohlhaas," the tall one, Jacques, said in accented English.

"Bonjour," Kohlhaas responded with a slightly forced smile.

He was Danish by birth, fluent in four languages, a necessity in an interconnected world, but his employees usually defaulted to English in deference to Kohlhaas' New York upbringing.

Kohlhaas went through the scanner, received an apologetic patting down around his chest pocket, where he'd mistakenly left his Montblanc pen. "Very sorry, Mr. Kohlhaas," Jacques said with a small wince. Kohlhaas waved the inconvenience away with a tired smile.

Then he was through to the building's interior. The long hallway took him past a heavy steel door secured with yet another layer of electronic locks, leading to what Kohlhaas jokingly referred to as the most expensive bugs on the planet.

In addition to their grievous cost, the bugs inside the well-secured incubators were among the deadliest on earth. They had been an absolute bitch to procure. All were heavily regulated. As a result, many of them had been acquired without authorization. Some had been bought under the table, obtained from an otherwise upstanding lab supervisor or chief of infectious diseases with a bit of a gambling problem, for example, or one too many alimony payments. Others had been grown in Synergique's own labs. Still others had been stolen. Most of them had to be carefully hidden from the health inspectors, because Synergique didn't officially own them.

They had procured just enough of the bacteria samples through official channels to provide plausible deniability for the elaborate biological containment facilities they'd constructed. But if Kohlhaas hadn't taken matters into his own hands, they'd never be anywhere close to completion. They'd still be kissing government ass, bribing mid-level bureaucratic functionaries, and wading through miles of red tape.

Kohlhaas took the stairs to the executive offices. His secretary met him with a printout of the day's agenda. Someone from the US Food and Drug Administration had called again, she said, still hoping for an interview. Kohlhaas waved a dismissive hand. And another venture capital firm had called. Kohlhaas didn't care to hear the name. He had no interest whatsoever in taking on additional equity partners. He preferred his profits undiluted, thank you very much.

He stepped into his well-apportioned office, poured a cup of coffee, and sat at his gargantuan mahogany desk.

It was completely clean and devoid of lingering work, as was his custom, with one exception: on the middle of the desk sat a manila envelope. There was no writing on the outside, and it was sealed. "What is this?" he asked his secretary, waving the envelope.

She didn't know. Was he sure he hadn't left it there before his trip to New York several days earlier?

Kohlhaas was sure. Papers left on his desk implied loose ends. He hated loose ends.

He felt the package. Seemed harmless enough. It was full of papers. He retrieved the letter opener from the center drawer of his desk, sliced expertly through the flap, and emptied the contents onto his desk.

He looked at the pages. The blood drained from his face. Fear, hatred, and rage filled him. And a heartbreak nearly beyond a man's capacity to bear. Kohlhaas' hands shook. His words stuck in his throat. "Get Barnes," he rasped to his secretary, his heart pounding.

It was clear that his world would never be the same.

Chapter 3

Peter Kittredge sat alone in the interrogation room. It was simply apportioned, with two utilitarian chairs at a scratched table. There was no clichéd two-way mirror, but Kittredge did notice three video cameras, located in various spots on the ceiling.

He'd been in this kind of situation before. Several times, in fact. But unlike those occasions, which were ultimately of his own making, Kittredge knew that he had absolutely nothing to do with the grisly scene that he and Nora had discovered in his bed several hours earlier.

But they'd so far treated him more as a suspect than a witness, and that pissed him off. Fingerprints, photographs, the local version of the Miranda rights, even a ride in the backseat of the squad car to the station — it all smacked of intimidation. And Kittredge had had his fill of intimidation, which meant that he didn't respond well to it these days. And who the hell were *they*, those smug Polizei in their little German eyeglasses with their German abruptness, to even hint at assigning guilt before asking any questions?

The interrogation room door opened. It was the small guy, the one with the face that was overly serious, even by Teutonic standards. *This is going to be interesting.*

"How long have you known Sergio Delafuentes?" Jürgen Strauss, the police investigator, asked after Kittredge stated his name for the record.

"I didn't know his last name was Delafuentes," Kittredge said.

"That is not the question I asked," Strauss said, his face inscrutable despite what could certainly have been interpreted as a truculent statement.

Kittredge bristled. He wasn't drunk, but neither was he sober, and the three large cocktails he'd enjoyed with breakfast still held some sway over his tongue. "No, Franz," he said, knowing full well that the investigator's name wasn't Franz, "you didn't ask me that question. But I was trying to illustrate for you that I didn't really know Sergio very well at all. We met last night, as a matter of fact."

If Strauss was put off by Kittredge's petulance, he didn't show it. "Where did you meet?"

"You've already asked me this twice before."

"The answer should be easy in that case," the investigator said.

Kittredge shook his head, cursed silently, and ran through the whole thing for what was now the third time. He and Sergio had met at a club, drank and danced, and one thing had led to another.

"This man slept in your bed?" Strauss asked with a look of disdain. Germany was famously tolerant of alternative lifestyles, but that was on average. This particular sample size of one didn't appear to buy into the magnanimity, Kittredge observed.

"No, he Harry Pottered himself there, just in time to be beaten to death." Kittredge knew he probably wasn't helping himself out, but he couldn't help it. This little prick was annoying the hell out of him.

"This is a very serious situation, Herr Kittredge."

"You think? I found a man bludgeoned to death in my bed.

There's really no need for you to emphasize the seriousness with me."

"How do you know he was bludgeoned?"

"Isn't that the word you use when someone's head is bashed in?"

"And you know this because you got a view of his head."

"He was lying in my bed," Kittredge said, barely containing his impatient annoyance. "I got a view of his head."

"You weren't in an argument?"

Kittredge was taken aback. "Of course not."

"And you would have no reason to want to harm Herr Delafuentes?"

"None whatsoever. As I said, we had just met the night before."

"But you knew him well enough to invite him to your bed," the inspector said.

Kittredge shook his head. "I didn't know him. I just wanted to sleep with him."

The investigator's look of disgust returned. "But there was also a girl."

"Yes," Kittredge said. "People do these things from time to time. The lucky ones do, anyway."

"And the woman, Nora, had no quarrel with Herr Delafuentes?"

"None that I saw. In fact, I'd say she was more than a little sweet on him."

"How long did she know him?"

"You'll have to ask her."

"Did she know that Delafuentes was not his original surname?"

Kittredge shook his head. "You should take better notes. I didn't know Sergio's last name before you told me. Now you're asking me if *I* know whether *Nora* knows that Sergio was using a *fake* last name. How the hell would I know that?"

"So she did not know that Delafuentes was not his original surname."

Kittredge felt annoyance turn to anger. "I didn't say that, Franz. Maybe you should ask Nora what's going on in Nora's head, and leave me out of it."

Strauss remained unruffled. "Have you ever been to Copenhagen?"

Left field. Kittredge shook his head. "What?"

"I want to know whether you have ever been to Copenhagen," Strauss repeated.

Kittredge had to search his memory. He'd been somewhere up north, but he couldn't quite remember where. There was a museum with Viking ships in it, and a park with a lot of sculptures of a famous children's author, but that could have been just about any Scandinavian city. Oslo, he concluded finally. He'd been to Oslo. Not Copenhagen.

"No," he finally said. His eyes returned to the investigator, who had evidently noticed — and possibly misinterpreted — the relatively long silence before Kittredge delivered his answer. *This is not good.*

"Are you certain, Herr Kittredge?"

"Fairly," Kittredge said. "I've been to some city up there, and I was trying to recall which one. Turns out it was Oslo, I'm pretty sure. I was drinking a lot at the time."

"Were you drinking a lot last night?"

Kittredge didn't like where things might have been headed. "I enjoyed myself a little, yes," he said carefully.

"How many drinks did you have?"

"I don't know."

"Was it two?"

Kittredge laughed.

"Four?"

"I don't know," Kittredge said.

"Was it more than five?"

By noon, Kittredge didn't say. He nodded.

"Is it then possible, Herr Kittredge, that you might have quarreled with Herr Delafuentes, and not remembered it in the morning?"

Kittredge shook his head. "Not at all. I did very many things with Herr Delafuentes, and none of them were remotely related to quarreling."

"So you have complete recollection of the evening, despite drinking heavily?"

What was this guy getting at? "I'd say so, yes."

"How did you get home from the club?"

Kittredge exhaled. "We drove."

"Whose car?"

"Mine."

"So you drove?"

Kittredge nodded.

"Drunk?"

Kittredge didn't respond.

"Would you submit to a blood alcohol test?"

"Sure. But I've had a little hair of the dog this morning, so I don't think it would tell you much. Anyway, what does my drinking have to do with Sergio's murder?"

The investigator's eyebrows raised slightly. "That is what I am hoping to ascertain."

"Let me help you out. It had absolutely nothing to do with it. Not a damned thing. Unrelated entirely. Nora and I went to breakfast. When we came back, Sergio was dead. Next question."

"You seem agitated," Strauss said.

"How the hell am I supposed to feel? He was killed in my own damn bed! His brains and blood are all over my sheets! And you're giving me the criminal treatment?"

The investigator rose. "Thank you, Herr Kittredge. Here is my card. Please call me if you think of anything else that might be important."

Kittredge nodded, rose, and followed the investigator out of the interrogation room. "Hey, one thing," he said.

The investigator turned around.

"Two things, actually," Kittredge corrected himself. "What is Sergio's real last name, and what does Copenhagen have to do with it?"

The investigator shook his head. "I'm afraid that is information that I cannot discuss with you, Herr Kittredge." He turned on his heel and walked into an adjacent office, shutting the door behind him.

* * *

Kittredge waited half an hour for Nora, only to subsequently discover from the desk officer that Nora's interrogation had wrapped up several minutes before his. She hadn't waited for him, and he found that he was a bit hurt by that.

And he didn't have her phone number, which he wanted very badly. Conventional wisdom had it that relationships that began under traumatic circumstances were more likely than average to end in heartbreak, but Kittredge didn't pay much attention to conventional wisdom. Wisdom wasn't conventional, he was fond of saying, and whatever the masses thought, it usually wasn't wise.

He had an almost unbearable urge to compare notes with Nora. His interrogation had been decidedly unpleasant, at least in his estimation, and he wondered whether hers was similarly hostile.

Kittredge went straight from the police station to his favorite Kneipe, or public house. He wanted nothing to do with his apartment at the moment. The police had gathered all of the bed linens, and had even taken the mattress, so there wouldn't be much in the way of blood and guts for him to clean up. But he still had no desire to be alone in the place where someone had been murdered.

His favorite spot was open at the Kneipe, as it usually was shortly after noon. He eschewed beer, which was a German passion, almost its own food group, but failed to get the job done with sufficient speed. He favored schnapps, which he considered to be the local vodka equivalent. It was often flavored, which made for interesting vomit when he overindulged, which seemed to be upwards of a couple of times per week these days. He ordered the usual, downed it with gusto, and smiled as the bartender brought the second round.

As the alcohol hit his bloodstream, Kittredge seemed to gain a little perspective on his police interrogation. Had the investigator really been all that unreasonable? After all, Sergio was found in *his* bed, and his only alibi was someone he'd met the night before, someone whom the police might easily consider to be a likely accomplice. Hell, if he didn't know the truth, he might be tempted to suspect himself, too. From the outside, it sure looked an awful lot like Kittredge could be the guy who had killed Sergio.

That wasn't all. Whoever had killed Sergio had somehow gotten into Kittredge's apartment without breaking in. There was no sign of forced entry, and Kittredge was positive that he had locked the door when he and Nora left for breakfast. Did they have a key? Had they bribed the building's super?

And why hadn't they stolen anything? They hadn't even taken Sergio's wallet. Kittredge had expensive audio equipment, a high-end television, and an authentic Rolex on the nightstand. Nothing had been disturbed, much less taken.

The German police had been thorough, with the same plodding Teutonic eye for detail that produced BMW, Porsche, and Mercedes, the same inexorable German-ness that had nearly exterminated an entire race of people. That had pissed Kittredge off as much as anything — the machine-like march through the facts, never once acknowledging the devastating emotional aspect of the hideous travesty Kittredge had discovered in his bed.

The whole thing was miles beyond messed up. Meet a nice boy, have a nice time, go to breakfast, come home to brains splattered all over the bedroom. The violation of it, the sense that there was nowhere safe for Kittredge to go, no place that couldn't be accessed, no way to keep his possessions or his life safe from harm, was reminiscent of... Venezuela. Quinn, the giant assassin with wolf's eyes. Bill Fredericks, the fat, vile piece of shit CIA case officer who still held Kittredge's hand receipt. A dead Venezuelan with a ridiculous nom de guerre, El Grande.

And *her*.

He couldn't get the image of Sergio's bloody body out of his mind. It was horrible enough on its own. But it reminded him of her, of the whole thing, the thing he'd been trying desperately to drink from his memory, the thing that he'd been running away from for the past year. Unsuccessfully. Kittredge had discovered, like so many others who had enlisted geography's assistance to cope with internal problems, that no matter where you went, there you were.

Could it have been *them*? Could they have found him? Could the whole thing have been a bloody message, a murderous calling card with an unambiguous caption: *we still own you, bitch?*

It was certainly possible. There were bad people in Kittredge's past. And try as he might to think and drink it different, there was no escaping the fact that he still belonged to them. Lock, stock, and barrel, Kittredge was owned.

If they ever found him.

Goddamned Venezuela. He hadn't been in terrific shape before the whole thing, but afterwards, he was a complete mess. He had simply walked away from his job, not bothering to resign, not caring enough to collect a severance check, just needing to get as far away from the whole situation as possible.

His asshole old man had died around the same time, leaving him an unexpectedly large sum, which was likely the only reason Kittredge wasn't sleeping in a gutter somewhere.

But the gutter would probably have been a terrific place to hide. Homeless people don't tend to leave much of a digital footprint. And homeless people have no trendy Cologne flat to break into, and probably have no boyfriends to bludgeon to death.

A word popped into Kittredge's inebriated mind. Copenhagen. Had he ever been to Copenhagen. What the hell was that about? What did a city in Denmark have to do with the Cologne murder of a man named Sergio Delafuentes?

Or a man whose *false* name was Sergio Delafuentes. Kittredge sighed. As he walked deliberately to the restroom, taking care not to stumble, he determined that he had little better to do than figure it all out.

He also had the inchoate notion that figuring out what had happened to Sergio might also serve to prolong his own life.

Because Peter Kittredge had *those* kinds of acquaintances. And maybe they had caught up to him.

Get the #1 Bestselling noir thriller from
Author Lars Emmerich

DESCENT

What readers say:

"The best writing in decades. Move over, Lee Child."

"Some of the best thriller fiction you will ever read."

"Right up there with Patterson, Baldacci, Forsyth, and DeMille."

"The best thriller I've ever read."

"LOVE LOVE LOVE this series!"

Made in the USA
Columbia, SC
31 October 2021